RAVE REVIEWS FOR *USA TODAY* BESTSELLING AUTHOR JOY NASH!

A LITT

"Ms. Nash writes thi_____
very quirky character_____
heart of the matter in_____

"If you love a romantic romance, filled with hunky heroes, funky family members, and a remarkable heroine, then *A Little Light Magic* is the novel for you."
—Long and Short Reviews

"Joy Nash is one of those treasures . . . As a hard lover of completely character driven romances, I am definitely on board for Nash's future contemporary releases."
—All About Romance

IMMORTALS: THE CROSSING

"I read this book in one sitting because it is just too good to put down. Don't miss out on one of the best paranormal romances of the year!"
—Romance Junkies

"Nash's latest hero is a charming rogue with a compassionate heart, while her heroine is a desperate mother willing to sacrifice everything to save her son . . . Mac Lir is a hero to die for."
—RT Book Reviews

IMMORTALS: THE AWAKENING

"Nash takes readers on a fast journey, keeping the action going from beginning to end. Cutting edge drama, creative characters and a plot that moves like fire all create a great read. The Immortals series just keeps getting better and it may be hard to top this fantastic addition."
—Paranormal Romance Writers

"This book is fantasy romance done right and done well."
—All About Romance

SEDUCING THE WARRIOR

"I understand now why you rejected me that day at my father's house. I know why you flung all those hurtful words at me. I was too young for what I was asking of you. But, Rhys, that was four years ago. I'm no longer that girl. I'm a woman now."

He clenched his teeth. *Gods.* Aye, she was a woman. A lush, tempting . . .

Her words battered him. "There's no longer any need to push me away. Don't you see? I love you, Rhys. I always have, and I always will. And I think you l—"

Something snapped inside him. He spun around, and stalked toward her. "Breena, stop. Before you say something you'll regret."

"No! I won't. I'll say what's in my heart. I lov—mmph!"

He'd covered her mouth with his palm. His other hand gripped her shoulder. "Don't," he pleaded. *"Don't."*

Her lips parted. Her breath bathed his palm. Before he could react, before he could even *think*, she tasted his skin with the tip of her hot, wet tongue.

The tiny point of moisture caused his brain to seize. And still, he might have resisted. Might have pulled back completely, and retained some shred of his honor.

If she hadn't pressed her open palm on his stomach. And slid it downward, slowly.

JOY NASH

Silver Silence

LOVE SPELL NEW YORK CITY

*To my biggest fans in the world—my kids. Please don't
ever lose your sense of wonder.*

LOVE SPELL®

November 2009

Published by

Dorchester Publishing Co., Inc.
200 Madison Avenue
New York, NY 10016

ISBN 10: 0-505-52717-0
ISBN 13: 978-0-505-52717-2
E-ISBN: 978-1-4285-0766-1

The name "Love Spell" and its logo are trademarks of Dorchester
Publishing Co., Inc.

Printed in the United States of America.

10 9 8 7 6 5 4 3 2

Visit us online at www.dorchesterpub.com.

Silver Silence

Chapter One

$\mathcal{S}$he really shouldn't be doing this.

But, dear Goddess, she just couldn't help herself.

A tide of guilt battered the shore of Breena's conscience. Still . . . what she was about to do wasn't so very wrong, was it? She wasn't hurting anyone. The spell wasn't dangerous. She wasn't calling forbidden deep magic.

She only wanted to *See*.

And only for a moment. She needed to make sure Rhys was all right.

The past month had been dreadful. Her terrifying night vision had returned. Even after waking, the shadow of the dream lingered. Some days, her chest remained so tight she could not manage a full breath until midday.

Rhys wasn't part of the silver vision that had plagued Breena for the past four years. He never had been. But in her current unrelenting state of anxiety, she'd become obsessed with his safety. Perhaps it was her mind's attempt to avoid dwelling on her disturbing dreams. She wasn't sure. She only knew she couldn't rest until she'd seen Rhys alive and well, with her own eyes.

She knew it was wrong. And most likely, unnecessary. Rhys wasn't some novice traveler. Just the opposite. He'd roamed Britain for fifteen years seeking

Druid initiates for Avalon. In all that time, he'd not come to harm. But this time, he'd been gone so long. Nearly a full year. According to old Mared, Avalon's healer, Rhys had never before stayed away so long.

What if, this time, he did not return?

What if, this time, something had happened?

What if Breena never saw him again. . . .

No. She would not think it. She could not bear a world without Rhys in it. She'd loved him for so long. Nearly all her life. And that was the problem, wasn't it? Rhys did not take her love seriously. He did not take *her* seriously. He was eleven years her elder, and her brother's best friend. Like Marcus, Rhys considered Breena nothing more than an amusing, and sometimes annoying, little sister.

Her chest was hurting again, her ribs squeezing too tightly. It had been a month since she'd gotten a full night's rest. She was so, so tired. She wouldn't be able to close her eyes at all tonight unless she knew Rhys was well.

She would look quickly, and be done with it. No one need know. Not Gwen. Not Marcus. And certainly not Owein. As Avalon's only other Seer, and her mentor, Breena's uncle would be especially disappointed if he knew what she was about. And if Owein learned that this was not the first time she'd misused her Druid power? She shuddered to imagine how angry he'd be.

The afternoon sunlight was fading quickly, sinking into the mist surrounding the sacred isle. The air carried a hint of the coming winter. The leaves had begun to drop from the apple trees, exposing branches heavy with fruit. But the ancient yew that sheltered the Grail spring was ever green. The pool of red-tinged water that bathed its roots was the most powerful scrying surface Breena knew.

Calling a vision of the present or past was not so

difficult—seeking knowledge of the future was infinitely harder. Scrying for Rhys was not likely to give her more than a dull headache, or a faintly sour stomach. Small price to pay for her peace of mind.

If Rhys ever found out . . . No. Breena would not think of that, either. Rhys was an intensely private man. He would be furious.

The autumn grass crunched under her feet. She approached the Grail spring with reverence. The sacred water collected in a deep, moss-ringed pool before spilling in a crooked rivulet down the hill. Sinking onto a smooth, flat rock at the edge of the pond, she crossed her legs under her skirts and leaned forward.

She drew several deep breaths, and, with some difficulty, emptied her mind. Her vision blurred. She grew heavy, as if she were sinking into the earth. Becoming part of the Great Mother's body.

Vast currents of life energy vibrated just under the soil, collecting and flowing in much the same way as streams and rivers did on the earth's surface. This was true the world over. But nowhere were those unseen paths of power so strong as here on Avalon. An ocean of power rested beneath the sacred isle of the Druids.

It was to this awesome force that Breena surrendered her mind and her magic. Into that vast sea, she cast a Word, and spoke Rhys's name.

The power answered. Light and shadow played across the pond's surface. Dancing. Merging. Separating. She concentrated on a memory of Rhys's face: high brow, clear gray eyes, harshly angled cheekbones. Her breath hitched a notch. Great Mother, but she loved him so.

She imagined his strong jaw, stubbled with his close-cropped beard. He wore his hair short as well. The color, an unusual shade of white blond, was perhaps his most distinctive feature. He looked very much like his sister, Gwendolyn, Avalon's Guardian. Gwen and Rhys were twins, after all.

The light and shadow on the pool shifted, creating the illusion of substance and depth. There was a pulling sensation deep in Breena's belly. A scene formed on the water's surface, as plainly as if it were happening at arm's length, rather than miles and miles away.

Rhys strode a muddy road, his leather pack slung over one shoulder. Breena's chest eased. He was alive! Thanks be to the Great Mother.

He was alone. That was not unusual. Rhys most often traveled alone, save for Hefin, the small merlin falcon that was his companion. Ah, yes. She caught a glimpse of brown wing and speckled breast sailing overhead.

She returned her full attention to Rhys. His breeches were rough and torn, his old linen shirt frayed at the collar and sleeves, his cloak spattered with mud. He'd gone perhaps a sennight without a razor. He wore no sword, but he looked more than a little dangerous nonetheless. And that was no illusion. Rhys was a powerful Druid. Beneath his facade of geniality, he was without doubt the most dangerous man Breena knew.

She'd meant to break the vision once she'd seen him. But the longer she looked, the faster her good intentions crumbled. Rhys's tread was weary, his shoulders hunched as if against a chill wind. He'd just entered a village. Well, perhaps "village" was too generous an assessment. The settlement was little more than a handful of ragged structures clustered at a crossroads. Mud and rubble walls supported roofs of sagging thatch. Weeds crowded thick against the unkempt dwellings. A ragged chicken pecking in a garbage heap looked hardly worth the trouble of plucking.

The thin rays of the setting sun slanted into Rhys's face. He looked as tired as the village. The lines around his eyes and mouth were deeper than she remembered. His usual easy gait had become heavy and plodding.

She watched as he approached the largest building of the small group, the only one that boasted an upper story. A hostelry, Breena thought. Rhys shoved open the door.

The public room inside was hazed with smoke from guttering tallow candles. A poor establishment indeed, if the owner could not even afford oil for proper lamps. The ceiling was so low that Rhys, who was very tall, had to duck under the blackened ceiling beams.

Two long plank tables, dark with scars, boasted three disreputable-looking patrons. Celts all, and male. A stout matron delivered mugs of *cervesia,* the bitter Celtic beer few Romans—including Breena—could stomach. From the looks of the establishment, Breena doubted whether a cask of wine had ever crossed its threshold.

An idle barkeep leaned his beefy arms on a waist-high counter. He looked up as Rhys entered, and a wide grin instantly appeared on his ruddy face. Rhys gave him a half smile in return. Crossing the room, he sank down on a stool opposite the man, and lowered his pack to the ground. The barkeep was already filling a mug with ale. He shoved it into Rhys's hands, at the same time shouting something toward an open doorway that Breena assumed led to the kitchens.

A young boy of about ten years appeared almost immediately. The lad's eyes lit up when he saw Rhys, and Rhys smiled in return. The barkeep spoke to the lad. The boy nodded and dashed between the tables, and out the front door.

Rhys's lips moved. The barkeep leaned on the counter and answered. Breena expelled a sigh of frustration. How she wished she could hear his voice! But it was an inconvenient fact that Breena's visions—the unbidden

night terrors as well as those she called deliberately—
were always silent.

Ah, well. At least she'd learned what she needed to
know. Rhys was well. She should allow the vision to
fade and try to forget she'd violated his privacy. But,
just as she prepared to speak the Word that would have
dissolved the vision, a woman emerged from the
kitchen, drying her hands on her apron.

She was not young. Her clothes were patched, her
hands reddened. But even worn and work-weary, she
possessed an earthy, sensual beauty that caused every
male eye in the room to swing in her direction.

She beheld Rhys, and her eyes took on an eager light
that disturbed Breena in a way she did not fully understand. The woman's lips formed Rhys's name, then
curved in a slow smile. Rhys looked up from his mug,
and nodded a greeting. In reply, the woman leaned
across the bar and kissed him full on the mouth.

Rhys did not protest. Far from it. He threaded his
fingers though the woman's hair and plundered her
mouth for several long moments. A hot knife of pain
sliced through Breena's chest. The blade twisted when
the woman came around the table and slid into Rhys's
lap.

The barkeep guffawed. Breena's fingernails bit
through the linen of her skirt and into her thigh.

Stop looking.

She couldn't. Instead of ending the spell, as she knew
she ought, she drew a deep, painful breath and continued watching.

Rhys released the wench with a playful swat on her
bottom. With a smirk on her lips, and a swish of her
hips, she disappeared into the kitchen. She returned a
short while later with a bowl of stew and a basket of
barley bannocks. Rhys bent his head over the meal and
began to eat.

The woman returned to the kitchen, emerging a moment later with a large tray laden with mugs and bowls. The tavern was filling, Breena belatedly realized. The kitchen boy had returned with a good number of men, women, and even children. Why, it looked as though the whole village had suddenly decided to take the evening meal in the tavern.

Breena understood why when Rhys pushed aside his empty bowl and reached for his pack. Every eye in the room was on him as he withdrew a bundle and unfolded the well-worn oiled cloth. Breena could almost feel the excitement rippling through the room as Rhys's harp was revealed. A visit from a bard of Rhys's talent would be a rare and treasured event in such a poor settlement.

The barkeep had already set the tavern's best chair before the hearth. Rhys sat, cradling the harp's polished wood frame in the crook of his arm. His long, graceful fingers moved swiftly over the harp strings.

Breena felt the touch on the strings of her heart. When Rhys began to sing, a lump rose in her throat. Unshed tears burned her eyes. Though the vision was silent, Breena had no trouble imaging his song. Her memories of Rhys's music stretched as far back as she could remember. She'd been a small girl when the lanky Celtic boy had first appeared at the gates of her father's farm on the outskirts of Isca Silurum, carrying little more than his harp. He'd begged to trade a song for a night's shelter, and had ended up staying a fortnight.

It was the first visit of many. Rhys was of an age with Breena's half brother, and, despite the fact that Marcus was the son of a retired Roman army officer, and Rhys a homeless Celt, the pair had become close friends. Rhys never stayed long at the Aquila farm, but he returned often over the years. Breena had looked forward to every visit.

The tall, handsome bard utterly entranced her. At first, it had been a childish fascination. But as Breena grew to womanhood, the attraction became so much more potent. It squeezed her heart and pulled at her belly. It pulsed between her legs in the small hours of the morning. She'd lain awake so many nights, wanting him. Imagining what it would be like to be in his arms. But Rhys did not want her. Not in that way. To him, Breena was still a child.

At the encouragement of several patrons, the bold barmaid had abandoned her tray. Laughing, she tore off her mobcap and pulled the thong from her hair. Thick blonde curls tumbled over her shoulders.

She began to dance, lifting her skirts above her ankles as her feet flew in a graceful, complicated pattern, her steps coming faster and even faster. A half smile played on Rhys's lips as he played her accompaniment. At the end of the dance, the woman draped her arms about Rhys's shoulders and kissed him deeply. The audience stomped and applauded; Rhys laughed.

Breena's hold on the vision faltered. A tear trickled down her throat. Eyes blurred, she watched Rhys sing several more songs. Finally, he rose and bowed. Someone brought his pack, and he rewrapped his harp with care. The barmaid, standing to one side, watched his every movement, a gleam of anticipation in her eye.

He looked at her and she smiled, her invitation unmistakable. Rhys's expression was harder to read. He watched as the woman turned and walked slowly away, hips swaying. Her destination was the narrow stair that rose along the wall. One foot poised on the bottom step, she turned and looked back.

The barkeep was at Rhys's side. He clapped Rhys on the shoulder and made a comment that set two men nearby laughing. They raised their mugs in Rhys's direction. Rhys returned a wry smile. The barmaid glided up the stair. Rhys shouldered his pack, and the barkeep gave him a shove in the same direction.

The air was squeezed from Breena's lungs as Rhys crossed the room and followed the woman up the stair. Her throat closed as he disappeared into the gloom at the top.

Her vision shattered.

She gasped with the sudden violence of the broken spell. Pain pounded her head, her stomach twisted violently. She might have emptied her stomach of her last meal, save for the fact her ribs had contracted too tightly to draw a full breath.

Hugging herself, she rocked forward and back, her eyes squeezed tight against the tears.

She never should have looked.

Great Mother, but his mood was black.

The meal had helped a little. Ciara had even managed to find a few chunks of meat to float in his broth. She must be feeling generous. Or perhaps just very needy. Not many travelers found themselves stopping at this godsforsaken crossroads.

Rhys's weariness had receded a little upon Fergus's warm greeting. No doubt the man anticipated the profit Rhys's harp brought to his tavern. But Rhys sensed honest regard, too. A minstrel's song, even sung with half a heart, was a joy Fergus did not often experience.

And so Rhys had worked to keep the darkness at bay. His music flowed easily, as it always did. After fifteen years, his harp was almost a part of him; he could play in his sleep, if need be. Now it was done. He found himself looking forward to Ciara's bed. At least with her, he did not have to pretend. She understood what he wanted.

It shamed him, this burning, angry need. And yet,

he could not summon the strength to resist it. If it was wrong, so be it. He was tired of fighting.

Fatigue dragged at his bones as he followed Ciara up the stair. He felt old. Far older, even, than his nine-and-twenty years. Fifteen years, he'd wandered. More than half his life. His youth had been worn to dust on the road. Aye, he did his duty to Avalon. Every day, he fulfilled the promise his grandfather had forced him to give, knowing he would never be done with it. Knowing he would never be free.

It angered him. It had from the beginning, though in those early days, panic had been his foremost emotion. He'd conquered his fears long ago—but his rage? That remained, simmering beneath the genial facade he presented to the world. He could not fight for his life, nor could he escape it.

He could only forget. For a few hours, at least.

Ciara climbed the stairs swiftly. She lit a candle in her small room under the eaves, then shut and bolted the door. Turning, she leaned against it.

Rhys set his pack in a corner, then straightened and looked at her. She was thin—if he wished, he might have counted her ribs. But her breasts were high and full, and she was more than willing to give him what he wanted.

"Strip," he said softly.

Her fingers went immediately to the tasseled cord at her waist. She unknotted the braided leather, and let it drop. Her blouse dropped next. Then her skirt. By the time her undertunic joined the heap of clothes on the ground, she was trembling.

He ordered her onto her knees. She obeyed swiftly. Her eyes, sharp with excitement, fixed on his groin. He unlaced his breeches; his shaft sprang free. She made an appreciative sound in the back of her throat, and licked her lips.

He used her mouth first, holding her head in place and plunging into her almost desperately, seeking that rush of dark lust that blotted out every other thought. Her ripe red lips worked him, encouragement vibrating deep in her throat. Her hands clutched his buttocks, her nails digging deep. But oddly, the pain seemed very far away. As did the pleasure. It was as if his emotions were wrapped in a death shroud.

Unsatisfied, he left Ciara's mouth, and ordered her onto the bed, which was little more than a straw-stuffed pallet laid on a wooden frame. She lay with arms flung overhead, watching hungrily as he removed his clothing. Naked, he bent to retrieve something from the floor.

He crawled over her on all fours and entered her with one hard thrust. She gasped, hips arching. Catching her wrists, he wrapped them with the braided leather cord she'd worn at her waist. He looped the free end around the end rail of the bed frame and pulled the rope taut.

The sight of her lying bound and helpless brought a rush of dark, erotic satisfaction. In this one small area of his life, at least, he was master. Ciara enjoyed playing the slave. Her inner muscles milked his hardness; a shudder of pleasure ran through her. Her full breasts beckoned. He took one hardened nipple in his mouth and suckled.

"Aye!" she gasped. "Like that. Harder, Rhys! Harder—"

He drove his flesh into her with anger and lust and hopelessness. But try as he might, he could outrun none of it. His shame spread over him like a vermin-ridden blanket, until he all but choked with the ugliness of it. Ciara, oblivious to his inner turmoil, urged him on.

He was glad, he supposed, that one of them would take some fulfillment from their joining. With an odd detachment, as if he were spectator rather than participant, Rhys watched the frantic union of their bodies. His lust had long gone cold; he could have easily withdrawn and walked away. But Ciara would not appreciate that insult.

So Rhys closed his eyes and summoned a fantasy—one as forbidden and shameful as it was exciting.

In his mind's eye, the woman beneath him was not a whore. She was young, and innocent, and trusting. Freckles danced across a proud nose that was decidedly Roman. A gap showed between her front teeth. Her pointed chin hinted at her stubborn nature, and her hair . . . ah, her hair was a rare luxury. Long and bright as flame, it spilled and curled like a river of fire, circling her glorious round breasts. . . .

His lust returned with a vengeance. His cock hardened past endurance. Every stroke into Breena's lush, ripe body was the most agonizing bliss. . . .

Ciara cried out, convulsing with pleasure beneath him. Rhys yanked himself from her body just in time to groan his own release. His seed spilled milky white on her stomach and thighs.

Shame rushed in, hot on the heels of his climax. Heartsick, he fumbled with the knot on Ciara's bonds. When she was free, he jerked to his feet and strode the short length of the room to its single window. Throwing open the shutters, he braced one arm on the sill and looked out on blackness.

"Rhys? Is something wrong?"

The genuine concern in Ciara's voice made him hate himself even more. He pressed his forehead to the window frame, cold sweat beading on his forehead. Gods. How could he have imagined Breena naked, servicing him like a whore? She was just a girl. An innocent. The sister of his best friend. For years, Rhys had thought of her as his own sister.

Until her breasts and hips had rounded, and the

youthful worship in her eyes had turned to something sweeter and darker. And she began to speak to him of love, and of marriage.

Even now, the thought caused a bitter laugh to rise in his throat. He and Breena, married? He had nothing to offer her—not even the meanest roof to shelter her. But gods help him, he could not stop imagining her in his bed.

Someone should kick him in the head. No doubt Marcus would be more than pleased to do so, if his friend ever suspected the thoughts Rhys entertained.

"Rhys? Love?" Ciara's nude body pressed against his back. Her hands came around to stroke his chest. "Something is troubling ye, aye? Whatever it be, come back to bed. I'll help ye forget."

He only wished it were that easy. "I think not, Ciara. I am . . . just weary, perhaps. I've been traveling hard for days now, in the rain and mud. . . ."

"Lie down and sleep, then." She smiled. "And perhaps, in the morning . . ."

But morning found Rhys slipping from under Ciara's blanket without waking her. He dressed silently. He hadn't found the relief he'd sought in her bed. Just the opposite. Their bedplay had left him feeling more hopeless, and lonelier, than ever.

Perhaps his advancing age was catching up with him. By the gods, he was nearly thirty. He remembered a time when he could not have imagined being so ancient. He was too old, perhaps, to be seeking comfort from whores. By the time a man had seen thirty winters, he should have a wife tending his hearth. Children to teach. But Rhys would never enjoy those simple blessings.

He took up his pack. Was Breena wed? He'd been away almost a year; she might very well be someone's wife by now. Penn's, perhaps. During Rhys's last visit to Avalon, he'd noted an easy friendship between them. Penn was only a few years older than Breena. He was earnest and good, and strong in the Light. Aye, Penn would make Breena a fine husband.

His stomach turned. Last night's meat, perhaps. He thought it had been a bit off.

He paused at the door to slip a silver denarius from his purse. He laid the coin on Ciara's wash table. It was far more than she would expect from him. But she was more than welcome to it.

He would not, he thought, be coming back.

Chapter Two

Leave Avalon?" Rhys stared at his grandfather. "But . . . where would I go?"

"Many places," Cyric replied. "Britain is vast."

"I do not care how vast Britain is. I do not want to see it. I am content here, on the sacred isle. I want to live here forever."

A shadow passed through Cyric's eyes. "That is not possible, Rhys. It is not your destiny. Avalon is but your stopping place."

"It is not! It is my home!"

"No longer," Cyric said gravely. "The Great Mother has need of your magic elsewhere."

Fingers of dread wound through Rhys's chest. Leave Avalon? It was not possible. It had to be a jest! But he knew with sickening certainty it was not. Cyric never jested.

"Elsewhere?" Fear dripped through his veins like rancid oil. "To . . . to Isca Silurum, you mean?" It was the only place in the outside world he knew.

"Aye, there and to other cities and towns. Ye will travel with your harp, as a bard."

Rhys closed his eyes so Cyric would not see his abject panic. "But, Grandfather, why must I go? I do not understand."

"Ye will seek initiates for Avalon," Cyric told him. "It is a mission of grave importance. We are a small *settlement, Rhys. Without new blood, new magic, we will soon be gone. But ye will change our fortunes. Ye have the rare talent of seeing a Druid's magical soul. Ye will know those with great powers of Light, and ye will bring them to us."*

"I may return? Once I find someone with magic?"

"When ye come to me with an initiate for Avalon, ye'll be permitted to step onto the isle. But only for a fortnight. No more. Then ye must leave us again."

He was to be an outcast. His tears burned. How could Cyric do this to him? Rhys had always tried so hard to please him. It was Gwen who challenged their grandfather's authority at every turn.

Rhys opened his eyes. A tear trickled down his cheek. "But, sir, Gwen can see auras as well as I can! And she wants to leave Avalon. It is all she talks about. She would welcome a chance to hunt for Druid magic. Send her on this mission! Not me."

Cyric, eyes grave, shook his head. "That is not possible. Gwen's destiny lies here, on Avalon. She will one day be Guardian."

Nay! Rhys wanted to shout. That was to be his destiny, not Gwen's! His twin did not love Avalon as Rhys did. No one did.

But Rhys did not say these things, because Cyric was already turning away.

"Grandfather . . ."

The old man stopped and looked back at him. "Prepare yourself, Rhys. Ye leave us at dawn."

"It's Rhys! *Rhys!* I saw him! He's coming!"

A child's squeal set Breena's heart pumping so fast she thought her ribs might burst from the pressure. Her fingers cramped on old Mared's wooden pestle. Tears sprang into her eyes. The dried bits of root and seed blurred.

She didn't ever realize she'd dashed to the door until she found herself shoving it open. The others were already beginning to gather. Breena spied Gwen hurrying from her roundhouse, drying her hands on a rag.

"Rhys is coming!"

"Thank the Great Mother." Gwen's relief was palpable. Breena realized with a start that Rhys's sister had been as worried about Rhys as Breena had been.

Behind Breena, Mared stirred from her seat by the hearth. "What is all the commotion about, child? My ears are not what they once were." The old healer planted the tip of her oaken staff on the packed dirt floor and struggled to rise. Her thin arm trembled with the effort. Breena abandoned the scene outside the door and went to assist her.

"Rhys is coming across the swamp." Just saying his name tightened her chest.

Mared's wrinkled face broke into a smile. "Great Mother be blessed!" She motioned for Breena to help her to the door. "The lad has been gone far too long. I'd begun to fear I would not see him again in this life. Come, let us greet him."

By the time Breena had guided Mared from the hut, the entire population of the Druid village had collected in the common area. Marcus and the twins had joined Gwen. Breena's uncle, Owein, and his wife, Clara, were present with their own young son. Trevor, Penn, and the all the rest had abandoned their harvest in the orchard. Excitement shimmered in the air.

Owein approached, and Breena delivered Mared onto her uncle's arm. But when Owein escorted the old healer into the center of the crowd, Breena hung back. The others might not have seen Rhys for a year, but Breena had seen him only a fortnight past. She was not completely certain how she was going to look Rhys in the eye, with the memory of him kissing a tavern wench vivid in her mind. Every time Breena thought of it, she wanted to cry.

"I wonder if Rhys has brought Avalon a new initiate," she heard Penn say to no one in particular. "Let us go to the dock to greet him."

Some perverse force compelled Breena to follow the villagers down the steep path to the shore. She arrived in time to see Rhys's merlin, Hefin, circle the cove once and alight on a high branch. Rhys jumped from one of the rafts the settlement kept moored on the far side of the swamp.

Trevor waded into the water and greeted Rhys with as much emotion as Breena had ever seen the man display. Rhys returned a wide smile to the tall, taciturn Caledonian.

Breena stood half-hidden behind a curtain of yellowing willow fronds, reluctant to join the welcoming party. Taking the raft's pole and ropes from Rhys, Trevor bent to moor the craft. Rhys lifted his pack, slung it over one shoulder, and waded toward dry land.

A small girl splashed through the mud and threw her arms around Rhys's waist. Laughing, he lifted the child off her feet and swung her in a circle before plopping her down on the grass.

A burning lump formed in Breena's throat. Not so many years had passed since Rhys had greeted her that way. Every one of his visits to her family's farm was indelibly etched in her memory. In the early years, he would swing her about, muss her hair, and deliver some small treasure from his pack into her grasping hands.

As she grew older, their greetings had become more dignified. But no less exciting, at least to her. Her fingers crept to her throat, to the last gift Rhys had ever given her, when she was just fourteen. The silver pendant bore the sign of the Druids of Avalon. The charm was powerful protective magic: the triple spiral of the Great Mother Goddess merged with the cross of the Carpenter Prophet, whose teachings of Light had been brought to Avalon by the mysterious woman known as the Lady. Every female Druid on Avalon wore a similar pendant. The men bore the same mark, tattooed with woad, on their chests.

But soon after receiving that gift, Breena had made a serious mistake. Whenever she thought of that horrible afternoon at her father's house, she flushed hot with mortification. Ever since that day, Rhys had treated her with nothing more than polite indifference. He was almost a stranger to her now.

He was laughing, his thick white blond hair falling into his eyes. He pushed it back. He was so handsome. Bending, he opened his pack and extracted some small object. It promptly disappeared into the little girl's hands.

"Ooh!" she exclaimed, holding it up for all to see. "A pretty blue rock!"

The other Druid children clamored for treasures of their own, jumping and chattering all at once. Laughing, Rhys let himself be pulled down onto one knee. He opened his pack and produced a handful of stones and other trinkets, which he soon handed all around. He knew each boy and girl by name, of course. Indeed, he'd brought most of them to Avalon himself, from all over the Celtic isles, having discerned each child's powerful Druid talent by the color and strength of his or her magical aura.

"Get on with ye, ye ruffians." Gwen laughed as she pushed her way through the children. "I would embrace my brother before ye pick his bones dry."

Rhys straightened, his teeth flashing white as he held out his arms to his twin. "Gwen. 'Tis good to see you."

Gwen fell into his embrace. Her voice was uncharacteristically gruff as she gently chided him. "It has been far too long since Avalon has seen ye, Rhys. What do ye mean, staying away from home for almost a year?"

He stiffened slightly, and it seemed to Breena that while his smile remained on his lips, it faded from his eyes. "There was no reason for me to come," he said. "In all that time, I encountered no one with power strong enough to need Avalon's guidance."

Gwen slipped her arm around his waist. "Grandfather's old rule no longer keeps ye away. Ye may come and go as often as ye like."

"I know," Rhys said, planting a kiss on top of his sister's head. "Am I not here now?"

He greeted Marcus next, then clasped hands with Trevor and Owein, and produced a grin for Owein's wife, Clara, and their son. He laid a brotherly hand on Penn's shoulder, and drew him into animated conversation.

Breena drank in Rhys with her eyes, both craving and dreading the moment when he would look in her direction. It came soon enough, first with a stiffening of Rhys's shoulders, then with a slight frown as their gazes touched. In the next instant, his expression went blank, as if a dirty rag had wiped the joy of his homecoming right off his face.

There was no gift or exuberant hug for Breena; there was not even a handclasp or a smile. A slight dip of his chin was all the acknowledgment she received.

Breena swallowed hard and somehow kept her eyes dry, even though her heart was cracking to pieces. Why did Rhys treat her this way, when he knew how much she loved him? He gave his love and friendship to the other Druids. He'd given his passion to a nameless tavern wench. What did he give Breena?

Nothing.

Their gazes had held too long; the others were starting to notice. Marcus, especially, was narrowing his gaze. Rhys flicked a glance in the direction of his brother-by-marriage. Then he looked back to Breena, his careful smile as empty as a cracked jug.

"Breena," he said. "Well met."

"Blessed be your coming," she replied hollowly.

Rhys turned back to his twin. Arm in arm, they led the procession back to the village common, where Mared and Padrig waited. Rhys bowed to each Druid elder in turn. Mared raised her hand and murmured the blessings of the Great Mother and the Carpenter Prophet. Padrig followed with a prayer of thanks to all the gods and goddesses of Annwyn for Rhys's safe homecoming.

Rhys was soon relieved of his pack, and drawn into conversation with the men of the village. The women gathered to begin preparations for an impromptu feast. Breena did not join them. Instead, she returned to Mared's roundhouse and pounded roots until her hand ached.

But she could hardly miss the evening meal. Despite the chill, a large fire was built in the center of the common, and benches and plank tables set up all around, so the entire community could celebrate together.

Gwen claimed a seat at Rhys's right. Breena sat at another table entirely. Penn took the seat beside her, as he often did.

"Rhys does not look so well," he remarked in a low voice.

"He is very tired, I think."

"Aye. More weary than I have ever seen him. His is a hard life, and it can do him no good traveling in the wet and cold. I hope he stays through the winter in Avalon."

As the meal progressed, Rhys regaled the gathering

with tales of his year of wandering—some humorous, others filled with suspense. The children listened with round eyes.

When the meal was done, the calls for a song began. Rhys agreed with a smile, and his harp was soon brought to him. He cradled the instrument in his arms with all the care of a lover. His head bent, and his long fingers caressed the strings.

It was as if he were plucking Breena's body, causing it to ripple with sensation. She prayed desperately for numbness, but it was no use. Where Rhys was concerned, she couldn't *not* feel. Neither could she hold onto the anger she'd harbored since the night she'd seen more than she'd wanted.

Each note he played, each syllable he sang, stripped away a bit of her resentment, until there was none. Until there was only love, and longing, and that sweet, aching pull in her belly. And an even fiercer yearning between her thighs.

She hardly knew what Rhys sang. A ballad, perhaps. Or a song of Annwyn. She only knew that when his beautiful tenor touched her, she softened. Opened. For him.

His hair glinted silver in the dancing fire. Its light cast into stark relief the angles of his face. He sang one song after another. But as the night deepened, so did the shadow in his eyes, and Breena wondered if he wouldn't rather seek his bed.

And she wondered what woman he would dream of.

The shore was cold and damp. The seat of Rhys's breeches was wet where his arse touched the ground. The discomfort was welcome. Or, if not exactly welcome, tolerated. It allowed Rhys to focus on the wretchedness of his body, rather than the wretchedness of his soul. For that small distraction, he was grateful.

Silence spread like a woolen blanket over Avalon. Far off, a raptor screeched. Perhaps it was Hefin, hunting. The village, however, slept. Rhys had tried to do the same, on the spare pallet in Trevor's roundhouse. He was as tired as he could ever remember—exhausted in soul as well as body. But sleep would not come.

Sleep never came to him easily, here on Avalon.

Aye, he could drop off at a moment's notice camped by the road, under trees and sky. He slept effortlessly in vermin-ridden haylofts, or wrapped in a thin blanket in front of some stranger's hearth. And he'd slumbered soundly in any number of beds belonging to widows and whores.

But here in Avalon, surrounded by the people he loved, and who loved him in return, he could not sleep. His loneliness was too profound, his hurt too deep.

He wanted what he could not have. Desperately.

Gwen had scolded him soundly for staying away so long. He was sorry to have frightened his twin. Once they had been so close, they had shared nearly every thought, but now Gwen's husband was first in her heart, and her connection with her twin had faded. Still, his sister loved him deeply, even if she understood him less well. He wondered if she suspected that Breena was the reason Rhys had stayed away so long.

Now that he could no longer tell himself she was too young to give herself to a man, he could not look at her without wanting her beneath him. Or on her knees, her red lips parting eagerly. Or bent over a bed, or chair, or even a log, as he slaked his lust like a rutting beast. Or with her wrists bound—

He broke that sickening thought with a shudder of raw guilt.

Marcus would kill him for even imagining such things about Breena. But Rhys couldn't help it. He might travel to Hibernia, or the far northern isles . . . he might warm the beds of a thousand whores . . . he might drink himself to oblivion, or walk until he dropped. . . . And still he would not be able to wipe Breena from his mind.

The worst of his torment, perhaps, came from the knowledge that had he truly belonged to Avalon, he would have been able to have her. If his grandfather had not condemned him to a life of homelessness. Even though Cyric was dead, Rhys did not for one moment imagine he could give up his wandering on Avalon's behalf. He'd seen, through Cyric's magic, the terrible future Britain would face if Rhys abandoned his search for Druid magic. Only by bringing the most powerful Druids to Avalon, to be trained in the Light, could he ensure that darkness would not overtake his land and his people.

Aye, Cyric's vision of Britain's precarious future meant that happiness was a blessing Rhys would never know. Perhaps there might have been hope, had Breena been raised in poverty, as Rhys had been. Until four years ago, Breena's home had been a prosperous Roman estate. She'd been born to luxuries Rhys hadn't even known to dream of during his own childhood. The comfort and security of the Celtic settlement of Avalon was a primitive life for her. The hard life of a wandering minstrel's wife? He almost laughed. Unthinkable.

He stared into the fog and the darkness. He should not have come. Visiting Avalon, far from comforting him, had only driven loneliness and hopelessness deeper into his cold heart.

"Rhys?"

He would have known her voice at a hundred paces. As it was, she spoke from only a few steps behind his back. He dropped his head and pressed his forehead to his bent knees. He could not face her. Not now. Perhaps if he gave no answer, she would simply leave.

He should have known better. Even as a small lass, Breena had been too stubborn for her own good.

"Rhys, what are you doing here all alone? Are you . . . all right? You're not ill, are you?"

He admitted defeat by lifting his head. "Nay."

He didn't look back as she approached. His body tightened as she neared, the scent of roses wafting before her. He could not suppress the wholly inappropriate hardening of his cock.

She stood beside him, just visible in his peripheral vision, hesitant, shivering. His first instinct was to pull her into his arms and warm her. But because he had some measure of honor left, he did not.

"Why are you here?" Her teeth chattered a little. She rubbed her arms. "The whole village is asleep."

"You are not."

She did not answer. He did not rise, nor did she move to sit. He glanced up at her, but could not discern her expression in the darkness.

"But you should be asleep," he said. "Did you follow me, Bree?"

"Yes," she confessed. "I woke and . . . I needed air. I opened my shutters, and saw you leave Trevor's roundhouse. When you did not return . . ."

"You should not have come after me. You should be in bed."

She hugged herself more tightly. "I . . . have not been able to sleep much of late."

He caught the tremor of fear in her voice. "The silver visions?" he asked sharply. "Have they returned?"

"Yes, the visions . . ." She blew out a white plume of breath. "But that is not all. You were gone so long. Even Gwen was frightened for you. As for me . . . I think of you often, Rhys. Especially at night, when I . . ." Her voice faltered.

Dear gods in Annwyn! He did not want to hear this.

She stood so close now, her skirt brushed his knee. Exactly when she'd moved, he did not know.

She sat down beside him. He fought the urge to put his arm around her. Or get up and run. He wasn't sure which he wanted to do more.

"The ground is wet," he said.

"I don't care."

A heavy silence fell between them. It lengthened into awkwardness. The night seemed to contract around him, until the darkness contained nothing but the lap of water on the shore, the shush of Breena's breathing, and his own pounding heart.

He inhaled her scent. She must have put rose oil in her bathwater. It was a Roman fragrance, very much prized by wealthy women. The aroma seemed to draw a thin, straight line between them. He did not try to cross it. He knew better.

Unfortunately, she did not. "Will you stay the winter in Avalon? I . . . I do hope so. Everyone has missed you." She paused. "I have missed you."

He was ashamed at how fiercely he drank in those four words. She had missed him. His cock responded, even as he fought to remain detached from a rush of tangled emotions. In the grand scheme of things, it did not matter that Breena missed him.

"I'll stay perhaps a sennight," he said. "Until the harvest feast. After that . . . I must go."

She uttered a sound of dismay. "But that is hardly any time at all! Gwen will not have it, Rhys, I am telling you that right now. She will not allow you to—"

"My sister has no authority over my comings and goings." The words were harsher than he'd intended.

Breena sucked in a breath. "I . . . I didn't mean to imply that she did. Only . . . only that she loves you. She misses you dreadfully when you're gone."

"No one should miss me. I am not a part of Avalon."

"How can you say that? Why, you're the most important part of us! Without you, the sacred isle would be all but deserted. Most of us are here only because you brought us."

It was true. Of Cyric's original small band of Druids, only Mared and Padrig remained. And Gwen, of course. All the others . . . dead. Or lost.

As Rhys was.

"I'm used to wandering," he told her. "I am more comfortable on the road."

"What nonsense! You could not possibly be."

He made no reply.

"Mared says in the past, when Cyric was alive, you visited far more often, and stayed longer. But now that your grandfather is dead, and your freedom greater, you stay away. Rhys, is it . . . is it because of me? Do you . . . do you hate me so much?"

He turned so abruptly she lurched backward. He grabbed her arm to steady her. He released her an instant later, as if he'd touched a hot coal.

"I could never hate you." He swallowed. "How could you imagine such a thing? You are like a sis—"

"I am not your sister! I never was, and I don't want to be. Rhys, I lo—"

"Gods in Annwyn, Breena!" He jerked to his feet. "Do not say it. Please."

She stared up at him. "Why not? It is the truth."

"What you want from me can never be the truth between us."

Slowly, she pushed to her feet, regarding him with sober eyes. "Rhys. You are shaking."

He was. He turned and paced a few steps away. His hand went to the back of his neck. He needed some space.

But her voice followed. "I understand now why you rejected me that day at my father's house. I know why you flung all those hurtful words at me. I was too young for what I was asking of you. But, Rhys, that was four years ago. I'm no longer that girl. I'm a woman now."

He clenched his teeth. *Gods.* Aye, she was a woman. A lush, tempting . . .

Her words battered him. "There's no longer any need to push me away. Don't you see? I love you, Rhys. I always have, and I always will. And I think you l—"

Something snapped inside him. He spun around, and stalked toward her. "Breena, stop. Before you say something you'll regret."

"No! I won't. I'll say what's in my heart. I lov— mmph!"

He'd covered her mouth with his palm. His other hand gripped her shoulder. "Don't," he pleaded. "*Don't.*"

Her eyes were huge. In the moonlight they looked gray rather than the clear blue he knew them to be. And in them . . . a spark of dangerous, feminine knowledge.

Her lips parted. Her breath bathed his palm. Before he could react, before he could even *think,* she tasted his skin with the tip of her hot, wet tongue.

The tiny point of moisture caused his brain to seize. His cock, already more than half hard, flashed into full arousal. And still, he might have resisted. Might have pulled back completely, and retained some shred of his honor.

If she hadn't pressed her open palm on his stomach. And slid it downward, slowly.

He grabbed her wrist and yanked it away. The sudden movement caused her to pitch forward. Her body fell against his, her soft round breasts squashed against his chest. He opened his mouth to scold her.

She went up on her tiptoes and kissed the words from his mouth.

Her lips were sweet honey and spice. He could not

summon the strength to resist claiming a small taste. He licked them, parted them, drank in her innocence like water from a pure stream. She opened beneath him like a spring blossom. Her artless response fired his blood; the kiss turned hot, and hard. He pulled her close, one hand anchored at her nape, the other slipping down to cup her bottom.

Mindlessly, he ground himself against her, thrusting his tongue into her mouth in a savage parody of what he wanted to do to her body. She should have protested. Should have pushed him away, slapped him, screamed for help . . . anything to stop this madness. Instead, she ignited like living flame in his arms. She returned his kiss, in full measure. She clung to his neck, and purred deep in her throat. Like a cat, she rubbed her body against him.

He was an instant away from throwing her down and taking her right there, in the mud. Gods. Nay. He couldn't. Panic closed his throat. His next breath caught no air at all.

He grabbed her wrists and wrenched them from his neck. She gasped, but did not protest. He meant to release her, push her away, but some dark demon inside him would not allow it. Instead, he forced her wrists to the small of her back, and anchored them in one hand.

Her head fell back, and a low moan escaped her lips. The lust that surged through him then was stunning in both darkness and strength. His hand, trembling, covered the lush globe of her breast. The peak hardened against his palm.

"Gods, Rhys," she gasped. "Yes . . ."

He dropped his head to the crook of her neck, his chest heaving, his body and brain battling like gladiators in the arena. This yearning, this torment . . . it was too much for a man to bear. More than anything, he wanted to surrender. But it was wrong. Very wrong.

Her lips nuzzled his ear. "Gods, Rhys, I've missed you. I love you so. And . . . I knew you loved me. I knew it. Marcus and Gwen will be so glad. . . ."

Marcus.

Marcus, glad to find Rhys mauling his beloved little sister on a muddy beach? Rhys thought not. The man would be enraged, and rightly so. A homeless wanderer was no fitting mate for Breena. Even worse, Marcus was the one man who knew the kind of sexual encounters Rhys craved—they'd often hunted whores together in their youth. On occasion, when they'd been short on coin, they'd even shared a woman between them.

Aye, if Marcus were to stumble upon Rhys right now, he would waste no time in beating him to a bloody pulp. And Rhys, for his part, would not lift a finger to defend himself.

It took every dram of his strength, but at last he forced his hands to his sides and stepped back. Released from his grip, Breena swayed, blinking up at him with hazy eyes.

"Rhys? What is it? What is wrong?"

"Everything. This . . . this cannot happen between us, Breena. It is not right."

"What?" She lifted her hands. "Of course it is right! We belong together. I have always known it."

"Nay," he said. "We do not."

A beat of silence ensued. "But . . . you wanted me. Just now. Don't try to tell me you didn't! I *felt* it, Rhys." Her throat worked. "Quite plainly. You cannot deny it."

He forced a laugh. "What you felt was the natural reaction of any man, to any woman. It meant nothing."

Her breath hissed through her teeth. "I do not believe that for a moment. You want me. Why can you not admit it? I'm no longer a girl. I can be your wife now. I can travel with you. Help you find initiates for

Avalon. Why, I am certain that my Sight can be of help—"

"No," he ground out. "You cannot travel with me. The very thought is absurd."

"Why? I would like to travel. Marcus has covered the distance from Rome to Caledonia! I've never even seen Londinium."

"Breena, my travels are not a lark. I do not visit fancy inns. Just the opposite. I seek out the lowest, meanest places. Or the wildest ones. That is where I am most likely to find what I'm looking for."

He felt her hesitation. But it lasted no more than a heartbeat. "I'd happily stay in those places, Rhys, if it meant we could be together."

"You only say that because you cannot imagine what it is like. The privations of Avalon are trial enough for you, even with Marcus's improvements! You could not be content sleeping before a stranger's hearth, or on a low tavern's flea-ridden pallet. Or perhaps a stinking stable or barn would please you? Or sometimes, Breena, there is no roof at all. I often sleep in the open, even in the rain, and count myself lucky if a brigand does not murder me in my sleep."

"Rhys—"

"I have nothing, Breena. Nothing but the clothes on my back, my harp, and my duty."

"Oh, Rhys, that's just not true! You have a family, and people who love you. And a home. Right here, on Avalon."

His laugh was low and bitter. "Avalon is not my home. My grandfather made certain of that."

"Cyric is dead. And you said yourself that Gwen has no control over your comings and goings. You could live here if you wanted."

"Nay," he said. "I could not. And you know that. You know of Cyric's visions of Britain's future."

"I know he saw two possibilities. One was a nightmare—Britain torn by war, plundered by barbarians from over the sea. The second was a bright dream—a strong, peaceful Britain, ruled by a Druid king. But Rhys, to my mind, neither vision makes sense! Where is the Roman army in Cyric's vision? Britain is one of Rome's most prosperous provinces. The legions would never tolerate barbarian raiders. Still less, a Druid king."

"Aye, I know. Gwen and I have discussed the mystery at great length. Both visions seem unlikely. But Cyric was a powerful Druid. These visions cannot be devoid of meaning."

"What if they are? What if Cyric was wrong?"

"Then I will likely never know it. But I cannot take that chance." He sighed, and dragged a hand down his face. "I cannot say I understand any of it. I can only tell you that even with Cyric in his grave, I do not dare go against his command. My grandfather's visions came from the Great Mother."

Breena gripped his arm. "If you tell me it is the will of the Great Mother that you wander, Rhys, I believe you with all my heart. But it doesn't have to keep us apart! If you love me even half as much as I love you, we can find a way. I am not as pampered and as fragile as you make me out to be. I can travel with you, truly I can. It would be hard, yes, but you would not hear a word of complaint from my lips."

"And when you are with child, what then? Am I to allow my pregnant wife to sleep on a stranger's floor? Have you birth my babe in a barn? Shall I haul our children the length and breadth of Britain in the rain and snow?"

"No." Breena's voice cracked a bit. "Of . . . of course not. I . . . . I suppose I could stay on Avalon then."

"So you can watch the swamps for my infrequent return? What kind of life would that be? You'd be miserable. And you'd soon come to hate me."

She hugged herself and turned away. "I would never hate you. There must be a way for us to be together."

"Breena, surely you are intelligent enough to realize it would not work. You are better off marrying a man who can give you a real marriage. A man who will live here on Avalon and be a father to your children." He cleared his throat. "Someone like Penn, for instance."

She spun around, and flung her arms wide. "I do not love Penn! And he does not love me. Not in that way."

"Then you will choose someone else," Rhys insisted. "Trevor, perhaps? He is a good man."

Her voice trembled. "I don't want anyone else, Rhys. Can't you understand that? I love you. I want you."

And gods help him, he wanted her.

"Breena, please. Let us not speak of this again. Do not even think of it. I will not marry you. And I will not change my mind. I beg you, find another man on which to fix your fantasies."

He heard a sudden *whoosh,* as if all the air rushed from her lungs. "Oh. So I'm to find another man for my fantasies, am I? While you find whores for your bed?"

"I am a man," Rhys said quietly. "I am not celibate. I won't pretend that I am."

"Of course you are not. How could you possibly be celibate when there are no end of public-house wenches ready to lift their skirts and dance to your music? And invite you above stairs after? What man could resist such an invitation?"

He stilled. "I don't know what you're talking about."

But it was a lie. Her description matched too closely that last, awful night with Ciara. The night that had left him feeling so shamed and hopeless that dawn had found him fleeing to Avalon on a knife's edge of desperation.

A horrible suspicion took shape. "Breena. What are you saying? What . . . what do you know?"

She hugged herself tightly. A defensive posture. But her eyes were spitting sparks. "Tell me, Rhys. How was that blonde whore? Did she please you?"

Shock and shame gagged him. His mouth dropped open, but no sound emerged. He could only stare at her, aghast.

"No doubt she knew her business." Breena's voice shook. "She looked as though she'd bedded every man in that dingy outpost. Did she put her tricks to good use? Did you enjoy fu—"

A red rage washed over him. He didn't remember moving, but suddenly his hands were on her shoulders, and he was shaking her, brutally, trying to stop the ugly words from spilling out of her mouth.

"You used your magic to spy on me! You *watched* me, while I—" He choked, and shook her again, hard.

Her head snapped forward and back. "Rhys—" she gasped. "Please—"

"By all the gods in Annwyn, Breena, what did you see? *What did you see?*"

Gods help him. Had she watched Ciara strip? Take him in her mouth? Had Breena been a silent specter over his shoulder when he tied Ciara's wrists and used her like the whore she was? The thought enraged him. Shamed him. And aroused him.

And that shamed him all the more.

He shook her again. "Did you watch us?" he asked hoarsely. "Did you see—"

"No! Gods, no!" She clawed at his hands. "I saw nothing! Nothing! Please, Rhys, stop shaking . . . let me go. You're hurting me—"

He released her so abruptly, she stumbled and nearly fell. She backed off a few paces, arms wrapped around her torso, trembling, her eyes round.

"I didn't watch you . . . having relations with that woman. Do you really believe I could stand that? I only watched you enter the tavern, and play your harp. When you started up the stairs . . . I broke the vision."

Relief flooded him. He drew a ragged breath. "Breena, you should not have been looking at all."

"I-I know. I'm sorry! But I couldn't help it. I was worried about you. You'd been gone so long. I had to see if you were all right."

"That would have taken but a moment."

She rubbed her arms and didn't answer.

"Have you learned nothing from Gwen and Owein? Druid magic is sacred. One does not use it for personal amusement."

"Believe me, Rhys. I was not amused."

"Nay. I imagine you were not. But Breena, it is none of your business if I bed a hundred women."

Her voice broke. "But . . . those women cannot love you as I do. How can you go to them, when I—"

"When you are what? Waiting for me here, in Avalon? Weaving fantasies of a life that can never be? The gods know I have tried my best to cure you of your delusions."

She was crying now, sucking in big gulps of air. Each sob felt like a dull knife goring his heart. "I love you. I always have. And I'll never love anyone else!"

He had never hated himself quite so much as he did at that very moment. "Bree, please, listen to me. Whatever your feelings, you must put them aside. There is nothing between us. There never can be. The sooner you believe that, the sooner your heart will be free to love another."

His words tasted like bitter ash on his tongue.

"I wish that were true," she said through her tears. They were running down her cheeks, but she made no move to dash them away. "I wish I felt nothing for you.

I even wish that I could hate you. I've tried, you know. I've tried very hard to hate you. But somehow, I just . . . can't."

She waited a moment, as if hoping for a reply. When Rhys said nothing, her shoulders slumped. She whirled around. After a long moment, she squared her shoulders and walked away without a word.

Just before she faded into the gloom, he whispered, "Perhaps, in time, you will."

Chapter Three

*B*reena returned to her bed, only to toss and turn all night. But it was no use. One moment her body was hot with the memory of Rhys's mouth and hands, the next she was shivering with the cold of his rejection. At last, she abandoned even the pretense of sleep. She rose and lit a lamp. And forced herself to face reality.

It was really, truly over.

Over? a small voice in her head taunted. *Why, it never began!*

The walls of her small room squeezed tightly. It was too warm. She couldn't breathe. She had to get out. She padded through the common room and slipped her cloak from its hook by the door. Her twin niece and nephew, cuddled like puppies on their pallet just outside their parents' door, did not stir. Once in the open, Breena paused.

Her first impulse was to go to the Grail spring, but the place reminded her too keenly of the night she'd used her magic to spy on Rhys. The high slope? No. That holy place was forbidden, save for certain rituals.

Perhaps it would be best to leave the island—and Rhys—for a short time. She knew a place in the hills sacred to the Great Mother; she would go there and seek her counsel. Decision made, she gathered her cloak around her shoulders and hurried down the path to the dock.

Separating a raft from its mooring, she thrust its long pole into the shallow water and shoved the craft into the thick of Gwen's protective mist. The magical fog clung to the vessel, as if reluctant to allow Breena's escape. She gritted her teeth and stabbed her pole all the harder.

Scant moments later, the sacred isle disappeared into the mist. Gray fog spread in every direction. Breena shoved her raft through the void, hoping her sense of direction had not failed her. She emerged from the mists some time later, the slopes of the Mendips rising before her.

Dawn already lightened the eastern sky. Breena moored the raft behind a screen of willow fronds and murmured a lookaway spell. Though Avalon was remote, travelers did occasionally pass this way.

The sun rose as she climbed, brambles snagging her skirt. By the time she reached the summit, she was panting in the crisp autumn air. The dawn colors had given way to a brilliant blue sky.

She did not like it. Heavy gray clouds, or even a storm would have been more appropriate to her mood. But the exercise did her some good. Her heart remained heavy in the hollow space that was her chest, but by the time she reached the high meadow, her tears had mostly subsided.

From this vantage, the misty swamp seemed to stretch on forever. There was no sign of the steeply sloping island that was her home; Avalon was well hidden by Gwen's protective mists. Even knowing exactly where the sacred isle lay, Breena could not discern so much as a hint of its outline.

The long meadow grass, yellow and stiff with hoarfrost, crunched under her shoes. A fertile hollow existed in the circular depression created by a ring of barren rock, like a treasure hidden within cupped hands. A massive blue-gray stone, eroded by age and pitted with scars, stood in the center of the small field. Patches of lichen and moss mottled its surface. Deep spirals, carved by an ancient hand, marked the megalith as sacred to the Great Mother.

The Druids of Avalon often prayed before the stone. Breena approached it now with an air of great respect. If she held herself very still, and closed her eyes, she could feel its deep magic as a subtle vibration beneath her feet.

The stone's color did not match that of the surrounding rock; it was clear the megalith had been brought to this place from afar. Breena thought it must have been very deep magic indeed that had moved such a giant. Bowing her head, she placed her palm on the stone's cool surface and uttered the prayer she'd brought in her heart to this sacred place.

"Help me . . . help me forget Rhys. Help me find someone else to love."

She forced a swallow past the unshed tears burning her throat. "Help me find a man who will love me in return."

It was a difficult prayer to speak. Her vision blurred as the words left her lips. Her heart felt as though someone had cut it open with a jagged piece of glass. Rhys would never again kiss her. Never take her to his bed. Never love her.

Tears spilled onto her cheeks. She sagged against the stone, turning to press her shoulder blades against its comforting solidity. Her prayer had not assuaged her grief. If anything, it had made it worse. She closed her eyes, willing the tears to stop.

"'Tis far too fine a day, lass, for so sad a face."

She gasped. Her eyes flew open. If her prayer had only encouraged her tears, now pure shock dried them. The mild comment had been uttered by an old man, white of hair and long of beard. He held a stout oaken staff.

She knew her expression showed her shock; her reaction seemed to amuse him. The corners of his light-colored eyes crinkled. But humor was not the only emotion she read in his expression. Another emotion, wistful and intent, was etched in the lines bracketing his eyes.

He stood not five strides before her, oddly dressed in a long gray robe. He was a Celt, of that she had no doubt. He was very tall, taller than any Roman she had ever seen. His long beard, white with a few fading blond strands, was braided in the Celtic style. He'd seen at least sixty years, Breena judged. Despite his age, he retained the erect bearing of a much younger man. She was sure he did not carry his wooden staff for support.

He had not been in the meadow when she'd entered. He must have been hidden behind one of the boulders ringing the field. But where, beyond that, had he come from? Avalon was the only settlement for miles. But the man was hardly dressed for travel. Perhaps he'd camped in one of the many caves nearby? He might be a pilgrim, come to pray at the Great Mother's stone, as she had.

"Who are you, sir?"

He did not answer. Instead he tilted his head and studied her. As the moments tripped by, she began to wonder if he had even heard her question. Unease crawled up her spine. The man might be old, but that did not mean he was harmless. In fact, she was beginning to suspect that he was a Druid. Was he of the Light? Or did he serve darkness? She had no way of knowing.

She shifted her weight to her left foot, considering a prudent retreat. His sharp eyes followed the movement.

"I assure you, lass. I mean no harm."

She stared at him, uncertain how to answer. His lips crooked in a smile. He was an utter stranger to her, but for some reason, her initial panic was fading. He took a step forward, his hand lifting. For a moment she thought he might reach for her. But then his hand dropped.

"So young," he murmured. "So, so young. Just a child, really."

She stiffened. "I am not a child."

His smile widened. He inclined his head. "Of course not. You are a woman grown. Please. You must forgive the ramblings of a foolish old man."

She sniffed, trying to place the old man's accent. He spoke British Celtic, but with an inflection that was almost Roman. And yet, she was certain Latin was not his first tongue.

"Who are you?" she asked again. "How have you come to be here? You must have traveled far—there is no village for miles."

"No?" The word conveyed mild surprise. "Then you, too, must be far from your home."

Heat crept up Breena's neck. Curse her quick tongue! It was forbidden to speak of Avalon to outsiders, but it had to be plain that she had not traveled far to this place.

"I've come to the Great Mother's stone to pray," she answered vaguely.

"You've been crying."

There was no point in denying it. "Yes."

"Let me guess on the reason." The old man paused. "The man you love is giving you trouble."

Breena was astonished. "Why, how did you know?"

He laughed. "My dear, when a lass of your age is troubled, the cause can usually be traced to a man."

She grimaced. "He has been nothing but trouble, if you must know. He is a very difficult man. He believes that since he is so much older than me, we can never be together."

"Ah, well. Doubts are to be expected in an older man. They have so many more uncertainties than young ones."

"I would think the opposite true."

"It is youth that is so certain of its path," he said. "As a man ages, black and white merge to become shifting shades of gray. But this older man of yours, if he is blind to your worth, then he is very foolish."

"And very stubborn! There is no reasoning with him."

"So you came to pray? To ask the Great Mother to change his mind?"

"No. I asked her to help me stop loving him."

Surprise registered on the old man's face. "Truly?" he murmured. "You have given up hope? Then this man of whom you speak is even more foolish than I first imagined."

Breena shrugged. "He does not think he is foolish. He thinks I am. We fought last night, terribly. That's why I had to get away. I couldn't stand to see him this morning."

"And you didn't tell a soul where you were going, did you?"

She peered at the old man more closely. "You cannot know that."

He shrugged. "I know many things. Others, I can guess. I have lived a long life."

He stepped closer. Breena tensed when he halted within arm's length, but he simply reached past her shoulder and laid a reverent hand on the stone behind her.

"You feel the life coursing in the rock," he said. "As I do."

"You are Druid," she said.

"Yes."

"If that is so, then you should come—" She broke off. It was not her place to invite anyone to the sacred isle—that was Rhys's task. And it was no accident Rhys brought mostly children to Avalon. Older Druids had already chosen their paths. Light, or darkness.

Which had this old man chosen?

"Eh, lass?" He cocked his head. "Where should I go?"

"Nowhere," Breena mumbled. "I spoke hastily."

He stroked the stone. "That is true. You should not speak of Avalon to outsiders."

Her jaw dropped. "You know of the sacred isle?"

"I once encountered a man who spoke of it. A wandering bard."

"Rhys?"

"He may have called himself by that name. He thought to bring me to his Druid isle. But at the time, I was . . . unable to make the journey."

"Rhys is in Avalon now," Breena said. "I . . . could send him to you if you'd like."

The old man seemed to consider it. "No," he said at last. "I think not. I did not come all this way to see him. Nor his sacred isle."

Breena was confused. "I don't understand. Who *are* you? And why would you travel all this way, if not to seek Avalon?"

A scant smile touched the old man's lips. "My name is Myrddin, my dear. As for the reason I am here . . . why, Breena, can you not guess? I have come for you."

Breena gaped at the old Druid. Several long moments passed before she found her tongue. "You know my name?"

Myrddin nodded. "You are Breena, daughter of Rhiannon, who is herself a daughter of the great northern queens. You are a Druid. A Seer." He paused. "Your aura is very strong."

"But . . . how do you know of me? Did Rhys tell you? Or are you a Seer yourself?"

"I am not a Seer. But I am . . . close . . . to one who is."

"And this person . . . has Seen me?"

The old Druid spread his hands. "She has Seen that you are troubled by terrible visions you do not understand."

She hesitated. "That is true enough."

Myrddin's gaze was intent. "Tell me what you have Seen, Breena."

She did not even think to hold the truth back from him. "I have had the dream for years, but recently, it has come more frequently. And . . . it has changed. I think . . . I think that is what frightens me most."

"Go on."

"It starts with a series of disconnected images. First, a falcon circles once around an army watchtower, then flies off. I see a silver goblet, filled with wine. I hit it with the back of my hand, and it tips over. As I stare at the spilling wine, it fades. I find myself standing before a window. One of the panes suddenly cracks in a jagged line. Then a full moon rises, bloodred, over a sea cliff. Behind the broken glass, it looks as though it is split in two.

"I try to think what it all means. But I cannot understand. And then there is a reflection in the window, and I turn. There is a woman standing before me. She is tall, and shapely, and though I cannot make out her features, I know she is very beautiful. A silver mist rises, to swirl all around her. After that—"

She broke off with a shudder. What came next was by far the worst part of the nightmare. She did not want to continue, but when Myrddin nodded, eyes grave, she swallowed and forced herself to speak.

"A man appears, from behind me. I can see only his back as he halts before the woman. He raises his hand, and . . . and slaps her. She cries out, but of course I cannot hear. And then his hands go to her throat. I try to move, but my feet are frozen. He shakes her. Chokes her. I try to shout, but I cannot breathe. She fights at first, but in the end she goes . . . limp. He releases her and she falls to the floor and does not move again. And then the darkness rushes in, and everything goes black. . . ."

Myrddin's arm came around her. Breena became aware that she was trembling like a dry leaf. With an effort, she stepped away.

The old Druid's gaze remained upon her. "Breena, the woman in your vision—she is known to me. That is why I have come."

Breena's pulse leapt. A low hum vibrated in her ears. "You know her? She is real? Who is she?"

"Her name is Igraine, and, yes, she is as real as you or I. And she is . . . in need of your magic. Will you go to her?"

"Go where? Is it far?"

"That," Myrddin replied, "is an exceedingly difficult question to answer. In one sense, it is not so far. In another, farther than you can imagine."

"You speak in riddles."

"Life is often a riddle, is it not? And magic—ah, magic!—that is always a riddle." He held out a hand. "Will you come?"

The question was more than Breena could absorb on a moment's notice. "You mean—right now? But . . . that's preposterous! I cannot just go off with you."

"Time is of the essence, Breena. Igraine is in danger, and I do not have to describe to you the evil that is poised to strike. You have seen it many times. We must act swiftly if we are to stop it."

Breena's gaze flew to the misty swamp. "But—"

"You would run back first, to ask permission? Like a child?"

Her jaw tightened. "I am not a child. But the others will worry if I don't return."

"And if you go home, and explain, do you imagine they will allow you to leave with me?"

She hesitated. Myrddin spoke the truth. There was not a single chance in Hades that Marcus would be inclined to allow her to go anywhere with this stranger. Gwen would question Myrddin thoroughly, of course. But even if Avalon's Guardian determined the old Druid was sincere, Marcus would insist on accompanying Breena to wherever it was Myrddin meant to take her. Marcus would probably invite Owein as well. And Trevor. And Rhys. . . .

Anger flooded her cheeks. Gwen had told Breena many times that her vision came from the Great Mother. The dream carried a purpose. *Breena's* purpose. She'd been waiting all her life to discover what it might be. Was she to seek it now with an army of overprotective family hovering over her shoulder?

Still, she could hardly just disappear with a stranger. What she needed right now was Gwen's advice. Gwen understood the significance of Breena's vision better than anyone. As Guardian of Avalon, Gwen would not permit even her husband's most violent protest to interfere with the will of the Great Mother.

"Perhaps . . . perhaps I can bring Avalon's Guardian to you," she told Myrddin. "The three of us may discuss what is to be done."

The old Druid gave a shake of his head. "There is no time. You must come with me now. Or not at all."

"But—how can I? They will be frantic! They will think I've . . . fallen to my death, or been set upon by brigands. My brother will tear the hills apart, looking for me."

Myrddin's eyes softened. "It will be difficult for those who love you, I know. And I am sorry for it. I wish the decision could be easier for you."

"Why give me a choice at all if it is so important? I begin to believe you are powerful enough to take me against my will."

His jaw tightened. "Only a servant of the dark would seize you against your will. I would like to believe I am yet a follower of the Light. You will come of your own free will, or not at all."

Breena considered the old Druid's words. Surely they proved his sincerity? And yet. . . . "I am not sure."

He ran a hand down his face, ending with a tug on his beard. "No one is ever sure, lass."

"If only I could tell the others. . . ."

"No. It would not be wise."

She shut her eyes briefly. "Then . . . I cannot go with you. I am sorry."

Myrddin gazed at her in silence for a long moment. Then he simply sighed, and bowed his head. When he raised it again, she was struck by the vast weariness in his eyes.

"As you wish. I see I was mistaken in thinking you were old enough to follow this path. In truth, you are still a child." So saying, he planted his staff in the dirt. Turning, he strode toward a cleft in the rocks edging the meadow."

"I am not a child!" Breena called after him.

He paused and looked back. "Then prove it. Come with me. I give you my word that I walk in Light, and do the will of the Great Mother. But then," he added softly, "you know that, do you not?"

She inhaled a sharp breath. Though Myrddin's aura was not visible to her, she could feel his magic, vibrating with the same perfect frequency as that of the Great Mother's stone. In that moment, she would have staked her life on the old Druid's sincerity.

"I do know it," she said.

"Then come with me. Your magic is needed. Not only by Igraine, but by tens of thousands of Britons whose lives and future depend on her safety."

It was the hint of desperation, and the vivid fear in Myrddin's clear eyes that decided her.

"All right," she said. "I will."

Chapter Four

Rhys was, at heart, a coward.

Why else had he awakened Trevor before dawn, to mumble a ludicrous tale of an errand in the coastal town of Isca Dumnoniorum? Because it required a sennight to travel there and back. A sennight in which he would not have to face the hurt in Breena's eyes.

Rhys did not for a moment think Trevor believed his story. The taciturn Caledonian's eyes had narrowed in suspicion. But in the end, he had merely grunted and turned over on his pallet. Rhys had collected his meager belongings and fled.

He did not actually mean to go to Isca Dumnoniorum, of course. He'd simply camp in the hills across the swamp. His harp and Hefin would be company enough. When had he ever had more?

The village was silent, and the journey through the mist uneventful. Scant hours later, Rhys lounged at the mouth of a south-facing cave, a small fire warming the morning's chill. Leaning back on his elbows, he watched Hefin draw lazy arcs against a blue sky.

Briefly, he considered joining his animal companion aloft. All he'd need to do was shuck off his clothes and call his shape-shifting magic. What a relief it would be, to take to the sky in his falcon form, leaving his human troubles far below on the ground. But much as Rhys craved the mindless oblivion of his animal self, he knew he would not cast the spell to throw off his humanity. Shape-shifting was dangerous deep magic.

When Cyric had been Guardian of Avalon, he'd forbidden deep magic. Now, with Rhys's grandfather dead, the stricture was not absolute. But that did not mean the Druids of Avalon called such power lightly. They did not. Rhys had shifted to falcon form only a handful of times in his life, when the need was dire. Gwen, who possessed similar magic, was more familiar with her wolf form. Thus far, Rhys's shifting had not resulted in disaster, though more than once it had been a near thing. It was not wise to tempt the gods.

Heart heavy, he gazed out over the swamps. A braver man would have stayed on the island, and faced the hurt and humiliation in Breena's innocent eyes. But Rhys's courage failed miserably where Breena was concerned. He hoped that seven nights hence, when he returned for the harvest feast, it would not be so difficult to face her. By that time, surely, the burning in his stomach would have lessened, and the horrible feeling of having destroyed something indescribably precious would have settled into a dull ache in his heart. Once the feast was done, he would leave Avalon.

It would be a long time before he returned.

He shifted his weight on the unyielding ground. Why had he imagined visiting the isle would soothe him? It would have been better to stay away. Aye, the road was harsh, but not so harsh as being an outsider among his own people. He lost sight of Hefin in the glare of the rising sun. With a sigh, he unwrapped his harp and picked idly at the strings.

The sun had passed its zenith when Rhys first sensed something was wrong. Hefin had offered up a young hare for Rhys's breakfast. Soon after it had been roasted and eaten, and his harp safely wrapped, Rhys found himself drowsing. He woke with a start when the merlin, screeching in agitation, alighted on an outcrop of rock above Rhys's head. Rhys's mind registered a flash of an image, relayed from the bird's mind to his. He sat up. Scant moments later, he caught a glimpse of pale gray fur on the trail below.

A she-wolf. But not just any wolf—Ardra was Gwen's companion, in the way that Hefin was Rhys's. Rhys moved not a muscle as the sleek beast loped into the clearing. To his great surprise, Ardra padded right up to him and clamped her teeth on his sleeve. She tugged, as if trying to urge Rhys to his feet.

Hefin flapped his wings frantically. Ardra gave a low growl and did not let go.

Rhys rose. Ardra's jaw relaxed. She bounded down the trail, then stopped and looked back, teeth bared.

"You wish me to follow you?"

Unease slithered through Rhys's gut. He grabbed his pack and slung it over his shoulder. "Go."

He followed the wolf down to the muddy strip of land separating the foot of the mountain and the swamp. Gwen and Owein were there, speaking in low, grim tones.

"What is it?" Rhys asked, hastening toward them. Ardra bounded to Gwen. "What is wrong?"

The pair turned as one. "Rhys!" Gwen's face showed a mixture of surprise and hope. "By the gods, I'm relieved to see you. Trevor said you'd gone to Isca Dumnoniorum."

"I stopped to rest in the hills," Rhys lied, "and fell asleep. Ardra found me—"

"And what of Breena?" Owein interrupted. "Is the lass with you?"

He stared at Breena's uncle. "Why would you think that?"

Gwen colored slightly. "We thought . . . hoped . . . oh, Rhys! Have you no idea where she is at all?"

His sister was close to tears. The sight sent icy fingers skating down Rhys's spine. His twin rarely cried. He gripped her arm. "What has happened to Breena? Is she missing? Tell me!"

Owein answered. The man's eyes were haunted. "No one has seen her since last night. She is not on the island, nor in any of the usual places on this side of the swamp. I have scried for her, but my Sight revealed nothing. That should not be possible. Breena is a Seer, and my own sister's daughter."

Rhys understood. Druid Seers, especially ones who shared the same blood, were very sensitive to each other's magic. "You Saw nothing at all?"

"I Saw nothing. I felt nothing. Her essence is gone. Completely."

The three Druids stared at each other in stark silence. A shroud of denial descended on Rhys, blotting all sound save the roaring in his ears. He tried to breathe, tried to move. He couldn't. It was if he'd died on his feet, and had yet to fall to the ground.

"You think she is—" He could not say it.

"No!" Gwen's arm came around him. "No, not that. Owein would have . . . would have Seen her body."

"Then what?" Rhys croaked. "What has happened to her?"

"Deep magic," Owein said grimly. "It is the only explanation. No other force could hide Breena's presence so completely from my Sight."

"What are you saying?" Rhys demanded. "That Breena was secretly practicing deep magic?"

"I do not believe she would be so rash," Gwen said. "But if she encountered someone else . . ."

"Someone else?" Rhys dragged a hand down his face. "But who?"

"I have no notion."

"Perhaps she is simply lost. Perhaps there is some other reason why Owein cannot See her. Did you find no sign of her at all? Her raft?"

"I found it in one of the usual mooring places," Owein said. "Marcus followed her tracks to the high meadow."

"Where the stone of the Great Mother stands?" Rhys asked.

"Aye. But there her trail ends. At least, Marcus could find no tracks leading down."

"Where is Marcus now?"

"On the far side of the mountain," Gwen replied. "With Trevor."

Rhys's gaze brushed the high slopes. "I will join them. And send Hefin flying overhead. Perhaps the falcon will see something Owein's magic missed."

Gwen placed her hand on Ardra's head. "Owein and I will continue searching on this side. We're all to meet here at dusk. I only pray she is found before then."

They clasped hands and parted. Rhys dispatched Hefin into the sky, then set out at a grueling pace up the path to the high meadow. The strap of his pack bit into his shoulder. He considered leaving it behind, then simply readjusted its weight on his back.

With each step he battled a tide of guilt. If any harm befell Breena, it would be Rhys's fault. His callous rejection had driven her from the safety of her bed.

He reached the high meadow. The trampled grass gave evidence of Marcus's and Trevor's search. The swamps and lowlands to the west were a mosaic of autumn orange and rust. A low line of clouds on the horizon threatened to blot the afternoon sun. Rhys shivered. The wind had picked up. It carried a portent of winter.

He scanned the ground, hoping to find a clue the others had missed, whether magical or mundane. As he paced a wide circle around the sacred megalith, the sun succumbed to the clouds. The daylight turned dull, erasing the contrasts of light and shadow.

Rhys closed his eyes and cast his senses, searching inward for his magic. When he again opened his eyes, the golden autumn grass at first appeared unchanged. He whispered a word and a subtle shift occurred in his vision. Glimmers of magic emerged from the earth and stone. The edges of the standing stone appeared translucent, as if a glow sprang from the heart of the rock. Sparkling lines of green earth magic radiated from the base of the megalith in several directions. One path, Rhys knew, led directly to Avalon. Another ran toward the ancient henge of stones that stood on the great plain near Leucomagus.

He searched for remnants of power. A Seer's aura was pure white. Rhys recognized Owein's magic, bold and wide. Breena's auric trail was more delicate. Rhys stood almost in her footsteps. She'd entered the meadow at nearly the same point as he had. She'd then moved in a straight line toward the standing stone.

And then an unknown Druid had slipped from a cleft in the mountain on Rhys's left. He almost missed the trail. The faint blue sparks the man or woman had left behind were all but invisible. The spell used to conceal the stranger's presence had been powerful—strong enough to fool Owein and Trevor, and even Gwen, who shared Rhys's rare talent of discerning Druid auras. But Rhys, unlike his twin, had spent fifteen years following scant trails of magic all over Britain and Hibernia. It was no surprise he'd found what the others had missed.

He straightened, gripping the straps of his pack. The evidence before him suggested a Druid who was very powerful in air magic, as Gwen, and Rhys, and even Penn were. It was a common enough talent—far more common than the rare Seer's magic Owein and Breena shared.

Both Breena's trail, and the unknown Druid's, ended at the foot of the Great Mother's stone. And then . . . nothing. But that made no sense. He turned away, searching. . . .

Light shimmered on the great stone, at the farthest corner of Rhys's vision. He swung his head back, eyes narrowing.

The light vanished. Frowning, he tilted his head just a fraction. Again, the glistening outline appeared, glowing silver against the gray-blue stone. Just as quickly, it disappeared.

A portal.

Rhys sucked in a breath. He had not known this stone guarded an entrance to the Lost Lands.

The Lost Lands lay between earth—the realm of men—and Annwyn, the Otherworld of the gods. Few mortals traveled to those shadowy midlands. Even fewer returned. Owein and his wife, Clara, were among those who had survived such a journey. If Breena had entered the Lost Lands, that would explain why she was now invisible to Owein's magic. The deep magic of that mystical place hindered every other magical force.

He bent and touched the ground. Its warmth surprised him. The standing stone itself was even hotter. Deep magic pulsed against his palm like a heartbeat. The unknown Druid had cast a powerful spell to open the portal. Blue sparks gathered at the edges of Rhys's hand. The stranger's air magic recognized him.

That was a very good thing. Without pausing to consider the wisdom or folly of his intentions, Rhys opened his mind to the remnants of the spell. The power of it nearly knocked him off his feet. By the gods! This magic was far deeper than any he'd ever encountered.

Its sheer strength took his breath; his heart commenced pounding as if he'd run down the mountain and back. The spell was awesome in its simplicity and elegance. The shape of it, the color, the Words—all the facets of the spell were familiar to Rhys, though he'd never thought to join the elements in quite this way.

Swiftly, he re-formed the spell and repeated the Words. Then he inhaled sharply. There was a single instant in which he might have pulled back; he did not.

The stone heated, searing his palm. Gritting his teeth, he battled the reflex to snatch his hand away. The hard surface softened. The essence of the rock dissolved into flame.

He felt himself fall.

"Dear Goddess," Breena whispered.

The Great Mother's standing stone had not changed. Neither had the meadow, nor the slope of the hill. The autumn wind still blew from the north, carrying the scent of the sea. To the southwest lay the swamps.

But . . . Gwen's mists! They were gone. Breena stared blankly at the sacred isle, rising steeply from the water. Naked to every enemy's eye.

Dread blossomed. "What have you done?"

The words emerged as a thready rasp. Her mouth felt as though she'd been chewing new wool. Her body felt strangely heavy; her limbs weak. It would take nothing for her legs to collapse beneath her.

Myrddin clasped her upper arm. "Take deep breaths. The magic that opened the passage is difficult for a human body to absorb, especially when one travels through the portal for the first time."

Breena's chest expanded painfully with the effort of breathing. Her knees wobbled. The old Druid pressed his staff into her hand. She leaned on it heavily as he helped her to a low, flat stone at the edge of the clearing. Once seated, she wondered if she'd ever have the strength to rise again

Myrddin did not seem to be similarly affected. The old Druid knelt before her, chafing her ice-cold hands. His eyes were grave. Breena was too tired to protest when he laid his hand on her head and whispered a spell. His light magic was powerful; immediately, she began to revive.

He rose and smiled down at her. "Better, my dear?"

After a moment's hesitation, she nodded. Vigor seeped slowly back into her limbs, but her chest remained tight with fear. Dear gods! Myrddin's power was beyond her imagining. He'd obliterated the mists! How could she have been so foolish as to trust him?

"How . . . how did . . . you do it?" Her parched tongue barely formed the words.

"Here. Have some wine, child. It will help."

She looked down. Myrddin had placed a wineskin into her hands. For a moment, she couldn't think what to do with it. The old Druid uncorked the spout and guided it to her mouth. The wine was unwatered, and very bitter. She pushed it away, choking.

"This . . . this is more vinegar than wine."

"I know. Very little decent wine makes it across the channel from Gaul these days. But somehow I did not think you would appreciate a skin of *cervesia*."

That was true. Even bad wine was preferable to barley beer. She forced herself to drink a few mouthfuls. Then she frowned. Another aspect of the Druid's comment hadn't made sense at all.

She tilted her head and looked up at him. "Good Gaulish wine may be expensive, true, but it's imported by the shipload. It is plentiful enough."

Myrddin corked the wine and stowed it in a leather pack before answering. "It once was," he said. "No longer."

That was absurd, but she did not wish to argue. At least not about something so trivial. "The mists," she said, her voice rising. "How did you destroy them? What manner of spell did you cast? You must undo it, at once."

He sent her an assessing glance as he fastened the buckle on his pack. Straightening to his full height, he picked up the pack and slung it easily over one shoulder. For an old man, Breena thought, Myrddin was certainly agile.

And tall. She did not like the way he loomed so far above her. Drawing a deep breath, she stood.

"It was not I who destroyed the mists," he said. "That was done long ago."

"You make no sense."

A wry smile touched his lips. "Indeed. My life ceased making sense quite some time ago."

Breena scowled. "Do not jest with me, old man."

Immediately, he sobered. "In truth, I do not jest. Though I am certain my words do sound like nonsense to you." He rubbed a hand down his face, ending with a tug on his beard.

"There is no gentle way to present it, so I suppose a measure of bluntness is in order." He looked at her intently. "Though we stand in precisely the same place you remember, we have traveled an incredible distance. More than three hundred years."

Three hundred *years*? Gods. Breena hadn't considered the possibility that the old Druid might be mad. Mad, and possessed of deep magic. A deadly combination.

"Please," she whispered. "Restore the mists. Avalon is no threat to anyone. But if the Roman army should discover us . . . we will be destroyed."

He shook his head, his eyes infinitely weary. "Believe me when I say, child, that I would never do anything to harm your home. But in this time, that is not even possible. The Avalon you know was destroyed long ago." He paused. "Do you remember nothing of your passage?"

"No, I—" She frowned. "Yes. I do recall . . . something. A land of shadows. You spoke a Word—no, many Words. I remember thinking I had never heard the language of the Old Ones used in quite that way."

"It took me many years to discover the pattern and cadence of that spell, I assure you." He planted his staff on the ground. "You know of the Lost Lands, of course."

"What Druid does not? They are the vestibule to Annwyn."

"Then you know the Lost Lands show a different face to each soul that enters."

"Is that where we are now? In the Lost Lands?"

"No," Myrddin replied. "We existed in that realm but a short time. You see, the Lost Lands are more than the vestibule to the Otherworld. They are a vestibule to time itself."

Breena's head had begun to throb. "I don't understand."

"Nor do I. Not completely. Deep magic, after all, is a complex power. That island lying across the lowlands? I assure you, it is Avalon. But it is not the Avalon you know. It is Avalon as it exists more than three hundred years into your future."

She studied Myrddin's face. His expression was grave. He appeared to believe the preposterous tale. "You cannot expect me to accept that."

"You are too intelligent to disbelieve it," Myrddin countered. "Look at the sacred isle, Breena. Really look. What do you see?"

She shaded her eyes and peered across the swamp. She had never seen Avalon from this vantage; the mists had always obscured it. But she had no trouble recognizing her home. The island rose steeply from the water, forming a mound that was roughly the shape of a lopsided egg. She could just make out the apple orchard at midslope, and the roofs of several long, squat buildings just below it. One boasted a square tower.

She blinked. There were no long, squat buildings on Avalon. No tower. Only Celt roundhouses, nestled among rowans and yews. They would not even be visible from this distance.

And the swamp. . . . When she examined it more closely, she realized the marsh was not as it should be. It was as if some giant hand had opened a drain and allowed some of the water to seep out. A wide swath of lowland forest hugged the base of the mountain, where there should have been nothing but a strip of muddy shore. What should have been a glassy expanse of water was broken by shoals and a network of shallow, grassy islands.

"This . . . this cannot be real. It must be an illusion. Or a dream you've cast into my mind."

"No. No dream, no illusion. This is reality." He paused. "The woman in your silver vision exists in this time. Lady Igraine is very real, indeed."

"She is here? On Avalon?"

"No. The duchess dwells some miles to the west, at Tintagel."

"Duchess? What is a duchess?"

Myrddin grimaced. "I forget how little you know. 'Duchess' is the Lady Igraine's title. Her husband is Gerlois of Cornwall. His title is 'duke.'"

"Duke? Do you mean *dux*? An army general? And where is Cornwall? I have never heard of the place."

"A British duke is somewhat like a Roman *dux*. Especially in a military sense. But Gerlois is a landholder as well. His dukedom is called Cornwall. It is part of the kingdom of Dumnonia."

"You mean Isca Dumnoniorum?" Breena asked.

"King Erbin's seat was once called Dumnoniorum. The king is very old, and his mind has gone weak. Duke Gerlois is Erbin's heir, and king in all but name. He controls Dumnonia's army, and administers all its laws."

Breena struggled to make sense of it all. "There is no longer a fortress, or a *dux*, in Isca Dumnoniorum. The Second Legion's home is Isca Silurum now. And there are no kings in Britain. The province is administered by a governor."

"Breena, I am trying to tell you—there are no legions in Britain. Nor any governor. The Roman army sailed from the island almost fifty years ago."

"What a preposterous notion—Rome would never abandon Britain! Though I know there are many Celts who yet consider that a pleasant dream."

For a long moment, Myrddin did not answer. Then his shoulders sagged. "No pleasant dream. Far from it. In truth, Rome's abandonment of Britain was a nightmare. One that has yet to end."

A nightmare. Like the vision Rhys's grandfather had seen of a brutal, hopeless future?

Breena's heart began to beat an uneven tattoo as her resistance to Myrddin's preposterous assertions cracked. Could it be true? Had Myrddin's deep magic brought her through time?

"There was a Seer in my time," she began. "He . . . he prophesized two possible futures for Britain. One dark, one light. Is this . . ." She swallowed. "Is this his dark vision come to pass?"

"I know of Cyric," Myrddin said. "His Sight was true. His dark prophecy has not yet come to pass, but Britain is careening toward that fate with sickening rapidity. Rome is gone. Druid magic is fading. Barbarians rape the shoreline while petty kings squabble among themselves. And yet, there is still hope. That is why I need your help, Breena."

She hardly understood what the old Druid was saying. All she could think of was her home, long gone in this time. "If we are truly in the future, then . . . are they all dead? My parents? My brother and his family?"

Owein and Clara. Penn. And oh, gods—*Rhys*. She squeezed her eyes shut against a crushing tide of grief.

Myrddin rested a hand on her shoulder. Reflexively, she gripped it. "In this reality," he said quietly, "yes, they are gone. But time, I have found, is not quite the logical concept I once thought it to be. I have discovered that all time happens at once. So in one sense, your loved ones are alive, and well, as they will always be."

"But . . . will I ever return to them?"

"Yes. You will. Once your task in this time is done. I promise you that, Breena, on my life."

She met his gaze. "You brought me here with deep magic."

"Yes."

"Then that is a promise you cannot truly offer."

The expression on his face told her she'd hit her mark. Myrddin might be the most powerful Druid Breen had ever encountered, but he was, after all, just a man. Not a god. And only a god could control deep magic.

The line of Myrddin's jaw firmed beneath his beard. "I will send you home, Breena. Do not doubt it."

She peered out over the swamps, drawn by the strange notion that the island rising above the water was a different Avalon than the one she knew.

"Do Druids live openly on the sacred isle in this time? Is Druidry legal? Have they no need of the mists?"

Myrddin's brows rose. "Do you believe me, then?"

"I'm not entirely sure what I believe," Breena confessed. "But I've decided to trust you."

He smiled at that. "Ever practical. Thank you, my dear." His gaze followed hers across the water, and he sighed. "I am sorry to tell you that there are no mists around Avalon because the Druids of Avalon are long gone."

"Gone! Where? And why?"

"They were driven from Avalon centuries ago. A pair of men, priests of the Christos, pierced the mist and exposed Avalon to the outside world. The legions dispersed the illegal settlement. The Druids fled."

"But . . . did they never return?"

"No. The priests, Faganus and Deruvianus, were wise enough to recognize the sacred power of the isle. They established their own settlement. The pair are long dead, but their brotherhood remains. More than fifty holy men of Christos live on Avalon."

Breena's brow furrowed. "Who is Christos?"

"A god," Myrddin said. "You know him as the Carpenter Prophet."

"But . . . the Carpenter Prophet was a man! The Lady brought his Grail and his teachings to Avalon. The Druids of Avalon walk in his Light. His priests would not have had any reason to hate us."

"So one would think." Myrddin's voice had gone hard. "But the holy, it seems, are not always known for their tolerance. It mattered little to Faganus that the Druids honored the teachings of the Christos. Not when they also revered the Old Ways. The priests of the new religion believe the ancient gods and goddesses of the Celts are servants of the evil one they call Satan."

"But surely, the Druids would have gathered elsewhere."

"Some did, for a time. But as more people flocked to the new faith, they came to view Druid powers as evil. Many Druids were put to death because of their magic.

Others, frightened, rejected their own power. And now Druidry is all but gone." Myrddin's lips pursed. "Precious few of us retain the heritage of our ancestors."

Her eyes widened. "Why . . . you are a descendant of Avalon! Are you not?"

"I am. I follow the Old Ways." He tilted his staff so she could more clearly make out the carving on the knob at the top: the triple spiral of the Great Mother merged with the cross of the Carpenter Prophet.

"You carry the symbol of Avalon." Breena drew her silver pendant from beneath her tunic. "It is the same as mine."

"Indeed."

"But your power is very great. Greater than any Druid in my time."

He inclined his head. "In this time, those with Druid power are far fewer. But those who do possess magic are very strong."

Something in his unwavering gaze made her shiver. "The gods do not grant great power without equal recompense. What have you paid, Myrddin, for your gifts?"

A shadow passed through his eyes. "A price you cannot possibly imagine, child."

Chapter Five

*D*eath could not possibly feel worse.

Rhys pressed his cheek against the dirt and willed his stomach to stop heaving. The ground was cold, very cold, but his body . . . that was still on fire. No wonder. He'd plunged through a maelstrom of flame to come to this place.

Wherever it was.

How much time had passed since he'd fallen into the standing stone? Without moving, he opened his eyes. The sun was directly before him, low in the western sky. It had dropped little, if at all, since he'd cast his spell.

The straps of his pack burned his shoulders. *His harp.* Shoving himself up on rigid arms, he heaved his body into a sitting position. The ground lurched, then steadied. Easing the pack from his shoulders, he cradled it between his bent legs. Astonishingly, neither the leather bag nor its contents was so much as singed.

Rhys was unharmed as well. His clothing was whole, his skin unmarred. Only his soul had been seared, by magic so deep that one might have stacked ocean upon ocean within it.

He tried to rise. A wave of debilitating fatigue struck. It was an effect of the deep magic he'd called to come to this place. Humans did not easily tolerate the power of the gods. This spell had been so powerful that

Rhys's own magic, along with his physical strength, had been drained severely. It would be a day at least, he estimated, before he recovered fully.

He tried to lift his pack. It might have been a leather-wrapped boulder for all he was able to budge it. Pain cut through his skull with the ragged edge of an unhoned ax. With a low curse, he dropped into a crouch and pressed his fingers to his temples.

Deep magic had wrung him out like a soiled washrag, then pounded him into the dirt for good measure. Gritting his teeth, he resisted the urge to lie down. If he did, he feared he might not regain his feet for a very long while.

He could do nothing but wait. Bit by bit, the pain and fatigue retreated. When he thought his legs could bear his weight, he drew a shaky breath and stood.

He'd done it. He'd followed the unknown sorcerer's spell into the Lost Lands. He wondered if Breena had passed through the fire, as he had. Most likely, she'd experienced a different trial. Was she nearby now? He could only hope. . . .

He looked about—truly looked—for the first time since opening his eyes.

A curse sprang to his lips. He stood in the same meadow! The stone of the Great Mother stood just steps away. A hot wave of frustration assaulted him. He had not traveled anywhere. The Lost Lands had simply sucked him in, and spit him back out. He was seized by an urge to throw his head back and howl. Instead, he clung to his usual custom of bottling his rage, and scrubbing a hand down his face.

He was so sure he'd recreated the sorcerer's spell exactly. His utter failure was evidence that he had not. What error had he made? He did not know. Should he try again? Or find the others and tell them what he'd discovered? Perhaps it would be best to join forces with

Gwen and Owein in this. Together, they might succeed where Rhys had—

His thoughts ceased abruptly. His gaze had fallen on the swamp. Gwen's mists were . . . gone.

Avalon was plainly visible, awash in a halo of late afternoon sunlight. Rhys's first thought was for his twin. Gods! What disaster could have befallen her in the short time since he'd left her? Panicked, he grabbed his pack and ran toward the head of the trail leading down to the shore. But when he reached it, he paused.

Something was not right. The swamp—it was not as it should be. Clumps of grass dotted the watery flatland. Where the water should have been smooth and blue, it was instead a bumpy, brackish green. What Rhys knew as a wide, glassy lake, was now shallow fenlands. Silty shoals broke its surface. The smell of the sea was faint. The tidal waters had receded to an impossibly low point.

And Avalon itself? Shielding his eyes against the sun, he peered at the sacred isle. A cluster of stone buildings, one boasting a tall stone tower, was clearly visible in a place where there should have been nothing but grassy meadow. The play of light and shadow on the flat roofs created a patchwork of charcoal and gold. The settlement appeared to be prosperous.

Whatever this island was, it was not the Avalon he knew. He allowed himself a grim smile. He had not failed. The wall of fire had indeed led to the Lost Lands. Which, for him, at least, had manifested as eerily similar to the place he'd once called home.

He began a slow circuit of the meadow, combing the ground for remnants of Breena's aura, or that of the Druid who'd led her astray. A short time later, his cautious optimism had deserted him. He could discern nothing.

Fighting his frustration, he considered his options.

At one point, he looked skyward, reflexively, for Hefin. But the merlin was nowhere in sight—Hefin had not followed Rhys into the Lost Lands. Rhys felt the bird's absence keenly. Hefin would have been an invaluable ally in the search for Breena.

Where to look? The logical place to begin his search, he supposed, was on the island that looked so much like Avalon. Hiking his pack onto his shoulder, he set out down the trail to the shore.

It was well past noon on the following day by the time Rhys drew close to Avalon. His first obstacle had been the swamp—unlike in his own world, there were no Druid rafts, conveniently hidden along the shore. He'd been forced to follow the high ground in a wide arc along the water's edge.

His next problems had been the starless night, and his fatigue. He'd tried to walk in the dark, but succeeded only in stumbling. He'd sat down to await the dawn, and had fallen asleep. When he'd awakened, it was nigh onto midday.

At least the delay meant his magic was once again at full force. That gave Rhys a measure of confidence. He only prayed he would find Breena on the isle that was not Avalon.

The island came into view as he rounded a corner. The low waters revealed a spit of sandy land that reached from the foothills to the isle. A long bridge, over sparkling water, spanned the last part of the distance.

Across this lake, the settlement looked even more extensive than it had from the mountain. A gatehouse stood at the end of the bridge; beyond it lay an unpaved plaza, bordered by a stable and several windowless storehouses. A gated, arched entryway led to what looked like a courtyard, enclosed by several long, squat, buildings. He could see the top of the tower beyond the slate roofs. An apple orchard spread across the upper slope, just as it had in Rhys's Avalon. And a great, ancient yew stood in the precise location of the similar, younger tree that shaded the Grail spring on the island he knew.

The juxtaposition of familiar and strange elements disturbed him. He approached the bridge warily, traveling on a dirt track from the north. A wider, paved road to the south was clearly more frequently traveled; a rather large party was visible now, moving toward him. Rhys summoned a lookaway spell and eased behind a screen of tall grass.

Two men on horseback rode in the lead, carrying standards marked with a white cross. Six mail-shirted cavalry soldiers rode behind, flanking a silk-draped litter carried on the shoulders of eight stout porters. A cluster of dark-garbed riders followed. Four baggage-laden mules brought up the rear.

Subtly, Rhys cast his senses toward the travelers. His attention sharpened on the litter. A crimson glow clung to the edges of the hangings. *Magic.*

It was not, however, the blue glow of Breena's abductor. This magic was sparkling crimson. Whoever was inside the litter possessed fire magic, not air magic.

Rhys's eyes narrowed as the party turned onto the bridge to Avalon. The structure was a sturdy affair of logs and planks, wide enough for two men walking abreast. The lead riders called ahead; a brown-robed figure immediately appeared in the doorway of the gatehouse. A bell was rung, prompting more robed figures to appear, along with a few men dressed in more familiar garb.

The entourage moved past the gatehouse and into the plaza. The soldiers dismounted; the baggage was lifted from the mules. The litter, its hangings still closed, disappeared through the archway. Rhys emerged from his hiding place and strode the last distance to the bridge. A tiny bird darted amid the yellowing swamp grass hugging the timber pylons.

He hesitated, unsure of his welcome on the island. It would be best to cloak himself in an illusion before crossing the bridge. He was preparing to call the spell when the improbable sound of a singing man, accompanied by the equally improbable song of a flute, reached his ears.

Rhys's gaze turned to the south. A new party of travelers, much smaller and more ragged than the first, had appeared over a rise in the road. The group consisted of three grown men and one slender boy, all on foot. Scruffy and splashed with mud, they wore ragged shirts oddly accented with scraps of brightly colored cloth.

They were in high spirits, their music accompanied by laughter and good-natured insults. The singer, whose voice was really quite melodious, sported a bald head, a ruddy complexion, and a very large stomach. The musician, by contrast, was a pale, dark-haired young man with little meat on his bones. His graceful fingers flew over the holes in his flute. The resulting melody was so light and sweet, it seemed to dance on the air.

The third member of the quartet was a hulking giant, his blond hair pulled back in a tight queue. He topped Rhys's own impressive height by a full two hands. The tall man sang a bass counterpoint to his fat friend's tenor, hitting notes so low they vibrated in Rhys's bones. Bounding alongside the trio, sometimes running ahead, sometimes hanging back, was an energetic, wiry lad with cropped black hair.

Rhys's shoulders relaxed. He let the strands of his

lookaway spell drop. While mysterious magicians and soldiers on horseback demanded caution, this odd little band required none. Entertainers were one society Rhys understood exceedingly well.

Minstrels knew the lay of the land, and, to a man, they were inveterate gossips. Rhys could not have asked for a better source of information about this strange world into which he'd been flung.

He waited for the group to notice his presence. The lad had whipped around to walk backward in front of his musical companions, his arms pumping encouragement. The song was sung in Celtic British, mixed with a good bit of Latin, as well as some words that were wholly unknown to Rhys. Nevertheless, Rhys had no trouble grasping the gist of the bawdy ditty. It chronicled the story of a poor farmer who taught humility to his shrewish wife with the aid of a very large carrot.

The ruddy man hit a high, sour note. The flautist winced, and cut his melody. The giant looked skyward and groaned. The younger lad halted in the middle of a backward step, threw up his arms, and let out a stream of profanity foul enough to singe the hair from a pig's ear.

"Blast and devil take you, Floyd! Did that pox-ridden wench you had last night cut off your stones? Sing like that at the festival, and we'll be tossed over the cliffs and into the sea!"

Rhys swallowed a gasp of laughter. The lad was no lad at all—his voice was a man's, strong and rasping. The sound of it was oddly incongruous with his slender frame, thin arms, and smooth chin.

"Perhaps we should simply heave Floyd into the fens now, lads, and save the good people of Tintagel the trouble." This from the blond giant, whose chortle of laughter gave the lie to his threat.

The general chorus of agreement with the giant's

plan brought a scowl to Floyd's flushed face. "'Tis difficult to sing well when I'm hungry!"

"If that be the case," the giant retorted, "ye'd nay hit a single true note."

"The good brothers of Glastonbury Abbey will fill our bellies," the thin-faced flautist interjected. "Their tables are sure to be heavily laden in honor of Bishop Dafyd's arrival. Perhaps tomorrow, Floyd will hit a right note or two."

"Bishop Dafyd," snorted the small man with some disgust. "Aye, he eats like a king, but, unlike Floyd here, a full belly ne'er improves the bishop's temper. I have ne'er in all my life seen a man more in need of a good swiving."

The giant laughed, showing a set of large white teeth. "True enough, by God! One only wonders if the good bishop prefers a woman's arse or a lad's!"

"Or a ewe's!" chortled Floyd. The young flautist was not amused. "For the love of the Christos, Howell, guard your loose tongue!" He darted a fearful glance at the bridge, as if expecting retribution to come rushing across it. "'Tis a man of God you insult so lewdly. Have you no fear for your soul?"

"None at all," Howell replied easily. "My concern is for my belly. Bread is my religion."

"And mine," declared Floyd. "If bread be lacking, Kane, a jest and a song will inspire someone to fill my stomach far quicker than any prayer would."

Kane scowled. "There's no food in the fiery pit of Hell. Think on that as you blaspheme."

"Ah, lads, lads." The small man quickly stepped into the center of the altercation. "Fighting amongst ourselves serves neither the Christos nor our empty bellies! Kane, you must learn to accept a jest. Howell, if your highest concern truly is your stomach, have a care! Lewd jests within earshot of the abbey will sooner earn all of us a night in a sinner's cell than a place at the good monks' table."

The giant accepted the smaller man's scolding with surprising humility. "Aye, ye have the right of it, Trent."

"Now make your apologies to the lad, man. God knows we will have no peace, nor any music, if you don't."

Howell snorted, but did as he was bid, bowing his head to the flautist. "Kane, apologies. I didna mean to wound your tender sensibilities." The giant punctuated the apology with a companionable, and very firm, slap between the youth's shoulder blades.

Kane stumbled forward under the strength of the blow. His face would have ended up planted in the mud, if Floyd hadn't caught his arm. The youth swung about to face Howell, brandishing his flute like a club.

"You swine!"

Howell hooked his thumbs in his belt and grinned.

"Good Lord, men, can you not stop bickering for even a moment?" The small man—Trent—jumped up nimbly, grabbing Kane's arm. "Have a care, you young fool! Crack that flute in two and we will all go hungry!"

Kane twisted out of Trent's grasp and folded his arms over his flute. Spinning around, he kicked at the muddy road.

"Ah, that's better," Trent declared. "Now. If we're all in agreement, let us proceed across the bridge. You fishwives may not have noticed, but the sun is sinking fast, and we are in danger of missing vespers. Not to mention the supper that follows."

There was a general grumble of agreement. Rhys chuckled. Trent might be small in stature, but his outsized personality clearly held sway over his three larger companions.

Rhys's amusement drew the giant's attention. "Lads," Howell said sharply. "Look about! We have an audience."

The other men turned.

Rhys met Trent's gaze first, with a slight nod. He then made eye contact with Howell, Floyd, and Kane in turn. "Well met, friends."

Trent's lips twitched, acknowledging Rhys's deference to his position as leader, as well as the stranger's quick assessment of the troupe's pecking order.

"Ah, an audience," he declared. He unshouldered his pack and handed it off to Howell. The dagger at his waist followed. Then he clapped his hand together and rubbed his palms. "How I do love an audience."

Before Rhys could react to this statement, Trent took two running steps and launched himself into the air. Knees tucked to chest, he spun a graceful midair roll, landing lightly on his feet not two strides from where Rhys stood.

He bowed. "Trent Masterson, at your service."

Rhys brought his hands together, clapping slowly as his astonished grin widened. "Well done, man! Very well done indeed. Will you require a coin for your efforts?"

Trent eyed Rhys appraisingly, then grimaced. "'Twould be a waste of breath, I'm thinking. From the looks of you, you're worse off than we are. I reckon I could not snatch an *as* from your lily white arse."

Howell and Floyd guffawed at the poor pun. Kane only rolled his eyes. Rhys gave a diplomatic snort. An *as* was a common denomination of Roman currency. He dug into the small pouch hidden under his shirt and produced the coin in question. With a grin, he tossed it at Trent.

The little man snatched it from midair and tested it between his teeth. A broad smile broke over his face.

"Well, now! For another like this, we might be persuaded to sing a song as well."

Rhys forced a laugh, but in reality, his anxiety was rapidly expanding. This scene in which he found himself did not feel right. Every tale he'd ever heard of the Lost Lands described the realm as misty and dreamlike. The midlands between earth and Annwyn were known to be vague and illogical. Time and form shifted constantly, without warning. This world—with its swamp, its mud, its ribald minstrels who spoke of Roman coins—was far too familiar for Rhys's comfort.

Which begged the question: where, exactly, *was* he?

He had not the faintest notion. But Rhys was well used to finding himself in foreign places. He knew from experience that the first thing a stranger in a strange land wanted was an ally among the local populace. Or, even better, four such allies.

"Perhaps I might offer a song of my own, in the faint hope of regaining my meager coin."

He slid his pack from his shoulder and unbuckled the flap. When he unfolded the oiled cloth inside, Kane's eyes went wide as twin moons.

"By the Christos," he breathed. "A harp. Are you a bard?"

"Aye."

"God in heaven!" Trent's shrewd gaze turned speculative. "Are you any good?"

"So I've been told."

"Then play, man! Let us hear your skill."

Rhys's lips twitched. "For an *as*?"

"For the satisfaction our pleasure gives you," Trent said dryly.

Rhys laughed and plucked a short, complex melody. Improvising, Kane joined in with his flute. At the end of the piece, the pair took their bows amid the enthusiastic applause of the other men.

"Well done!" Trent exclaimed. "Indeed, I have never heard the like—your fingers are as golden as your hair—damn me, but I don't even know your name. What are you called, man?"

"Rhys." Rhys rewrapped his harp and stowed it in his pack.

Trent took his own pack and dagger from Howell. "Do you travel alone, Rhys?"

"Aye."

"From where, might I ask? Your accent is none too familiar."

"I'm newly arrived from the north of Cambria," Rhys smoothly lied.

"Gwynedd, do you mean? Ah, but that would explain both the lilt in your speech and the harp in your pack. A wild place, Gwynedd is, or so I've heard tell. But to travel all that distance, alone, with no sword on your belt? That, my friend, is as astounding as it is foolish."

"I'm well skilled in the art of avoiding trouble. Besides, what thief would bestir himself to rob a poor minstrel?"

Trent spat in the mud. "Such perfidy is not above a Saxon sea wolf. But I suppose the raiders do not often venture as far north as Gwynedd. Here in the south, though, you'd be wise to find yourself a weapon. And some traveling companions. Are you headed to Tintagel for the festival? If so, you are welcome to join us. A harp would be a fine addition to our show."

"Festival?" Rhys wondered how far this Tintagel might be.

"Never say you know nothing of Duke Gerlois's harvest festival!"

"I am afraid they do not speak of it in Gwynedd."

"Well, my man, 'tis famous in the west country. Seven days of feasting, all at the duke's expense! Rich and poor alike partake. This year, there's to be a tournament among the knights pledged to Gerlois and his lords."

"Knights?" Rhys asked.

Trent shot him an odd look. "Cavalry, man! Do you not know the Germanic name? Surely they are not so backward as all that up in Gwynedd."

"I know the cavalry, of course," Rhys murmured. The horsemen were the swiftest arm of the Roman military. This Duke Gerlois must be their general.

"'Twill be a spectacle well worth the journey," Trent said, squinting at the sun. "But for now, we'd best be across the bridge. The abbey bell will toll vespers any moment."

Rhys nodded and followed the others. Trent fell into step beside him as they crossed the planks. "So what do you say, man? Will you join up with us?"

Rhys hesitated, considering what his next step might be if he failed to find Breena on Avalon. A large gathering might very well be the next logical place to look. "Aye, I might consider it."

"What's to consider?" Trent asked. "Why, half of Dumnonia will be at Tintagel. Think of the coin!"

"And the wenches," cut in Howell, who was openly eavesdropping.

"And the food," added Floyd.

"And the wenches and food," repeated Trent. "All to be had for the small price of singing a verse or two in praise of warriors stupid enough to be slaughtered in battle."

"Is Tintagel far?" Rhys asked.

"Much closer than Gwynedd," Trent replied. "Five days by foot, if we set a quick pace. If the weather holds, we should arrive in time for the opening feast. What say you, man? Are you with us?"

Rhys was saved from answering by the group's arrival at the gatehouse. Beyond, in the wide plaza, the soldiers Rhys had seen arriving earlier now stood in a loose knot, talking. A few of the island's brown-robed inhabitants—monks, Trent had called them—hurried to and fro, eyes fixed on the ground. A scrawny lad drew water from a well.

Trent seemed well acquainted with the gatehouse attendant, greeting the man with surprising humility. "The blessing of our Lord Christos be upon you, Brother Fergus."

"And upon ye, Trent." The man's lilting accent marked him a native of Hibernia, or Eire, as it was sometimes called. "May ye ever be worthy of our Lord's mercy."

Rhys was beginning to understand that this Avalon, like his own, housed a religious community. But these holy men honored not the Great Mother, but a god called Christos.

While Trent and the monk conversed, Rhys scanned the activity in the plaza. Dropping back, he spoke in a low voice to Floyd. "Where are the women of the community?"

The portly man's face registered his astonishment. "Women? In a monastery? My God, man, are you insane?"

Rhys was taken aback. "You mean there are no women? None at all?"

"Of course not!"

"Not even in the kitchens? Or the laundry?"

"Nay, not even there," Floyd confirmed. "The monks take care of their own needs."

Howell met this assertion with a snort.

Kane landed a subtle kick to the giant's shin. "Whatever vulgarity you are thinking, Howell, pray do not speak it. Or we are like to find ourselves sleeping in the swamp."

"My comrades and I humbly request shelter for the night," Trent was telling Brother Fergus. "We journey to Tintagel for the festival."

"Sure and many are the travelers who have sought shelter at Glastonbury in the past fortnight. Why, we are blessed to have Bishop Dafyd himself in residence. His litter arrived not an hour past."

It was this Bishop Dafyd's aura, then, that Rhys had seen shining from the depths of the litter. Rhys was not surprised to discover that the man was spoken of with respect.

Trent nodded sagely. "His blessed grace journeys to Tintagel's festival."

"Aye, to lend much-needed piety to his brother's revels. Else many weak souls would be drawn into sin by the pagan customs of old, and damned to hellfire." The monk shook his head. "I suspect 'twould be best to ban the festivities entirely. But Duke Gerlois is loath to disappoint the people of Dumnonia."

"That dilemma is why my men and I have traveled so far to attend," Trent said solemnly. "If a festival there must be, then may the entertainment provided be offered to God's glory! My troupe sings the loftiest of hymns, and we stage scenes from the life of the Christos. God willing, our art will save many souls from Hell's fires."

"'Tis a miracle," Rhys heard Howell whisper to Floyd, "that Trent's tongue does not split in two under the strain of his lies."

"May God shower his mercy on you lads," Brother Fergus declared.

A bell began a low, mournful tolling. At once, all activity ceased. Every man in sight streamed toward the archway.

"Vespers." Brother Fergus gestured Trent and the others to proceed in the same direction. "Bishop Dafyd leads the community in prayer. Please, advance to the chapel."

The troupe passed under the archway, entering a smaller courtyard dominated by the square bell tower. They joined the queue at the entrance of the tall building beside it. They soon found themselves in a large, barrel-vaulted room thickly packed with bodies.

A dozen or so monks gathered at one end of the hall, around a stone altar. The holy men had dropped the hoods of their brown robes, revealing closely cropped hair and shaved chins. Rhys quickly scanned the group for signs of magic, but found none. The bishop had not yet entered.

A handful of chairs faced the altar. The seated occupants were richly dressed.

"Nobles," Trent explained. He nodded toward a short, dark, bearded man. "Lord Clarence of Tregear. The sallow-looking young one is Lord Maddock of Bolerium. They are bound for Tintagel as we are. No doubt they, and Bishop Dafyd, will take the sea route, and arrive well before us."

Soldiers, monks, and servants filled the rear of the chapel. The poorer travelers jostled cheek by jowl in the rear. Rhys tugged at the collar of his shirt. The chapel was not meant to hold so many bodies. The heat was prodigious; the odor even worse. And the evening prayers had not even begun.

The monks began a chant. The entire assembly, save for the nobles, knelt. With a sigh, Rhys followed suit. And waited for Bishop Dafyd to appear.

Chapter Six

"There's the lad. A pretty one, isn't he?"

Rhys stiffened, then relaxed. The Celt halfway down the tavern table could not possibly be talking about him. His illusion was firmly in place. Anyone who looked would see a man of two-and-twenty, not a boy of fifteen.

In the early days of his exile from Avalon, he'd kept to the wilderness, but soon realized that was not practical—he sought Druids, not solitude. He had to go where they were to be found. But there were many places a very young man could not venture except with extreme care.

This was one of those places. A rough dockside tavern on the banks of the River Thamesis, in the Roman provincial capital of Londinium. Before Rhys had dared enter, he'd fashioned a disguise of sorts. A spell of illusion, woven from the Words of the Old Ones.

He'd added seven years to his age, broadness to his chest, and a beard to his chin. Illusion-making was a skill Rhys had just begun to master; his magic this night was tenuous at best. If anyone looked too closely, Rhys very much feared his illusion would crumble.

This tavern had been a dangerous waste of time. The patrons were sailors and thieves. To a man, they were hairy, ugly, and stinking, without a single spark of magic among them. Rhys would have been better served making his bed in the forest outside the city. At least the animals in that place were predictable.

"He's got a lily white arse, I'll wager," the ruddy Celt sailor was saying.

"I've got first go at him," warned his Roman companion, a thin, cruel-looking man with a long scar across his bald head. "I hope he's worth the quadran I paid."

The object of the pair's attention was the slave boy who had just emerged from the kitchens. The lad, who could not have been more than eight years old, carried an armful of peat for the fire. Upon hearing the sailors' remarks, he froze. Raw terror washed over his face.

Rhys's stomach sickened. Life in Avalon had at times been very hard, but he'd never imagined the misery that lurked beyond the sacred isle's shores. The young slave's master had sold him for the night, willing or no. The lad knew what pain and degradation were in store for him—indeed, he'd probably suffered the same before. Yet he was powerless to stop what would happen. Rhys felt a rush of aching sympathy.

Then he blinked. A shimmering blue glow of air magic bathed the lad's head and shoulders. The slave boy possessed latent Druid magic. His power was more than strong enough for Avalon.

The lad dropped the blocks of peat by the hearth and scurried back in the direction of the kitchen, no doubt hoping to put off his ordeal. It was not to be. The bald sailor snatched him up by the scruff of the neck. "You'll come with us now, boy."

"Please, sirs, nay—"

The ruddy man backhanded him across the face. "Shut up."

Rhys rose as the pair hauled the lad out the door and into the street. Dropping a coin on the table, he hastened after them. But what could he do? He could *hardly fight two hardened sailors bare-handed. And yet, he could not allow this evil to take place.*

He found the trio in the stinking alley beside the tavern. The Celt held the boy. The Roman was untying his breeches, eyeing the lad with an avid expression. The boy twisted, and kicked, and earned a cuff on the ear for his defiance.

Rhys enhanced his illusion, adding years to his face and richness to his garb. He was now a prosperous merchant. Upon further consideration, he added the illusion of a sword at his belt. He did not think the false weapon was very convincing, but then, the night was dark.

Doing his best to project a confidence he did not feel, he hailed the sailor. "Stop. Stop now."

The bald man looked over at him, a sneer on his face. "And who might you be, to issue such an order?"

"This slave's new owner," Rhys said. "I bought him not an hour ago."

The lad's eyes widened.

"Did you? Well. Old Marcellus did not say anything of it when he sold us the use of this whelp for the night."

"I have his papers right here." Rhys hoped they would not reach for the scroll in his hand; it was nothing more than magic and air. "Now give him to me."

The Celt did not release his hold on the lad's thin arms. "But we paid good money for him!"

"And we mean to receive our due," his companion said. "We'll give him up when we're done with him. Not a moment sooner."

Rhys placed his palm on the hilt of the sword that was not really there. "How much did you pay to use him?"

A calculating light gleamed in the bald sailor's eye. "A denarius."

It was a blatant lie. The man could have bought far more than a sniveling boy for that price. But Rhys's tenuous illusions would never hold up to a fight, if it came to that.

"Very well," he said, fishing in his money pouch. He tossed something in the ruddy man's direction.

The Celt released his hold on the boy to catch it. The lad darted behind Rhys's back. The Roman snatched the coin from his companion and tested it between his teeth.

He smiled broadly. "Take him. We'll find us another. Perhaps two."

The pair trod down the alley, toward the tavern door. Rhys looked down at the trembling lad. "What's your name, lad?"

The boy sniffed. "Penn, sir."

"Well, come on, then, Penn. Let's get out of here."

He did not move. "Did ye truly buy me from Marcellus?"

"Nay," Rhys admitted. "I am stealing ye from him."

"But . . . why? Do ye . . . mean to use me as those men wanted?"

"Of course not." In his utter shock at the lad's assumption, Rhys lost his hold on his illusion.

Penn's eyes went round. "Why . . . ye are not a merchant at all! You're hardly even a grown man! How—"

"Magic. Illusion. I'll explain later. "Now move, lad!" Rhys gave the lad a shove in the direction of the forest. "It will not be long before those two bastards realize that *denarius* is nothing more than a bit of glass."

"Sorcery!"

Bishop Dafyd's eyes blazed with zealous light. His

flaccid jowls trembled. The priest's ranting showed no sign of abating, even though the twilight glow in the chapel's narrow windows had long since faded to black. He punctuated each sentence with a rap of his hooked staff against the flagged stone floor. Rhys's knees, protesting their long contact with the cold stone floor, had long since gone numb.

"Sorcery is the gravest threat to man's salvation. The power of the sorcerer is unnatural. Perverse! It is the might of demons. Seductive, its talons sink into a weak man's soul, bringing disease and infection of the spirit. The miserable mortal becomes Satan's instrument on earth—"

Dafyd's oratory was compelling; he held the larger part of his audience entranced. Kane's expression was rapt. Floyd's eyes were glassy, as if he had fallen into a trance.

"—magic fouls all it touches, and sends even righteous men into the embrace of the dark prince. Yes, my sons, beware the sorcerer, and his whore, the witch. Their souls are black, fit only for agony in the fires of Hell—"

Rhys slid a glance in Trent's direction. The small man's face was a careful blank. Howell, in contrast, wore an outright scowl. At a subtle nudge from Trent, the giant ducked his head.

Rhys wondered at the audacity of the bishop, to condemn the very power he himself possessed. Was Dafyd afraid one of the monks, or a nobleman, might rise up to undermine his authority with his own magic? If so, he needn't have worried. Rhys was the only other Druid present in the chapel. He noted with some relief that the bishop did not glance his way. If Dafyd were sensitive to Druid auras, as Rhys was, his gaze surely would have been drawn to Rhys.

The air in the crowded room was almost unbearable. At dusk, the monks had lit scented torches on the altar. They did not burn cleanly. Sweat and other, fouler bodily odors melded with the stink and smoke of incense to fill the chapel with a thick haze. Rhys imagined the miasma rivaled the foulness of the Hell the bishop described with such passion.

How much longer could the man go on? Surely this had to end soon.

"—the righteous man must be vigilant against evil, for Satan bears many faces—"

Rhys shifted his gaze to the tall monk who stood just behind Dafyd's left shoulder. While the other monks wore brown, this one alone wore black. The man was never more than a few steps from the bishop.

"—beware the murderer, the fornicator, the adulterer. The thief. Those who do not honor the Lord's church—"

Of all the monks, only the black-cowled acolyte had not dropped his hood. The edges of the thick fabric drooped forward, shadowing his face.

"—my sons, you must not rest your vigilance, not even for an instant! Guard against lust, against the sins of the flesh, for evil so often comes to a man in the guise of woman. The female soul is weak. She is easy prey for Satan, who ever seeks to drive men from the path of righteousness. She is the devil's handmaiden, eager to snare a man's soul for her master—"

The bishop's words were like insects tracking filth over Rhys's skin.

"—temptress. Woman is ever eager to defile a holy man's soul. For this reason, God has given man dominion over woman. A woman may reach salvation only through the guidance of her lord and master. A man must guide a woman under his care with a firm hand. He must chastise her often, and sternly, if she is to have any hope of seeing heaven—"

Gods. Rhys felt like plunging into the nearest spring and washing until he was red and raw. He tried to imagine Gwen's reaction to the idiocy spouting from Dafyd's mouth. He imagined his sister would have a few choice words—and a spell or two—with which to chastise the bishop.

He lowered his gaze, smothering a snort.

"—beware, my sons, for a woman imperils a man's soul. But woman is not the worst threat to salvation. Of all the evil that surrounds us, there is none so foul as those sorcerers of old—the Druids."

Rhys's head jerked up.

"—at the time of the birth of the Christos, in a humble stable in Judea, Druid vermin crawled thick in Britain. They once defiled even this holy island, this blessed ground to which the holy Joseph of Arimathea brought the Grail of the Christos, which even now lies in the very earth beneath our feet, feeding the red waters that flow from the Chalice Well—"

Gods in Annwyn! This Christos of which Dafyd spoke could only be the Carpenter Prophet revered by the Druids of Avalon. Rhys did not know who this man Joseph could be, however. According to Druid teaching, a mysterious woman known only as the Lady—Rhys's own many-times great-grandmother—had brought the Grail of the Carpenter Prophet to Avalon. While the Lady's male descendants, like Rhys, were very strong in magic, it was the Lady's direct female descendants—her Daughters—who inherited the vastness of her power. In Avalon, Gwen and Clara, and now Gwen's female child, were Daughters of the Lady.

"—the filth of the Druids once defiled this holiest of islands. The scum of their existence was scoured from this holy place by the holy brothers, Faganus and Deruvianus, blessed saints of the Christos. But do not be so simple as to believe our ancient enemy has faded from this land. No. A Druid walks among us still, brazen in his evil. This Satan's servant whispers blasphemy into the ear of Britain's high king—"

What was this? Rhys's heart thudded. He shifted on the flagged stones, straightening so as to get a better view of Dafyd. A sharp pain shot up his knee to his thigh.

"—the Druid Myrddin! King Uther professes to be a servant of the Christos, but how can that be, when he takes counsel from a foul Druid? I promise you, if our king persists in his folly, God will punish all of Britain! Yes, our shores are battered by godless Saxons. But the real enemy attacks from within. I tell you, unless a true man of God sits upon the throne of Britain, every soul in the land will be cast into hellfire!"

The bishop's sermon went on for some minutes longer, as Dafyd elaborated upon the qualities of an ideal king. And though he mentioned no name, Rhys had the idea every man in the chapel knew perfectly well of whom the bishop spoke. And what of this Myrddin, advisor to the high king called Uther? Might he be Breena's abductor?

At last Dafyd fell silent.

"About bloody time," Howell grumbled.

Kane glared at him. Howell snorted, and the youth's lips pursed.

A monk whom Trent had identified as the monastery's abbot now ascended the single step to the altar. He bowed to Dafyd before turning to face the worshippers. Arms lifted, he raised his voice and sang in a language Rhys was fairly certain was Greek.

"Kýrie eléison, Christé eléison, Kýrie eléison."

More prayer ensued, this time in Latin. Rhys added his own silent prayers that the end of the service was near.

He let out a long breath between his teeth as the monks made their final bow to the altar. Dafyd, followed by his gaunt hooded attendant, was the first to exit the chapel.

The monastery's dining hall was a utilitarian space, devoid of decoration save for a large wooden cross hanging above a raised platform. Several noblemen, Dafyd, and Glastonbury's abbot were already seated at a table on the dais, which was covered with a pristine white cloth. Rough plank tables, unadorned, served for the rest of the crowd.

Rhys and his companions filed past a table laden with bowls of thin stew, hunks of bread that were only slightly stale, and rinds of too-fragrant cheese. Rhys accepted his portion, along with a cup of ale, from a round-faced monk with a pleasant smile.

"They've meat at the high table," Floyd grumbled as the troupe elbowed their way to an empty bench. "And wine."

Rhys looked down at the gruel in his bowl and shrugged. "I've eaten far worse."

Floyd sighed. "So have I, more's the pity."

"Chins up, men," Trent said as he slid into his seat. "In less than a sennight's time we'll be rolling fat in Duke Gerlois's bounty."

"Aye, and Dafyd's sermon only confirms what many are whispering," Howell said. "Duke Gerlois's tournament is naught but a show of force designed to taunt King Uther."

"Gerlois has been taunting Uther all summer," Trent remarked. "Despite all the fighting in the east, Gerlois has sent not a single knight to the high king's aid."

"One can hardly blame the man," Kane said. "The king insulted the duke quite blatantly last Eastertide in Caer-Lundein. Uther made no secret of his lust for Lady Igraine."

"If a lustful eye cast toward the duchess enrages Gerlois," Howell retorted, "the duke had best be ready to taunt every man in Britain! Lady Igraine is far too beautiful for any husband's peace of mind."

Rhys followed this interchange with great interest.

"'Tis beyond foolish for men to fight over a woman," Floyd commented, slurping his gruel. "Even one so lovely as Igraine."

"True," Howell said. He leaned across the table and lowered his voice. "But I canna credit how close to outright treason Dafyd came tonight. He all but called for Gerlois to replace Uther on the high throne."

"The bishop grows bold, aye," Trent said. "He is Gerlois's younger brother, after all. He knows there are many in Britain who would pledge fealty to the duke rather than Uther. But I cannot like it. Gerlois holds Dumnonia and the west country well enough, but can he protect the east of Britain, which lies on the Saxons' very doorstep? I think not."

"I agree," Howell said. "Uther is Britain's fiercest warrior. He may not be the most ardent follower of the Christos, but what of it? Prayers are no match for arrows and swords."

Kane's cheeks reddened. "For shame, Howell! If all Britain's faith proves as weak as yours, the Saxons will certainly be our masters."

"'Tis only due to Uther we dinna all wear Saxon slave collars," Howell retorted.

"Some of Lord Vectus's subjects already do," Kane countered, "seized as they were after their master fell to Saxon raiders, not even a month past! 'Twas Gerlois's warriors, not Uther's, who answered the pleas of Vectus's people. Else even more would have been taken."

"It was Gerlois's duty to aid Lord Vectus," Howell said. "Vectus was Lady Igraine's kin. Must King Uther personally hold every mile of western coast for Gerlois, as well as the south, north, and east for the rest of Britain's dukes and petty kings?"

A sour silence descended, each man frowning into his cup.

"Only the Christos can grant Britain victory against the Saxons," Kane muttered eventually.

The bottom of Howell's mug hit the table with a thud. He looked right, then left, then leaned forward to hiss in Kane's face. "If your Christos is so concerned with Britain's defense, where was he fifty bloody years ago? He might have prevented the Roman army from abandoning Britain in the first place!"

"What of the Druid the bishop mentioned?" Rhys asked Trent. "This Myrddin?"

"Ah, Myrddin," Trent replied. He took a long draught of bitter ale, frowned into his mug, then put it aside. "Uther's old Druid is an enigma, to be sure. No one seems to know whence he came. Eire, perhaps. At least that is where he first became known as Uther's advisor, during the campaign Uther waged as King Ambrosius's general. Many believe Uther's victories in Eire, and all the ones after, were aided by Druid magic. 'Tis even said Uther changed his battle standard, and took a new surname, solely because of a vision Myrddin received from his pagan gods."

"Indeed," Rhys murmured.

"Aye, 'twas a dream of two dragons—one red, one white—locked in battle. At first, it seemed the white would be victorious, but then the red prevailed. Shortly after, Ambrosius was murdered, and Uther took his half brother's throne. He raised a standard to the red dragon, and named himself Pendragon—son of the dragon. From that day to this, Myrddin has rarely strayed from Uther's side."

"'Tis an incredible story," Rhys said.

"Many say Uther's own mother was a Druid priestess," Howell put in. "And that Myrddin is her kin."

"Small wonder, then," Rhys mused, "that Bishop Dafyd should desire a new king for Britain."

"Duke Gerlois almost certainly shares Dafyd's ambitions," Trent said. "To my mind, the tournament is but an excuse to keep his lords and knights close, in case Uther and his knights decide to pay Cornwall a visit. But I believe the duke overreaches in his aspirations. Gerlois may be popular here in the west country, but the dukes and petty kings of the east prefer Uther. Despite his youth and arrogance—or perhaps because of it—the Pendragon is the fiercest warrior king Britain has ever known."

"Now that the Saxons' raiding season has ended, I would not be surprised should Uther decide to ride," Howell said. "He must put Gerlois's disrespect to rest once and for all. Perhaps he will even claim the beautiful Lady Igraine as his own."

Two bright spots of red appeared on Kane's pale cheeks. "Bite your tongue, Howell! That would mean war!"

Trent dipped his bread in his gruel and ate a messy bite before answering. "Aye, and perhaps that is the only way to put the matter of Dumnonia's loyalty to the high throne to rest once and for all. Uther has Myrddin at his side. Many say he cannot fail."

"What good is Briton killing Briton?" Kane said. "Saxons raid our shores with impunity, while Britain's lords bicker like washerwomen! A king should value diplomacy as highly as swords."

Howell grunted. "To what purpose? King Ambrosius was a fine diplomat, and a bloody fool! He sat down to make peace with his enemies and got a knife in his back for his trouble."

"Hush, man!" Trent placed a cautioning hand on

Howell's arm. "Our discussion has begun to attract undue attention."

The minstrels fell silent, bowing their heads over their bowls. Rhys ate the rest of his meal in silence, mulling over what he had learned. The pieces of the puzzle were coming together into a picture that was, in a word, preposterous. And yet, it was the only explanation that made sense.

He was now certain he was not in the Lost Lands. This was a land of real men—a war-torn country assaulted from without by a brutal enemy and torn from within by political turmoil. And he was very much afraid he knew exactly where this dangerous land was.

Or, more precisely, *when* it was.

It was well known that Druid Seers, like Breena and Owein, could cast their spirits into the future. Rhys had never before considered the possibility that a Druid could transport his flesh and bones there as well. But Rhys was certain that in casting the unknown Druid's spell, he'd unwittingly done precisely that.

He was no longer in his own time. He existed in a violent future Britain—the one Cyric had foreseen.

And Breena was lost somewhere in the nightmare.

Chapter Seven

$\mathcal{H}$ow does she fare? Any change?"

"Nay. Just the same."

The answer was expected. Why, then, did it descend upon Myrddin's heart with all the weight of a millstone? His gaze cut to the doorway. Vivian's room was dark.

"The light bothers her eyes," the village woman explained. "Do ye wish a candle? There are coals in the brazier. . . ."

"No," he said. "A candle won't be necessary."

He approached the door with something like panic clawing at his innards. The crisis at Tintagel was fast approaching; Vivian, if she were able, would scold him for being here with her, rather than at Igraine's side. But how could he stay away? She was everything to him. He had not expected her to improve during his absence. The clawing disappointment he felt now told him he'd been hoping, nonetheless.

At least his wife was still alive, he told himself. There was yet hope.

She looked up as he entered. "Who is there?"

"It is I, love. Myrddin."

"Myrddin?" She blinked. "I do not think I know that name."

Gently, he eased himself into the chair by the bed. Vivian looked unnatural. The aura of magic—the light he was so accustomed to seeing about her head and shoulders—was gone. She lay, still and pale in the center of the mattress. He remembered the day he'd brought that mattress to her. He'd been so proud. Stuffed with down, rather than straw, it had been one small luxury he'd been able to provide for her. She deserved far more. And yet, in all their years together, she'd never complained.

It was so difficult to see her like this. It was even more difficult, knowing he was to blame. He should have sensed the darkness gathering at Uther's court. He should have watched over her more closely.

He picked up his wife's hand. It was limp, her skin cool. He held it tightly, tears burning his eyes. She did not protest.

"You do know me, Vivian. You know me very, very well."

He longed to kiss her. How many times had he kissed her? Too many to count. But today, he would not. He was not sure how she would react.

A bitter laugh passed his lips then. Just imagine— the great wizard Myrddin, did not even dare kiss his own wife. A harsh irony indeed. No doubt Vivian, with her quick wit and quicker laughter, would have been the first to point it out.

If her mind had not been . . . elsewhere.

Damn caution. Easing onto the mattress, he slipped his arm beneath his wife and gathered her into his arms. She fit perfectly, as always. She struggled a bit, her eyes flaring with alarm. But when he shushed her, and rubbed the back of her neck, she settled.

He could feel her heart beating. He concentrated on the sound. As long as her heart was beating, there was hope. The spell Dafyd had cast was deep, but not impenetrable. Now that Breena had taken Vivian's place at Igraine's side, he could, perhaps, fight it.

Vivian's eyes roamed the room. He was not sure what she saw.

He began to speak. More for himself than for her. But then, speaking to Vivian was as natural to him as thinking. After so many years, it was as if they shared one mind.

"I found her," he murmured, "just where I knew she would be." He grimaced. "Do you know, it was not even difficult to persuade her to come with me? She is so innocent. So trusting. And so very, very young." He fell silent for a beat. "I cannot remember what it was like, being so young. Can you?"

He stared at a shadowy point on the wall, head cocked, as if awaiting an answer. Vivian said nothing, of course. He was not even sure she had heard him. But he knew exactly what she would have told him, if she'd only been able to.

"It is a grave risk, I know," he said to her. "Deep magic . . . it is always dangerous. And so often deadly. And to tamper with time itself. . . ."

A chill ran up his spine. He'd been so sure of himself when he'd gone to fetch Breena. Now, doubt crept in.

"Was it wrong? Perhaps. But Vivian, what choice did I have? The stakes are far too high! I could not bear to risk you. But the timing is critical, as our enemy knows. We set our course long ago . . . and perhaps that is where we went wrong. Certainly we had doubts. But we made our decision then, and now there is nothing to do but see it through. And Breena, truly, is the only Druid able to play your role in this."

He could almost feel Vivian's frown. But when he looked down at her face, her expression was blank. A black fist squeezed his heart. How often in their long life together had he fled her disapproval? Now he would welcome it, if only she would come back to him.

He smoothed a white curl from her forehead, and tucked it behind her ear. She allowed him the small liberty; he even imagined he saw a slight smile on her lips.

"I cannot let you go," he said, more to himself than to the silent woman in his arms. "Not without a fight. I had no choice but to find Breena, and bring her here. She will be fine. Her magic is strong, her instincts excellent, and I have set a magical protection about her. I've left Gareth with her as well. I will find you, and then I will go to her. Once Igraine is free, I will send Breena home."

Myrddin prayed it would all be so easy.

But he very much feared it would not.

"This is never going to work."

"I beg to differ, my lady. The great Myrddin's magic paves our path."

"It is not Myrddin's magic I doubt," Breena muttered, "It's my own. And . . . my balance on this stallion. I—"

A gasp stole her breath as the warhorse pranced sideways, snorting as his nimble hooves avoided a deep rut. If Breena could have tightened her death grip on the beast's mane, she would have done so. As it was, her fingers were already so tightly clenched in the horsehair she'd begun to wonder if they would ever uncurl.

The young warrior guiding the beast chuckled. "I will not let you fall."

Breena was not so sanguine. Sir Gareth's warhorse—Jupiter—was nothing like the Celtic ponies she'd grown up with. The beast was by far the largest and surliest equine Breena had ever seen. Its owner, a knight in the service of Duke Gerlois of Cornwall, had been waiting for Myrddin and Breena at a sea port near Avalon. Sir

Gareth had told her his magnificent stallion's blood-lines had been cultivated by a wild people known as Sarmatians, horsemen from the eastern fringe of the Roman empire.

Jupiter had boarded the boat with Breena and Gareth, to sail west along the rocky Cornish coast. The pitch and roll of the sea had unsettled Breena's stomach. Riding the last miles to Tintagel on Jupiter's back had not improved it.

Myrddin did not accompany them. He would rejoin them at Tintagel, he'd said, as soon as he could—but certainly before the rise of the harvest moon. That was the night the old Druid expected the events of Breena's vision to unfold.

Breena did not know what Myrddin meant to do in the meantime. When she pressed him, he would tell her nothing. He spoke only of Breena's mission.

Igraine was a Druid. A Seer, like Breena. But the duchess's power was weak. At Tintagel, Breena was to form a link between her magic and Igraine's, and protect her until Myrddin's arrival. Breena only hoped she was worthy of the trust Myrddin had put in her.

She was not even sure she would arrive at Tintagel with her bones whole. Gareth's warhorse was so large! Gingerly, she peered down at the ground passing rapidly beneath her. She tried not to imagine her body's impact on the road.

Gareth's arms were solid and sure on either side of her torso; his hands held the reins loosely before her. "Relax, my lady. It wants but three miles to Tintagel. I promise you, I will not allow you to tumble to an untimely death."

Untimely death? Now, there was a jest. How could it be untimely for a woman to meet her death some three centuries after her birth?

Breena wondered if Gareth knew she'd traveled

from the past. She did not ask him. Even Breena had difficulty believing what had happened. Gareth had no magic—very few people in this age did. The young knight all but worshiped Myrddin, but could he accept magic as deep as the power that had brought her here?

Gareth was a knight pledged to Duke Gerlois. His first loyalty, however, lay with Britain's high king, Uther Pendragon, and with Myrddin, the king's counselor. Though Gareth had no magic of his own, he revered Druidry and the old ways. Breena had been astounded when he'd shown her the mark of the Druids of Avalon—the triple spiral of the Goddess, merged with the cross of the Carpenter Prophet—on the hilt of his sword.

Her pendant bore the same symbol, as did Myrddin's staff. Gareth was, bluntly put, the elder Druid's spy in Cornwall.

"Myrddin charged me with your safety, my lady." The young knight was very earnest. "I will not fail him. Or you."

Breena twisted in the saddle to meet Gareth's gaze. He was perhaps only a year or two older than she. It was impossible not to notice how handsome he was, with his thick chestnut hair and green eyes.

"I did not mean to suggest you would fail in your duty. Of course you will not. It is only that I am . . ." She swallowed around the lump in her throat. " . . . somewhat frightened."

Gareth's ocean gaze gentled. She was all too aware of his arms around her, shifting with the stallion's gait. Her left shoulder pressed against the chain mail he wore under his tunic. Embarrassed, she fixed her gaze on a small scar on his right cheekbone.

"Do not worry so, my lady. Myrddin is a great man, and a powerful Druid. He is never wrong."

"Never?"

"No, my lady. At least, I have never known him to be."

Breena could almost believe it. An intense magical energy surrounded Myrddin. Even she, who had no special talent for detecting magic, could feel it. When Myrddin had explained how she was to protect Lady Igraine, it had sounded so simple.

But now, deprived of the his immense magical presence, doubts flooded in. Oh, she did not question the importance of her task—far from it. She knew with a bone-deep certainty that the Great Mother had set her on the path she now tread. No, it was her own abilities, and her magic, that she doubted.

"My lady—"

"Please," Breena said. "Stop calling me that."

Gareth nodded. "You are right. I should call you Lady Antonia, so that you may become accustomed to the name."

A shiver ran through her. "I do not like the notion of assuming a dead woman's identity."

Gareth guided Jupiter around a puddle with little more than a subtle press of one knee. "The ruse will bring you quickly to Lady Igraine's side."

"I feel like a thief. I've taken Antonia's name, her life, and her history."

"She is dead," Gareth said grimly. "She is beyond protest."

Another shiver raced through Breena. Yes, Lady Antonia was dead, as was her family. Her father, Lord Vectus, had been a minor landowner and cousin to Lady Igraine. The entire family, and a good number of their tenant farmers, had been killed in a Saxon raid a month earlier.

"How can Myrddin be so certain I will be accepted as Antonia? Lady Igraine is sure to know I am not her cousin's daughter."

"Antonia was but a child when the duchess last saw her. As for the duke, Gerlois has never laid eyes on Vectus's daughter. But Myrddin told you all this. Do you not trust him?"

Oddly, she did. "I'm just apprehensive, I suppose. What if I fail? What if they question my story?"

"They will not. Your Latin is that of a noblewoman. Your hair is the color of fire, as Antonia's was. It is not a color often seen in the south. You could hardly be anyone other than Antonia. Nay, the danger in Tintagel lies not with the duke, but with his brother, Bishop Dafyd, who has traveled west for the festival."

Dafyd possessed dark magic. Myrddin had lectured Breena at length about the danger the sorcerer posed. He'd even cast a spell to veil her magic from Dafyd's senses. Until Myrddin arrived at Tintagel, Breena was to stay close to Igraine, and avoid catching the bishop's attention.

A hare darted across the road. Gareth's stallion sidestepped neatly, causing Breena to shift in the saddle. Her bottom bounced hard between Gareth's spread thighs. The knight shifted backward immediately, but not before Breena felt something hard and blunt prod her left buttock.

Heat flooded her face. Gareth cleared his throat.

"Er . . . my apologies, my lady."

"Do not think on it," Breena said hastily. She moved as far forward as she could. "Um . . . how much farther is it to Tintagel?"

Gareth shifted the reins to one hand and gestured ahead. "When we gain that rise, we will see the island below us."

"Island?"

"Did Myrddin not mention it? Tintagel Castle is built on an island that lies but an arrow's flight offshore."

Gareth reined in Jupiter as they crested the hill. Tintagel Castle perched like a dark jewel atop sheer cliffs polished by the crashing spray of surf. A deep channel, spanned by a narrow, rocky ridge, connected the island to the shore. Above the battlements, seabirds circled.

"It is said to be impregnable," Gareth said.

Breena could well believe it. The island's cliffs dropped a dizzying distance to the sea. The natural stone bridge spanned about twice as far as a man could throw, and was scarcely wide enough for two horses to travel abreast. The road ended at an open area before a massive pair of timber gates. Anyone requesting entrance would stand exposed to archers on the battlements above.

Breena imagined even a Roman legion at full strength would have difficulty taking the island. Any enemy who dared try to rush the gates would be shot full of arrows before he reached his goal. His body would be consumed by the rocks and sea below.

The castle's most prominent feature was a tall, square tower. "It looks like a Roman army watchtower," Breena said, an uneasy feeling creeping over her.

"Aye," Gareth replied. "It once was. When the legions withdrew from the west country, the outpost was claimed by the local lord."

The fortress, large as it was, did not cover the whole of the island. Breena glimpsed fields and orchards beyond. "Why, the island is as large as my father's farm," she said, "barring our outlying fields." Large enough to be self-sufficient. "Is there a source of fresh water?"

"Cisterns catch rainwater," Gareth replied. "Tintagel castle, fully provisioned, can easily withstand half a year's siege."

The castle village, resting firmly on the mainland, was a small, but prosperous, settlement. A second village of tents, bustling with activity, sprouted in a neighboring field.

"They've come for the festival," Gareth explained.

"It looks to be a popular event."

"It is. Gerlois provides food and drink for all. Minstrels and other entertainers will be about, too. The market offers a chance to barter for one's needs before winter sets in." He pointed to a field close to the castle access, where carpenters labored to erect a raised viewing platform along one side of a broad, flat field. "That is where the tournament will take place." His tone hardened. "The duke's show of strength to the high king."

"You do not approve."

"Gerlois plays a dangerous game. If there is opposition to Uther in Dumnonia, it has been stirred by the duke's hand."

Myrddin had told Breena that three years ago, Igraine had been forced to wed Gerlois, though she had been secretly pledged to Uther. Last spring, in Caer-Lundein, Uther had planned to reclaim his intended bride. But Bishop Dafyd's sorcery interfered, and Gerlois carried Igraine back to Cornwall. War had prevented Uther's chase until now.

"We must remove Lady Igraine from Tintagel before the king's forces arrive," Gareth continued. "If a siege is enacted, casualties will be high."

"Surely, with Myrddin's magic, it will be not be so difficult to rescue Igraine."

"It may be harder than you think. Since his return from Caer-Lundein, Gerlois holds Igraine in near seclusion in the castle tower. She is only rarely seen."

Dear Goddess. What if they were already too late? What if Breena's vision had already come to pass, and Igraine already lay dead? "Are you sure Gerlois has not harmed his wife?"

"He has announced she will preside over the harvest feast. It is vital that you find your way to her side, and advise her of Myrddin's plan. We must see her safely away, and quickly."

Gareth pressed his knees to Jupiter's flanks. The horse began a trot down the hill to the castle. Breena's gaze snagged on a bird flying toward Tintagel. A small falcon. A merlin, if she was not mistaken.

Her heart tripped a beat. She'd seen Rhys once, in his merlin form, sailing overhead, looking much the same as this bird did now. But of course this falcon was not Rhys. It was just an ordinary bird, no doubt on its way to cull pigeons from the cliffs for its breakfast.

Breena's eyes followed its flight. The merlin flew straight ahead, toward Tintagel. Her initial uneasiness multiplied a thousandfold when the bird flew in a slow circle about the old Roman tower.

Just as it had in her dream.

Gerlois, Duke of Cornwall, was a large, well-muscled man of middle years. He was possessed of unbounded arrogance, a loud voice, and a hard, round stomach that put Breena in mind of a woman about to give birth.

His beard and hair were cropped short, and his long tunic was trimmed with purple and gold, in the style of a Roman senator. He wore a twisted Celtic torc about his neck, however, and a belt inlayed with a Celtic scroll design. His features, and his mien, were all Celt warrior. His shrewd blue eyes took in Breena with a single hard glance.

Anxiety kept her gaze cast downward. The mosaic floor of the duke's receiving chamber had been poorly repaired in more than a few places, with new stones that did not quite match the color of the original ones. Breena stared at one patch of yellow amid faded gold and prayed the duke believed she was stricken with grief for her lost family.

At the duke's right sat his younger brother, the flaccid, frowning Bishop Dafyd. Breena carefully avoided meeting his gaze, studying him through her lowered eyelashes. He wore a long brown robe, devoid of decoration, and held a staff with a hooked end.

A woman of middle age sat on Gerlois's left. She was introduced as Lady Bertrice, the duke's widowed sister. Bulky and sour-faced, she resembled her brothers greatly. She, too, wore a mix of Roman and Celtic garb.

Two soldiers were also present, standing at attention near the door. A second monk, a gaunt figure draped in a black-cowled robe, stood a few steps behind the bishop, head bowed.

Breena was grateful for Gareth's confident presence at her side. The knight bowed to his lord and proceeded to relate Antonia's sad tale.

"After the Saxon dogs were driven back into the sea, I remained behind as my brothers-in-arms returned to Tintagel. I thought to search the forest for friend or foe. I discovered Lady Antonia and her servant huddled in a cave."

Breena dared a glance at the duke. Gerlois's attention was fixed on Gareth.

"How is it the women did not return to the village upon the Saxons' withdrawal?" Gerlois's Latin was precise, his inflection that of a patrician.

"Lady Antonia was delirious with fever. Her maid could not carry her, and was loath to leave, lest Antonia die in her absence. Indeed, Antonia's fever did not break until several days after I carried her to the village. Another fortnight passed before she was strong enough to make the journey to Tintagel."

The duke did not appear to disbelieve Gareth's lies. Breena's shoulders unclenched a fraction.

They tensed again when Bishop Dafyd's staff struck the floor. The cleric rose. Breena tried not to flinch under his narrow gaze. "The girl escaped the Saxon attack."

"Yes, Excellency," Gareth replied.

Dafyd addressed Breena directly. "Lady Antonia."

Reluctantly, Breena raised her eyes.

"Did you escape *all* of it?"

A long, blank moment ensued before Breena understood. Dafyd was asking if she'd been raped.

She wet her dry lips. "Yes, Excellency. By the mercy of the Christos," she added belatedly.

"Saxons are godless demons." Dafyd's statement sounded like an accusation—not of the Saxons, but of Breena. "They are not easily thwarted in their unholy lusts. How did you evade them?"

Breena dared a glance at Gareth. The knight's expression was carefully neutral. She inhaled, and launched into the tale she'd practiced with Myrddin.

"My maid woke me before dawn, as the attack began. We ran through the kitchens to the pig yard, where we blacked our faces with muck. We escaped through a postern gate and fled into the forest. The Saxons took no note of us."

"This maidservant. Did she not accompany you to Tintagel?"

"No, Excellency," Gareth said. "Lady Antonia permitted the woman to remain with her daughter's family."

Dafyd nodded. Silence ensued, during which Breena felt the bishop's scrutiny like a crawling insect on her skin. She stood very still, her eyes fixed on a point behind his shoulder. Her gaze fell on the black-cowled acolyte. The man had not moved a muscle during Breena's interview. Now he lifted his head. His cowl fell back just far enough for Breena to see his face.

She swallowed a gasp. The monk was hideous.

The left side of his face looked as though it had been boiled in oil. The hair above his missing ear had been burnt away. From temple to jaw, his flesh was raw and puckered. No lashes grew on his left eyelid. The eye over which it closed wandered blankly to one side.

By the gods! What tragedy had the poor man endured?

The monk's good eye, dark and intelligent, took note of Breena's horror. Immediately, Breena looked away, embarrassed to think the poor man had caught her gawking at his misfortune.

Bishop Dafyd resumed his seat. Leaning toward the duke, he conversed with his brother in low tones. Breena strained her ears, but could not make out more than a few indistinct words.

Honor . . . shame . . . sin . . .

At last, the duke rose, and his siblings with him. "I thank you, Sir Gareth, for the mission of mercy that has brought my wife's cousin to Tintagel. You may take your leave."

Gareth bowed. "At your command, my lord." Pivoting with military precision, he strode from the room without a backward glance.

Breena's lungs squeezed. She'd known, of course, that she would not have Gareth constantly by her side until Myrddin's arrival. But that did not prevent her panic from welling.

The duke addressed her. "Antonia. I give thanks to the Christos that you were spared your father's fate. It is good and right that you have come to us at Tintagel."

Breena's knees nearly buckled with relief. Gerlois believed her! "I am honored by your kindness, my lord. May I . . . may I go to my cousin now?"

"In good time," Gerlois said. "First we must settle the matter of what is to be done with you."

"What is to be done with me?" Breena echoed.

"Your hair, of course, makes things difficult."

Breena brought her hand up, uncertainly, to touch her hair. What was the duke talking about?

Bertrice made a disapproving sound with her tongue. "Such bold color is the devil's work, I do not doubt."

"Indeed," said Dafyd. He gazed at Breena thoughtfully. "How old are you, child?"

"Seventeen," she said, still confused. The real Antonia had been a year younger than Breena.

"You claim your virtue is intact. But a woman's soul is deficient. Even a virtuous woman utters many untruths. A woman with hair the color of hellfire cannot be trusted at all."

Breena stared dumbly at the bishop. He believed she lied? Because of the color of her hair?

Gerlois's expression was grim. "If there is to be a mongrel babe, we will soon know it."

"Even if no bastard yet grows in her belly," the bishop said, "I very much doubt even Bertrice's vigilance will prevent one from taking root soon enough."

Breena's mouth fell open.

"I advise that you place her under a husband's control immediately," Dafyd told his brother.

Husband?

Gerlois stroked his chin. "Yes, there is merit in that plan. She will wed as soon as possible."

"But who will offer for a girl tainted by Saxon swine?" Bertrice asked.

"Vectus's wealth was not inconsequential," Gerlois replied. "Even if his treasure has been sacked, many will be willing to fight for his holdings alone." He slashed the air with his hand. "I will open the harvest tournament with a contest for Vectus's lands. Lady Antonia's hand will, of course, be part of the bargain. The wedding will take place immediately."

"A fine notion." Dafyd nodded his agreement.

Breena briefly shut her eyes. This was insanity. The festival was set to begin on the third night before the full moon.

What would she do if Myrddin did not arrive before then?

Chapter Eight

*I*f one wished to travel the Lost Lands in the flesh, one had to pass through an ancient standing stone. A human mind, however, could enter the shadow realm from any point. In either case, the journey was fraught with danger and deep magic. Time unfolded illogically in the Lost Lands. An hour in that mystical place might be a day, or a year—or ten—in the human realm. A man could return to find all he knew was lost forever. Myrddin did not count the cost. Detaching his mind from his body, he followed his wife's path to the Lost Lands, which was a more complex problem, especially as she had not traveled the route by choice.

He had little time to reflect on the wisdom or folly of his actions. Vivian lay sleeping, her face pale as death. Her body, stripped of its soul, had steadily deteriorated these past months. All summer, while he battled at Uther's side, his mind had been here, with Vivian. Now, with Breena ensconced in Tintagel, and the night of her prophecy drawing near with sickening speed, he had a short span of time in which to search for his lost love. He could not fail. She was his life. He did not know how he could go on without her.

Her hand in his was cold, her skin stretched like parchment over fragile bones. She was his anchor in the storm that was his life, and he clung to her. If he failed, he did not know if he would have the strength to keep living.

The trail of Vivian's soul led into the sky. Following it was like plucking the dimmest stars from the night darkness. But her magic was as familiar to him as his own. He did not falter.

This was not like traveling through the standing stone to Breena's time. He had been in control of that magic. Or at least, he'd held the reins as firmly as any man could when he'd harnessed deep magic. This journey into the Lost Lands, with only his mind, was different from treks he had made in the flesh. His life essence was dust tossed by merciless storm winds. All he could do was pray the gods would not blow him off course.

He did not remember entering the midlands. He became aware of his surroundings abruptly, as if he'd fallen asleep in one place, and awakened in another, with no memory of how he had come to be there. He found himself in a forest of towering trees. Jagged overhead branches blotted out the sun.

His sense of hearing was heightened—every bird's cry, every creaking tree limb, every whisper of wind, was almost deafening. Even the insects scurrying beneath his feet did not escape his notice. His smell was keen, too. Moss, and mold, and grass.

Vivian?

He tried to speak her name, but the sound formed only in his mind. The faint trace of her life essence was gone. The earth magic of the forest was so deep it obliterated every power but its own. The world stretched endlessly before, and behind, and to his right and left. Each direction identical. He did not know which way to turn.

Hesitantly, he took a step forward. And stumbled. His feet were not his own. Looking down, he was stunned to discover paws covered with white fur. His body was not a man's. It was rounded, with plump belly, short forelimbs, and long, powerful hind feet.

He did not remember shifting. Had not felt the pain. He was a hare, an animal in whose form he did not feel comfortable. It took some concentration to command four feet instead of two. He hopped forward, nose twitching, wondering if he could scent Vivian's magic. Going up on his hind legs, he sniffed the air.

And froze.

The dog appeared as if out of nowhere. He caught a glimpse of a gaping maw lined with razor-sharp teeth, drool dripping. The stink of *predator* exploded in his nostrils.

The beast snapped at his ears.

Myrddin ran.

"You are in sore need of a bath."

Lady Bertrice's nostrils flared. Not without cause, Breena admitted. It had been three days since she'd bathed—three days of travel by boat and horseback. She did not smell like a rose.

"Yes, my lady."

The duke's audience chamber gave onto a covered walkway circling Tintagel castle's main courtyard. The wide space was crowded with servants hustling to and fro, carrying foodstuffs, firewood, coal, and linens. Bertrice cut a diagonal across the court, skirting two serving women drawing water from a well. Breena caught a glimpse of an arched passage leading to what looked like a large feasting hall. Five or six soldiers lounged with tankards at one of the long plank tables. Reflexively, she searched the group for Gareth. He was not among them.

"Come along then," Bertrice said briskly. "We go to the laundry."

"But . . . am I not to see the duchess now?"

"In that dirty dress? Smelling like a pig sty? You are touched in the head to even suggest it. No, you'll have a bath first, and don some suitable clothing. That rag you are wearing is little more than peasant's garb. If one of Gerlois's knights must be burdened with you, you should at least look like a lady."

Gerlois's sister traversed a long hallway, still muttering. "As if I have time to play nursemaid! What with festival guests arriving daily. The bishop's retinue alone took up an entire floor of the castle's main wing. And there is much left to do before the harvest feast."

"You oversee Tintagel's servants, my lady?" Breena ventured.

"I am the castle's chatelaine. In Lady Igraine's stead, of course."

"Does the duchess not tend to her own home?"

"The duchess!" Bertrice shot Breena a look over her shoulder. "Why, that is ludicrous. The duchess cannot even tend to herself most of the time. She cannot be left alone for long, lest she harm herself."

"Harm herself? Why would she do such a thing?"

Bertrice sniffed. "The woman is melancholy. For all her beauty, she is malcontent. Her mood only worsened after the babe was born. . . ."

"Igraine has a child?" Breena blurted out, before she realized that Antonia would have surely known this.

But Bertrice did not seem to think the question odd. "She had a child. It died scant days after its birth. I am not surprised you do not know of it. My brother did not announce the babe's birth, or its death. It was only a female, after all."

"I'm sure the duchess was inconsolable just the same."

"To be sure. Igraine's condition deteriorated alarmingly after the birth."

"She fell ill? A childbed fever?"

"No. Your cousin's deficiency is of the spirit, and of morality. Not of the body."

Breena did not quite know what to make of that. "I do not understand."

"Lady Igraine fell into melancholy when her babe died, and her bleakness of spirit only became worse after she visited Caer-Lundein this spring. She tolerates very few attendants. Myself only, and one or two maid servants. The rumors in town have been rife. The duke has not been pleased."

Lady Bertrice's lips compressed in a thin line. "Perhaps she will accept you, since you are her kin. I can only hope that is the case. It would be a great help to me, I tell you. With the festival fast approaching, my direction is sorely needed in the kitchen. At the same time, the duchess is in need of constant care. She is greatly agitated by Gerlois's command that she appear at his side during the harvest feast and tournament."

"I will try my best to be agreeable," Breena said.

"See that you do." Bertrice bustled into the laundry. Three women, engaged in folding linens, looked up. They curtsied to the duke's sister, and eyed Breena with curiosity.

Bertrice clapped her hands. "A bath. At once."

The servants abandoned their work to comply with their mistress's order. Two women erected a screen in front of a copper tub, while the third hurried through a doorway leading to the outdoors, where fires burned under three large cauldrons. Two sweating women employed in stirring laundry abandoned their task to draw clean water for Breena's bath.

When the tub was filled, Breena waved off offers of assistance and ducked behind the screen to undress. She tucked her Druid pendant inside the linen towel she'd been given. It would not do to have Lady Bertrice notice that Breena wore the symbol of the mother goddess.

When she emerged from her bath, she found an undertunic, blouse, and overskirt laid out for her. The cloth was very fine, and the colors dark and rich. Her muddy shoes had been replaced with leather slippers. She dressed, and quickly slipped her pendant under her bodice.

One of the maids braided Breena's hair, and wound it tightly about her head. Lady Bertrice, watching Breena's transformation with a critical eye, produced a veil as a finishing touch. No doubt to hide the ungodly color of Breena's hair.

Lady Bertrice surveyed Breena from head to toe and gave a curt nod. "Come along."

Back in the busy central courtyard, Bertrice halted before an iron-strapped door. The soldiers guarding the portal snapped to attention.

"My lady."

A stout wooden crossbar was raised. Breena passed into a small atrium garden, planted at the base of the old Roman watchtower. The door to the main courtyard shut behind her; the crossbar thudded into place on the other side. The only other exit from the garden was the door in the base of the watchtower. The structure stood some six stories high; Breena tilted her head back and looked up. Though the lower stories retained a watchtower's small windows, the windows of the upper three stories had been widened and set with mullioned glass. The lowest of these three levels gave out onto a narrow terrace on the roof of the abutting building. This, then, was where Duke Gerlois kept his beautiful wife.

Lady Bertrice strode swiftly across the garden. The arching cane of a rose, heavy with bloodred hips, snagged her skirts. The atrium's fountain was adorned with a carving depicting a stone maiden tilting a jug. But the vessel was cracked, and no water flowed. Slime edged the rainwater in the basin.

Inside the watchtower, flickering torches illuminated the steps of a stone stairway, winding somberly upward. After four complete turns, the stair opened into a narrow vestibule. The room boasted two doors. The one on the outer wall likely led to the roof terrace Breena had glimpsed from the atrium. The other, Breena discovered, led to Lady Bertrice's bedchamber.

Light poured from the window, illuminating furnishings—table, chairs, trunk, desk, and bed—that had once been opulent. Now they were worn with use, the upholstery faded. In the window, Breena noted, fully half the glass panes were cracked. In one panel the glass was missing entirely; parchment was tacked in its place. The room did not lack for heat, however. Coals smoldered in an iron brazier, with more in a bucket nearby.

Bertrice crossed to a narrow door in the corner of the room and pulled it open. "You may sleep here until your marriage."

Breena peered into a small storage room containing folded linens and discarded furniture, including a narrow bed. "Thank you, my lady." With difficulty, she kept the impatience from her voice. "May I greet my cousin now?"

"Yes. Igraine is above, in her solar." Bertrice blew out a short, irritated breath. "Let us hope the duchess is not in one of her moods."

Myrddin had told Breena that Igraine's beauty was renowned. Gareth, too, had proclaimed the lady's loveliness. Their paltry descriptions fell far short of reality. The Duchess of Cornwall was nothing short of sheer feminine perfection.

Upon entering Igraine's solar, Breena tried her best not to stare. Igraine's skin was the finest, most fragile ivory, blushed with roses. Her blue eyes, high cheekbones, and red lips merged in graceful perfection. Lush hair, gold with a touch of dawn red, was piled high on her head. A few loose curls dangled, emphasizing her slender neck.

Her figure was flawless as well. Tall and slender, with generous breasts, a narrow waist, and lushly curved hips, Igraine rivaled any Greek goddess. Or perhaps it might have been more accurate to compare her to Helen of Homer's *Iliad,* whose beauty had been famed, more so than that of Hera and Athena. For just like Helen's, Igraine's beauty was destined to launch a war.

When Breena entered the room, the duchess was seated on a chaise with a maid in the chair beside her. Igraine's brows drew together; she put aside her embroidery and rose. Her maid did likewise.

Igraine was dressed in Roman style, as elegantly as any patrician's wife. Her undertunic of saffron linen was overlain by a *stola* of heavy golden silk, embroidered at the edges with gold thread and seed pearls. Her jeweled girdle was set with topaz and amber, and the pins at her shoulders and sleeves were twisted silver and gold. Her slippers were jeweled. And none of her garb was old, or worn, or mended, as everything else in Tintagel castle seemed to be.

She looked at Breena with a question in her eyes. Breena, quite nervous now, met Igraine's gaze.

Breena's eyes widened. Faint white sparks, shifting and swirling, clung to the duchess's head and shoulders. The magic of a Seer. Myrddin had told her Igraine possessed Druid magic, but Breena had never expected she'd be able to see the duchess's aura. For a moment, she just stared, wondering if her mind was playing tricks. Then, as quickly as it had appeared, Igraine's aura vanished, fleeing before a dull silver pall.

Without a doubt, Breena knew that Igraine was the

faceless woman of her dream. The silver magic was only part of it. Her height, her graceful carriage, her air of sadness—it was all so familiar. And the painting on the wall—Breena noticed it now for the first time since entering the room. The beautiful, sad young man held a shepherd's staff in one hand, and cradled a lamb in his other arm. This, too, she'd seen in her vision.

A bone-deep shudder ran through her. First the falcon circling the tower, now this. Myrddin had been right. This place, this time, this woman. All of it was Breena's fate.

Her breath caught in her throat, making a sound like a hiccup. Lady Bertrice sent her a quelling frown. Breena closed her eyes against what felt like a sudden, dizzying dip of the floor.

"Duchess," Lady Bertrice said. "Why, you look quite well today! I am pleased to see it."

"Thank you. But whom have you brought to . . ."

Igraine's question faded as the heavy, familiar silence descended upon Breena. Silver mist rose from the floor like a fog rising from a lake. Gray fingers of smoke reached upward, encircling Igraine, enveloping her, caging her . . .

A shadow moved to the left, at the edge of Breena's vision. She swung her head in time to see the darkness materialize into the form of a man. He shoved past, his angry footsteps shaking the floor. It happened just as it always had, more times than Breena could count. Igraine's eyes widened as the shadowy figure approached. He halted before her and raised his hand.

The man's arm descended. Breena's throat closed. She tried to move; she struggled to breathe. She could do neither. Blackness seeped into her vision.

And she was falling, falling, falling. . . .

* * *

"Dear Christos! What has happened to her?"

"'Tis just a faint, I think, my ladies—"

"Perhaps it is as my brother suggested. She carries a Saxon mongrel."

Breena groaned, trying to make sense of the voices. Three women, talking at once. The cacophony of their speech only added to the pounding in her skull. She tried to bring her hand to her temple, but somehow could not figure out how to make the two connect.

"She's waking," a woman with a broad Celt accent said.

"But . . . who is she?" An utterly melodious voice uttered the question.

"Why, she is your own cousin! Lord Vectus's daughter. Do you not recognize her?"

"Antonia? I thought . . . the Saxon raid . . ."

"She escaped. One of Gerlois's knights found her. They arrived this morning."

Breena struggled to fill her lungs.

"God be praised," the lovely voice exclaimed.

"Poor thing." It was the maid who spoke. "Only think what she must have suffered, if she is carrying a Saxon babe! 'Tis too horrible to contemplate." Breena felt a light touch on her cheek. Then, as before, "She is waking, my ladies."

With an effort, Breena opened her eyes. Three faces hovered above her. Bertrice, Igraine, and the unnamed maid.

"I am not," she gasped through gritted teeth, "carrying a Saxon babe."

Lady Bertrice's pointed chin jabbed downward. "So you claim."

"Bertrice!" Igraine admonished. "Surely fatigue and grief are sufficient cause for a faint."

Bertrice sniffed. "I suppose."

Breena sucked in a deep breath at last. Her lungs

spasmed. Black and red swirls blotted her vision. She felt the room fade. . . .

Unsympathetic fingers tapped firmly on her jaw. "Antonia! Stay with us, girl!"

Breena opened her eyes, twisting her head to avoid Lady Bertrice's blows. "Please. I am fine. Or I will be, in a moment."

"Thank goodness." Igraine smiled her relief. The effect was dazzling. "Do you think you can sit up, Antonia?"

She was lying on her back on the floor, though she hadn't felt herself fall. She pushed herself up with one arm, wincing as the movement brought a stab of pain to the back of her head. Tentatively, she touched the lump blossoming there.

"Nesta," Antonia said. "Bring Lady Antonia some wine."

The maid rose and crossed to a sideboard. She returned a moment later with a silver goblet, which she pressed into Breena's hand. Obediently, Breena sipped. The wine was passable. Better, at least, than the sour swill Myrddin had carried. She dared not drink much, though. Her waking vision had left her stomach churning.

Lady Bertrice harrumphed. "I hope that blow to her head did not addle her brains."

The duchess laid a cool hand on Breena's forehead. "I am sure it did not."

"Well. Perhaps you are right. Perhaps she fainted from exhaustion. But she'd better recover quickly, if she is to be married."

"Can you stand, do you think, Antonia?" Igraine asked gently. "Nesta, help Lady Antonia to the chaise."

The ground lurched only once or twice as the maid helped Breena to a padded bench. A pillow was placed under her head, and Bertrice ordered Nesta to the kitchens, to fetch meat broth and bread.

"Is my cousin betrothed?" Igraine asked Bertrice after the maid had gone. "I had not heard of it."

"She is not, as of yet," Bertrice admitted. "But the duke believes it prudent she should have a husband within the sennight."

"So soon? Why, she has just lost her family!"

"All the more reason why she needs a husband," Bertrice countered. "Especially if there is to be a babe."

"There is no babe," Breena said.

"Humfph," Lady Bertrice snorted. "So you say."

"I do not—"

Igraine placed a hand on Breena's shoulder. "Lie back, Antonia. Try to relax. You'll feel better in a moment."

"I'm fine," Breena lied. She was not fine. The waking vision had frightened her badly. And the prospect of a forced marriage did not help.

The duchess pressed the forgotten wine into her hand. "Drink again. It will help with the dizziness."

Breena accepted the cup. The piece had once been very fine; now the intricacies of the silverwork were worn almost smooth in places. More fading opulence. Remnants of a safer, more prosperous time.

Lady Bertrice addressed the duchess. "Nesta will soon return with refreshment. I trust you and Antonia will be all right until then? I am wanted in the kitchens. There is much to do before the harvest feast."

Igraine nodded. "Go with the Christos, sister."

The door closed on Lady Bertrice. Breena let out a long breath. For a moment, silence ensued as Breena and Igraine exchanged a long look. Breena wondered at Bertrice's comments about the duchess's weakness of spirit. Igraine did not seem melancholy at all.

But there was something odd about the duchess. Breena tilted her head. The white glow reappeared, clinging to Igraine's head and shoulders. Igraine's

Seer's magic was stronger than Myrddin had led her to believe. And yet, Breena was certain Igraine could not reach her power. Dull silver strands flowed with the white, trapping it as if within a cage. The effect was so overpowering that Breena wondered if Igraine was aware of her power at all. There was some force holding it in check.

She wondered why Myrddin had not explained Igraine's magic more fully. She understood much better now the task the old Druid had given her. Igraine had need of another Seer to protect her because her own magic could not.

Swiftly, hiding her lips with a feigned sip of wine, Breena murmured the Words of the joining spell Myrddin had taught her. She felt her power fly to Igraine. The link formed like a perfect knot joining two strands of silk. But if Igraine felt the connection, she gave no sign of it.

The duchess took Breena's cup, and set it on a table. "How are you feeling?"

"Better," Breena said. "I'm sorry to have caused such worry. I cannot think what came over me. I never faint."

"You have good reason to feel fragile. You have lost your family. And now, you have the prospect of marriage to contend with."

"There is no reason for me to wed," Breena said. "I am not carrying a babe."

Igraine's hand rested on the chaise. "If my lord Gerlois has ordered you to wed, then wedded you will be. The duke does not often change his mind once he reaches a decision."

The speech was delivered with an undercurrent of wretchedness. Breena felt a rush of concern for this sad, beautiful woman.

"Do you never question your husband's decrees?"

"It is not my place to do so. A husband is the protector of his wife's soul. It is a wife's duty to obey her lord."

The rote words were spoken in a whisper. Breena's eyes searched the duchess's face. When Igraine would not meet her gaze, Breena impulsively covered Igraine's hand with her own.

The gesture lifted the edge of the duchess's sleeve. Breena stared in shock at the ugly purple bruise encircling the delicate wrist. She inhaled sharply.

Igraine gasped and snatched her hand back. Standing abruptly, she shook her sleeve down.

"Igraine," Breena said softly.

The duchess's eyes met hers. The beautiful blue of her irises were shadowed with shame.

"Is it also a wife's duty to bear the mark of her husband's anger?"

Igraine reared back. "You overstep yourself, Antonia."

"I think I do not. Does the duke abuse you?"

"He is my husband. My lord. It is his right." The duchess rose and moved away. The discussion was over.

For now.

Chapter Nine

Rhys avoided the Aquila bathhouse, choosing instead to wash in the forest stream just beyond the farm's barley fields. He had not relished the prospect of submerging his mangled back in a steaming hot bath. The thought of answering Marcus's questions appealed even less.

He should not have come to the Aquila farm. He should have taken refuge on Avalon after his escape from the Roman army prison. But he had not. He told himself he'd dragged his battered body to Lucius Aquila's gate because it was closer than Avalon. That was a lie. Though he'd first sought out the Aquilas at his grandfather's command—to secretly gain information about a child Seer Cyric had sensed with his own Seer power—Rhys had gradually come to think of the Roman farm as home, and the Aquilas as his family.

Still, he had not shown the Aquilas his back. Only slaves and criminals endured the flagellum. He was not a slave, and he had no wish to explain the crime that had led to his arrest. He had said only that he had been ill. That was true enough.

The morning air was brisk. He stripped off his shirt, but left his breeches on. The scabs on his back itched terribly; he wished he could apply a salve, but the wounds were too difficult to reach on his own.

Cold water would help. The first shock on his heal-

ing skin brought a gasp. A moment later, all he felt was blessed relief. He waded to the deepest part of the stream. Crouching, he let the water run over his scabs.

It was too cold to stay there for long. Reluctantly, he dunked his head, scrubbing his hair with clean grit scooped from the streambed. Standing, he shook like a dog. And froze when he heard the small, feminine cry behind him.

Pollux.

He turned slowly. She stood on the shore, her herb basket anchored to one hip. Her free hand covered her mouth; above it, her blue eyes were wide with shock. Thanks be to all the gods in Annwyn he had not shed his breeches.

"Breena," he said unsteadily. "I did not know you were here."

The color had leeched from her face, making her freckles stand out like dark pebbles on white sand. Her dress was old, her feet bare. She looked more like a Celt wood sprite than a half-Roman girl of ten winters.

"Rhys," she whispered. "Your . . . your back. What happened?"

He absolutely did not want to answer. He also knew there was no escape from Breena's curiosity. With a sigh, he waded to the shore. He bent to retrieve his shirt while he considered how much of the truth he could safely tell her.

He decided to start with the obvious. "I was flogged."

"With a flagellum. You were . . . arrested?" She swallowed. "Condemned to die?"

She was far too intelligent for someone so young, Rhys thought wryly. He shrugged into his shirt, trying not to wince as the fabric slid over his scabs. "Aye."

"*That is why you lost your harp,*" she said. She had been most distressed when he'd arrived without it. He'd told the Aquilas only that it had been stolen. Again, true enough.

"*I'll make another one,*" he said. And quickly, too, for without a harp to play, he would not eat.

"*Why . . . why did they arrest you? Was it a mistake?*"

Aye, it was a mistake, but not in the way she meant. He'd been beyond careless in casting magic too close to the Roman fortress at Londinium. A soldier had seen Rhys emerge from an illusion and had immediately sent up a cry. Scant moments later, Rhys had found himself arrested and charged with Druidry. Three brawny soldiers dragged him before their centurion, who had pronounced Rhys's sentence with little ceremony. Forty lashes less one, and burning at the stake at dawn.

The flagellum was in itself an instrument of death. Multiple strips of leather, the ends tied with bits of metal and broken glass, flayed skin from muscle with ruthless efficiency. Rhys had borne only the first few blows in silence. After that, his screams had attracted a crowd.

But he could not tell Breena any of that.

"*Aye,*" he said. "*A mistake.*"

"*And when they discovered their error, they let you go?*"

A muscle in his jaw twitched. He'd gotten out of the mess the same way he'd gotten into it—with illusion. When the soldiers had opened his cage at dawn, he'd been simply—not there. Hidden by magic, he'd crawled away during the confusion of their search. But, again, he could not tell Breena. Not without admitting he was Druid. The Aquila family did not know of his magic.

"*Roman legionary soldiers do not admit their mis-*

takes," he said. His tone was harsher than he intended.
"I managed to escape before they could kill me."

"Oh!" Her voice cracked. She looked down, and
toed at the muddy stream bank. "I . . . I am sorry . . .
that the . . . legionaries treated you so cruelly."

He cursed himself as a heartless brute. "I mean no
disrespect to your father," he said quietly. "He is a legionary I am proud to count as a friend."

She raised her head. "It must have hurt," she said.
"So badly." Her blue eyes filled with tears. For him.

The back of his throat hurt. In the days following
his escape, he'd lain in the forest, burning with fever,
wondering if he would survive. He'd craved a word of
sympathy; there had been none. He'd told himself it
did not matter.

He had lied.

"It did hurt," he admitted.

"Does it still?"

"Nay. It . . . itches. Fiercely."

"Oh!" She bent her head, sifting through her basket. "I have plantain. And I saw more, just upstream.
I'll make a cold poultice. That should help." She
pointed to a flat rock. "Sit down over there, and take
off your shirt. I'll be back in a trice."

She smiled through her tears and scampered away.
Rhys watched her go, a smile touching his lips. The
little lass was as practical as she was good-hearted and
impulsive. Slowly, he sat on the rock and pulled his
shirt over his head.

She returned with a great handful of broad green
leaves, which she wet in the stream and crushed
between two flat rocks. He hunched forward; she
knelt behind him. With great care, she spread the
leaves over his back. As she'd predicted, the itching
soon subsided.

His heart healed as well.

* * *

Four days came and went, in which Breena learned very well what Lady Bertrice meant when she'd muttered about Igraine's "moods." Breena found herself in sympathy with Gerlois's sour sister. After just four days, she felt like muttering, too.

After Breena had so unwisely pressed the subject of Gerlois's abuse, the duchess seemed to fade from the world around her, retreating into herself like a turtle into its shell. Igraine moved slowly, spoke little, and ate only when Nesta or Breena coaxed or threatened. During the times when Breena sat with her, she tried everything she could think of to break through the icy wall Igraine had constructed. Nothing worked.

She did not know what to do, other than count the moments until Myrddin arrived. Igraine's luxurious sitting room in the tower was little more than a prison. Lady Bertrice and Nesta came and went, but Breena was not permitted farther than the roof terrace, or the atrium garden. Gerlois's sister feared Breena's red hair would lure men into sin.

At night, Breena tossed and turned in Lady Bertrice's narrow closet. The silver vision intruded, more distinct than before. First came the signs—falcon, shepherd, spilled wine, a pane of cracked glass, a blood-red moon. Then Igraine's face, clearly visible now. Her silent scream as her attacker struck. The man's visage remained shadowy, but Breena recognized his shape and manner. It was Gerlois.

The day preceding the opening of the harvest festival dawned clear and cold. Preparations for the great feast, which was to take place the following evening, were well underway. Breena watched the activity in the castle forecourt from the window in Igraine's solar. The duchess had not spoken a word since Breena had so unwisely pressed her about Gerlois's abuse. Breena could not even reach her through the link of magic they shared—when she cast her senses toward Igraine, it was as if she hit a stone wall. Breena had thus far done nothing to gain Igraine's cooperation in her own rescue.

The tournament for her hand, to take place in two days, loomed large in her thoughts. She could hardly think for worrying about it. She needed help. She needed Gareth.

She scanned the forecourt, and the mainland beyond, hoping to catch a glimpse of him. Perhaps Myrddin had arrived in Tintagel village. Perhaps he and Gareth were already together, plotting a way to free Breena and Igraine from the tower. If only Breena knew more!

At noon, Nesta arrived with a tray of flatbread and cheese, and a pitcher of wine. Breena coaxed Igraine to the table by the window. When the duchess was seated, Breena returned to the sideboard to help the maid.

"It has been four days. Does the duchess often withdraw from the world for so long?" she whispered. "How long might this last?"

Nesta bit her lip. "It happens often enough, when something has upset her. But it has been quite some time since she's left us for so long. Not since her babe died last winter."

"Do you think the loss has something to do with her melancholy?"

"Oh, aye, to be sure. Childbed melancholy sometimes lingers, even when the babe thrives. Often 'tis worse when the child dies."

"Was the babe stillborn?"

"Nay. She was born live, but weak. The duchess even put her to breast. Perhaps it would have gone easier if she had not."

"The child was a girl?"

"Aye. My lady called her Morgan. The duke was

sorely displeased. He expected an heir. He would not even look at the little lass."

Breena darted a glance at Igraine. The duchess sat like a statue. "How long did Morgan live?"

"Two days. On the morning of the third day, when I came to attend my lady, I learned she had died in the night."

"How sad," Breena murmured.

Igraine stirred. "She did not die. She did not."

Breena's head whipped around. Nesta all but flew to her mistress's side. Dropping down on her knees, she chafed Igraine's hand.

"Please, my lady, do not think on it."

The fog had fled from Igraine's eyes. "Morgan. My daughter. She did not die. She did *not!*"

Breena moved closer. "Why do you say that?"

Nesta shot Breena an apologetic glance. "She often went on so in the beginning," she murmured. "It will pass."

Igraine's gaze clung to Breena's. "Gerlois wanted a son. When he came into my room, and saw our daughter at my breast . . . he flew into a rage."

Breena sucked in a breath. *Gods.* What had Gerlois done?

"He took her." Tears ran down Igraine's face. "He took her away. But he did not kill her."

Breena's arm went around the older woman's shoulders. "I am so sorry. Nesta, please. Bring your mistress some wine."

Nesta rose, frowning, but moved to the pitcher on the sideboard.

"You believe me?" Igraine asked, her voice low.

"I do."

"Then you are the first."

Nesta pressed a goblet of wine into Igraine's hand. Igraine took a few sips, then placed the vessel on the table.

"Leave us," she said to Nesta. Her voice was steady.

"My lady! You have not eaten."

"Antonia will attend me. I am sure there is much for you to do in the kitchen."

"But Lady Bertrice—"

"Go, Nesta."

"Do not worry," Breena told the woman. "We will be fine. If Lady Bertrice is displeased, I will speak with her."

The maid gave a reluctant curtsy and withdrew. Breena took a seat and covered Igraine's hand with her own.

"You cannot stay here, my lady. Not if you truly believe your husband stole your daughter away."

Igraine's laugh was short. "Of course I must stay. How can I leave? It pleases Gerlois to keep me locked away in this tower. I am to provide him with an heir. That is my only purpose."

"You cannot believe that. To my mind, you owe the man nothing. He beats you, he tore your babe from your arms—"

"He is my husband."

"He was never meant to be your husband. You were promised to Uther!"

"Yes," Igraine said slowly, "I was. But that was a very long time ago."

"You loved Uther. You danced with him only months ago, in Caer-Lundein."

Igraine stiffened. "I had no choice. He all but dragged me from my chair at court. I went because . . . because I have known Uther forever. He is a distant cousin. He fostered with my uncle, King Erbin, as I did. He was such an arrogant boy! But we were great friends, the three of us."

"Three?"

Igraine sent Breena an odd look. "Myself, Uther,

and Geraint, Erbin's son. But surely, you know that, Antonia? Geraint was your own kin as well."

"Of course," Breena said quickly, though she had no idea of whom Igraine spoke.

"Uther and Geraint were as close as brothers. They were like puppies, constantly snapping and wrestling, but they loved each other deeply. And I loved them both. Geraint was like a brother to me. But Uther . . . my dreams of him were not sisterly at all."

Igraine raised her head, and seemed to stare intently, but Breena knew she saw nothing but the past. "I am older than Uther by three years. An eternity when one is young. When we first met, I was taller than he. Even after he became much larger and broader, I never missed a chance to remind him that I was his elder."

Breena smiled. "How did he respond?"

Igraine laughed. It was a musical sound. "Absurdly! He'd fall to his knees at my feet, and tell me . . . and tell me he meant to wed me, so he might stay forever humble." Her smile faded. "We began slipping off alone together, whenever we could. My old nurse, Vivian, aided our mischief. I promised myself to Uther when I was seventeen, and he fourteen. But even at such a young age, he was so strong, and so very confident."

"Did King Erbin not consider it a good match?" Breena asked. "I cannot think why he would not. Uther was the king's brother."

"Erbin would not entertain the notion. He thought Uther too young, and too wild. He wanted the tempering of age, my uncle said. I vowed to wait for him. Less than a year later, Uther joined Ambrosius's knights and rode to war. Barely a month later, the Saxons struck Llongborth. Geraint died defending the town. King Erbin was stricken with grief."

Igraine brushed a strand of hair from her eyes. "Gerlois drove the Saxons off after Geraint fell. He became my uncle's new heir. When he asked Erbin for my hand, my uncle gave his blessing willingly."

"But what of your promise to Uther?"

"It crumbled like dust. We never had Erbin's consent; the betrothal was not legally biding." Igraine lifted her gaze. "But how could you know of my childish promise to Uther, Antonia? Almost no one did. Your parents certainly did not."

Breena could not think what to reply. She was supposed to be Antonia, but lying to Igraine felt very wrong."

"Myrddin told me," she said at last.

Igraine's eyes went round. "Uther's Druid counselor? But Antonia, how—?"

"I am not Antonia."

The duchess drew a sharp breath. "But . . . of course you are! You survived the Saxon raid. One of Gerlois's knights brought you to me."

"No. I was nowhere near the massacre. I am not your cousin. Saxons killed the real Antonia. Myrddin arranged for me to come here, using her name as a ruse. So I could speak to you."

"Antonia . . . is gone, truly? That poor, poor child. . . ." Igraine shook her head, as if trying to dislodge the remnants of a dream. "If you are not she . . . then who are you?"

"My name is Breena. Myrddin—and Uther—sent me to you. I am here to help you flee."

Igraine's eyes flared with alarm. "Surely you are not serious. I cannot flee. It is impossible."

Breena leaned across the table. "It is entirely possible. Myrddin is coming for you, on Uther's order. Indeed, he may already be here." *She hoped.* "He will take you to Uther."

"But . . . Gerlois is my husband."

"He struck you," Breena said. "He rejected your

child. Under the old Celtic law, you have the right to put him aside."

"How strangely you speak! What do the old laws matter? The church is the only authority now."

"The church follows the teachings of the Christos. Is he not a god of love? I cannot believe he would smile on a husband who beats his wife. You loved Uther once. Do you love him still, as he loves you?"

"My feelings matter little," Igraine said, clearly shaken. "What you propose is insanity. Gerlois will not give me up to the king. Not without a war."

"If you do not leave him, it will mean your death."

Igraine gripped the edge of the table and stood. "No. Gerlois may strike me, but he would never—" She broke off as Lady Bertrice's plodding footsteps sounded on the stair.

"We will speak more of this later," Breena whispered as the door swung open.

Igraine seemed to fade into herself. "Speak all you want," she said. "It will make little difference."

Bertrice bullied the duchess into eating, then took up a seat in a cushioned chair. "Fetch my embroidery," she ordered Breena.

Breena was only too glad for the excuse to leave the solar. She hurried down the stair to Bertrice's chamber, but she did not immediately disturb Bertrice's needlework. Instead, she went to the sideboard, and poured a goblet of wine.

She hurried to her small room and shut the door. Setting the cup on the table, she lit the lamp that lay beside it. Bracing her hands on either side of the cup, Breena dropped her head forward and let her mind fall into a trance. The harvest feast, and the tournament for her hand, approached with frightening rapidity. She had to know if Myrddin was near.

Her magic gathered. Light and shadow emerged on the surface of the wine—shifting, breaking, re-forming. The world faded; the heavy quiet fell like a blanket around her. She whispered a Word, and then added Myrddin's name to the silence.

A dimly lit room sprang into view. A sliver of sunlight shone through the shutters, which were not quite closed. Thorny rose canes arched over the sill. Her gaze fell on the figure of a man, sitting upright in a chair.

Myrddin.

The Druid's posture was rigid, his hand on his staff, as if preparing to rise. But his body was utterly still. For a moment, she feared he might be dead. But no. If he'd died sitting upright, he'd have fallen to the ground.

His eyes were open, staring unblinkingly at some point in the distance. Or, more likely, at some world visible only to him.

Gods. This was not what she'd wanted to See. She'd wanted to find Myrddin inside Tintagel's gates, or in the village—or at the very least, approaching at a quick pace! Not deep in a trance, sitting in a dark cottage that was gods knew where.

The scene was lightening now, as her eyes became accustomed to the dimness. Myrddin was not alone. He sat beside an iron-framed bed. An old woman lay upon it, her white hair spread out over her pillow. Her eyes were closed; her sleep restless. Her lips moved, as if she were mumbling something, but of course, Breena could not hear.

Myrddin's right hand gripped his staff; his left clasped the old woman's hand as if anchoring her in this world. As Breena stared at her face, she was seized with sudden fear.

There was magic in that room. Deep magic. Magic beyond her understanding. Panic struck; she recoiled, yanking her mind away. The vision shattered. A shudder ran through her body. Her arm jerked, the back of her hand hitting the goblet.

The goblet tipped, the rim smacking the table. Wine spilled across the scarred wood. Breena stared at what she had done, aghast.

Another premonition from her vision, come to pass.

The deep magic she'd disturbed vibrated around her. As her shaking hand righted the goblet, she became aware of yet another force, rising from the ground and seeping into the space around her. Dark magic.

Dafyd! It had to be. Her own magic was hidden by Myrddin's spell. The sorcerer must have sensed the deep magic she'd touched in her vision. And now he was looking for its source.

Dear Goddess. What had she done?

"God's teeth, tongue, and cock!" Trent exclaimed. "What a crowd!"

"Aye," Howell said. "'Tis much bigger than last year. They've all come for the tournament, I reckon."

Trent clapped his hands briskly and rubbed. "There's a sack of coin to be earned here, lads."

Rhys rolled his shoulder, and winced. He was getting too old for sleeping on rocks. The troupe had bedded down in the open on the road from Glastonbury to Tintagel. The few inns they'd passed had been filled with paying guests. There was scarcely an empty stable loft to offer a group of scruffy minstrels. But at least they'd eaten well. A song and a bit of entertainment could always be trusted to earn a meal.

Their brisk pace had paid off. The troupe had arrived in Tintagel the day before the festival. The village was abuzz with last-minute preparations.

The merriment had already begun in the city of tents on the field north of town. Trent, Howell, and Floyd were in their element, laughing and jesting with every soul they passed. Even Kane seemed less dour. Rhys trailed after them, but the commotion going on all around meant nothing to him.

His entire attention was focused on Tintagel castle.

It was the most impressive fortress Rhys had ever seen. And that was saying something, for Rhys was well acquainted with the Roman legionary fortresses in Londinium, Eburacum, and Isca Silurum. The sprawling structure, surrounded by high, thick walls, perched atop sheer rock. A dizzying drop ended in jagged rocks and turbulent sea. It might have been the stronghold of a god.

But the castle's form, and its situation, was not the reason Rhys could not drag his eyes from it. When the troupe had first caught sight of the castle, at the top of the rise outside town, the atmosphere around it had been bright and clear. As Rhys entered the village, a dark glow streamed skyward, rising from the walls of the fortress. Magic. And not of the benign sort.

Before his eyes, the spell burgeoned into a blanket of darkness. It wrapped the structure with evil in much the same way Gwen's mist protected Avalon with Light. Rhys did not mistake the crimson sparkle intertwining with the dark strands. This was surely Bishop Dafyd's work.

Dafyd was not the sorcerer who had brought Breena through the standing stone—of that, Rhys was certain. But there seemed to be so few Druids in this Britain. In the past sennight, Rhys had encountered many people—monks, servants, villagers, farmers, innkeepers, travelers. And now, he was faced with the crowds assembled for the festival. Rhys could not detect even a wisp of minor Druid talent among all of them.

With so few rivals, the few Druids who did exist in this time had to be well aware of each other's movements. Disputes were likely. Breena might have been brought from the past by one Druid, in order to provide an advantage over a rival. Or perhaps the two Druids Rhys knew of—Dafyd and Myrddin—were working together.

"My God, men!" Trent's exclamation roused Rhys from his brooding. The little man had spun around to walk backward before the troupe, as was his habit. He spread his arms wide. "Will you but look at the people! I have never seen the like."

To Rhys, the festival crowd did not seem exceptional. More people visited a regular market day in Aquae Sulis. A week of games in Londinium easily drew ten times the crowd. Apparently, the population of Britain was in decline.

He'd cobbled together a history of sorts from the troupe's idle banter. The Roman Empire was on the brink of collapse. The legions had abandoned Britain and the other frontiers. Germania was overrun with barbarians, and even Rome's forces in Gaul were in retreat. There was speculation that within a few years, the city of Rome itself would fall. In Rhys's time, such a notion would have been unthinkable.

Upon the Roman army's withdrawal from Britain, many nobles, and a good portion of its merchant class, had also fled. Britain had been quickly divided among the various Romano-British lords and chieftains who had remained. The Saxon barbarians, immediately recognizing a weakened enemy, had wasted no time in attacking.

The noble family of the present high king, Uther Pendragon, had been among those who fled, after the murder of Uther's father, King Constans. Uther had spent most of his childhood in Brittany and in remote Dumnonia, far from the violence brought to the eastern shores by Saxon raiders. He'd been barely more than a boy when he joined Ambrosius, his older half brother, in a quest to unite Britain's fractious rulers under one high throne.

King Ambrosius had been a true diplomat. But diplomacy had eventually earned him a knife in the back, delivered by a treacherous Saxon during a sham peace treaty conference. Since that dark day, war in Britain had been constant.

"Aye, audiences aplenty we'll have here," Howell said to Trent. "As for earning coin, I'm not so hopeful. I wager few in this swarm have even seen an *as* this past year, let alone a *denarius*! More likely, we'll be offered payment in skillets and brooms."

It was true. The market was busy, but almost every transaction, from what Rhys could see, was bartered.

"Ah, well," Floyd said, sniffing at the aroma of roasting mutton. "If sacks of bronze and copper are not forthcoming, at least we'll be fed."

They made their way through the village of tents. Some were elaborate structures, others little more than blankets tied to sapling frames. A pair of grubby children darted across the path. One clipped Floyd behind the knee—on purpose or not, Rhys could not tell.

Floyd went down hard, his arse hitting the ground with a solid thump. He spit curses at the urchins, who neatly vanished between the rows of tents. Laughing heartily, Howell and Kane gave their friend a hand up.

Floyd was soon grinning ruefully, rubbing his arse. "Ah, well, at least I missed the worst of the mud."

Rhys smiled. Despite his fear for Breena's safety, he could not help being amused by the antics of Trent's troupe. The four men were like good-natured puppies, snarling and scratching, then just as quickly rolling and licking.

Floyd's fall had attracted attention of the surrounding market-goers. Trent, ever quick to note an opportunity, elbowed Kane in the ribs.

"Quick, man! Your flute."

The youth obliged. A murmur rippled through the crowd.

"Give us a song, minstrels!"

"Aye, do!"

The troupe suddenly found themselves in the center of a wide circle. "Ah, and so our dinner is cooked and served," murmured Trent. "Good God, Rhys, what are you waiting for? Let's see that harp!"

With wry amusement, Rhys slung his pack from his shoulder and obliged him. Trent flung his arms wide, pacing a wide circle around his companions. He bowed right, then left, then to the front and back.

"Gather 'round!" shouted Howell.

Kane began a lively tune. He'd played the same melody in a tavern two nights before. Rhys picked out a countermelody on his strings. Floyd's tenor mingled with Howell's deep bass.

> Gather 'round, gather 'round,
> Journeymen and homeward bound!
> Feast your ears, feast your eyes,
> God hath made a man who flies!

On the final note, Howell dropped down on one knee. Using the big man's thigh as a springboard, Trent launched himself skyward. He executed a midair flip before landing lightly on his feet.

Shocked exclamations arose. As it happened, Trent had landed not two steps before an elderly woman. He bowed low to the wizened crone.

"My beauty, I would fly to the moon for the merest chance to kiss your feet."

The old woman laughed. "Cheeky lad."

The crowd roared. The troupe sprang into action, taking new positions, and launching into a new song— a bawdy ditty that soon had the women shrieking and the men laughing heartily. More acrobatics from Trent followed. Rhys joined the well-rehearsed show as best he could with his harp and voice.

The short exhibition drew to a close when Trent climbed onto Howell's shoulders, balancing with ease. The giant sprang skyward, launching his friend into the air. Trent executed three complete flips before landing with a bounce and a flourish.

Much as Howell had predicted, the impromptu performance did not produce much in the way of coin. Trent added only two *quadrans*—half of an *as*—to the communal purse. But he gained a string of painted wooden beads, and a hat with a plume, which pleased him well. And of course, many offers of food and drink.

The stew was simple fare, but filling. The meat and turnips had been provided by Lord Gerlois's bounty. Hard barley bannocks were plentiful. There was even *puls,* a sweet mixture of curd cheese, grain, and honey. Ale flowed like water from a mountain spring.

Howell and Kane had erected the troupe's tent at the edge of the field. Their position—a too-windy bit of hillside—overlooked the tournament grounds. Tintagel castle rose from the cliffs beyond, its dark cloud hanging above it like a pall. The troupe's hearty laughter seemed incongruous to Rhys. He had to remind himself none of the others could sense the malevolent magic.

He eyed the line of colorful banners hung over the castle gate. "Bishop Dafyd's standard is the one with the white cross, aye?"

"To be sure," Howell said around a bite of stew. "No doubt he's been here several days already. His party would have come by sea, rather than jostle his Excellency's tender arse over the road."

"And the rest? To whom do they belong?"

"Why, to just about every noble in Dumnonia. Clarence of Tregear's standard is the lion; Allan of Seaton, the oak leaves. The stag belongs to . . . " Howell frowned, looking toward Trent.

"Maddock of Bolerium," the little man supplied promptly. "Lord Timon of Siluria has the bear, and the double-headed eagle belongs to Hyroniemus of Carn Brea."

"The castle is likely filled to the rafters with nobles," Floyd commented.

"Gerlois of Cornwall's standard must be the black tower," Rhys said. It was the largest banner, and hung directly over the gate.

"Aye, that's right," Howell said. "Only Dewnan's flag is missing. That is old King Erbin's seat. He is too infirm to travel."

"What of the high king? Will he impose on the festivities with his Druid counselor?"

Trent frowned. "If he does, 'twill be with an army at his back. To meet the army Gerlois has assembled here."

"I'd welcome Uther's attack," Howell declared. "Gerlois's defiance of the high king must stop. If that means war, so be it."

"Ho, man! Are you mad?" Floyd shook his head. "I have no wish to be caught in the middle of a war."

Rhys was inclined to agree with Floyd. He would like to investigate Gerlois's island fortress before any war began. He turned his attention once again to the pall hanging over the castle. He had to get in. He could, perhaps, slip into the gates under the cover of a look-away spell. Such a spell worked best when those near it were largely inattentive, preoccupied with their own business. It would be difficult to pass through an active checkpoint undetected. He might cast an illusion, and give himself the appearance of a local lord. Though, presumably, the guards would know who was expected.

Shape-shifting was another option. A falcon could fly easily over the castle walls. But shifting involved deep magic. It was dangerous of itself, and doubly so in this situation. When Rhys's deep magic touched Dafyd's pall, there was a danger the sorcerer would sense it. And Rhys was not willing to give up the advantage of anonymity just yet.

"With so many noble guests in residence," Rhys said slowly, "surely there is a great need for entertainment inside the castle."

Trent gestured with a half-eaten bannock. "Oh, to be sure. No doubt the castle forecourt is teeming with minstrels and actors rehearsing for tomorrow's feast."

"Therein lies our opportunity," Rhys said. "Surely if we are to be paid in coin, rather than in chickens or pottery, we must perform inside the castle."

Howell's mug thunked on the board that served as their table. "Are ye mad? The sorry likes of us, inside Tintagel castle?"

"Why not? Our talents are many and varied."

"But our costumes are not," Howell countered. "My God, man! What castle guard worth his salt would allow a ragged bunch like ourselves past his gates?"

"I'm afraid Howell has the right of it," Trent said with a sigh. "'Tis a pleasant dream, but I fear the market square must be our stage. There are merchants galore in Tintagel village. I anticipate a tidy fortune—if not in copper and brass, then, aye, in poultry and pots."

"Coin is far more portable," Rhys persisted. "Surely you agree that the best talents must be displayed on the highest stage! And surely our talents are the best. It would be a disservice to the duke to stay away."

Trent laughed at that. "Until this very moment, Rhys, I did not think you an ambitious sort."

"If 'tis possible to gain glory, why not try? Why should we grub among peasants, when we may dine with nobles? And surely, with this wind, it is much warmer inside Tintagel's walls."

"Aye, all true enough," Trent said, eyeing the roof currently over their heads. It was nothing more than an oiled cloth, one corner whipping in the stiff breeze gusting off the sea. "'Twould be very grand, I am sure, to pitch our tent in Tintagel's forecourt, and make our bow at tomorrow's feast."

"Who chooses the entertainers for the duke's table?" Rhys asked.

"Why, the castle steward, I imagine," Trent said.

"Then why not beg an audition?"

"Dressed in rags?" exclaimed Kane. "The guards at the gate would laugh us into the sea! We would never even see the steward."

"New clothes can be had easily enough," Rhys said. "I saw several textile merchants in the market."

"And with what, pray tell, shall we pay for these new garments?" Howell demanded. "Our good looks and charm? Our music and wit? We could sing for a solid month and nay earn a single costume fit for the duke's stage."

"Ah." Rhys opened his pack. He removed his harp, a spare shirt, and a few other personal items.

Howell peered inside the satchel. "As empty as our own pockets. What are you about, man?"

Rhys drew his eating dagger. With a swift stroke, he reached inside the pack and cut a swift slash in the bottom. Then, sheathing his knife, he turned the satchel upside down and shook.

Three shining bits of metal spilled into the dirt at Trent's feet. The little man was on the coins in a trice.

"Will they be enough, do you think?" Rhys asked.

Howell, Floyd, and Kane were all on their feet, crowding around their leader.

"Good God," Howell breathed. "Silver!"

"Are they real?" asked Kane.

"Aye, of course," Rhys said.

"We shall see." Trent reached for his own dagger, his gaze intent as he scraped the tip across the face of each coin. He squinted at the coins, then tested each between his teeth.

"They *are* silver! Not coated copper or brass at all." The little man's eyes narrowed on Rhys. "Where did you get them? Surely not in Gwynedd."

Rhys hesitated, unsure how to answer. Pure silver *denari* were common in his Britain—he hadn't anticipated the troupe's amazement. In this time, it seemed, silver coins were a rarity. How to explain?

He needn't have worried. Trent kept right on talking, inventing his own tale. "You must have the devil's own luck! 'Tis many an abandoned villa or fort I've searched, but I've yet to find a single cache buried by the liver-hearted nobles who fled across the channel. Where did you come across these?"

"Er . . . an abandoned villa." The Aquila farmstead was the first possibility that popped into his mind. "Near Isca Silurum."

"Caer-Leon, ye mean? Aye, that was once a rich bit of countryside." Trent peered at the three coins, front and back. "Two from Hadrian's reign, one from Trajan's. Why, these coins are more than three hundred and fifty years old! And yet, they look all but newly minted."

"Is that a problem?" Rhys asked warily.

Trent grinned. "Not for the right people. And trust, me, my good man. If anyone knows the right people, 'tis I."

* * *

"Ah, don't ye look the fine dandy," Trent declared to Rhys the next morning. "With that bright tunic and your lofty, fair head, the lasses will swoon at your feet."

"Or, more likely, cover their eyes against the glare," Rhys replied. Dressed in his new yellow tunic, he all but rivaled the sun itself.

Trent had been as good as his word. He'd taken the first of Rhys's silver coins and traded it for bolts of colorful silk. Overnight, the second coin had transformed the silk into tunics and breeches. Rhys was not sure what the little man had done with the third coin. He suspected it was deep in Trent's pocket.

"Aye," laughed Howell, tugging at his own sky blue shirt. "The other minstrels will fade into the shadows."

Floyd wore a tunic of crimson, Kane of chartreuse. Somehow, Trent had managed to secure a purple costume for himself. Rhys suspected he might have paid more for that one small tunic than all the rest put together.

"I look like an apple," Floyd complained, smoothing the fabric of his crimson shirt over his belly. "What were you thinking, Trent, to garb me in such a color? I would have much preferred Kane's green."

"The green cloth was cut too narrow for your girth," Trent said.

"Why would you want the green?" Howell demanded. "Kane's shirt is the color of goose turd."

"Aye," Kane added darkly. "If goose turd be lit from within. Be thankful, Floyd, that you have the red."

"The color 'twill likely not last, anyway," Howell said, clapping a heavy hand on Floyd's back. Floyd staggered forward two steps. "I'd wager the dyer ne'er clapped eyes on a madder root. Your shirt will run pink in the first rain."

"Oh, aye, and that's a relief," Floyd muttered.

Kane interrupted. "What I cannot understand, is why Rhys would waste a fortune to clothe us."

Trent clapped the youth on the shoulder. "Why, as an investment, of course! We're sure to double his coin! And think of the food on the duke's table."

"I am!" Floyd said. "'Tis the only reason I donned this humiliating costume." He looked heavenward. "Where is my dignity?"

"Dignity's a grandly overrated commodity," Howell said. "It does not fill bellies. But a fine show, delivered with daring and color, will make us rich."

"Let us just pray the sun shines until the festival's closing trumpet," Kane muttered.

"Lads, lads! Stop your whining." Trent waved a wooden card. "Let us thank God above for this seal from the castle steward! The Brothers Stupendous will play this very night at the harvest feast, before Duke Gerlois himself!"

"The Brothers Stupendous?" Howell's bark of laughter rang out. "Good God, Trent, I fear your brain took more damage than I'd thought, when that black-haired lass's father came at ye with an ax last month."

Trent grimaced. "It is cruel of you to remind me of that incident, Howell. How was I to know the lass was a virgin? Anyway, we have far more important matters to attend to at the moment. Do you know, 'tis said the beautiful Lady Igraine herself will stand at the duke's side at tonight's feast? And 'tis rumored she will also appear at the ceremonies on the field this afternoon. Time is growing short—we must decide on our show. We should open with a ballad, methinks." He turned to Floyd. "What do you suggest?"

Floyd considered. "Oh, without doubt, it must be the tragic tale of the Battle of Llongborth. The heroic Prince Geraint was kin to Lady Igraine."

"Ah, a brilliant proposal." Trent shot a glance at Rhys. "You know the tune, I trust?"

Rhys cleared his throat. "Actually, I do not."

"My God, man, 'tis most popular!"

"Not in Gwynedd."

Trent huffed his irritation. "Ah, well, no matter. We'll sing of Uther's victory at Mount Damen. Surely ye know that one?"

Rhys shook his head.

"Nay? Truly? Well, then, what of the Night of the Long Knives? That tale of Saxon treachery never fails to stir the blood."

"I will learn it quickly, if Kane will but teach me."

The little man shot Rhys a look of pure incredulity. "How can it be, man, that you do not know the ballads sung in every public house in every town in Britain?"

"The songs I prefer are older," Rhys said. "The tale of Rhiannon and Pryderi. The sagas of the Sons of Llyr. Or the ballad of Ceridwen and Taliesin."

"You sing of the old gods and goddesses?" Kane was aghast.

Even Trent's chin went down. "Fine enough, perhaps, for a tavern, but in Tintagel's great hall? With Bishop Dafyd at the high table? It will not do. You'd best learn one of the popular ballads, and quickly."

"Nothing would give me more pleasure," Rhys agreed.

"Fine. Well, come along then, lads. Rhys, Floyd, Kane—you find a quiet spot—if you can!—and rehearse your music. Howell and I will practice the tumbling. Come this evening, we'll give the duke a show he'll not soon forget!"

Chapter Ten

*M*yrddin ran in blind panic, forest flashing past in a blur. The dog's teeth snapped at his tail. His mind, submerged inside the brain of the hare he'd become, could not reach its magic.

Water. Up ahead. The crisp scent teased his nose. A river. Deep and swift. Fear gaped like a ravenous jaw. A dead end. The dog would win.

No. He angled his course over smooth, wet rocks. His hind feet slid too fast. Paws scrabbled for purchase, and found none. The ground fell away . . .

A splash. Cold! Water closed over his head. He twisted, frantic, lungs bursting. He could not breathe. And then . . .

He could. Air, blessed air, flowed through his gills. The current rippled over his shining scales. Water magic bathed his new body—that of a fish. The dog could not catch him now! With a flip of his tail and a twitch of his fins, he glided downstream.

Up on the riverbank, out of sight, the dog stood at point. Magic skimmed over its fur. Its body melted, reforming into a brown-pelted otter. The creature splashed into the water and renewed the chase.

Trent was too short to see over the heads of normal-sized men, and too proud to ride on Howell's shoulders. Rhys wasn't quite sure how the wily little man had managed it, but somehow he'd secured the Brothers Stupendous a prime bit of dry ground in the front row of spectators. Every man, woman, and child from the village crowded behind them, eager for a glimpse of the beautiful Igraine, Duchess of Cornwall.

On the far side of the field, the viewing stands erected for the nobles stood well above the muddy ground, awaiting the lords and ladies who would fill them. Colorful canopies topped the padded benches, allowing the sun to warm the spectators from the south while blocking the wind from the north. Below the high platforms, several rows of benches had been provided for the wealthier merchants.

A pair of horns blew. Anticipation rippled through the crowd. The gates of Tintagel opened, emitting a slow procession of horses and litters. The nobility rode out first, each lord preceded by his standard bearer and flanked by his knights, whose bright tunics bore their lords' colors. If a lord's wife or daughters were present, they rode behind. As each party approached the field, the knights who were to compete in the upcoming tournament turned their horses onto the field. The nobles dismounted and climbed to their places in the viewing booths.

Howell, standing at Rhys's right elbow, kept up a running commentary. "There's Clarence of Tregear . . . Maddock of Bolerium . . . Ah, Lord Maddock has brought his lovely lady wife, Honoria. A stalwart female she must be—not many noblewomen are willing to brave the indignities of the road."

The next group came into view, prompting the giant to snort. "What a sour-looking wife Lord Hyroniemus has! I do not envy that man. Here's Timon of Siluria— his heir will surely make a fine showing on the field tomorrow . . . Lord Allan of Seaton . . . that poor bastard has only daughters—five of them! But they are young yet, and I see he's left them at home."

Howell paused, squinting back toward the castle gate. "I wonder if Lady Igraine will truly appear. 'Tis said she has not left the castle since returning from Caer-Lundein last Eastertide."

A small group of brown-clad clerics followed the nobles. Rhys's gaze sharpened as he picked out Bishop Dafyd's litter. The drapes were pulled back, revealing the round form of the bishop seated upon a red velvet chaise. He raised one hand in blessing.

Rhys's skin crawled. The aura of menace clinging to the hypocrite was sickening. But the crowd, it seemed, held their duke's brother in high reverence. The spectators lining the path of the procession bowed low as Dafyd passed. Some held their children aloft, seeking added blessings. To Rhys's mind, they would have been far better off fleeing in the opposite direction.

Bishop Dafyd's attendants bore their burden to the viewing platform. The bishop alighted with the help of the tall, black-cowled attendant Rhys had seen at Glastonbury Abbey. The pair climbed the steps to the duke's center box.

Trumpets sounded a second time. All eyes turned to the castle. The booming voice of a herald rose over the commotion of the crowd.

"All hail his grace, Gerlois, Duke of Cornwall, honored heir to King Erbin of Dumnonia!"

Gerlois, mounted on a huge white stallion, rode out from Tintagel. A thunder of applause greeted him as he crossed the narrow path to the mainland.

Rhys eyed the duke's approach with open curiosity. Gerlois was Dafyd's brother—Rhys had wondered if the duke might also possess Druid magic. But nay. There was not the merest spark of an aura about Gerlois.

Rhys was surprised to see the duke arrayed in full Roman armor. The polished iron segments gleamed in the sun. A crimson Roman army cape fluttered from his shoulders, and the hilt of a *gladius* glinted on his belt. The Roman garb contrasted oddly with the twisted torc about Gerlois's neck, the symbol of a Celtic chieftain's royalty. In Rhys's time the Celts and Romans were only beginning to blend as a people. Three hundred years, it seemed, had completed the transformation.

Gerlois was a large man, his bearing that of a hardened warrior. Only his large girth hinted at his age, which Howell guessed to be near forty. Rhys eyed the man's armor. It was clearly a relic; the soldiers he'd seen in this time wore lighter and more maneuverable chain mail. Their swords were longer than the ones worn by the Roman legions—*spathas,* Howell called them. In a low voice, Rhys questioned his friend about the duke's affinity for the trappings of Rome.

"Aye, to be sure, Gerlois loves to flaunt his Roman ancestors," the giant replied. "He hopes to convince us the glory of Rome is not quite gone from Britain's shores. Bah! Rome is nothing but a hulking carcass, being picked clean by Visigoths and Vandals! There are none of us so foolish as to pin our hopes upon a set of antique armor. Uther would never stoop to such inane pageantry."

Gerlois halted his mount at midfield. His subjects, their bellies full of the duke's mutton, roared their enthusiasm. Gerlois lifted his arms in acknowledgment. After a moment, he reined in his warhorse and rode to the center viewing booth. He dismounted, but did not immediately climb the stair. As an attendant led his prancing stallion to the far end of the field, he looked toward the castle.

Murmurs of awe wove through the crowed. For the third time, trumpets blared.

"By heaven!" Kane's voice trembled. "The rumors were true! The duchess approaches!"

Rhys could hardly hear his own thoughts over the roar of the throng. The woman might have been a goddess for the adulation she inspired. Curious, he shaded his eyes to get a better look at her. He caught sight of not one, but three noblewomen. Each rode a white mare decorated with colorful streamers. The trio was escorted by no fewer than eight knights on horseback.

"I give you Lady Bertrice of Cornwall," the herald cried.

"Gerlois's widowed sister," Howell shouted.

"I give you Lady Antonia of Vectus!"

"Truly?" The giant craned his neck. "Why, I thought Vectus's daughter died in the Saxon raid along with the rest of her family. Now it seems she was spared. By the Christos, look at those bosoms! And that hair peeping from under her veil—why, 'tis like a living flame . . ."

A low buzz sprang up in Rhys's ears. The roar of the crowd faded. Nay. It could not be.

The herald's voice seemed very far away. "I give you Igraine, Duchess of Cornwall!"

The spectators sent up a deafening cheer. "God's teeth!" Howell yelled directly in Rhys's ear. "I am stunned. Lady Igraine is even more beautiful than they say!"

The Duchess of Cornwall might have been a withered old hag, for all Rhys noticed. He did not see her. How could he, when his eyes were fastened on the red-haired woman riding at her side?

The buzz in his ears became deafening. A wave of overwhelming relief threatened to turn his legs to molten wax. He had to lock his knees to keep his limbs from folding.

Great Mother. He'd found her.

And she did not look wretched, or frightened, or desperate. On the contrary. Garbed in flowing green, her brilliant hair swept up under a scrap of a silk veil, seated on a white mare decorated with ribbons, Breena looked like a princess.

Rhys could hardly wait to throttle her.

She had to find Gareth.

That thought was uppermost in Breena's mind as she entered the duke's booth in the tournament stands. Igraine, draped in a white cape embroidered with silver thread, took the seat on Gerlois's right. Bishop Dafyd and Lady Bertrice sat with the duke and duchess in the fore of the box, Dafyd on Gerlois's right, Bertrice on Igraine's left.

Breena moved into the rear of the booth, where two empty chairs waited. One, it seemed, was meant for Dafyd's disfigured acolyte, but the monk had not availed himself of it. Instead he stood stiffly behind it, his cowl draped forward to shadow his face. Breena felt a rush of sympathy for the man. But when she nodded in greeting, his only response was the barest nod. He turned his face away.

The autumn day was crisp and clear; she clutched her cloak tightly about her shoulders as she sat. The garment was lined with fox fur. It did little to warm her icy panic.

Myrddin was not coming to Tintagel. He was trapped in a trance. What in the name of the Goddess was she to do? She scanned the tournament grounds for Gareth, her only lifeline in this time.

She spotted him at the edge of the field, with Gerlois's tournament knights. Mounted, they wore the green and white of Cornwall over shirts of mail. Gareth's Jupiter looked eager for action. The warhorse's big body shied to one side.

As if the young knight had felt her regard, he looked up, tilting his visor with one gloved hand. Their eyes met, and he gave a nearly imperceptible nod.

It wasn't enough. She had to speak to him. She had to tell him about her vision of Myrddin. And of the evil spell that had descended over Tintagel when she'd touched the elder Druid's deep magic.

There was to be no competition this first day, merely introductions of the lords and their champions, followed by a display of horsemanship. Afterward, the duke was to present Breena—or rather, Antonia of Vectus—as his cousin and ward, and announce the contest for her hand.

Gareth would be shocked. She wished she could warn him before the announcement was made. She'd briefly contemplated using Nesta as a messenger, as the maid had free run of the castle. But there was neither pen, parchment, nor ink in Igraine's tower, and Breena did not trust Nesta to deliver a verbal message; the maid was far too friendly with Lady Bertrice. And so Breena had been forced to bide her time. She hoped to snatch a few moments alone with Gareth at tonight's feast.

More than thirty mounted knights arrayed themselves behind their lords' standards at one end of the field. The crier called each nobleman's name, then announced the warriors competing under his banner. How many would vie for Breena's hand? Gareth had sworn to Myrddin to keep her safe; he would likely add his name to the lists. But could he win? She eyed his competition. She had no way of knowing.

Unsettled, she cut her gaze to the crowd of commoners across the field. The unruly mob shifted like a drab mosaic—the dominant colors of their dress were gray, brown, and a dull green—except for five bright flashes of color in the very front row.

She focused first on a figure in cerulean. The man was a veritable giant, standing head and shoulders above every other person present. His four companions were as vibrantly garbed as he. A fat man in crimson, a slight young man in putrid green, and a very short fellow amazingly garbed in royal purple. A step to one side, stood a tall, fair-headed man clothed in brilliant yellow.

The man in yellow was not looking at the field, but toward the duke's booth. In fact, Breena thought, it almost looked as if he were staring directly at her. Her cheeks heated, despite the chill in the air. He was tall—though not as tall, nor as brawny, as the giant in blue. The man in yellow had very fair hair. Silver blond, in fact. Just like Rhys's.

Her heart skipped a beat.

The man, still staring, lifted his hand in a sort of salute. And the distance between them seemed to vanish.

Breena closed her eyes, swallowed hard, then opened them again.

It could not be. But it was. She would know him anywhere.

Dear Goddess. Somehow, he had followed her. And she did not have to guess how he felt about the journey. Even from across the field, she had no trouble reading the emotion on his face.

Rhys was furious.

Chapter Eleven

*T*intagel's forecourt was wide and unpaved, enclosed by high, forbidding stone walls and crowded with tents. Rhys breathed a sigh of relief as the guard waved the Brothers Stupendous through the castle gate and onto the hallowed ground on the other side with little more than a grunt. They were delivered into the care of the assistant to the castle steward, a man called Dermot. He sported a flushed face and a harried air.

"Brothers Stupendous?" He gave the troupe a dubious once-over. "You jest."

"Nay, my good man, we do not," said Trent, puffing up his chest. "We are the finest minstrels and players in all of Britain."

Dermot snorted and began a trek across the castle forecourt. Dafyd's dark spell hung in the air above Rhys's head; he could feel the weight of it on his limbs and in his heart. But if the others noticed, Rhys could not discern it. On the contrary, his "brothers" were in excessively fine spirits.

As for Rhys, he wanted nothing more than to slip away and begin his search for Breena. Dear gods, she'd been offered as a tournament prize! He could not believe it. What was she doing, masquerading as Lady Igraine's dead cousin? Rhys had to extract her from whatever scheme she was involved in, and quickly, before Dafyd became aware of her magic.

Rhys had veiled his power with a spell, so as to stay invisible to Dafyd's magical senses. Now that he'd gained admission to the castle without magic, the longer he avoided using his power, the safer his search for Breena would be.

It would be a difficult task, though, without magic. The castle was filled to bursting with soldiers and servants. With Floyd at his left elbow and Howell on his right, Rhys could not simply disappear without explanation. He hitched his pack higher on his shoulder, tried to convince himself that Breena was not in immediate danger, and followed his stupendous brothers across the court.

"God's lungs," Howell said with a whoop. "I have never seen so grand a place."

The castle was large. It was also square and hulking. To Rhys's eye, it compared poorly to the grace and opulence of the Roman estates of his own time. The villas in the vicinity of Londinium had been especially extravagant. Tintagel looked more like an army fortress than a patrician's home. Which, given the old Roman watchtower at its core, was an apt comparison.

The forecourt was an irregularly shaped plaza, large enough for military training. To the west, the entrance to the castle's great hall was festooned with flags. The remaining walls hugged the island's cliffs. A collection of low outbuildings—gatehouse, stables, barracks, storehouses—abutted the gray stone. On the battlements above, soldiers paced, watching the crowds below.

Something in the sky above caught Rhys's attention. His eyes narrowed on the form of a small raptor, flying with wings outstretched. A merlin. For a moment, he'd thought it was Hefin. But nay, that could not be.

"Water may be had at the cistern well," Dermot was

saying. "Minstrels are to bed down in the yard beyond the temporary stables. This area here is reserved for the visiting knights and their squires and pages. Dressed so prettily as you are," he added with a snort, "I suggest you tred carefully around them. The tournament knights are a randy lot."

"Myself, I'll take my chances with the serving wenches," Trent said easily. "Where might I find their beds?"

Dermot laughed, and pointed to a cluster of tents. "That's where the villagers engaged as extra hands for the festival are housed. But if it's a swiving you're looking for, you'd have been better off in the village. The lasses here make eyes at the knights and squires. Not the minstrels."

Trent grinned. "Aye, well, we shall see, eh?"

Dermot led them past the structure set up for the visiting knights' horses. The minstrels' tents were erected in a rough circle. Several musicians and actors were on their feet in the common area, running through various repertoires.

Trent eyed a trio of lute, lyre, and timpani. "Amateurs," he said after a moment. "Why, just listen to that pox-faced brute mangling his lyre! He might as well take a hammer to the strings. That melody sounds like dung."

Dermot barked a laugh. "Dung has a sound, does it?"

"Most assuredly. 'Tis the buzzing of horseflies, which is precisely what that fellow's music sounds like."

"Your tent," Dermot said, still chuckling.

"You cannot be serious!" protested Trent. "Why this is hardly more than a rag set on two sticks." He sniffed, and grimaced. "And it is downwind of the latrine. This is not acceptable."

"'Tis the best I can do on short notice. If you don't like it, return to the village."

"We'll take it," Trent grumbled.

"I thought you might. Now, then. There's food to be had in the large tent—the one with the red flags atop. No fires at all in the sleeping areas, mind you. We're sheltered from the worst of the wind here in the fore-court, but a rogue flame could whip through these tents in a trice. I'll be making regular inspections. If you're caught with a fire, it's back to the village with you."

The man paused, but only long enough to draw a quick breath. "Minstrels are allowed in the feasting hall only while awaiting their performance. Keep to the back of the hall beforehand, and leave directly afterward."

"What about payment?" Trent demanded. "How much? And when do we receive it?"

"At the festival's end, according to the duke's pleasure. If you please him, you'll do well for yourselves. If not . . ." The man shrugged.

Trent's chest puffed. "We'll be the best the duke has ever seen, I daresay! Now, tell me, man. Who arranges the order of the performers?"

Dermot smiled slightly. "I do."

"Well, then, 'tis your aid we beseech! For we do not wish to take the stage at the start of the dinner. No one pays any mind to the first entertainers. But neither do we wish to be the last. By the end of the night, no one is sober enough to attend to the entertainment. Surely," Trent continued, smoothly pressing a coin into the man's hand, "there are a few empty seats at some poor corner table in the feasting hall where my lads and I might await our time on the duke's stage. We play so much better when warm and nicely fed."

With a gleam in his eye, Dermot palmed the coin. "Aye," he murmured. "I believe there just might be."

* * *

A fanfare blared.

The thousand or so butterflies that had taken up residence in Breena's stomach fluttered their wings in response.

She stood in a small antechamber between the castle's main wing and its feasting hall. Gerlois and Igraine were to be the last to enter Tintagel's great hall, preceded by Breena, Bertrice, and Dafyd. Once again, the duke had dressed in the trappings of Rome. Garbed in a snow-white toga edged in purple, he might have been standing in the Senate.

Igraine stood beside her husband. She wore a *stola* of aquamarine blue; glittering diamonds adorned her girdle and sleeve pins. She looked as beautiful as she did brittle; the day had not worn well on the duchess. The ceremony on the tournament field had been taxing, and the prospect of again being on display at the feast had her trembling. Breena feared Igraine was close to withdrawing into another strange melancholy.

Gerlois offered no comfort to his wife. Indeed, despite the duke's insistence that Igraine attend the ceremony and tonight's feast, he seemed barely aware of her. His head was bent in conversation with Dafyd, who stood rigid, hooked staff in hand. Lady Bertrice edged closer, clearly eavesdropping on her brothers' dialogue.

A glimpse through the door showed the expansive hall already filled to overflowing. The most important of the noblemen and their ladies were already seated on the dais, while the lesser ranking nobles, and the tournament knights, filled the main floor. The tables had been arranged encircling the perimeter of the room, with an area in the center left open for the entertainers.

Servants scurried among the tables, delivering goblets of wine and mugs of ale. Breena craned her neck, realizing only after she'd started looking that she was searching for Rhys. Commoners were not permitted in the castle, and with Dafyd's spell hanging in the air, Rhys would have to be very careful with his magic. Still, she had no doubt that he had found a way into the castle. He was a very persistent man.

The relief she felt at not being alone in this dangerous future world was overwhelming. And yet . . . she could not forget their last meeting, when Rhys had rejected her love. She suspected that when she next spoke to him face to face, he would treat her like the child he believed her to be. He would be appalled at the danger she was in, and would want to yank her out of it.

If he thought he could draw her away from her purpose, he was sadly mistaken. She would not leave Tintagel before she ensured Igraine's safety. Tomorrow's tournament weighed heavily on her mind. She needed to speak with Gareth. Rhys could wait.

"You look very beautiful tonight, my lady."

Startled, Breena turned. To her surprise, Dafyd's acolyte stood not two steps away. It was the first time she'd heard the monk's voice. It was rich and low, beautiful as his ruined face was ugly.

"Thank you," she said. Then, "What is your name?"

"I am Brother Morfen."

"I am pleased to meet you," Breena said. "I am Br— Antonia of Vectus."

"I know, my lady." She did not miss the hint of amusement in his tone. Morfen's voice was very fine. She wondered if he ever sang.

"You have a lovely lilt to your accent." She forced herself to look directly into his ruined face. "I find myself wondering where you were born."

"I am from Gwynedd. In the north of Cambria, or Cymru as the locals call their land. Do you know it?"

"I hear it is a land of mist-topped mountains."

"That is so. The tallest is the seat of Idris the giant. It is said that the hounds of Annwyn hunt on its slopes."

Breena smiled. "I have heard that story. It is very old." Even older, in this time, than in hers. "But, I confess, it surprises me to hear you speak of Annwyn. I do not think Bishop Dafyd would approve."

A shadow darkened Morfen's expression. "No doubt he would not. It is a sin to speak of Annwyn."

An awkward pause ensued. Breena returned her gaze to Brother Morfen's face. She couldn't quite suppress a wince of pity.

He noted it. "You think my face is hideous."

"No," she said quickly. "It merely requires getting used to."

His lips twisted, the unmarred side rising more than the burned side. "There can be no getting used to it. I have had years, you see, and still have not done so."

Breena's face reddened. "I am sorry."

"Do not be." He paused. "You are wondering how I came to be this way. Shall I tell you?"

"If you would like."

He studied her. "Oddly, I believe that I would." His hands rose, and he pushed the cowl back far enough to reveal the puckered skin that covered the right side of his head. The shell of his ear was almost completely gone. Wisps of black hair sprouted all around it.

"I am a monster."

Breena swallowed. A protest would be a bald lie. "Many would think so."

"And you?"

"I think . . . the first sight of you is a shock. But after that. . . ." Her gaze moved over his disfigurement, and this time she did not flinch at all. "Once one is accustomed to your scars, one sees only the character that lies beneath your ruined skin."

He gave her the ghost of a smile. "A pretty speech, I am sure."

However ugly his face might have been, his voice was pure beauty. The sound sent a tingle down her spine.

"I was little more than a lad when it happened. I was playing in the kitchen, when a boiling cauldron overturned."

"How awful! You must have been in agony."

"I screamed for days, I am told. I do not remember much of it. The entire household prayed most fervently for my death."

Breena could think of no reply to that.

"Their prayers were not heard, and I did not die. It would have been better, perhaps, if I had. My demon's face agitated the village. A year after the accident, I was turned out."

"But you were just a boy!"

"Only ten winters," he agreed. "I might have died then, of starvation or cold, but again God intervened. I found my way to a monastery. The good monks cared for me, but even they saw Satan in my face. Only Father Dafyd was blind to my appearance. I have served him ever since."

"You must be devoted to him."

"Must I?" His single eye seemed to bore into her soul. "Do you believe that gratitude breeds love so surely?"

"Why, I do not know. I never considered it, truly."

"The bishop is rigid in the dogma of the new religion. He has no reverence for the Old Ways."

"And you?" Breena asked curiously. "What do you revere?"

"I have not forgotten the gods and goddesses of my youth. But the land and the people are changing, even in such a far-flung place as Gwynedd. Men like Dafyd rule with iron fists. The old ways will soon die, and Annwyn will be forgotten."

"I hope not," Breena said softly.

"Ah, hope," he murmured. "What a fragile commodity that is. And yet, man does not hesitate to grasp at it."

Brother Morfen raised his cowl, and retreated into gloom once again. As Breena stared after him, the crier announced Bishop Dafyd. With a parting glance, Morfen followed the cleric into the hall.

Breena and Lady Bertrice entered next, and took their seats upon the dais. The duke and duchess processed to the high table amid deafening cheers. Standing at the high table, Gerlois said a few words to the assembly, then asked his brother to invoke the blessing of the Christos.

Morfen, who had been standing in the shadows, came forward with a small book. As Bishop Dafyd droned his prayer, Breena let her eyes roam the hall. Gerlois's guests were a curiously mixed group. While most of the lords dressed in Celtic style, a good number followed their duke's example and wore various types of Roman clothing. The knights and soldiers also wore a mix of Celtic and Roman armor.

Breena spotted Gareth standing among a group of Gerlois's knights. When their gazes caught, the steady confidence in his expression helped Breena breathe a bit easier. Gareth was a warrior. With the young knight at her side, perhaps she would not need Rhys's help.

She looked toward the door that led to the privies, hoping Gareth would understand. When he gave an almost imperceptible nod in return, she was sure that he had.

Dafyd's prayer ended; the duke and duchess sat. Their guests took their seats as well. Breena perched on the edge of her chair. Once Lady Bertrice's attention was engaged elsewhere, she'd slip off to the privy alone.

The servants climbed the dais to serve the first course. Breena's eyes roamed the hall. Three massive chandeliers, every lamp within them lit, hung from the arched ceiling. Banners rippled on all four walls.

She spied a flash of bright yellow at the opposite end of the long room. At the same time, she felt the weight of Rhys's disapproving gaze.

Her spine stiffened. She flushed, feeling like a child caught with a stolen sweetmeat. He stood against the back wall of the hall, near the door leading to the kitchens. The colorful men she'd seen on the tournament field—dressed in red, green, blue, and purple—were seated nearby. The man in green held a flute. Rhys had joined a troupe of minstrels! She had to admit it was a clever ruse.

Their eyes met and held.

Breena's heart thudded. With the lines of his face set in anger, and his chin covered with a fortnight's worth of beard, he looked every bit the dangerous man she knew him to be. She suspected he wished to turn her over his knee and spank her like a defiant child. An odd twinge in her belly accompanied the thought. Her head lightened, and for a moment, she felt faint.

And overly warm. She fanned her face. Was it possible to feel the heat of a man's anger from thirty paces away?

Rhys's companions were occupied with bread and ale; he was not. He stood a bit apart, one shoulder propped against the wall, watching her. The expression in his eyes put her in mind of when she was nine years old, and he'd caught her plucking the strings of his harp. He'd hauled her to her feet, brought her to her father, and Breena had gone to bed with no dinner.

She inhaled sharply. He had no right to look at her

that way now. She was no child—she was a grown woman! A Druid following a path set by the Great Mother. She belonged in this place and time.

If Rhys disapproved, that was his problem. She would not allow him to impose his rules on her. He should not even have come after her! He was not her husband, nor her keeper . . . nor, for that matter, was he even her friend. For the last five years, he'd treated her as little more than an annoyance.

Irritated, she turned away.

"Something troubles you, my lady?"

It was Brother Morfen who spoke. The monk stood but a few feet behind her.

"Do you never sit?" she asked.

"Rarely." His chin lifted, and he met her gaze. Lamplight from the chandeliers caught him in the face, exposing his scars.

This time, Breena managed not to flinch. Her heart twisted with pity. Morfen was truly hideous. What must it feel like to be so disfigured? Did anyone, apart from Bishop Dafyd, even talk to the poor monk? Or did Morfen experience only faces averted in horror?

She sent him a small smile. "The bishop has left a chair empty for you. You should take it, join in the feast."

Morfen's good eye widened. "I would not dare." He paused. "But . . . thank you."

Nodding, he stepped back into the shadows. Breena studied the oysters before her. She wasn't at all hungry, but she supposed she should at least try to eat. She picked up her knife.

A trio of players took the stage, bowing low to the duke. They were not Rhys's group. Thank the Goddess. She wasn't quite ready to have him so close.

* * *

"Come on now, men, look lively!" Trent paused to bat down the curling hem of Kane's tunic. "We're to take the stage once those three imbeciles drag their sorry white arses into the privy where they belong!"

Trent prowled back and forth before the table, his small body alight with energy. The rest of the Brothers Stupendous stood ready, awaiting their signal to advance.

Rhys, who had been glaring at Breena, shifted his gaze to Floyd, who was busy brushing crumbs from his chest and belly. Chuckling, Rhys bent to retrieve his harp.

"Dermot is beckoning," Howell said suddenly.

Trent whirled around. "So he is. This is it, lads! Our first performance in Tintagel Castle! Can the high king's court in Caer-Lundein be far behind?"

They gathered at the edge of the open area below the high table. On stage, the aforementioned trio, whose intelligence and posteriors Trent had maligned, concluded a play in which Humility, represented by a whey-faced young man, triumphed over two masked villains, Greed and Lust.

Bishop Dafyd leaned forward in his seat, his jowls quivering with approval, his crimson aura shimmering about his head and shoulders. Gerlois, by contrast, reclined almost lazily, sipping his wine. To the duke's left, the beautiful Igraine sat like a statue, a slight, false smile on her face. There seemed to be an odd spell muting her magic, glinting around her like tarnished silver. Beneath it, her impotent Seer's magic showed in flashes of white.

Rhys sensed the binding spell on Igraine was a very old one. It must have been cast when the duchess was a child. Who would do such a thing? And why?

His gaze continued down the table. Gerlois's large, pinched-faced sister was a dark smudge on Igraine's left. The end seat belonged to Breena. Dressed in a *stola* of emerald over a long-sleeved tunic of lighter green, she put Rhys in mind of a lush fern. He did not want Breena anywhere near these people. He vowed to get her out of the castle, and headed toward home, as quickly as possible.

Breena kept her eyes on her plate. Rhys was aware of a confusing mix of anger and fear, and aye, of lust, when he looked at her. She'd always been the most troublesome female he'd ever encountered. As a girl, she'd wrapped him around her little finger. As a woman, she tied him in knots.

The players exited the stage amid a polite spatter of applause. Dafyd looked hugely gratified by their performance. Gerlois shifted in his seat, frowned, and drank deeply of his wine.

Trent rubbed his hands. "All the better to follow those fools."

At Dermot's signal, the little man stepped forward. Plumed hat in hand, he swept a low bow. Then, tossing his headwear to the floor, he took the stage at a run.

With a bounce on the balls of his feet, he launched himself into the air, turning heels over head. He landed just below the duke's place at the high table, one knee bent, head bowed.

Duke Gerlois raised his brows and set down his wine. "What is this? Something new?"

Floyd stepped onto the stage, bowing low. "My lord duke! My lady duchess! I present to you the finest players and acrobats in Britain! The Brothers Stupendous!"

Rhys stepped forward with Kane and Howell, joining Trent and Floyd in the opening bow. As he straightened, his wry gaze met Breena's astonished one.

He sent her a small shrug.

Her blue eyes laughed.

* * *

The Brothers Stupendous?

Breena covered her mouth, stifling a spurt of horrified laughter. Five less likely "brothers" could not possibly exist.

A giant, a midget, a horse-faced youth, and a fellow almost as wide as he was tall? Not one matched another in either features or coloring. She could hardly believe Rhys had consented to wear that blinding yellow tunic. His fellows were dressed just as garishly. Taken together, they formed an outlandish human rainbow.

Brothers Stupendous? More like Brothers Ridiculous.

Scant moments later, her mouth hung open in astonishment, and she was compelled to revise her hasty assessment. The small man in purple executed another amazing jump, flying through the air like a bird. The round man's rich tenor, and the giant's bone-rattling bass, blended with the flautist's trilling melody.

Enthusiastic applause ensued. The small man bowed. Then the young flautist joined Rhys at the side of the stage. Harp and flute blended seamlessly. The giant crouched on one side of the stage, while the round man took a position directly opposite.

The small man scampered nimbly up the giant's back. As he reached the man's broad shoulders, the giant leaped out of his crouch, launching his "brother" high into the air. The audience gave a collective gasp. The acrobat, his body a purple blur, spun two complete turns through the air.

He landed neatly atop the round man's shoulders.

The hall erupted in cheers. The smallest "brother" jumped to the ground, bowing to the front and back, right and left. Most of the hall was on its feet, shouting wildly. Gerlois himself stayed seated, but the duke looked impressed. Lady Bertrice nodded and applauded. Even Bishop Dafyd's permanent scowl relented.

The show of acrobatics continued, one marvelous feat after another, involving differing combinations of Rhys's four companions. Through it all, Rhys stood to one side, his long fingers moving across his harp's strings, his eyes on the action onstage. Breena watched him surreptitiously. She had never seen him like this, wearing the persona he adopted for the world outside Avalon. He was entirely natural as a performer. One might have thought he'd played with the Brothers Stupendous for years.

Rhys's unusual life had taught him to blend with all types of people. For the first time, Breena realized what a useful skill that was. As valuable as his beautiful voice, and his talent with the harp.

His eyes met hers, briefly. She felt the jolt of sensation all the way to her toes. He'd chased her though the Lost Lands. At one level, the thought thrilled her, even though she knew it was duty, not love, that had compelled him to come after her. Then she remembered the anger in his eyes, and her excitement changed into something more unsettling.

The little man in purple executed a handstand, flipping his body into the air. He landed on the dais, directly before the duke and duchess. Passing one hand behind his back, he conjured a perfect apple, as if from thin air. The audience murmured in amazement.

With a flourish and a grin, he offered the fruit to the duchess.

Igraine stiffened. She sent a glance toward her husband, and accepted the gift after receiving Gerlois's nod. The acrobat bowed again. Then he flipped neatly off the dais. Someone tossed him his plumed hat. Catching it neatly, he made a sweeping bow.

The applause was generous. But the show was not yet over. Rhys strode to the center of the stage, his harp cradled in his bent arm. He bowed low before Gerlois, his fair head catching the light from the torches. His yellow tunic shone like gold. He spoke in perfectly accented Latin, his voice filling the hall.

"My lord duke. I am honored beyond words to stand before you. May I offer a humble song?"

Gerlois raised a hand. "You may, minstrel."

Rhys bowed a second time, and began to play. Music rippled like water. A soft gasp arose from the audience. The melody was so beautiful, Breena's heart squeezed.

Rhys added his voice. His song was a ballad. Breena had never heard it, but the audience seemed to know it well. The poem was an ode to Prince Geraint, Igraine's dead cousin. The verses were long and complicated, and yet Rhys, who had certainly only just learned them, did not trip over a single syllable.

By the time the last lingering note of Rhys's voice had faded, every woman in the room, Breena included, was in tears. Even Lady Bertrice's expression had softened. Lady Igraine was particularly affected; so much so that Gerlois, in a rare show of care, took her hand.

Rhys made his bow. Gerlois eyed him with open curiosity. "Your tongue is pure silver, minstrel. How is it I have never seen you before, neither here at Tintagel, nor at the high king's court in Caer-Lundein?"

"I am recently come from Gwynedd, my lord."

"Gwynedd? I cannot believe they breed such fine minstrels in that wild land."

"Did not God create both music and wilderness, my lord?"

Gerlois grunted. "Well said, minstrel. See that you and your companions return for tomorrow's dinner."

Rhys bowed again. "As you wish, my lord." He turned to join the rest of his troupe.

"Wait," a voice said.

Breena twisted in her seat, shocked. Brother Morfen had spoken. The acolyte had abandoned his silent post in the shadows. He advanced to the table. His cowl drooped low, shielding his disfigured face from the chandelier's light.

Bishop Dafyd frowned. Morfen did not seem to notice his master's displeasure. He spoke directly to Rhys.

"Gwynedd is my homeland as well, minstrel. Will you play a song from my youth?"

Rhys's gray eyes flashed with curiosity. He looked from Morfen to Gerlois. "If I know it, brother. And if my lord duke allows it."

Gerlois waved a hand. "I am not unwilling to hear another song. Pray, continue."

Rhys bowed to the duke, then turned to Morfen. Breena wondered how much he could see of the acolyte's face. If he was repulsed, his expression did not show it.

"What is your wish?"

"The ballad of Ceridwen. Do you know it?"

Rhys's brows rose. "Aye, of course."

Dafyd's frown deepened; he leaned forward in his seat. For a moment, Breena thought the bishop would deny his acolyte's request. But then he seemed to change his mind. He sank back in his chair.

Rhys's gaze fell to his harp; he began to play. Breena knew the ballad; she'd heard Rhys sing it countless times. But a glance around the hall told her the song was not a familiar one for the people of this time.

She was not surprised. The ballad of Ceridwen was a song of the magic of the Old Ones. As the poem unfolded, Dafyd's scowl deepened. His fingers tightened on his goblet. Breena half expected the bishop to leap to his feet and denounce the pagan song. But he did not.

Rhys's voice rose, rich and full. The tale told of a goddess crone, Ceridwen, who was possessed of a magical cauldron. Her son, Afagduu, had been born with a dark and hideous face. Filled with love and pity for her child, Ceridwen brewed a potion with dangerous deep magic. She was determined that if her son could not have beauty, at least he might have wisdom.

Due to the difficulty of the spell, and the immense power of its magic, only the first three drops of the potion would hold boundless knowledge; the rest would be poison. The concoction required constant stirring for a year and a day. Afagduu refused to do the work, so Ceridwen charged a kitchen boy, Gwion, with the task.

Afagduu eagerly awaited his prize. But, as is so often the case with deep magic, disaster struck. The instant the potion's magic blossomed, the cauldron tipped. The first three drops fell on Gwion's lips, not Afagduu's.

"Thief!" the goddess cried. Enraged, she lunged for Gwion; the lad barely dodged his mistress's ire. He fled the cottage, the crone chasing after, screaming threats and imprecations.

The hapless lad, desperate to escape and overwhelmed with deep magic, transformed into a hare, then a fish, then a dove. The crone countered by shifting into the forms of a dog, an otter, and a hawk. Finally, Gwion became a grain of wheat; Ceridwen changed into a hen, and ate him.

The magical meal caused Ceridwen to become heavy with child. Nine months later, she gave birth to a new son. The child was beautiful. His fair hair shone upon his brow like silver. When he became a man, he took up the harp. His music and song spread wisdom and Light in Annwyn, and among the people of Gwynedd.

"Thus," Rhys sang, drawing the ballad to its finish. "The great bard Taliesin was born."

The harp song faded on a final, plaintive note. Rhys took a step back, and inclined his head.

Morfen bowed in return.

"I thank you, minstrel."

Chapter Twelve

The otter cut through the current, its sharp claws swiping at Myrddin's fish body. Myrddin twisted and flipped his tail—too late. Pain slashed along his side.

Black terror consumed him. He could not die this way. What would happen to Vivian? With his last strength, he leaped, breaking the water's surface.

The warm air singing across his scales shocked him. The sun's rays blinded. He flailed, wildly, reaching out . . . for what, he did not know.

Wind caught under his outstretched wings. The downy feathers on his breast ruffled. Air magic bathed his face. He blinked, and looked down, and saw the ground fall away.

The laugh in his throat emerged as a warble. He was a dove, wild and free. Elation struck. The otter could not harm him now.

But the otter was no more. In its place, on the river bank, stood a hawk.

The great bird spread its wings, and took to the sky.

"'Twas a fine show, my handsome bard."

Rhys looked up. The serving wench was very shapely, and very bold. Her eyes held that inviting look common to loose women. Rhys had known a hundred like her. He was not interested in knowing another.

Earlier, when she'd caught his eye and smiled, he

made the mistake, out of habit, of smiling back. That had encouraged her to ply him with food and ale. All evening, she'd made a point of returning to his table. She spoke with Trent and the others, but her eyes kept returning to Rhys.

Rhys wasn't given to vanity, but he was not so modest that he did not know there was something about him that attracted women like geese to water. His height, he supposed, and his unusual coloring. And his harp, of course. A tragic song never failed to leave a woman sighing.

He'd ignored the black-haired wench, in favor of watching Breena. Her color had risen during his performance, but now that it was done, she looked paler, and anxious.

The players that had followed the Brothers Stupendous were having a difficult time engaging the audience's attention. This troupe also boasted a harpist, but the instrument was smaller than Rhys's, and the pitch was higher. Rhys could not decide if he liked the difference.

He hardly noticed the serving wench sliding onto the bench beside him, until he felt her breast press the side of his arm. Startled, he jerked around, nearly knocking her over backward. Reflexively, he reached for her. His hand stroked down her arm and locked on her elbow.

"Ah." Her blue eyes danced. "So the fair son of Taliesin remains with us after all. Here I thought he'd flown to Gwynedd, so far away were his eyes."

She brushed a strand of hair from his forehead. "There. Ye can see me better now. I'm called Nesta. And ye?"

"Rhys."

"Ye've traveled far, to attend the festival, if ye hail from Gwynedd."

"Aye." His gaze drifted to Breena, at the high table. "I've put a fair bit of road behind me."

"It must be a grand thing, to see the world. Me, I've spent all my life here at Tintagel castle. But I do not normally serve in the hall, except for grand feasts such as this one. Most often, I attend the Lady Igraine."

Abruptly, Rhys gave the lass his full attention. "Do you, now?"

She laughed. "Aye, and I thought that would capture your interest! If there is a man born who is not awed by the duchess's beauty, I have never met him."

"A blind man, perhaps."

"The high king himself lusts after Lady Igraine," Nesta confided. "Uther made his intentions clear last Eastertide in Caer-Lundein. 'Tis why the duke now guards his wife so jealously. She rarely leaves her chambers in the tower."

"Indeed."

"Gerlois could not very well keep his lady wife locked away during the festival. The villagers have been restless, clamoring to see her. But Gerlois will not allow Igraine to dance, or even to speak to any save her close companions."

"You mean the pinched-faced matron?"

Nesta chuckled. "Lady Bertrice may have a sour face, but she is tireless in her devotion to Tintagel. She is the duke's sister."

"The resemblance is strong," Rhys agreed. "And what of the red-haired lass? The one offered as a tournament prize?"

"Lady Antonia. Poor thing. Her family recently fell to the Saxons."

"All Dumnonia is abuzz with the story of that raid."

"'Tis glad I am the Saxon wolves rarely wander so far as Tintagel." Nesta shuddered, pressing her breast against Rhys's arm. "Enough talk of death. I would rather talk of beauty." She touched his hand. "Your songs entranced me tonight, Rhys. Your fingers on the harp . . . they are very clever."

Nesta had clever fingers of her own. Presently, they were skating up Rhys's thigh. Gods. He did not need this. Subtly, he shifted away. "You flatter me falsely."

"Ye are too modest. Your song was so bittersweet, it brought tears to my eyes."

"'Twas the tale that moved you. Not me."

She picked up his hand and turned it over, stroking from the base of his forefinger to the tip. "Perhaps we could put that to the test. Play a song just for me, after the feast is done."

"'Tis doubtful I could. My companions . . ."

"Surely your friends would not begrudge ye a few hours of pleasure?"

"There would be little privacy. The castle forecourt is crowded with—"

"Nay, not in the forecourt! In the castle. I know a place where no one will disturb us. Lady Igraine's private garden. 'Tis at the base of the tower."

Rhys stilled. "Aye? Truly? But surely there are guards. How would I get past them?"

Her eyes danced. "You will not need to. There is a second entrance to the atrium. 'Tis a secret. A hidden door in the floor of the old Roman tower, under the stair. It leads to a storeroom below the kitchens. I do not think even the duke knows of it."

"Indeed." He pitched his voice low. "And how might I find this storeroom?"

"Slip through that door just behind you, but do not go as far as the kitchens. There's a stair to the right, leading to the cellars. Go past the wine and oil, and the baskets of apples. There is a small room just beyond, in the foundation of the old watchtower. It is filled with

old wine casks. Look up at the ceiling, in the far corner, and ye'll see the trap door."

Her gaze fell to Rhys's lips. "Will ye come, then?"

He hesitated. "Perhaps."

In the next instant, before he could react, Nesta's
lips were on his. She kissed him, deeply, her round
breasts pressing against his chest, one hand sliding
down to stroke him beneath the cover of the table. His
cock couldn't help responding, and he knew she felt it.
His hands went to her shoulders, to push her away, but
before he could do it, she pulled back of her own ac-
cord.

She rose, and propped her empty tray against one
hip. Her eyes fairly smoldered as she smiled down at
him. "I'll wait for ye near the old fountain."

Hips swaying, she walked away.

Breena pushed back her chair and lurched to her feet.

"Lady Antonia!" Lady Bertrice frowned. "Whatever is the matter with you?"

"I . . . my stomach. . . ."

"You are ill?"

Sick at heart, perhaps. "No. Not ill. I . . . just need a
bit of air."

Bertrice glanced down at her plate. "The third
course has just been served. Sit, and I will accompany
you to the inner courtyard when I am finished."

"You needn't trouble yourself," Breena said swiftly.
"I would not hear of it. I can go on my own. There is no
reason for you to interrupt your meal."

She felt Bertrice's resolve waver. Appetite won over
duty. The lady picked up her eating dagger and skew-
ered a succulent morsel of pork. "Very well. But do not
stay away long."

The courtyard was blessedly cool. Servants rushed
to and fro, none giving her more than a quick glance.

Breena gulped in a lungful of crisp air. Welcome as it was, it did little to ease the pain in her heart.

Rhys, kissing Nesta! Gods. Breena wanted to rip the woman's hair out. And after that, she would very much enjoy taking a knife to Rhys's—

A hand caught her arm. "Breena! At last."

She whirled around, then sagged against the wall in relief. "Gareth! Thank the gods."

His green eyes, clearly worried, passed over her. "Come," he said, drawing her into the shadow of the walkway bordering the courtyard. "We must talk."

She followed him. Opening a door, he pulled her into a small room. An office of some sort, judging by the parchment on the desk.

He was forced to leave the door partially ajar, to catch the light from the courtyard. "Breena. Are you all right?"

"Oh, Gareth. Myrddin is not coming!"

"What? How do you know?"

Breena described what she'd Seen in her scrying. "He almost looks dead. Do you know who the woman might be?"

He hesitated. "It is certainly Vivian. Myrddin's wife. She was stricken at court last spring."

"Myrddin has a wife?" The notion struck her as odd. But she had little time to dwell on the thought. "Gareth, there is a more immediate problem. When I touched the deep magic surrounding him, a dark spell rose here in the castle. It surrounds the castle now. I fear . . . I fear Dafyd sensed my magic, and is looking for me."

The knight swore. "We must take Igraine and flee. Tonight."

"But how can we? Igraine refuses to be a part of our scheme. She vows she will not be the cause of a civil war. We can hardly steal the duchess from the feasting hall by force. I need more time to convince her she must abandon Gerlois and Tintagel. I will plead with her again tonight." She would even confess her Druid powers, and tell Igraine about her vision, if that was what it took to gain her consent.

"The contest for your hand is tomorrow," Gareth said. "I have already entered my name in the lists."

Breena's heart tripped. "You have?"

"Of course. Did you imagine I would let any other man touch you? The tournament will work to our favor. Once we are betrothed, you will present me to the duchess, and we will smuggle her out of the castle."

"How?"

"There are caves beneath the castle gardens. It is possible to anchor a boat at low tide. Tomorrow evening, when I make my bow to the duchess, you will request a stroll in the gardens behind the castle. The entrance to the caves is just beyond the smokehouse."

"But, Gareth . . ." Breena hesitated. "What if you do not win the contest?"

He smiled. "Have you so little faith in my abilities?"

"It is not that. It's just . . . the other knights look very capable, too." Older, and more battle hardened, as well, but she did not say that.

"Breena. Not one of those men wants you as much as—"

Footsteps sounded in the courtyard, very close. Gareth put his finger to Breena's lips and drew her away from the door. When the servants' steps had faded, Breena opened her mouth to speak. Her words evaporated as Gareth's finger traced the curve of her lips.

"You are very beautiful, you know."

Her eyes widened. "I'm . . . I'm not. Not at all."

He cupped the side of her face. "I would be proud to call you wife."

"Wife? But—"

His mouth came down on hers, absorbing her startled protest. Gods! Gareth wanted to marry her in truth? It was not possible. She wanted to tell him so, but his lips were insistent, and she couldn't catch her breath. She felt him lift her hands and place them on his shoulders as he backed her against the wall.

She slid her palms to his chest instead. "Gareth, stop."

He pulled back, his breathing labored. "Breena. I am sorry. I meant no disrespect. I have wanted to do that since the first instant I laid eyes on you."

He had? "I . . . I have to return to the feast. I have been gone far too long."

"I will escort you."

"No! That would only rouse Lady Bertrice's suspicions. You go first. I need . . . a moment to compose myself."

"All right." He stepped away. A moment later, his footsteps retreated in the direction of the feasting hall.

Breena sagged against the wall. Gareth's kiss had felt . . . strange. Like the kiss she'd shared with Penn. Not at all like the times she had kissed Rhys.

"What a touching scene."

She nearly jumped out of her skin. "Rhys!"

He sketched a mocking bow. "At your service . . . Lady Antonia."

"You were spying on me! How long have you been lurking outside that door?"

He shrugged. "Long enough."

She met his gaze. His tone might have been light, but his eyes flashed with icy fury.

Her own tumultuous anger answered. "*Are* you at my service, Rhys? I confess I'm surprised to hear it. I thought you'd offered your *services* to Nesta."

"The duchess's maid is brazen."

"And you encouraged her! You stroked her arm. You kissed her in front of everyone!"

"Rather than slip away, you mean, to meet my lover in the castle steward's office? By the gods, Breena, I could throttle you! What is going on? Why are you masquerading as a dead woman, under the nose of a sorcerer? I am telling you, your folly ceases this instant."

Air hissed through Breena's teeth. The arrogant swine! How dare he order her about. "Just . . . stop it, Rhys. My *folly* is none of your business. Now step aside. I must return to the feast—"

"Nay," he said, grabbing her wrist as she tried to brush past him. "You are not going anywhere, Bree. Except out of this castle with me. Tonight."

His voice vibrated with rage. His fingers pinched. Dear Goddess. Rhys's anger had frightened her at a distance. In close proximity, it was terrifying.

But she would not bend. He was in the wrong, not she. She drew herself up to her full height. Unfortunately, her full height put her eyes hardly higher than his chest.

"Let me go," she said quietly. "You are hurting me."

"Too bad." He did not release her. "You are lucky I do not turn you over my knee. By the gods, Bree! I thought you were kidnapped."

"I was not. I am in this time and place of my own free will."

"I see that," he growled. "And it ends now. We are going home."

She stiffened. "You have no say in this. None at all. How did you even find me? You should not have been able to follow us."

"Us." The word dropped from Rhys's lips like a stone. "Who is this 'us,' Breena? You and Uther's Druid, I suspect."

"You . . . you know of Myrddin?"

His eyes were intent, even in the gloom. "There are very few Druids in this time. So far, I've seen but two, and heard tell of only one other. The magic I followed through the Lost Lands was not Dafyd's. Nor is it Lady Igraine's. That leaves me with one possibility. Myrddin." Abruptly, he released her. "Am I right? Or is there another Druid of whom I am not yet aware?"

Breena rubbed her wrist. "No. You are right. Myrddin brought me here."

"Where is he now?"

"I . . . do not know."

"He left you here unguarded?"

"No. Gareth protects me."

"That pup?" He swore. "I will have the sorcerer's head for that."

"Myrddin is not a sorcerer. He is descended from the Druids of Avalon. He even claimed he once met you."

"Then he is a liar as well as a sorcerer," Rhys said. "I am sure I have never encountered the man."

"He is not evil," Breena insisted. "He follows the Light."

Rhys snorted. "I am not inclined to call artful manipulation a service to the Light."

"Myrddin did not manipulate me. I knew what I was doing. And I trust him, Rhys. He carries the symbol of Avalon, carved on his staff."

Rhys made a cutting motion with his hand. "I would expect nothing less from a charlatan. The man practices deep magic, Bree. Deeper and more dangerous than any I have ever known."

"In our time, perhaps. But Rhys, magic is different in this Britain. There are fewer Druids, it is true. But the Druids who do exist possess power far greater than ours."

"I can well believe that," Rhys muttered. "Dafyd's power is very strong. The magic Myrddin cast to bring you here is lethal. We are both lucky we are not dead. I cannot believe you would involve yourself in such a spell."

She glared at him. "Then you are a hypocrite. Because you would not be here unless you cast Myrddin's spell yourself! You may preach against deep magic, Rhys, but time and again, when it suits your purposes, you do not hesitate to call it."

"You speak of my shifting. I cannot deny calling that magic, when the need is great. Each time, I feel my human soul slip a bit farther from my grasp. Aye, shifting is dangerous magic. But it is nothing, Breena, compared to the magic that brought us to this place. How can casting magic so powerful possibly be in service to the Light? You are a child if you believe that."

She lifted her chin. "Myrddin does serve the Light. And so do I, in coming to this time. It is necessary."

"And was it necessary to vanish so suddenly, without a trace? Marcus, Gwen, Owein—By Annwyn, Bree! They were frantic when I left them."

"Oh, gods." She closed her eyes on a rush of guilt.

"And more than a sennight has passed since then," Rhys continued mercilessly. "Just think how anguished they are now. They likely believe we have both perished."

"Then . . . they don't know you followed me into the future?"

"Nay. I was alone when I found the remnants of Myrddin's spell. When I followed it into the Lost Lands, I had no idea where it would lead."

"I am sorry for their pain. I truly am. But they will understand, once I return—"

"Ah." He crossed his arms. "So you do intend to return, at least."

"Of course I do! Myrddin has promised to send me home. As soon as my task in this time is done."

"You do not have a task in this time. You *cannot*. You have no right to even breathe the air around us. And neither do I." He dragged a hand down his face. "Breena, nothing either of us do in this Britain could be right or good. On the contrary, the longer we stay here, the more likely it is that we'll do great harm. We have to return at once to the standing stone, and retrace Myrddin's cursed spell. And hope to Annwyn we can find our way home."

"You are welcome to leave, Rhys, if you think it right. But I am not going anywhere. I trust Myrddin."

He cursed. "You were always too trusting, even as a child."

She stiffened. "What I was as a child has no bearing on what I am doing now. I did not follow Myrddin into the future blindly. I have my own purpose in coming to this time."

He grasped her shoulders and gave her a shake. His scent—angry, male—filled her nostrils. "If that is true, then you are suffering a delusion. You have no purpose here. And you are not staying. We leave tonight."

She grabbed his forearms and tried to break his grip on her shoulders. He responded by shoving her against the wall.

Pure rage pounded in her ears. "Let me go. I mean it. If you do not, I . . . I will cry out. There are soldiers in that courtyard. They will be on you in an instant."

He shifted his hold on her, anchoring her more firmly. "You would betray me? Stand by and watch them drag me away? I would not be able to use magic to escape. Not without Dafyd learning of it, and that I will not do, for it would lead him to you." His fingers bit into her shoulder. "So? What are you waiting for, Bree? Scream."

Tears gathered in Breena's eyes. "I would not do that, Rhys. I would not betray you, ever. You are . . . you are far too dear to me."

Stark silence ensued. Their gazes locked. Rhys's eyes were shadowed; Breena could not begin to guess what he was thinking.

Air hissed between his teeth in a long, weary sigh. "Oh, Breena. You foolish, foolish lass. Whatever am I to do with you?"

His grip on her shoulders relented. His hands slipped up to frame her face. His head dipped; his body became her cage. He pressed his lips to her forehead. She felt the scratch of his stubbled jaw against her skin.

It was a chaste gesture—not what she wanted from him. But as his mouth lingered too long, and his arms tensed, she felt his turbid emotions churn into something darker.

His hips moved, surging forward to pin her lower body against the wall. His arousal burgeoned, throbbing against her lower belly. A shocked thrill ran through her.

A sweet, desperate longing twisted inside her chest. She'd wanted him so badly, for so long. Her breasts were pressed against the hard planes of his torso. His lips moved to her temple; a deep shudder ran through his body.

He bent his knees and moved his body downward, aligning his hips with hers. His phallus, rock hard, lodged in the cradle of her thighs. His hardness rubbed a spot that made her knees go weak. Instinctively, she parted her legs. He moved again, and she whimpered.

He responded with a groan. One of his knees intruded between her thighs, urging them to part wider, as wide as her skirts would allow.

Her hands stole around his torso, stroking and clutching. He was so solid—all muscle and sinew and bone. A heated tremor flashed through her. Her head went light. Her body softened in some places; it tightened in others. She was aware of a series of rapid, delirious thoughts.

Rhys had never wanted her as a woman.

He wanted her now.

His fingers touched her chin; he tilted her head.

His breath bathed her cheek. Her jaw.

Her lips.

In another instant, she was going to kiss him.

No.

Rhys was going to kiss *her.*

Chapter Thirteen

Rhys had lost his mind.

He was not sure he cared. Breena's body was soft and round beneath his, and welcoming, despite her anger. His mouth brushed her jaw, and a sweet little moan left her lips. His cock, already hard as a stone, stiffened even more.

He was going to kiss her. Gods! He could not. This would never stop at a kiss.

He pressed his lips to her ear instead. "Now would be the time, Breena. Cry out. Let the soldiers come for me."

"It . . . it would serve you right."

She wriggled a little in his arms. He dropped one hand, grazing the outside of her breast. His palm lingered, memorizing the curve.

"Do it, then."

Her breathing hitched. "No."

Her small hands roamed on his back, igniting fire everywhere they touched. Roughly, he grabbed her wrists and pressed them to the wall over her head. She gasped, her spine arching, her lush breasts thrusting toward him. Before he quite knew what he'd done, he'd transferred both her wrists to his left hand.

The sight of her, stretched and vulnerable, made him shudder. His right hand covered her breast. Her nipple beaded against his palm. He flicked his thumb over it. A wave of something raw and primitive rippled through her. He felt her body soften beneath his solidity.

A moan was torn from her throat. "Rhys . . . please. . . ."

"Breena." His voice was a rasp. "We cannot do this. It is wrong."

She looked up at him, wide eyed. The tip of her tongue darted out to swipe at her lower lip. He knew an exquisite torture.

"Is it, Rhys?"

"Aye. You know it is."

"I know nothing of the sort."

Of course she didn't; she was little more than a child. He struggled to remind himself of that fact. But it was difficult. She did not look like a child. Not with her lush woman's body pinned beneath his. Not with her quick breaths caressing his ear. The scent of her musky, female arousal fogged his brain. The white sparkle of her magic clung to her head and shoulders, calling to his own Druid power.

He wanted her, desperately. But Rhys was a man long used to self-denial. With a shuddering breath, he forced his grip to loosen. Flattening his palms on the wall on either side of her head, he prayed for the strength to step away.

Though he was no longer holding her arms, she had not lowered them. Wrists crossed above her head, she stared up at him, her eyes huge, her breath short. For a long moment, she just stared, and he could not quite read the emotion in her expression. And then a small smile curved her lips, and her hips arched. The warm, welcoming vee of her thighs cradled his cock.

The last frayed thread of his control snapped. His mouth came down on hers. His kiss was not gentle, not what she deserved. It was hard and bruising. Demanding. An assault on her all-too-knowing innocence.

He expected her to struggle. To slap him, or push him away. Instead she softened impossibly. Her body sagged against the wall. Her hands clutched his shoulders. Her toe stroked up his calf.

He kissed her ruthlessly, his tongue plundering her sleek, wet mouth. He caught her nipple and rolled it between his thumb and forefinger. The sound that emerged from her throat was part moan, part whimper.

"*Pollux.*" The crude Roman curse, whispered, sounded like an endearment. His knee rode high between her legs. His hands on her breasts were not enough. He tore his mouth from her lips and kissed a hot, wet trail down her neck. He buried his face in the cleft between those soft, perfect globes.

He wanted to tear through her *stola* and tunic, but somehow he retained his presence of mind and did not. He pressed his cheek atop the pillow of her breast instead, inhaling deeply of her scent. She cradled his head, holding him close.

"Rhys," she whispered. "Oh, gods, Rhys. I . . . I love you so."

He tensed. Gods in Annwyn. He could not do this to her.

He thrust himself back from the wall. Breena blinked up at him with hazy eyes.

"Rhys? What's wrong—"

She broke off, her eyes flaring with hurt as he took a second step back.

"Breena, I—" He swallowed and dropped his arms to his sides. "I am sorry. That never should have happened."

She lowered her arms and hugged herself. "I see."

He made a sound in the back of his throat, and shut his eyes briefly. "My disrespect is inexcusable."

"Disrespect," she repeated. Heat radiated from her body, but her tone was like ice.

His apology stumbled on. "It will not happen again. Now, please, let us leave this place."

She drew herself taller, and tighter. "No, Rhys. I've told you. I am not going anywhere."

"You cannot stay here. There's a pall of dark magic over this castle."

"I know that. It is my fault. The spell rose when I scried for Myrddin."

He swore. "Dafyd is certainly searching for you. The longer you stay here, the more likely it becomes that he will find you."

She seemed to falter at that. "I will leave before that happens."

"Aye, you will leave with me. Now."

Her head came up. Anger caused her aura to crackle. "You have no right to order me about. I did not ask you to follow me here."

He made a sound of disbelief. "You thought I would just let you vanish into the Lost Lands?"

"Hard as it might be for you to believe, I was not thinking of you at all. Why should I? You'd made it very clear the night before I left that you did not care what I did or where I went."

Rhys muttered a curse. "You are twisting my words. You know I care for you. I always have. You are like a—"

"Do not say it!" she hissed. "I swear to you, Rhys, if the word 'sister' passes your lips, I will scream loud enough to bring fifty soldiers running!"

If Breena's blue eyes had been daggers, Rhys would have been lying on the ground, flayed and gutted. "Breena. Please. We can fight later, if you like. Once we leave this cursed castle."

"I am not going anywhere. I have a task to complete.

Have you even asked me what it is? No. If you would shut your arrogant mouth and listen for but a moment, you would understand! Myrddin told me—"

"Myrddin!" Rhys spat the sorcerer's name. "I am sick to death of hearing you utter that man's name. He is a menace. He deals with deadly magic. Do you know, Uther Pendragon has not lost a single battle since his Druid counselor appeared at his side? I am sure Myrddin wins the high king's wars with deep magic."

"I do not know if that is true," Breena said. "If it is, Myrddin has good reason to cast that magic. He serves the Light."

"He uses deep magic as it suits him!"

"So do you."

His jaw tightened. "It is not the same."

"It is just the same. Don't you see? Myrddin is desperate. He needed a Seer at Igraine's side. Rhys, her life is in danger!"

"And now yours is, as well, because Myrddin saw fit to bring you here."

"It was necessary. I am the one destined for the task. And Igraine's life is much more important than mine."

"Excuse me if I do not agree," Rhys said tightly.

Breena's grip was hot and urgent on his arm. "You will change your mind when I tell you who she is. Rhys, Igraine is the woman in my vision. The one I've seen murdered more times than I can count."

Abruptly, Breena's willingness to involve herself in deep magic began to make sense. "Myrddin knew this? Even before he came looking for you?"

"Yes. Rhys, don't you see? This is the purpose that Gwen spoke of, when she told me the Great Mother had sent my vision for a reason. I am here to prevent my nightmare from coming to pass. I have Seen it happening very soon—at the rise of the harvest moon, four nights hence! If Igraine dies then, evil will erupt. Myrddin knows of your grandfather's prophecies. He has worked all his life to prevent the chaos Cyric foretold in his dark vision. As you have."

Rhys was silent for a long moment. "Myrddin told you all this?" he asked finally.

"Yes."

"And you believed him?"

"I did."

"How can you know he spoke the truth? How can you be sure the woman in your vision is the duchess? In your dream, you have never seen her face."

"Since I've arrived at Tintagel, I have. Igraine's face has been very clear in my nightmares."

Rhys began to pace the tiny room. "Your vision changed when you met the duchess?"

"Yes."

"It could be her stifled aura, affecting your Sight. Igraine is strong in magic, Breena, but her power has been trapped."

"I know that. I can even see Igraine's aura. She is a Seer. Or should be. That is why Myrddin chose me to protect her. I've linked my magic to hers."

"What has been done to Igraine is despicable. I can only wonder who cast such a spell."

"Dafyd," Breena suggested.

"Nay. The spell is very old. Dafyd would have been a child when it was cast." Rhys's lips thinned. "But Myrddin would have been old enough."

"No." Breena's eyes snapped. "He would never do such a thing. Myrddin is of the Light."

"He is ruthless."

"Believe what you want. I see I cannot change your mind. But know this—Igraine is in danger. Rhys, Gerlois beats her! She carries the bruises. Myrddin and Uther planned to take Igraine from Gerlois. But now that Myrddin is trapped in a trance, I fear Uther will not arrive in time to stop Igraine's murder. That is why Gareth—"

"Aye," Rhys interrupted. "The boy knight. That one is eager to get under your skirt."

Breena scowled. "That is why Gareth and I have decided to take Igraine out of the castle tomorrow night."

"I know. I heard his plan."

"You are welcome to help us, Rhys," she said quietly. "In fact, I would be very much relieved if you did."

"I have no wish to be a part of any scheme of Myrddin's," Rhys told her. "But I see I have little choice if I am to get you out of this place. So I will help. You will promise to leave with me afterward."

"I will. Of course. Once Igraine is safe."

"Fair enough." He paused. "But it will be my plan we follow. Not Gareth's. Where do you sleep?"

She blinked. "In the tower."

"With the duchess?"

"No. Two levels below, in a storage room adjoining Lady Bertrice's chamber."

"Good. I will come to you tonight, and I will tell you what you are to do tomorrow."

"But—"

He stepped back, and gestured toward the door. "Not now. I have much to consider, and you have been away from the high table for far too long. Go back to the feast, before someone comes after you."

The feasting went on until midnight. The Brothers Stupendous lingered, drinking and gambling. Dermot had, apparently, turned a blind eye, for no one arrived to shoo the errant minstrels from the feasting hall.

The highest ranking nobility, Breena included, had already withdrawn. A good number of guests remained; many would bed down in the hall once the tables were cleared and shoved to one side. Servants bustled about, clearing tables and sweeping away the debris of the feast.

Trent was exultant. "The duke loved us! He will surely heap rewards upon our heads."

Howell threw his dice, and grunted. "I'll believe it when I have the coin in hand. Ah!" he said with satisfaction as he counted his roll. "My win."

"You have the devil's own luck," Floyd grumbled, pushing a pile of small stones in Howell's direction.

The outstanding success of the performance had increased the troop's luck in other directions, as well. Trent, Howell, and Floyd each had a woman at his side—or, in Howell's case, the wench's arms were draped over his shoulders from behind.

Kane sniffed his disapproval. "Put away the dice, I implore you. It is unseemly, here in the duke's feasting hall."

"Do ye imagine anyone cares, man?" Howell retorted.

"True," declared Trent. "Why I can see four games of chance from where I sit! If I were a great hulking beast like Howell, no doubt I'd see a dozen." He laughed. "And Howell and Floyd do not even wager real coin."

Howell threw the dice, then cursed at the roll. Floyd chortled, and took back every marker he had lost.

Howell's woman grinned at Kane. "You are far too young to be so . . . rigid. You need a lass to soften you, lad."

The men laughed; Kane reddened. Howell's wench waved across the hall. In a trice, a fourth woman— barely more than a girl—had joined them. She made eyes at Rhys, who sat alone, but her friend chided her. "Not that one. He belongs to Nesta. Take the youth."

Nesta, thankfully, had not yet appeared to assert her claim on Rhys. The new girl, smiling, slid onto the bench next to Kane, and bent her blonde head to his dark one.

"You are the flautist, nay? I have never heard such music as you played this evening."

Rhys was amazed to see Kane actually reply to the lass. An hour later, when Dermot came by to shoo the troupe from the hall, it seemed a pleasant night was in store for each of Rhys's companions.

"Go on without me," Rhys told the others. "I mean to stay behind for a bit."

Unbuckling his pack, he pulled out his old shirt, and quickly divested himself of his ridiculous yellow tunic. "Kane, would you be so good as to take my harp to the tent?" Rhys knew the young flautist would treat the instrument with care, even with a wench on his arm. He could not say the same for the other three.

"Gladly," Kane said, taking the pack, "but you cannot stay—Dermot will not allow it."

"Dermot will turn a blind eye," Howell said. "He willna want to anger the duke's favorite players! Rhys is off to corner that black-haired serving wench, I dinna doubt."

"Aye," Trent said with a grin. "The way she was fawning over you, I thought she'd drop to her knees and service you right here in the hall. Be off, man. But do not spare us the details in the morning."

With a forced grin, Rhys took his leave of the troupe. After what Breena had told him, he was loath to call even the simplest lookaway spell. Grabbing a wooden trencher and an empty pitcher, he slipped through the door Nesta had indicated earlier, trying to look as though he belonged among the kitchen staff.

He found the cellar stairway easily enough. Two servants, chatting amiably, stepped onto the treads behind him. Once on the lower level, he abandoned his props and quickly hid himself amid the casks of wine. The two men turned in the opposite direction. Rhys eased from his hiding place and lifted one of the tallow tapers from the sconce at the bottom of the stair.

In the area beyond the wine, he found only clay amphorae, marked as carrying olive oil. He looked about. There were no baskets of apples. No fruit of any kind. He circled the area again, silently cursing. Finally, he located a root cellar. Similar enough, he supposed. He ducked into the empty room. A door in a far corner led to a tunnel. He followed it, not at all certain it led in the right direction.

The passage turned to the left. The floor was dirt, the odor musty. The dark all but swallowed his candle. He had definitely taken a wrong turn. He was sure the foundation of the tower lay farther to the east.

A deadening silence permeated the passage. With a sigh of frustration, Rhys turned back. A sudden noise drew him up short. The slap of a whip, followed by a grunt of pain.

The sound emerged from a side passage he hadn't noticed on his initial approach. Gripping his taper, Rhys moved silently down the corridor. The passage turned sharply to the right. Ten paces on, a vertical shaft of flickering light limned the edge of a stout iron-strapped door.

Another blow sounded. A staccato cry followed. Rhys jabbed his taper into a crack in the stone wall. With a sick feeling in his gut, he advanced.

The hiss of a whip. A man's sob. "Cleanse me, Father, for I have sinned."

"The devil must be defeated, my son."

Rhys dropped into a crouch beside the door, drew a breath, and peered around the jamb.

Bile rose in his throat. The room was lit by a single

blazing torch. The spitting flame cast Bishop Dafyd in harsh light. His raised arm held a Roman *flagellum*. Three leather straps hung from the wooden handle.

"For the glory of God!"

Dafyd's arm slashed. The whip struck its target— the thin, naked back of a man. His black robes hung limply on his hips. Of all the monks Rhys had seen, only Dafyd's hideous acolyte—the one who had requested Ceridwen's ballad—wore black. Arms spread and wrists bound, he was bent nearly double over a low wooden frame.

"Cleanse me, Father."

Thwack. Dafyd plied the *flagellum*. His victim did not beg for mercy; he begged for more chastisement. His body jerked with each blow, but he did not twist in his bonds, nor seek to escape. That was when Rhys realized that though Dafyd's victim's back was a mass of welts, there was very little broken skin, and only a trickle of blood.

When Rhys had found himself on the receiving end of a *flagellum,* there had been broken skin. And quite a lot of blood. The straps of Dafyd's whip were not tipped with bits of metal. Still, the bishop did not mute his blows. The monk's pain was very real.

"Your soul is black," Dafyd hissed. "Only Satan himself would take pleasure in a song of the demons of old."

Gods. This beating was on account of Rhys's song.

"I meant . . ." *Thwack!* ". . . no harm. I most humbly . . ." *Thwack!* ". . . beg mercy."

Dafyd paused, his breath heaving like a bellows. He'd at last struck hard enough to break his victim's skin; a stream of blood dribbled across the acolyte's flank. Almost reverently, Dafyd bent his head, and drew his tongue across the crimson line.

Dark magic rose in a noxious rush. Rhys's gorge

rose. He gripped the edge of the door, and fought a wave of pure revulsion. Blood magic was the darkest magic known to man.

So this was how Dafyd gained his vast power.

"Please, Father." The acolyte twisted in his bonds, sobbing. "Allow me my penance, I beg you."

Dafyd straightened. "You want it now?"

"Oh, yes. Now. *Please.*" The acolyte's moan sounded more like pleasure than pain. Rhys's stomach turned.

Dafyd's whip thudded on the dirt floor. With a trembling hand, he reached out to stroke the welts on his victim's back.

The acolyte arched, and hissed. "Hurry."

Rhys sickened to the core, watched as Dafyd bent to kiss the flesh he'd abused. Then he straightened, and opened his robes. Rhys caught a glimpse of his engorged member before the bishop turned his back fully to the door. Grasping the monk's drooping robes, he shoved them over his thin hips and onto the floor.

Rhys spun away. He pressed his back against the wall of the corridor, chest heaving, as Dafyd's grunts of pleasure melded with his acolyte's cries of pain. Or bliss. Rhys was not sure which.

Shaken to the core, he retrieved his candle and quickly retraced his steps to the wine cellar. The kitchen servants were gone. Sinking down on his haunches, he dropped his head back against an oaken cask and shuddered.

Rhys had done much, seen much, in his life. Some of it had been very dark, some of it had shamed him greatly. Never had he witnessed anything half so revolting as what he'd just seen.

The taint of perversion clung to his skin like a dark stain. He suspected he could rub his flesh raw and still not feel clean. At the same time, he was aware of a dark excitement, an unbearable restlessness. Despite the chill of the cellars, his face was flushed, and sweat heated his brow.

The pall that hung over Tintagel castle was seeping into his own soul. But he, at least, was no innocent. He'd known darkness, both in the outside world and inside his own soul. He would survive. What he could not bear was the thought of that same darkness touching Breena.

He had to get her out of this foul place.

"You came," Breena said.

Rhys slipped into the room and shut the door. "I said that I would."

"But Lady Bertrice—"

"Is a very heavy sleeper."

Breena knew Rhys could move like a wraith, even without magic. Still, she could not believe he'd actually gotten into the tower.

She drew up her legs as he sank down on the end of the bed. His long legs stretched almost to the wall. The flame of the hand lamp on the table by the door leaped erratically, releasing a curl of black smoke. She'd trimmed the wick, but the inferior oil did not allow it to burn cleanly.

"How did you get past the guards?"

"There's a hidden door under the tower stair. An escape built by the Roman soldiers who once manned the outpost." He hesitated. "Lady Igraine's maid told me about it."

"Nesta!" Her eyes narrowed. "You planned a tryst with her, didn't you? Why else would she tell you how to get in?"

"She planned a tryst with me. I made no promises."

Breena gave a tight smile. "Still, I imagine she was not pleased when you did not turn up."

"She'll find another man. Women like her always do."

Silence fell between them. Rhys did not look at her; he stared at the blank stone wall. He seemed restive, his dark energy coiled and ready to spring. He shifted one knee, then dragged a hand down his face.

"Rhys—"

"I hate that you are here, Bug, ensnared in Dafyd's darkness. The man is evil. More than you know."

His voice was so gentle, so filled with concern, her heart tripped. For once, the use of her childhood name brought no anger.

"In less than a day, we'll be gone," she said.

"We will," he agreed. "But we will not follow your knight's plan. It has more holes than a broken sieve."

"Gareth is not my knight."

Rhys shrugged.

Breena hugged her knees tighter against her chest. "What is wrong with Gareth's plan?"

"He wishes you to gain permission to walk in the gardens behind the castle. I was given to understand Lady Igraine's movements are restricted to the tower."

"That is true. But I will just have to find a way around it."

"Even if Gerlois was inclined to give his permission, he might very well insist on accompanying you and Igraine."

Breena frowned. "I had not thought of that."

"Neither, apparently, has the noble Sir Gareth. He has also not considered what would happen were he to fail in his quest to become your betrothed. If that happens, there will be no opportunity for escape."

"That is my fear as well," Breena confessed. "Gareth insists he will win, but . . ."

"I saw him during the exhibition. And in the feasting hall. He rides well, but he is very young. Some of his opponents will be far more battle hardened." He gave his head a shake. "Nay. We cannot risk waiting for the end of the contest. We had best make our move earlier. We will steal Igraine away during the tournament."

Breena's brows shot up. "You cannot be serious!"

He met her gaze and held it. "I assure you, I am."

"But . . . how?"

"I will weave an illusion around the duke's box. You and Igraine will simply slip away. Gerlois will not notice."

"Perhaps Gerlois will not, but Dafyd certainly will! He felt my magic, Rhys, when I scried for Myrddin. He will certainly feel yours."

Rhys rubbed his chin. "He felt the deep magic you touched. There is no sign that he is aware of my presence. I believe I can cast Light magic, at least, without his knowledge. Tomorrow, at the tournament, when I cast my illusion on the duke's booth, you and Igraine flee. The duke and his party will not discover the deception until the end of the contest. By that time, we will be well gone."

"Where?"

"We will ride to intercept the high king's army. Your knight can ride ahead, and inform Uther of our approach."

Breena turned Rhys's plan over in her mind. "It could work," she said slowly. "You will have to talk to Gareth, of course, and tell him to withdraw from the contest. Thank the gods he will not have to fight on my behalf. I've been sick with worry."

Rhys flexed his fist. His restless energy was back, in full force. Breena could almost see it, pouring off his body in waves.

He rose, and paced to the small window, as if seeking escape. "What is that knight to you, Breena?"

"Why, nothing! He is Myrddin's assistant. A friend."

"You allow his kiss. He speaks of marriage—real marriage, not a sham. Tell me, would you be willing? If you could not find your way home, would you take him as your husband?" He turned suddenly. Every muscle in his body was drawn taut. "Would you lie on your back for the noble Sir Gareth? Would you spread your legs for him?"

She gasped. "Rhys! That is crude."

"Aye, perhaps, but your knight is a man, like any other. That is what he wants from you." His voice pitched low. "That is what I want from you."

He did? She stared, stunned past words.

With two strides, he loomed over her. He placed one hand on the wall above her head and bent close, not touching, but filling her senses completely nonetheless. His scent—a heady mix of sweat, anger, and lust—stabbed at her nostrils.

The tips of her breasts tightened. Heat pulled at her belly. She became aware of slick moisture bathing her thighs. The sweet, twisting yearning of her girlish fantasies of Rhys sharpened on an edge that stole her breath.

She licked her lips. "Do you really want that from me, Rhys?"

Emotion stormed in his gray eyes. "That," he said, "is only the beginning of what I want from you, Breena."

Blood pounded in her ears. His hunger, stark in his expression, consumed her utterly. But what drove his passion? Breena wasn't completely sure. Not love. At least, not love in the way she had always thought of it.

She sensed the emotion driving Rhys was far more primitive than love. And far more dangerous to her heart. It scared her. The girl she'd once been wanted desperately to shrink back. But the woman she'd begun to be—the one who accepted the gravest risks, despite her fears—*she* would not turn away.

"Show me, Rhys. Show me what you want from me."

His nostrils flared. His eyes were hard, and hungry. "Do not tempt me."

She came up on her knees, facing him, so close that her breasts brushed his chest. He sucked in a harsh breath, and the arm he'd braced against the wall trembled. His free hand came up as if to embrace her. But he did not. It formed a fist instead, and dropped back to his side.

But he did not step away.

She met his gaze steadily as she unclasped the girdle about her waist. The bands of silver fell to the floor. Her silk *stola* loosened, her breasts no longer confined.

Rhys's throat worked. "Breena—"

She unclasped the pins at her sleeves and shoulders, dropping them one by one. The *stola,* freed from its constraints, slithered down her torso to puddle on the bed. She knelt amid the rumple of silk, clad only in her fine linen tunic.

Some feminine instinct prompted her to raise her arms above her head and clasp her elbows, in the pose she'd taken in the steward's office. The movement lifted her breasts. The tips were tight, and so sensitive that the slight friction of the cloth shot a flash of raw lust straight to her loins.

Her head tilted back; her eyes closed. She bit her lower lip to keep from moaning.

Rhys made a strangled sound. "Breena. Do not do this. . . ."

She opened her eyes. "You want me to do it, Rhys. You do not have the courage to do it yourself."

A tremor ran through his body.

"Gods help me," he said.

Their gazes locked in the flickering lamplight. For a moment, neither of them moved. Breena's arms remained crossed over her head; Rhys's hands remained fisted at his sides.

And then, slowly, Breena uncrossed her arms, and began plucking the pins from her hair. The heavy braids unwound, falling almost to her waist. She went to work combing out the fiery plaits with her fingers. Rhys did not move, did not speak. But by the time she was done, his chest was heaving.

Her hands went next to the neckline of her tunic.

Rhys's eyes followed the movement. His throat worked as he swallowed. There were three ties securing the linen; Breena's trembling fingers went to work on the first one. He drew in a harsh breath as the tiny bow disintegrated.

"Breena—"

She plucked at the second tie.

He shot a glance at the door. "Breena, stop this. Lady Bertrice—"

"Is snoring," she whispered. "You are right. She is a very heavy sleeper."

The second knot opened. Her right sleeve slid off her shoulder. Her fingers slipped to the third tie.

Rhys shoved off the wall. "This is madness."

"Then step back. Go to the other side of the room and turn your back. I will lie down on the bed and spread my legs. Then, if you wish, you may leave."

He cursed. Anger clashed with lust in his eyes. The dark energy radiating from his lean body made Breena shiver. She was frightened—there was no sense denying it. She was also unbearably aroused.

The tunic's last bow fell open. Her left sleeve slipped

over her shoulder. The garment whispered down her arms to her waist, baring her breasts.

She knelt motionless, the meager lamplight flickering across her skin. Rhys's eyes devoured her; his hands trembled. And she knew—*knew*—with feminine certainty, that this time, he would not turn away.

A sudden rush of feminine power made her head feel light. A scant moment later, when Rhys touched her, all thoughts of advantage evaporated. His gaze had gone so dark she thought she might drown in it, like a swimmer lost in a night sea.

Jaw clenched, he lifted a shaking hand and touched his forefinger to the tip of her left breast. The pad of his finger was calloused. It scraped across her tender skin; a hot knife of pleasure sliced through her body. Her stomach clenched. It was all she could do to keep from crying out.

Rhys's hand slid under her breast, weighing it in his palm. He did not watch her face, but his own hands. He rubbed her nipple again, with his thumb this time. His left hand soon began the same ruthless torture on her other breast. Fire flashed over her skin, heated her face. She did moan then, shamelessly. The expression on his face hardened into something like pain.

He urged her back. "Lie down."

The mattress seemed to rise to meet her. With swift efficiency, Rhys tilted her hips and stripped off her tunic. He rose up, looking down at her. Not at her face. At her breasts, and at the juncture of her thighs.

"Open them."

His command was low and hoarse. The abrupt order caused Breena's womb to convulse. Wet heat flooded her thighs. She stared up at him. Rhys was almost a stranger to her now, so foreign and hard was his expression. She was trembling, newly aware of an aching emptiness inside her.

"Spread your legs, Breena. As you said you would."

She swallowed hard, and obeyed.

He moved his weight to the bed, kneeling between her open thighs, but not touching them. The dark place between her legs throbbed. His gaze was fixed there. His face was flushed, and his breathing had gone shallow. The ache grew. She flexed her hips, more by instinct than by design.

Rhys made a sound low in his throat. He leaned forward, bracing one arm beside her head. His free hand covered her breast. His thumb and forefinger gently pinched her nipple. Breena's breath hitched. The throbbing between her legs transformed to a deep, empty longing. A moan rose in her throat and escaped before she could strangle it.

Dear gods. She could hear Lady Bertrice's snores on the other side of the door! "This . . . this is madness."

Rhys sat back on his heels, studying her with hooded eyes. "I have known that, Breena, for a good many years. And yet, you did not have the good sense to believe it."

"That is not what I meant," she whispered.

He continued as if she hadn't spoken. "Yes, the good sense has been mine all along, in this as in everything else. I am sick to death of good sense. Of right. Of duty. Tonight, I find I do not care. I am beginning to believe there are some things well worth an eternity of Dafyd's hellfire." He paused, his lips twisting. His beautiful eyes had turned bleak. Her heart hurt for him. Suddenly, she understood that, in a way, he was as frightened as she.

"Raise your arms, Breena."

He was not using magic, but he'd captured her in a dark spell nonetheless. She did not hesitate to do as he asked.

He closed his eyes briefly. When he opened them,

the misty gray of his irises had turned to iron. Wordlessly, he swiped her discarded tunic from the floor, and ripped a strip of linen from the hem. Before she quite realized what he was about, he'd looped the narrow length of cloth around her wrists. The backs of her hands brushed the carving on the bed's raised end.

She felt the linen go taut. She tugged, and understood with a shock that he'd tied her to the bed frame. There was almost no slack in her bonds.

"What—?"

The heat of his mouth absorbed her confusion. His kiss was bold and deep. He leaned over her, his body blanketing her with heat, though only their lips were touching. His tongue invaded her mouth. Claiming. Tasting. Taking.

The effect was that of a spark set to dry tinder. Her body burst into flames. Waves of desire rolled through her, melting her muscles, her bones, her will—and even her fear.

Perhaps she should have been afraid. This aroused male animal kneeling over her was hardly the Rhys she thought she knew. That Rhys was gentle, kind, and possessed of a wry humor. Not angry, and consumed with a kind of violent passion she had not even dreamed could exist between lovers. It was a dangerous force. Like deep magic, she sensed it was a power Rhys could not fully control.

The rough wool of his breeches scraped the delicate skin on the inside of her thighs. He was fully dressed, while she was completely naked, open, and vulnerable. There was a seductive eroticism to that. She felt herself surrender to it.

His tongue plunged in and out of her mouth with sinuous rhythm. She imitated the movement, plunging forward when he retreated. She wanted desperately to reach for him with her hands. Paradoxically, the fact that she could not—the knowledge that he'd rendered her captive—made her shudder with desire.

His breath whispered in her ear. "Lie very still. Try not to move until the pleasure becomes unbearable. And do not make a sound. Remember Lady Bertrice."

"But—"

He stopped the word with a press of his finger. His eyes pleaded. "Please, Breena. Do this for me. Otherwise . . . I cannot be certain what I will do."

She didn't understand. Not completely. She nodded anyway. He kissed her again, more tenderly this time. His lips trailed from her lips to her neck, across her collarbone, down her chest.

His mouth closed, hot and urgent, on her breast. She stifled a gasp, and tried to control her trembling. His teeth and tongue, relentless, tightened the coil in her chest and belly. When his hands joined the blissful torture, she couldn't help moving. Her head tossed from side to side, scrubbing the mattress. She pressed her lips together, and only just managed to stop herself from crying out.

The effort to be passive, when every nerve in her body screamed for movement, made the heat inside her flash hotter and darker. Her hips rose; she tried to still them. Rhys's tongue lashed at her nipple; she stifled a moan.

His mouth traveled to her belly, his tongue tracing a wet line around her navel. His hands slid up the inside of her legs, pausing high on her inner thighs.

"Wider," he said hoarsely.

It sounded more like a plea than a command. A shudder passed through her. Wordlessly, she did as he asked, then gasped as his fingers threaded through her curls and touched the wet, tender nub hidden within them. Dear gods! Her hips rose off the bed. She couldn't stifle a cry.

"Quiet," he whispered.

Fear of discovery honed the edge of her blissful torment. She nodded, and forced her body to go limp. Rhys's head dipped, and his tongue found the spot that his fingers had teased only moments before. Waves of exquisite sensation washed over her.

Her fingers tangled in her linen shackles. She clung to the cloth strips, and somehow did not cry out. But she could no longer lie still—that was impossible. Her hips bucked in Rhys's hands. His fingers dug into her buttocks. He lifted her toward his mouth, and she arched shamelessly, helping him.

His breath was hot. It seared her, branded her as his willing slave. He slid one finger inside her. Then two. She twisted, panting. Her skin flashed cool, then hot. His lips left her sated, then stoked her hunger anew. She needed . . . something.

He seemed to know just what it was. But he would not give it to her. He lifted his head, and took his hands from her body. She felt the loss in her heart.

He stood beside the bed. She lay dazed, bound, legs sprawled rudely, looking up at him. She longed to erase the sudden bleakness in his eyes.

He scrubbed a hand down his face. "I do not think, Breena, that this is precisely what you've dreamed of all these years."

"I might have," she confessed, "if I had only known what to dream."

She thought for a moment he would turn away. He did not. With precise movements, and shaking hands, he stripped off his shirt. His boots came next. He reached for the closure of his breeches.

She watched him greedily. She wanted to touch him; wanted to strip him as he'd stripped her. To open her mouth on his skin. She could have done it. She'd tugged so hard on her bindings that the linen had stretched. She could pull free with little effort. But she sensed he would not welcome that. Not yet. And so she waited.

He shoved his breeches over his lean hips. Her eyes went round at the sight of his phallus, thick and red and angry. Naked, he crawled over her on all fours. The blunt tip of his erection prodded her intimate flesh. Her belly spasmed. Instinctively, she arched her hips in welcome.

"Rhys . . . please. . . ."

He did not immediately respond to her plea. With his torso supported on rigid arms, he stared down at her.

"Breena. . . ." he whispered. "Tell me . . . tell me to stop."

The light was dim; his face in shadow. She could not read his expression. Heat radiated from his body. His breath was heavy, and his chest damp with sweat. She sensed his deep yearning, and an even deeper reluctance.

"I do not want you to stop, Rhys."

His head dropped, his forehead almost touching hers. His hair fell forward, brushing her temple. She wanted to slide her fingers through it. She wanted to scrape her palms on the heavy bristle covering his jaw. She wanted to tell him how very much she loved him. All of him. The dark as well as the light.

But she did not say it. She was afraid words of love would cause his misplaced guilt to surface, as it always had in the past. So she did not move, and did not speak. Neither did he. As the moments spun out, she thought she would go mad with wanting. How long could Rhys hold himself just . . . *there* . . . at the entrance to her body?

"I have tried to stay away," he said at last.

"Why?"

"You were . . ." He hesitated.

"I was too young. I know that. And far too bold. But Rhys, I have not been too young for some years now."

"Then perhaps . . . perhaps I am too old."

"You are not yet thirty."

"Old in spirit, then. I have seen more than a man four times my age. Cruelty, injustice, bigotry, perversion. And I cannot turn away from any of it, no matter how much I wish to."

She bit her lip. "You are alone far too much."

"Aye," he said simply.

"Rhys . . . look at me."

After a long moment, he raised his head.

"You don't have to be alone any longer. Not ever. You have me."

Turbulent emotion trembled through his long, lean body. A drop of water splashed on Breena's shoulder; with a sudden shock, she realized it was a tear. Rhys was *crying*.

Her heart turned over. He buried his head in the crook of her neck. A sob shook his shoulders. She let her wrists slip free of the linen strips and, hesitantly, touched his crown. When he did not flinch away, she threaded her fingers through his hair. She nuzzled him until he turned his head. His mouth found hers. Their lips met, and clung, in an achingly tender kiss.

"Come inside me. I want you so."

"Ah, Breena . . . I do not want to hurt you."

"It would hurt me more, Rhys, if you were to pull away."

He let out a breath. A sigh of surrender, perhaps. His body tightened, the head of his shaft slid through her folds, seeking welcome. She opened to him, planting her feet and arching upward.

"Bree—" With a flex of his hips, he slid inside.

She experienced an instant of sharp, burning pain. A gasp escaped her lips. Rhys froze. "Gods."

For long moments they lay that way, joined in body, breathing as one, hesitant to deepen the union. The sensation of being stretched, and filled, was very odd. But not unpleasant. The pain was already fading. A feeling of buoyant expectancy had replaced it.

She wriggled her hips. Rhys raised his head and looked down at her.

"Are you . . . uncomfortable?" His voice was strained.

"No. But I know there is more than this."

She thought she saw the ghost of a smile on his lips. "You are right," he said. "There is this." His hips thrust forward. "And this." He drew back.

"Oh!" The sensation was like nothing she'd ever known. Or had even dreamed of. It felt as though he caressed her soul.

He moved again, his hands sliding under her bottom, lifting her, guiding her. She caught his body's rhythm, and matched it, lifting her hips as he thrust downward. At last she touched him freely, a banquet of pleasure at her fingertips. Her palms stroked his shoulders, his flanks, his buttocks. He groaned, and dropped his head to her neck. His tempo quickened.

He became her world. The only solid thing in a universe of shifting, rolling pleasure. It came in waves, lifting her, urging her, ripping away her defenses, until every protection on her soul was gone. And she did not care, because it was Rhys. *Rhys.* She was making love with him at last.

The wild pleasure grew, and crested, driving every thought from her head. It was as if her body was made of pure sensation. Pure bliss. And yet there was more. She could sense it.

Rhys's soft urgings caressed her ear, his accent growing rougher as his own control slipped. "Aye, lass. Let go. Let it come. Let the end take ye."

It snatched her away hard and fast, hot pleasure slicing through her like the sharpest of blades. She shattered, a thousand bright lights flashing behind her eyelids. Rhys's mouth covered her, drinking in her cry. He moved inside her, harder, faster, until his own body stiffened, and she felt his seed spurt, warm and welcome, deep inside.

He collapsed atop her, his weight straining the ropes under the mattress. She wrapped her arms around him and tried to still the pounding of her heart.

"I love you, Rhys."

His body jerked, as if she'd struck him. He did not answer.

After a moment, he rose.

The cool air that rushed between their bodies was almost painful. He shoved himself into a seated position near her feet, and looked at her for a long moment. Then he turned, and rested his elbows on his knees. Dropping his head, he pressed the side of his fist to his forehead.

A sour feeling curdled in her stomach.

"Rhys?"

"Gods, Breena. I'm—"

"Do not say it," she whispered, horrified. "Do not tell me you are sorry."

He nodded and looked away. "Then I will not. It would be a lie, in any case."

He rose and found his clothes. Chilled by the odd shift of his mood, she drew up her blanket as he dressed.

He paused, his hand on the door latch. "There is a stand of oaks to the east of the tournament field, on a bluff overlooking the sea. Do you know it?"

"I do." She hoped her voice sounded as steady as his.

"Tomorrow, at the tournament, when my illusion takes hold, bring the duchess to the grove, as quickly as you can. Do not delay even an instant."

She nodded. He opened the door and was gone.

Chapter Fourteen

If he could find shelter, he'd be safe.

Myrddin plied his dove's wings. His destination was a sheer cliff dotted with gaps and fissures. If only he could reach it, he could dodge death.

A shadow passed over his body, and fell to the earth below in the shape of a hawk. The creature flew above. The cliffs were drawing near. But they were not close enough. He would not reach them in time. And yet, even knowing the truth, Myrddin flapped his wings, desperately.

The hawk screeched. He felt the rush of its dive even before it struck. *Gods, Vivian. I am sorry.*

He braced himself for the strike. It did not come. He was falling, falling, falling. His wings were useless. No, even worse, they had disappeared entirely.

He bounced on the ground, striking several times before rolling to a stop. He tried to move. He could not.

He had no body. Blades of grass loomed as high as trees. He had shrunk to the size of a grain of wheat. No. He *was* a grain of wheat. Ah, but at least a grain of wheat was safe from a hawk's beak. Perhaps, once the predator lost interest, Myrddin could find a way to regain the body of a man.

He heard the hawk land. Nearby, he thought, though he could not see it. He lay waiting, praying it would move off. When he heard the soft clucking, he did not at first understand.

Until the hen's black eye above him blinked, and her sharp beak descended on a single, discarded grain of wheat.

Breena thought she would never be able to sleep after Rhys left. Her skin tingled. Her emotions were in turmoil, and her thoughts of the day to come filled her with trepidation. Eventually, however, both mind and body succumbed to exhaustion.

Sleep brought no respite from her fears. Just the opposite. Her nightmare was more terrifying than it had ever been. The perspective had changed. In her vision, Breena was no longer a bystander watching Igraine's murder. Instead, she saw the scene unfold from the duchess's own eyes. The snatches of terror in her breast were not her own, but Igraine's.

Silver mist swirled all around her. It filled her lungs thickly. As beautiful as it was, she hated it. It separated her from . . . what? A power that should have been as natural as breathing. Someone had taken it from her.

A door opened. A man stood on the threshold. She couldn't see his face, but she could feel his anger. His footsteps were angry. She shrank back. . . .

Breena came awake with a start, heart pounding, head aching. Her lungs were tight; she gulped great mouthfuls of air. A shaft of moonlight tumbled through the musty storeroom's single window. Lady Bertrice's snores rose and fell beyond the door.

She would not sleep again tonight. The walls of her small room seemed to close in on her. She needed the open sky above her to feel whole again. She eased out of bed.

Blessed night air greeted her on the roof terrace. The gibbous moon, just shy of full, cast an ominous band of light on the sea. Morning could not be far off. The wind lifted her hair, causing it to stream behind her. She hugged herself tightly. Though she had no cloak, and her feet were bare on the cold stone walkway, she was loath to leave the small freedom of the outdoors.

She turned, giving her back to the wind. If she leaned over the wall encircling the terrace, and looked hard to her left, she could see over the lower roof of the great hall and into the castle forecourt beyond.

She stared down at the peaked roofs of the tents. Rhys was there, somewhere, with his minstrel friends. Was he thinking of her? Remembering the searing intimacy they had shared? If so, she suspected he was stewing in regret.

That thought hurt terribly. She had no regrets. None at all.

A hot flush rose up her neck, despite the bite of the wind. She touched her lips. The bottom one was still swollen. Her inner thighs tingled with the scrapes from Rhys's rough beard. Her more private parts twinged when she walked. Her arms ached, and there were faint marks on her wrists where Rhys had bound her. Dear Goddess. She'd spent years dreaming of how it would be when she and Rhys finally made love. The reality had been nothing like the fantasy.

The Rhys of her girlish imagination had been playful and gentle. So very romantic. He had not been angry, almost savage in his lust. The real Rhys frightened her. She could not deny that. When he'd tied her wrists, and she lay helpless as his hands roamed her body . . . A deep shudder ran through her. She could not deny that her fear was irrevocably entwined with dark desire. The sweet, twisting sensations he'd conjured . . . the exhilarating sense of being completely in his control . . . the blinding pleasure she'd experienced . . . She wanted to do it all again. She wanted to do it forever.

She suspected he did not. He'd been shamed by his

passion; he'd been on the verge of an apology. It did not matter that she had taken as much pleasure as he in their joining—he still sought to protect her. Gods. The man could be such an idiot sometimes. And so stubborn! Why could Rhys not accept the fact that they belonged together? As far as Breena was concerned, after last night, there was no going back.

She rubbed her arms. The fresh air had cleared her mind, but she'd catch her death if she remained barefoot on the terrace much longer. As she reached the tower door, a heavy tread sounded on the stair.

She'd left the door unlatched, and slightly ajar. She peered through crack just in time to see Gerlois disappear down the dim stairwell.

A chill seemed to blow right through her soul. She had not realized the duke had visited the duchess last night. But of course—why else would Nesta have been able to arrange a tryst with Rhys? Cold dread filled her stomach. She all but flew up the stairs. The moon remained three days from full, but last night, her vision had changed yet again. Had her new nightmare been Igraine's cry for help? One she had not heard?

One level above, the duchess's solar was empty. Without pause, she ran to the upper level. Soft sobs, muffled behind Igraine's closed door, flooded Breena with relief. The worst had not happened. Not yet.

Catching her breath, she eased the door open and stepped into Igraine's bedchamber. A pallet near the door—Nesta's, no doubt—was empty.

A large bed stood in the center of the space; Breena could just make out Igraine's huddled form, hidden behind the silk hangings. Her anguish tore at Breena's heart.

She approached with caution. "My lady?"

Igraine shoved herself upright, a pillow clasped to her chest. "Who . . . who is it?"

Breena fumbled on a table for flint and tinder. A moment later, the glow of lamplight chased the shadows into the corners. "It is I, my lady. Breena."

Igraine stared as if she did not recognize the name. She simply sat, motionless, her hair tumbling in a wild tangle about her shoulders. The neckline of her tunic was torn, revealing an angry mark on one breast. Her lips were swollen; her eyes red and puffy. Strands of pewter dulled her aura.

Breena's heart nearly broke. "Oh, Igraine! What has he done to you?"

The duchess blinked, then pulled the torn edges of her tunic together. "Breena. What are you doing here?" Her eyes flicked to the window. "It is not yet dawn."

"I could not sleep. I saw the duke descend, and I heard your sob. I thought . . . you might be in need of help."

"Help," the duchess repeated, her tone hollow. "Yes. I begin to believe you are right."

Breena sat on the edge of the bed. She could speak again of flight, but she sensed Igraine was in need of more immediate care.

She sent a rush of magic through their link. It disappeared as if it never was. The void that existed where Igraine's magic should have been was empty and desolate. How horrible a fate, to be so disconnected to one's power. Like touching the world with bandaged hands.

"Is there water?" Breena asked. "I could help you wash."

Igraine's eyes closed briefly. "There is water in the basin. I would very much like to wash. I feel so . . . dirty."

The water was cold, but Igraine did not flinch. Breena tended the duchess's bruises and scrapes as best she could. For the wounds of the spirit, she could do little.

She swallowed. "Did he—?"

Igraine understood. "Rape me?" She laughed. "No. Perhaps that would have been more bearable—or at least quicker—than his fists."

Heartsick, Breena discarded Igraine's torn tunic, and found another in a trunk. The room was chilled; she stirred up the coals in the brazier and added more from a nearby bucket. Taking up an ivory comb, she began to smooth the knots from Igraine's red-gold hair.

Breena concentrated on her task. Igraine stared at the window, watching the sky go from black to pink. The comb glided through the last of the snarls in the red-gold hair.

Breena laid the comb aside. Her heart broke for the duchess, who had so great a need of protection. On impulse, she lifted the chain bearing her Druid pendant and drew it over her head.

"Please," she said. "I want you to wear this. I believe you need it far more than I."

Igraine turned, a question in her eyes. She touched the dangling silver charm with her forefinger. "Why . . . I once had a charm like this. My old nurse gave it to me. But Gerlois took it away. He said it was pagan."

"The three-armed spiral in the center is the sign of the Great Mother goddess," Breena said. "But the four-pronged cross is the symbol of the Christos. I know him as the Carpenter Prophet. Dafyd calls the Old Ways evil, but that is not true. Both these signs, old and new, are of the Light. Together, they are very powerful protection. Will you wear it?"

Igraine searched Breena's eyes, and nodded. "If you wish it."

Breena put the circle of silver chain over Igraine's head, and drew her hair through it. Igraine looked down at the pendant, then tucked it under her tunic, saying nothing.

Breena separated the strands of Igraine's hair, and began to braid.

The duchess's shoulders slumped. "My husband hates me so."

"I cannot think why he should," Breena said evenly.

"Gerlois wants a son. I gave him a daughter. He was enraged, and threw her away."

"That is good reason for you to hate him. Gerlois has no reason to despise you, or to think you are incapable of giving him sons in the future."

A bubble of hysterical laughter erupted from Igraine's lips. "Give him sons! How can I? My womb cannot grow a son if my husband cannot plant the seed."

Breena's hands stilled. "You mean . . . the duke cannot . . . perform?"

"No. That is why he uses his fists."

"But—your daughter . . ."

"Gerlois was injured in battle shortly before Morgan's birth. Since then . . ." Igraine's shoulders lifted and fell. "He cannot . . . stiffen, no matter how I try to rouse him. He says the blame is mine."

"The fault cannot be yours! No man could fail to desire you. You are so beautiful."

Igraine's expression hardened. "My beauty is nothing but a curse."

"It is only a curse if you do not have the courage to leave him."

Igraine studied her clenched fingers. "I do not know," she said at last.

Breena finished the braid and tied off the end. "I do. You cannot remain here. Gerlois will destroy you. Uther is coming for you, Igraine. He will wage war on your behalf whether you wish it or not. You promised yourself to Uther, long before Erbin gave you to Gerlois. The time has come for you to keep your first vow. We leave today."

Igraine twisted around and met Breena's gaze. "Truly?"

"Yes. The plan is in place. All you need to do is agree to it."

Igraine looked down at her clasped hands. After a long hesitation, she nodded. "All right. I will do as you say. I will go to Uther."

Nesta arrived before dawn with a bucket of hot water, her head down and her forehead marred with a scowl. When she saw Breena with Igraine, her expression turned to one of surprise.

"My lady," she said as she emptied and refilled Igraine's washbasin. "Lady Antonia has already dressed your hair."

"I rose early," Breena said, "and thought to offer Lady Igraine my services."

Nesta eyed Breena's loose hair and bare feet. "Lady Bertrice is stirring. We are to be at chapel in under an hour. Bishop Dafyd wishes to offer a prayer on behalf of the tournament knights. We must hurry."

"I will dress quickly, then, and assist Lady Bertrice while you tend the duchess." Breena crossed the room, pausing at Igraine's wardrobe, where Nesta was already sorting through Igraine's gowns.

"You seem out of sorts this morning," Breena whispered. "Is something troubling you?"

"Only the usual," she grumbled.

"A man?"

"Aye, what else? That fair-headed minstrel, the one who sang so sweetly at the feast. Promised to meet me, he did. I waited half the night, and he did not appear." Nesta sniffed. "Faithless louts, men, the lot of 'em."

Breena hid a smile as she descended the stair.

*   *   *

Tintagel's chapel, with its lime-washed walls and tall, deep-set windows, might have been a place of Light, if not for Bishop Dafyd's darkness.

Breena fidgeted with one of her sleeve pins as Dafyd preached of Satan and sin. Her stomach churned. She had not broken her fast, but she doubted she could eat in any case.

Her nerves were wound tight. It was not that she doubted Rhys's ability to do what he proposed; it was that what he intended to do was so very dangerous. What if Dafyd became aware of Rhys's illusion before Breena managed to get Igraine away? The thought turned her heart to ice.

At least the cushion she'd been given to kneel upon softened the cold stone floor. Dafyd droned on. Breena's anxiety heightened. The bishop preached Light, but every word out of his mouth was darkness. She kept her head down, hoping he would not take notice of her. She'd been careful to tuck every strand of her hair under her veil. Nevertheless, the bishop kept glaring at her, as if he expected a demon to leap from her flaming head.

Brother Morfen, as always, stood just behind Dafyd. She was aware of him watching her with his single intense eye. Something in the young monk's posture and movement seemed odd. His lips were pressed in a straight line, and each movement of his body brought a grimace of pain. Something was wrong. She caught his eye and dipped her chin slightly. He did not acknowledge the greeting.

The private service, attended by only the highest ranked of the visiting nobles, ended at last. Dafyd raised his staff and blessed the worshippers. Gerlois, with Igraine at his side, paused for conversation with Lord Clarence of Tregear. Lady Bertrice chatted with Honoria of Bolerium. That lady's husband had claimed Dafyd's attention near the door of the chapel.

Breena hung back as the rest of the nobles filed into the receiving room. Morfen did not meet her gaze as he paced toward her. She stepped into his path, and forced him to halt.

"What is wrong?" she demanded.

His lips twisted. "Nothing, my lady."

"You are in pain. Are you hurt? Ill?"

"No." Morfen sent her a quick glance, then looked away. "Please, Lady Antonia, I beg you, do not press me. My affliction is less than nothing. It will soon pass."

"You are lying," she said baldly. "There is no reason to do so. Not with me."

She did not miss his nervous glance toward Dafyd. "Neither do I have reason to confide in you."

Her eyes narrowed. "It has to do with the bishop, doesn't it? What happened?"

"It is not your concern, my lady."

"Of course it is! I am your friend." Reaching out, she gripped his wrist.

He gasped his next breath and jerked his arm back.

"What—?" Before the monk could react, Breena grabbed his hand and shoved the sleeve of his robe up to his elbow. The skin on his wrist had been scraped raw, by what looked like the burn of a rope.

She met his gaze in horror. "Dafyd . . . bound you? And . . . and what? Beat you?"

Morfen's head dropped forward. "It is not your concern," he repeated.

He tugged his hand from hers. Reluctantly, she let it drop. "Why did he do it?"

"Punishment. For my sins."

"What sins?"

"Impiety. Pride. The sin of honoring the Old Ones, when they deserve only contempt."

Understanding dawned. "Dafyd punished you for asking R—the minstrel to sing the ballad of Ceridwen?"

Morfen nodded. "It is an evil tale."

"You do not believe that, any more than I do. Gwion stirred Ceridwen's cauldron when Afagduu refused. That is why Gwion, as Taliesin, gained wisdom, while Afagduu remained in hideous ignorance. The story teaches that the path to wisdom is not an easy one. That is truth, no matter the source of the lesson."

Morfen cut her a glance with his good eye. "Bishop Dafyd would not agree."

"That does not give him the right to beat you."

"You speak blasphemy. I suggest you do not do so out loud. If my master hears you, he will not stop with the *flagellum*."

Breena gasped. "Dafyd whipped you with a *flagellum*?"

His gaze shuttered. "Yes. For the good of my soul."

Breena did not know what to say. "I . . . I am sorry."

"I am not," he said softly.

Chapter Fifteen

The blackness was absolute. Myrddin drifted in the void. If he had a body, he did not feel it. Could not control it. Was this death? He thought it must be.

His grief, and his regret, overwhelmed him. He had been a prideful fool to think he could command the deep magic he'd cast to bring himself to this place. He believed he had lived long enough, had grown so great in magic and wisdom, that he could challenge the gods at their own doorstep and emerge the victor.

Idiot. There had been a time, long ago, when he would not have dared to insult the gods so boldly. Perhaps, after all, his younger self was the wiser man. He thought of Breena, whom he had trapped. And Vivian, whom he had lost.

He had failed them both.

Dafyd's dark magic accompanied the duchess's party from the castle to the tournament field. Rhys had expected this, and prepared for it. The haze of evil meant Dafyd was not yet sure where his enemy lurked. With luck, he would not know until it was too late.

"Ah, here come the fortune seekers!" Trent's cheerful commentary greeted the column of knights taking the field.

Rhys studied the warriors eager to fight for Lord Vectus's land, and the right to bed the woman posing as the dead lord's daughter. They numbered twelve. Rhys had no trouble picking out Gareth from his competition.

Proud idiot. To Rhys's mind, the young knight's big black stallion was more dangerous than its rider. Gareth's opponents were a battle-hardened lot. At least two of the hulking warriors, whom Trent named as Sir Berwyn of Tregear and Sir Hugh of Siluria, looked as though they'd cut their teeth on knights of Gareth's youth and inexperience.

It was not for want of trying that Rhys had failed to keep Gareth's name off the lists for the competition. Rhys had cornered Myrddin's spy near the privies at dawn. Gareth's eyes had narrowed when Rhys claimed to be a Druid, and Breena's friend. For a moment, Rhys had feared the knight would call out the guards and have him arrested.

Then Rhys had remembered Breena's assertion that Myrddin was descended from the Druids of Avalon, and carried the symbol of Avalon carved on his staff. He'd opened his shirt and shown Gareth the same mark tattooed on Rhys's left breast.

Upon seeing the mark, Gareth had become marginally more cooperative. He refused, however, to give up his place in the tournament, even after Rhys had outlined his plan. Gareth insisted that, should Rhys's scheme fail, Breena would need his protection all the more.

Fool. A wiser man would have leaped at the chance to abandon the tournament. Gareth was likely to find himself injured, or worse, and all for nothing. Rhys did not intend to fail.

He shifted his pack on his shoulder. He'd told the troop he did not wish to risk leaving his harp unattended in the castle forecourt. In reality, he'd kept it with him because he would not be returning to Tintagel.

"Fortune seeking is all very well," Howell replied to Trent's comment. "But bedding Vectus's buxom daughter would be no hardship, either."

"The lass's flaming hair alone would render me hard as a pike," Floyd put in with a smirk. He gripped the air as if it were a woman's hips, and made a crude thrusting motion.

The very notion of Floyd using Breena caused Rhys's blood to boil. With difficulty, he restrained himself from burying a fist in the singer's soft midsection.

He raised his eyes to the duke's viewing booth. When his gaze touched on Breena, the bottom of his stomach hollowed out. It was impossible to look at her and not remember her naked, beneath him.

She sat beside Igraine. Bertrice, Gerlois, and Dafyd were close at hand. As always, the bishop's somber, black-garbed acolyte stood a step behind his master. The perversion Rhys had witnessed in the cellars sprang into his mind. Nauseated, he shoved the memory back into the shadows where it belonged.

Breena wore a gown of deep blue. She had not looked his way, not even once, though the Brothers Stupendous had dressed for the tournament in all their rainbow glory, and Rhys's position at the front of the crowd was plain enough. No doubt she was humiliated by what he'd forced on her last night.

He closed his eyes on a wave of shame. He was the lowest brute imaginable. He loved Breena so much, and yet he'd used her like a whore. The memory of her nude body, stretched out on the bed, bound, awaiting his pleasure, was almost too much to bear. Her lush breasts . . . her gently rounded belly . . . her white thighs, parted to reveal her glistening feminine center, peeking from its veil of tangled red curls . . .

The light had been dim. That had not prevented him from burning the image of her nakedness into his brain.

He'd memorized the pattern of the spray of freckles dotting her shoulders and upper breast. He had wanted to nip at each red-brown dot. He'd wanted to take out his cock and rub it between her full breasts, until his seed spurted across those same fanciful freckles.

Gods.

Breena had looked at him with dreamy love. He had responded like an animal. She was far too precious to be subjected to his base urges. Aye, she had not protested, even when he'd tied her wrists, but that had most likely been due to shock. He'd worked hard to ensure she found her release, but no one knew better than he what shame such forbidden pleasure brought come morning.

What would she say if she knew how he longed to bend her over a table and mount her from behind? How horrified would she be if she knew he craved her on her knees, servicing him with her mouth? He could not bear to think of it.

He did not know what he would say to her when they next came face to face. He didn't think he could bear to see the contempt in her eyes. He was not the man she'd thought he was; after what had happened last night, she could no longer deny it. The loss of her good regard would rip a hole in his life that could never be filled.

Breena came forward in the ducal box, at the duke's command. She stood at Igraine's side as Gerlois presented her to the knights vying for her hand. She went still when the name of Sir Gareth of Cornwall was announced. Her head jerked up; she looked directly at Rhys. If she had shouted her accusation across the field, he could not have understood it more clearly. He wanted to shout back that it was not his fault, that Gareth was a proud, stubborn idiot. But he knew it would not make any difference if he did.

The crier announced the rules of the contest. A general melee would reduce the field of twelve contestants by half. Afterward, a mounted joust would eliminate four more knights. The two that remained would fight in hand-to-hand combat for the honor of Lady Antonia's hand.

The warriors split into two factions, taking positions at opposite ends of the field. Swords were drawn; shields raised. A trumpet sounded. Hooves thundered. The opposing teams collided in the center of the field.

Iron swords spit sparks. The crowd shouted insults and advice. But Rhys saw little of the action. His attention was consumed by Dafyd's pall.

The sorcerer's dark spell was a complicated bit of magic. It would take time and concentration to unravel just enough to slip Rhys's own illusion inside.

He drew a deep breath, and prayed Breena was ready.

A roar rose from the crowd. Rhys's attention snapped back to the field. The melee had been short and brutal, and Gareth's faction had prevailed. Fortunately, the young knight appeared unhurt.

"Sir Gareth put in a fine effort," commented Trent.

"Aye," agreed Kane.

"The brawny Sir Hugh has my coin," commented Floyd.

"Coin?" Howell scoffed. "What coin might that be?"

"Why, the markers I won from you last night."

Rhys ignored the banter. As the six remaining contestants prepared for a series of one-on-one mounted duels, he once again focused his mind on Dafyd's spell. The pall was like a thin, dirty blanket, knotted with threads of dark magic.

Summoning a subtle spell of Light, Rhys went to work moving and shifting the dark strands. Once he opened a narrow rift, he would cast his illusion. He hoped the ruse would blind Dafyd to the light magic being cast. If all went well, Dafyd and Gerlois would remain unaware of Breena's and Igraine's flight. To them, it would appear as if both women remained in their seats. Meanwhile, they would be riding east on the three horses Rhys had stolen the night before, hidden by the most powerful lookaway spell he could muster.

"My God," Floyd shouted. "Tristan of Seaton is down!"

"Not surprising," Trent declared dryly. "My own grandmother sits a horse better than he."

Rhys shook off the distraction of the jests flying around him. It was difficult work, lifting strands of dark magic with only light magic as a lever. Just touching his mind to Dafyd's spell made him feel ill. The spell was like slime—difficult to grasp, even more difficult to hold. Cold sweat broke out on his temple. His efforts would be far easier if he employed deep magic— but that, he did not dare. Not only would casting deep magic alert Dafyd to Rhys's magic, it would also render Rhys unable to cover their escape once he reached Breena and Igraine.

"Oh, well done, Sir Carden!" Floyd exclaimed suddenly. "Did you see that blow he landed to Sir Gareth?"

Rhys's attention wavered.

"Christos!" Trent peered across the field. "That's blood on Gareth's right arm, to be sure."

Floyd clapped Howell on the back. "My imaginary coin is safe, friend."

Howell shook his head. "The contest is not over. Sir Hugh took a mean blow as well. He is favoring his right side."

"We shall see," Floyd answered.

A sheen of cold sweat broke out on Rhys's brow. *There*. He'd succeeded in creating a small, open seam in Dafyd's spell. The bishop, watching the field as intently as any of the other spectators, did not seem to sense anything amiss. Holding the slippery strands of dark magic left Rhys few resources with which to fashion his spell of illusion, however. With great care, he eased part of his attention from Dafyd's spell.

His control on the dark magic faltered. The opening he had made narrowed, but did not close. Swiftly, Rhys turned his mind to the problem of crafting an illusion of Breena and Igraine.

"Ah," said Floyd with satisfaction. "The final contest is set. Sir Hugh against Sir Gareth." He rubbed his hands together. "Now we shall see who's to bed the flame-haired wench."

The spell formed in Rhys's mind. He was almost ready to whisper a Word and drop it into place. Once he did, Breena and Igraine would be free.

Breena's stomach rolled. Gareth had advanced to the last round, but blood stained the sleeve of his tunic. How could he face Sir Hugh? She glared at Rhys across the field. He had promised to stop this. But he hadn't.

Her sense of betrayal was sharp. Her anxiety was overwhelming. Why hadn't Rhys cast his illusion? She sidled a glance at Bishop Dafyd, who sat to her right beyond Igraine and Gerlois. His eyes were on the field, his expression impassive. If he suspected anything was amiss, she could not discern it.

Brother Morfen, standing behind Dafyd, shifted slightly. He gazed at Dafyd, the expression in his good eye steady and calm. It sickened her, knowing he'd endured a beating at Dafyd's hands. The monk was tireless in his devotion to his master. How could he stand such abuse?

The duchess sat with rigid spine, her hands clenched in her lap. If Breena's signal to flee did not come soon, she feared Igraine's resolve would crumble. She looked across the field and willed Rhys to hurry. And she willed Gareth to win his combat with the beastly Sir Hugh. Or at least, to come away from it unharmed.

Gareth and Hugh had each taken up two swords— double-edged *spathas*. Breena leaned forward in her seat, her fingers twisting painfully. Fighting with two weapons meant twice the chance of injury for the combatants. Fighting with no shield meant little chance for defense.

A blast of trumpets sounded. "All stand for Gerlois, Duke of Cornwall!"

The crowd surged to its feet. The duke stood last. All eyes turned toward Breena as Gerlois spoke. The duke proclaimed that, on the morrow at midday, Lady Igraine's cousin would wed the winner of the upcoming contest. Somehow, Breena managed a smile and a regal nod.

The two warriors saluted the duke. She wished she could see Gareth's eyes, but they were shadowed by his visor. Despite the wounds he'd sustained in the melee, he had fought well in the mounted duels. Hugh had also taken a mighty blow; likewise, the older knight showed little effect. Gareth's opponent was larger and heavier; Breena suspected the wagers flying about favored Hugh. She hoped them wrong, but in truth it hardly mattered who won the fight, only that Gareth came out of it unhurt.

Trumpets sounded, and the contest began. The combatants circled, taking each other's measure. Gareth's grip flexed on his swords; Sir Hugh came up on the balls of his feet.

The two knights lunged at the same instant. Swords struck high, then low. Sparks spit from the blades. Gareth moved with cunning; Hugh favored vicious force. It was soon apparent which strategy was more effective. Hugh's powerful reach was longer than his younger opponent's. He pressed his advantage, slashing and advancing as if he were harvesting a field of barley.

Gareth drew first blood, opening a gash on Hugh's thigh. Blood trickled, but the older knight did not miss a step. On a vicious lunge, his blade connected with Gareth's upper arm.

Gareth's weapon hit the ground amid deafening screams and jeers. His right arm fell limply to his side. His left, gripping his one remaining sword, angled into a defensive position.

And Rhys's illusion whispered over Breena's skin like a warm breeze.

Her gaze shot across the field. Rhys raised a hand, and circled it overhead. Her signal to flee.

But she could not move. She stood frozen, transfixed by the duel on the field. Hugh pressed forward swiftly, both swords raised; Gareth stumbled back. The crowd roared. Gerlois and Dafyd were on their feet, leaning forward over the railing. Even Morfen seemed intent on the violence below.

Rhys gestured again, angrily. He was moving now, coming around the field, on a course meant to intercept Breena and Igraine on their flight to the oak grove. There was no time to waste.

Panic bled into Breena's veins. Of course, they must go, no matter what Gareth faced on the field. Gareth himself would tell her the same thing. And surely Sir Hugh would not kill his opponent once he surrendered. She placed a hand on Igraine's shoulder, their prearranged signal. She met the duchess's frightened eyes with a brief nod.

She whispered the words of a lookaway spell. Holding her breath, she kept one eye on the bishop as she and Igraine eased from the booth. Neither Dafyd nor Gerlois so much as blinked in their direction.

She tugged Igraine down the stair. Halfway to the field, the duchess looked back and froze. "Dear Christos!" She started trembling. "We are here, and . . . and there, as well."

Breena glanced back, and felt her own moment of disorientation. It was eerie, holding the duchess's hand, while at the same time looking up to see herself and Igraine seated next to Gerlois and Dafyd.

"Surely this is sorcery," Igraine whispered.

"No. It is Light magic. Come. There is no time to lose."

"Perhaps . . . perhaps I should not go. Perhaps it is wrong. . . ."

Breena's patience with the woman's weakness of spirit had reached its end. "Would you rather remain," she hissed, "and die?"

Whatever color was left in Igraine's face drained away. "I—"

"Come. There is no time to argue. We are going." Breena all but dragged the duchess the last few steps to the grass.

The crowd on the ground had pressed as close to the combatants as the soldiers guarding the edge of the field would allow. With her lookaway spell firmly in place, Breena ducked behind the spectators and urged Igraine to the far corner of the field. She tried desperately to ignore the gasps and groans of the crowd as she urged Igraine toward freedom. She did not see Rhys, but she had no doubt he was near.

She rounded the last of the standing spectators just as a collective roar erupted from the throng. She spun about, catching Igraine by the arm as the duchess fell against her. Gareth was down. Hugh loomed over him, sword raised.

A cry tore from her lips as Hugh's arm slashed. Her heart missed a beat as Gareth rolled. Hugh's sword thudded into the dirt, missing Gareth by a hairs-breadth. Gareth—his right arm limp, his tunic soaked with blood—staggered to his feet and faced his foe.

Dear Goddess. He was not going to surrender.

The crowd sensed it as well. "To the death!" a voice shouted.

Instantly, the throng took up the cry. "To the death!"

A hand caught her arm. "Breena." Rhys suddenly loomed over her. "What are you doing? Run!"

She stared at him. "By the gods, Rhys! Why did you not tell Gareth of our plan?"

Rhys's gaze cut to Igraine, then back to Breena. "I did tell him. He refused to withdraw from the tournament nonetheless. The idiot thought to protect you if I failed."

"To the death!"

"He's not going to surrender! He's going to be killed."

Rhys's jaw clenched. "Then that is his choice."

"No!" She resisted Rhys's tug on her arm. "Rhys, we cannot let Gareth die because of me! Do something."

His gray eyes bored into hers as the frenzied chants grew louder. "What, Breena? What would you have me do?"

"I don't know. Cast another illusion. On the field. Give Gareth the advantage."

"Illusions take time to weave, and concentration to maintain. The spell in the duke's booth is difficult enough to hold. I can't create another at the same time."

Hugh slashed. Gareth leaped backward, too late. Hugh's sword sliced Gareth's tunic, gouging the mail shirt beneath.

Breena gripped Rhys's shoulder. "You must do something. You must! Could you . . . could you use deep magic?"

Rhys spit out a curse that made Igraine flinch. "Are you insane? Dafyd will sense it."

"And he will be distracted by it. You'll save Gareth, and we will get away while Dafyd is trying to figure out what happened."

"What about our escape? If I cast deep magic now, I will not be able to cover our flight."

"I can do it," Breena said. "My magic is strong enough. Please, Rhys! You cannot let Gareth die."

"This is madness." He dragged a hand down his face. "All right. I will try. If you go. Now." He shoved her in the direction of the oaks. "Run. Stay with the horses and do not let your lookaway spell drop."

"Thank you," Breena breathed.

"Thank me when it is over," Rhys muttered. "Now, go!"

Breena lurched toward the shelter of the trees. But Igraine, too long unused to activity, could not keep up the pace. Her slippered foot caught in a rut. Breena grabbed the duchess's arm just in time to prevent a tumble into the mud.

She glanced back at the field. Hugh had dropped one weapon; he stood with his second sword aloft, both hands wrapped around the hilt. Gareth was on his knees before him, struggling to rise.

The crowd was wild. "To the death! To the death!"

"No!" Breena shouted. "Surrender, you idiot!"

Oh, where was Rhys? Breena could not see him. But the fine hairs on the back of her neck were tingling. His magic was gathering.

Igraine screamed as Hugh's sword fell. Rhys's spell struck in the same instant. Gareth slid to one side, as if a giant hand had moved him. Sir Hugh's sword missed its mark. The blade plunged into the earth, sinking all the way to its crosspiece.

The spectators howled. Gareth staggered to his feet, sword in hand. A burst of unnatural energy renewed his charge. Hugh gripped the hilt of his buried sword. Muscles bulging, he tried to heave it from the ground.

It would not budge. Abandoning the weapon, Hugh lunged for another discarded sword, which lay on the ground nearby. Gareth reached the weapon first, and kicked it away. Hugh fell over backward. Gareth planted his boot on Hugh's chest and would not let him rise.

The tip of Gareth's *spatha* pressed at the base of Hugh's throat.

"To the death! To the death!"

Hugh lay supine, chest heaving, arms spread in surrender. For one dreadful moment, Breena thought Gareth might run him through. Her breath left her lungs in a whoosh when Gareth lifted his sword and stepped back.

"I accept your surrender!" he shouted.

Breena heaved a sigh of relief. "Come," she said, taking Igraine's arm. "We must be off."

A cool hand slipped under her elbow. Startled, she looked up, to find Morfen's single eye looking down on her.

"Lady Antonia. What are you and Lady Igraine doing so far from the duke's booth?"

Breena opened her mouth, but no sound emerged. Astonishingly, it was Igraine who answered first.

"The people. . . ." she whispered. "The blood . . . it overwhelmed me. I wished to return to the castle."

"The castle is in the other direction, my lady."

Igraine laid the back of her hand to her forehead. "As are the crowds. I sought to avoid them. I became . . . disoriented. Lady Antonia came after me."

Morfen offered his arm. "Then please, allow me to escort you to my lord Gerlois. He is frantic at your absence." His eyes touched on Breena. "As for Lady Antonia, no doubt she will wish to join her champion on the field."

Chapter Sixteen

So this was death.

A place beyond Light. Beyond hope. The knowledge that no matter how hard one tried, no matter how long one managed to stave off the inevitable, in the end, every fight was lost.

It was bitter knowledge.

Myrddin had so many regrets. So many things he had not done. So many failures. And yet, he did not know how he might have done anything in his life differently. He had always given all of his heart, and all of himself. If that had not been enough, perhaps the failure lay with his intrinsic human imperfection. Not with his choices, or his actions.

Perhaps.

When the light appeared, sparkling at the edges of his consciousness, at first he did not realize its significance. Then the magic flared, and the hope he had allowed to slip from his grasp came upon him like an avalanche.

Vivian.

He strained to reach her. But no matter how hard he tried, he could not drift closer. A rift separated them. Deep and unfathomable, it could not be crossed. Nor could they both enter. The fissure twisted like a river in a gorge, leading . . . away. Away from this place of despair.

And then he understood.

Only one soul would make the journey from this void to the human realm. And like so many decisions he had not wanted to make in his long life, the choice had been given into his hands alone.

He did not hesitate.

"Let it be she."

Breena was to be married at midday. To Sir Hugh.

Gareth was to be executed at dawn.

For sorcery.

Bishop Dafyd had leveled the charge. Sir Hugh, upon accepting his defeat, had gone to retrieve the sword he'd sunk into the ground. He could not do it.

Neither could Gareth, nor any of the knights. Much confusion, and more than a few curses, followed. Finally, the master of the castle guards called for shovels and picks. A quartet of brawny men began to dig; dirt was taken away from the hole in buckets. What remained behind brought gasps, then frantic prayers, to the lips of every man and woman present.

The blade of Hugh's *spatha* had sunk into the center of a large boulder.

The sword could not be moved. Not by any man, nor even by a team of horses. The iron had fused completely with the stone.

"Sorcery!" Dafyd had roared.

The bishop wasted no time in declaring Gareth the perpetrator of the heinous act. His victory in the contest was declared null, and Gareth was taken into captivity. Breena watched in horror as the young knight's companions-in-arms stripped him of his weapons and armor. A series of well-placed kicks rendered him limp and groaning.

Two stakes were quickly pounded into the ground, and chains were brought. Breena clung to Igraine as two of Gerlois's knights hauled Gareth to his feet and secured him between the posts. Duke Gerlois, upon grim consultation with his brother, announced Gareth's sentence: forty lashes less one at dusk, execution by burning at the stake at dawn.

Numb with shock, Breena looked desperately for Rhys. He was nowhere to be seen. The spell he'd cast would have drained his magic. She hoped it had not done worse than that. Two soldiers bowed low to Igraine, and declared their orders to escort the duchess and her ladies back to the castle. There was nothing for Breena to do but go.

Guilt crushed down on her shoulders. This disaster was her fault! She knew how unpredictable deep magic was. She never should have begged Rhys to cast it. She'd wanted to save Gareth; she had doomed him instead.

Dusk approached. Breena, sick with dread, paced Igraine's solar. The duchess herself stood at the window, gazing over the castle's outer wall to the tournament field. Nesta brought the evening meal. Only Lady Bertrice sat down to partake of it.

"To think," Gerlois's sister said between bites. "A sorcerer lurking among the duke's knights! God only knows what manner of evil the man has perpetrated without our knowledge."

"Dermot says 'tis certain Sir Gareth is the cause of the soured wine he found in the cellars," Nesta offered with an air of horrified awe. "And Cook insists he set maggots into the carcass of a pig that was slaughtered just yesterday."

"No doubt the brute caused the fever that killed that stable boy three nights past," Bertrice declared. "Dear Christos! My blood runs cold, Antonia! Just think of what hellish perversions the man would have forced on you as his wife."

Distant cheers drifted through the tower windows. Nesta moved to Igraine's side and peered out.

"They've begun the flogging, then," Lady Bertrice said with satisfaction.

"Aye, they must have done," Nesta said. "Though with the glare of the torches on the field, and the men crowded 'round the stakes, 'tis difficult to make out."

Breena thought she would be ill. She wanted to turn away, but some horrible compulsion drove her to the window. Hugging herself tightly, she joined Igraine and Nesta. As the maid had noted, the distance and angle of their view hid the flogging. But the eager cheers of the crowd, as they counted off the blows, were all too audible.

When it was done, and the throng had thinned, Breena was left with a clear view of Gareth sagging in his bonds. Dear gods. He looked half dead already. She touched the window, as if she could make contact with him from a distance.

She cried out as a sharp crack split the glass under her finger. A jagged fissure shot across the pane. Breena snatched her hand back and stared. Another image from her nightmare.

She thought of the dawn, and shuddered.

"Tell me again," Trent said seriously, "why this is a good idea."

"Because you and Howell are two men," Rhys explained patiently. Simple logic appealed best to a drunken sot. "And there are presently only two men guarding Sir Gareth."

"Ah." Then, "And tell me again what you will be doing whilst Howell and I distract the guards?"

"I will be freeing Sir Gareth."

"And why might ye be doin' that?" slurred Howell. "Damn me, but I've forgotten."

Why? Because Rhys would never be able to face

Breena again if he did not stop Gareth's execution. That is, if the poor bastard was even still alive. He might not be. His flogging had been horrific, enough to curdle Rhys's stomach with the memory of his own long-ago whipping.

"Because Sir Gareth is clearly innocent," Rhys said. "It was Sir Hugh, after all, who sank the sword into the stone. Hugh is the sorcerer. Not Gareth."

"But 'twas Sir Gareth who won the contest!" protested Trent. "Surely he is the sorcerer. Bishop Dafyd said as much."

Rhys looked right and left and lowered his voice. "If Sir Gareth were truly a sorcerer, do you think he could be held with rusty chains and two half-witted guards?"

Howell thunked his mug on the table and swiped the back of his hand across his mouth. "'Tis true, that. Dafyd is a fool. Rhys is right. Gareth is falsely accused. We canna let an innocent man die, Trent."

"But what of Sir Hugh?" Trent demanded. "Is the man to go free? Or shall we catch him and chain him in Gareth's place?" He grimaced. "With, perhaps, stronger chains and more guards?"

Rhys would have laughed at that, if the situation weren't so grave. "Who is to say any magic was involved at all? Sir Hugh is a beast of a man. I've no doubt he could pull whole trees from the ground if he had a mind to. No doubt he could easily thrust a sword into rock."

A sober Trent would have laughed this reasoning over the cliffs and into the sea. But drunk as he was, the small man greeted Rhys's daft theory with hearty approval. "Aye, and consider 'twas Dafyd who accused the poor bastard. The bloody bishop sees demons under every rock and stone."

Rhys stood. "So we are agreed, then."

Howell blinked up at him. "Agreed to what, man?"

"To rescuing Sir Gareth."

Trent's brow furrowed. "Did we say we would do that?"

"Aye," Rhys said, his patience growing thin. "We did."

"Oh," Trent said. "That's all right, then."

Howell heaved himself to his feet, and nearly lost his balance. He gripped the back of his chair. "Best get on with it, before I fall face-first in the mud." He grinned. "Or sober up."

At last. Rhys had waited all night for his magic to recover from his earlier deep magic spell. Dawn would be upon them soon. If they were to rescue Gareth before his execution, they had to act now.

Howell squinted down at Rhys. "Have we a plan?"

"We do," Rhys confirmed.

"Ah." He ruminated for a moment, then asked, "Is it a good one?"

"We shall see."

Trent drained his mug and leaped to his feet. Even stinking drunk, the nimble acrobat had no trouble finding his balance. Howell was less steady. Rhys caught him by the arm. If the giant fell, he'd hit the ground with the force of an oak.

Rhys herded the pair onto the hill overlooking the tournament field. He shifted the strap of his pack while he considered his quarry below. Gareth's arms were spread wide, his manacled wrists chained at shoulder height to twin posts. His naked back, a bloody mass of flayed skin, was enough to turn any man's stomach. Gareth had lost consciousness during the flogging. He'd sagged in his bonds like a dead man most of the night. Now, two hours before dawn, his head had begun to roll from side to side.

A short distance in front of the wounded knight, a merry campfire, shielded by a leather windbreak, crackled. The two soldiers charged with guarding the prisoner crouched on the ground, throwing dice.

Trent peered around Rhys. Wincing, he brought his hand up to shield his eyes. "The moon has set, but by God, that fire! It gives off too damn much light. We'll be seen."

"You want to be seen," Rhys told him. "Don't you remember? That's part of the plan. You and Howell are to distract the guards, while I free Sir Gareth."

"Oh," Trent said. "I forgot."

"Let's get on with it, then," Howell said, starting down the hill.

Trent grabbed the hem of Howell's shirt. "Wait just a randy cock's instant!" He looked at Rhys. "What are we to say to the brutes?"

"Anything. It does not matter. Just keep them occupied."

Howell nodded sagely. "Just as I thought."

"Go," Rhys said.

The pair went without further protest, staggering down the hill into the wind. Rhys crept after them. Crouching just beyond the ring of torchlight, he turned his focus inward. He could not afford a mistake. Gareth's life depended on the strength of the illusion he would cast.

Trent and Howell's forms blurred. Howell's hulking figure became slender, almost willowy. Trent's body stretched taller. The gaits of both men smoothed. Their clothing changed. Their hips rounded.

The last detail Rhys added to his illusion was a pair of very large breasts for each man. He had to make absolutely sure the guards did not look away.

His lips twitched as his friends glided toward the guards. Howell murmured a greeting. Whatever remark he'd truly uttered fell on the guards' ears as a suggestive purr. Rhys called a lookaway spell for himself and made his move.

The keys to Gareth's chains were attached to one of the guards' belts. He would have to pick the lock, then.

A tricky business, but not impossible. He kept a shard of iron in his pack for just such emergencies. He palmed it as he approached Gareth from behind.

Meanwhile, a farce played out at the campfire.

"Well, well. What have we here?" The taller soldier smirked. His gaze raked Howell from head to toe and back again.

Gareth's shredded back was a mess of dried blood and oozing fluids. A low moan issued from the knight's throat. Rhys crouched in his shadow.

"Sir Gareth," he whispered. "I've come to help. Can you walk, do you think?"

Gareth started. "Who's there?" he croaked. "Where are you?"

"Quiet," Rhys cautioned. "'Tis Rhys. Breena's friend. And I am just behind you."

The guards were on their feet now, circling Trent and Howell, their faces lit with lust. Trent's and Howell's alcohol-glazed eyes were glassy with confusion.

Standing slowly, Rhys reached toward the manacle encircling Gareth's right wrist. Wrapping his fingers around the metal, he inserted his iron shard into the lock. More time passed than he'd intended, and yet the lock would not give way.

"I cannot see you," Gareth said.

"I'm shadowed with magic."

Gareth squinted in the direction of Rhys's voice. "It was your magic on the field that sank Hugh's sword into the stone."

Air whistled through Rhys's teeth as the lock gave way. "Yes. Apologies. I never should have cast that spell."

"If you had not . . ." The effort of talking was taking its toll. ". . . I would be dead."

"You are almost dead now," Rhys said, circling to the second manacle.

"My . . . own fault. Should have . . . withdrawn. As you told me."

Rhys caught the second manacle as it fell free. He glanced back at the guards. The shorter man tried to drape his arm around Trent's shoulders, and stumbled when his goal turned out to be inexplicably closer to the ground than he had thought. His friend made a grab for Howell's elusive breasts. It would not be long before the guards, dim as they were, realized something was very wrong.

Rhys fabricated an illusion of Gareth's body hanging limply from its chains. The real Gareth wobbled a few steps away, his face drawn tight with pain. Rhys caught his arm and turned him away from the image of himself.

"Can you walk, do you think?"

"I can if I must," Gareth said through gritted teeth.

Rhys hoped that was true. He shot a glance toward Howell. The tall guard leaned in and stole a kiss. The giant flung the man back.

"You bloody swine! I ought to cut off your stones for that!"

"By Christos, you're a feisty piece. Come now, sweet. Do not tease a man."

It was past time to flee.

"Come." Rhys draped the knight's arm over his shoulders, and urged him across the field as fast as he dared.

"Enough play," the taller guard declared. "You two whores are comely enough. What's your price?"

Trent's reply burned Rhys's ears. The soldiers chortled. Rhys glanced back in time to see one of them slap a hand on Howell's rump.

Howell responded by planting his fist into the soldier's face.

Rhys shifted his illusion, melting it into a second

lookaway spell. The two whores blurred, then seemed to wink out of existence entirely.

The taller soldier's slap met nothing but air. He spun about. "Where is she? Where is the other one?"

"I don't know! They were right here."

"They cannot have just vanished!"

"Not without sorcery."

Swords hissed from scabbards as the men looked wildly around. Rhys allowed Trent and Howell to spot him, fleeing across the meadow with Gareth. The pair soon appeared at Rhys's side, panting.

Gareth stumbled, nearly dragging Rhys down with him. Trent's eyes widened.

"You have him? I did not think you even tried to remove him. A moment ago, he was still—"

"No time to talk," Rhys said as Gareth's knees buckled. "Howell, help me, man! The sky is lightening. We have to get him to the grove before the guards discover he's gone."

"Those nancy bastards?" Howell said darkly. "Let them come. I'll throw their arses over the cliffs."

"Good God, Rhys! The man is all but a corpse."

Trent's assessment was not far off the mark. The stripes on Gareth's back were jagged and deep, and already starting to fester. The gash Sir Hugh had sliced into Gareth's sword arm was a cleaner cut, but no less worrisome.

The knight was conscious, lying on his stomach in the dirt, gritting his teeth against his moans. The horses Rhys had stolen earlier were hidden nearby. Trent, sobering rapidly, helped Rhys assess Gareth's wounds, while Howell stood guard at the edge of the copse. Crouched behind a broad trunk, he peered toward the tournament field.

"Soldiers are running about like so many headless roosters. But none come this way. I canna think why.

'Tis the first place I'd look, were I searching for an escaped prisoner."

"Aye." Trent eyed Rhys. "'Tis very odd, isn't it?"

"Exceedingly," Howell agreed. "They've started in this direction more than once. Each time, they turn away."

"Almost as if by magic," Trent said.

Rhys shifted uneasily. "You and Howell should go. The others will be looking for you. This is my affair. I would not want you to suffer for it."

"Indeed it is your affair," Trent said. "But I find myself wondering, just what kind of affair is it? Swords sunk in stones. Guards who cannot tell men from whores. A wounded knight who appears chained to a post long after he's escaped."

Rhys met the small man's gaze. "Truly, it is better if you do not know."

For once, Trent's confidence faltered. "I daresay you are right about that."

Howell rose and abandoned his post. "You are a Druid. You have cast some sort of spell over this grove. That is why the soldiers turn away."

Rhys did not see the point in denying it. "Aye."

"Are you Myrddin's ally?" Trent demanded.

"I have never seen Myrddin," Rhys admitted. "I cannot precisely claim to be his ally, but yes, at the moment, I am aiding his cause. Sir Gareth is Myrddin's spy in Gerlois's camp. And even that is more than you should know. Please. Go back to Floyd and Kane. You do not want to know more."

Trent put his hands on his thighs and pushed to his feet. "I do not know what you and Sir Gareth are about, but I'll be damned if I'll just leave you to it. Druid you may be, but you are still one of my troupe. If the pair of you are Myrddin's allies, you aid the high king. And Britain. You have my support."

"And mine," Howell said.

from one man to the other, humbled by their loyalty. The truth was, he needed their help. Desperately.

"Thank you," he said quietly. "I must cast a healing spell. The magic will work better with the aid of clean, hot water. And willow bark." His gaze ran over Gareth's back. "And bandages."

Trent nodded. "Say no more."

In the hour before dawn, Breena lay in her bed, wide awake, stomach churning. When the faraway shouting of angry men sounded outside, she jumped up and ran to her small window. But the opening faced the ocean, and she learned nothing.

In the outer room, Lady Bertrice was just rising. "What is happening?"

"I do not—"

Breena broke off as Nesta barged through the door. Hot water sloshed over the edge of the bucket she carried. "Oh, my ladies!" The maid was trembling like a leaf in a gale. "The kitchen is abuzz with the news! 'Tis awful!"

"What? What is wrong?" Lady Bertrice snapped.

"What is not? First, Sir Gareth—he is gone. Slipped his chains in the night. By sorcery, they say!"

Breena's relief was so profound that her knees buckled. She all but fell into the nearest chair.

"The fools!" Bertrice muttered. "They should have killed the brute last night."

"He was all but dead, they say, after the flogging," Nesta replied. She set down the bucket. "He could not have escaped without help."

"Help?" Bertrice asked sharply. "Who would aid a sorcerer?"

Breena gripped the arms of her chair, and prayed that Rhys and Gareth were well hidden.

"They are saying 'twas Myrddin himself, my lady."

"Myrddin! How can that be? The Druid does not stray from Uther's side."

"That's just it," Nesta said, her face flushed. "Uther Pendragon is all but upon us! His knights ride in Cornwall! My lord Gerlois's scouts brought word just this hour past. The duke is gathering Dumnonia's forces. There is to be war."

"At last." Lady Bertrice voice vibrated with satisfaction.

Breena stared at Gerlois's sister. "The prospect of war pleases you?"

"But of course. My brother has cultivated this conflict for three years. Gerlois should be high king of Britain. Not that worthless whelp Uther. Now he will be."

Breena swallowed. "But . . . what of Myrddin? It is said Uther is invincible with his Druid at his side."

A smile touched Bertrice's lips. "No longer," she murmured. "Dafyd will see to that."

A chill ran the length of Breena's spine.

Gerlois's sister rose and moved to the window. "Tintagel prepares for siege, I see."

"Aye, my lady," Nesta said. "But 'tis only a precaution. Duke Gerlois vows war will not touch his duchess. He will lead his army to the pass at Dimilioc. They intend an ambush."

Bertrice murmured her approval. "An excellent strategy." She turned to Breena. "Come. Let us inform the duchess she will soon be queen."

Chapter Seventeen

Rhys's transformation took hold with a sickening wrench. Agony tore at his limbs. Muscles and bones melted in consuming fire; razor-sharp teeth flayed his skin. His body twisted, dissolved, changed. Skin thinned, limbs changed, feathers sprouted. Then came a sharp moment of blackness, when his entire existence seemed to stop.

When the world returned, it was sharper and simpler than before. Every sight was clearer, every smell sweeter, every sound louder. The sea breeze ruffled his feathers.

The merlin lurched to its feet, unsteady with its first hop. But the awkwardness soon fell away when Rhys spread his wing and took to the air.

The world looked very different from the sky.

As always, the view from on high filled him with awe. Man was not meant to see the moors rolled out far beneath him like a blanket. The sight was so sharp and pure it nearly hurt to look upon it.

Rhys tilted his falcon wings, catching an updraft. The overwhelming sense of freedom that was an integral part of his shape-shifting talent warred with the numbing fear that had driven him to call the dangerous deep magic once again.

He could not enter Tintagel as a minstrel. The castle gates had slammed closed upon the scout's report of

Uther's approaching army—for the duchess's protection, Gerlois had proclaimed. The castle prepared for siege, while Gerlois's army prepared to head off Uther's forces at Dimilioc. Trent had been correct, Rhys thought, when he'd asserted that Gerlois's tournament had been little more than a ruse to keep his lords and knights close at hand in case of war.

It wanted but two days to the full moon, when Breena believed the events of her vision would unfold. The fact that Uther was on the attack surely meant Myrddin had broken out of his trance. Uther did not fight without the Druid at his side.

But even if Uther prevailed against Gerlois, Rhys very much doubted the king could take Tintagel before the full moon's rising. Rhys was not willing to leave Breena trapped inside the castle past that night.

And so Rhys had once again called deep magic, and damned be the consequences. He flew toward Tintagel. He'd land on the duchess's roof terrace, and go to Breena. Sir Gareth, who remained under Howell's care, had revealed the location of the entrance to the caves below the castle. Trent had promised to have a boat waiting for Rhys's escape.

But as he approached Tintagel, Rhys discovered he could not even get close to the castle. Every time he tried, the surge of ill wind emanating from Dafyd's pall tossed him backward. In the end, he was forced to admit defeat.

He circled once around the tower, considering what to do next. Shifting back to human form would leave his magic useless for half a day; that was time he could not afford to waste. And so, swallowing his pride, he turned eastward.

He needed Myrddin.

He very much feared the king's counselor was the only man who could help him. He flew east with the greatest speed wind and wing could muster. He did not know the precise location of the king's army. Passing over Gerlois's advance, he prayed he could find Uther in time to prevent the king's army from riding into the duke's ambush.

It was nearly sunset by the time he spied Uther's army, setting up camp on the moors. A banner bearing a red dragon snapped above a large tent. Myrddin would be at his king's side.

He dived low, landing in a gully partially shielded from the soldiers' cooking fires. Folding his wings, he crouched close to the ground. His mind reached for the magic that would dissolved his falcon form.

He braced himself for the pain. It came in great rippling waves. Skin and flesh, muscle, bone, and sinew . . . stretching, contorting. Heat flashed in a shock along his limbs. It was far worse, changing from bird to human than the other way 'round. His human self craved the freedom his animal form granted, but his merlin form had no love of his humanity. He gritted his teeth, determined not to cry out.

He failed. He opened his beak; his bird's shriek emerged as a low moan, snatched away by the wind. He crossed his arms, suddenly cold and naked of feathers. The ground scratched his bare skin. He lay curled in a ball, shivering.

Footsteps sounded nearby. In the aftermath of using deep magic, Rhys could call no spell to cover his position. He froze, willing himself to sink into the ground. The footsteps came closer.

A rough hand grasped his upper arm. An instant later, he was on his feet, his shoulder nearly yanked from its socket.

"Ho! What have we here?"

Rhys, rallying as much dignity as possible while naked, regarded the knight impassively. "I've come to talk to the high king."

"Ye don't say? Well, at least ye have no place in which to hide a weapon."

The man chortled heartily at his own poor joke. His gaze flicked past Rhys, and encountered nothing but moorlands. "Where are your clothes, man? Your camp? Surely there is more than just you and your skin in all this desolation."

Rhys inhaled and took a gamble. "I bear a message for the king's counselor."

The man's demeanor abruptly changed. The corners of his mouth turned down. "A message for Myrddin?"

"Aye."

Suspicion flared in the knight's eyes. "From whom?"

"I will speak with Myrddin alone," Rhys said. "Or the king, of course," he added belatedly.

"Naked?"

Rhys felt his skin flush. "If I might beg a spare shirt and breeches. . . ."

The knight snorted. "Come along. We'll see about clothing, then inform the king of your request. Whether Uther deigns to listen to your tale, or whether the king orders you tossed off the nearest cliff, is another matter."

The rumble of conversation in the camp turned to laughter as Rhys, naked, strode between the rows of tents. The knight who had found him for the most part ignored his comrade's shouts, save to bark orders for clothing. Rhys was soon supplied with a dirty shirt and torn breeches. Uther, he was told, would speak with him.

The high king occupied the central tent of the camp. Uther, resplendent in full armor, his red and white tunic emblazoned with his dragon standard, stood before a makeshift table. A map was unrolled upon it; the officer on Uther's right pointed to a section of the parchment. A second warrior, on the king's left, spoke in low tones. Neither man, Rhys thought with keen disappointment, could be Myrddin. Both were far too young.

The king's discussion ceased abruptly when Rhys, accompanied by four guards, entered the tent. Uther raised his head, and regarded the newcomer with undisguised curiosity.

Rhys could not stifle his gasp.

Britain's high king was a powerfully built warrior. Whatever the rumors concerning his Druidess mother, his dark hair, olive complexion, and patrician nose proclaimed him a son of Rome. But Uther's Roman heritage was not the reason for Rhys's astonishment. Nay. What stunned Rhys was that Uther Pendragon might have been Marcus Aquila's twin.

Gods. Rhys scrubbed a hand down his face. Was he dreaming? Or had the deep magic he'd just emerged from scrambled his brain? Either possibility seemed more plausible than the fact of the man standing before him. The similarity between Britain's high king and Breena's half brother was so great that for one insane instant, Rhys considered the possibility that Marcus had come from the past.

But when Uther spoke, his accent and brusque manner were very different from Marcus's. "You were found lurking about outside the camp, I am told." His lips curved. "Stark naked."

"Aye. I have a message for Myrddin. Where might I find him?"

Uther gazed upon Rhys for a long moment. His eyes narrowed, and something in his expression shifted. He nodded to his officers, and to the two men who had accompanied Rhys into the tent. "Leave us. I would talk with this man alone."

The guards bowed and filed out. The knight on the king's left was not pleased. "Sire! You know nothing of this man."

The other knight agreed. "We will remain."

Uther clenched his fist, then seemed to force himself to relax the grip. "The man is unarmed, and my guard is outside. You will leave us."

"But, sire, he speaks of Myrddin—"

"Leave us!" Uther roared. "He is no threat to me. At least, not at the moment."

The men, frowning, saluted and exited the tent. Uther crossed to a side table and poured a goblet of wine. Sipping it, he eyed Rhys. "You come for Myrddin. And you employed deep magic to get here."

Rhys's brows rose. "How did you know?"

Uther met his gaze squarely. "Your aura. It is muddy."

Rhys sucked in a breath. Uther was Druid? This, he had not expected. Drained from his shifting, he had not attempted to view the king's aura. But it was apparent that Uther could see Rhys's.

Rhys peered through the numbness of his dimmed magic. He caught a snatch of blue light about Uther's head. With a shock, he realized the power was obscured by the same dull silver cage that crippled Igraine's magic.

"You are Druid," Rhys said steadily. "But your power is not strong. Can you do anything apart from reading auras?"

The king frowned. "You overreach yourself. Who are you? What do you want of Myrddin?"

"I need to speak with him about a matter of grave importance."

"You will speak with me, not Myrddin. Who are you? From whence do you come?"

"My name is Rhys. I come from—" He hesitated. "I come most recently from Tintagel."

"Tintagel?" For the first time, Uther's arrogance faltered. "You come from Tintagel?"

"I do. The situation there is grave, sire. Gerlois received reports of your army's movement. His forces are already on the march. They intend an ambush at Dimilioc. In the meantime, Bishop Dafyd holds the castle, and the duchess, in the grip of a foul spell."

"You lie. If you'd truly come from Tintagel, you would know the duchess is no longer in the castle. She is safe with Myrddin."

"She is not, sire. Myrddin was expected at Tintagel, but he did not arrive. He was snared by deep magic. I had hoped he had escaped by now, and had joined you."

Uther paled. "Who *are* you, Druid? How do you know of such dark doings?" Uther's eyes narrowed. "Unless you have had a hand in them."

"You think me an ally of Dafyd?" Rhys demanded. "I assure you, I am not. If I were, I would hardly be here, informing you of Gerlois's movements."

"I do not know that you tell the truth," Uther countered. "Perhaps you seek to misguide me."

"I seek only to enter Tintagel! There is a woman there—another Druid, my . . . friend. Myrddin brought her to the castle to protect the duchess. Now she and Igraine are both trapped. My own magic cannot pierce Dafyd's pall."

Uther's right hand curled into a fist. "The bishop's magic will not turn away swords and arrows. If Igraine is inside that castle, I will tear it down stone by stone to reach her."

"A pretty sentiment," Rhys said dryly. "You may succeed in fighting your way through Gerlois's army, but you will not succeed in breaching Dafyd's spell. Such magic can only be fought with magic. Magic far stronger than my own."

Uther appeared shaken. "We need Myrddin."

"Have you no idea where he might be?"

"He was to be at Tintagel! I was to meet him there!"

Planting his palms atop Uther's map, Rhys leaned across the table and repeated what he'd overheard Breena telling Gareth. "Three days ago, Myrddin sat entranced in what appeared to be a small thatched cottage. Rose canes arched outside the window, and an old woman, his wife, lay beside him upon an iron-framed bed. Do you know this place?"

"I know it well," Uther said. "I have been there many times. It is a cottage in Siluria. Myrddin and his wife often visit there."

Rhys looked down at Uther's map. "Show me."

Chapter Eighteen

By dawn Rhys's magic had recovered enough to allow him to regain his merlin form. As Uther's army rode in a wide arc, circling to surprise Gerlios's forces from behind, Rhys took to the sky. He flew north, over the wide stretch of the Sabrina channel to a swath of countryside he knew very well. The farmland of Siluria, now mostly fallow, lay to the north of the shrunken city of Isca Silurum, once the bustling home of Rome's Second Legion.

He found the cottage as Uther had described it, nestled in the foothills. If Rhys was not mistaken, Myrddin's cottage had been built, ironically, on lands that had once belonged to Breena's father, Lucius Aquila.

He circled above the dwelling, unwilling to land and shift unless he was certain his quarry was inside. Once back in human form, it would be sunset before he could summon the magic necessary to fly back to Tintagel.

The hut's single door was closed, as were most of its shutters, but smoke curled over the roof. Someone was inside. Rhys swooped low, landing on the branch of a tree near the only open window. Rose canes arched before it.

A sharp cry to his left arrested his attention. Another merlin perched on the branch of a neighboring tree. The bird eyed Rhys, its wings unfolding. Rhys mimicked the aggressive pose. For a moment, he thought the bird would attack to defend its territory. But after a moment, its threatening posture deflated.

Rhys returned his attention to the window. It was set, surprisingly, with glass. Weak blue sparks crackled behind the clear surface. Magic. The magical signature was one he'd seen before, in his own time, in the meadow of the standing stone.

He had found Myrddin at last. The aura of the woman with him gave off a faint sparkle of white— Seer's magic. Myrddin's wife had recently been very close to death, and remained as feeble as a newly hatched wren. As for Myrddin's magic . . . it was hardly any stronger than the old woman's. The Druid had only just emerged from a spell of very deep magic.

Troubled, Rhys flew to the ground. Had he come all this way, only to find Myrddin too weak to help him? If he shifted now, it would be midnight before he had the strength to return to Cornwall. Perhaps he should turn around and fly back to Uther, or to Tintagel. But there was no solution in either of those places. And no time to find one.

Myrddin, even weakened, knew more about Dafyd and his magic than Rhys could hope to discover by the time the full moon rose tomorrow eve. The old Druid was still Rhys's best hope of gaining entrance to Tintagel.

He gritted his teeth and endured the pain of his transformation. Lying in the grass, panting, he fought back the fatigue. Gaining his feet, he stumbled to the door and gave it a shove; it opened easily.

A figure stood waiting, just past the threshold. The subtle drift of the woman's aura trickled from an open doorway leading to the hut's back room.

"Rhys." The relief in Myrddin's voice was palpable. "At last."

Rhys was taken aback. "You . . . know me? You expected me?"

Myrddin held his staff in one hand, and a bundle in the other. He tossed it; reflexively, Rhys caught it. Shirt and breeches.

"I expected you long before this, if truth be told. But then, I did not properly consider how little you know."

Myrddin crossed to the table and struck a flint. He nursed the spark to flame on the tinder, and lit the lamp. Rhys shoved his legs into the breeches, and pulled the shirt over his head.

"You followed Breena here from the past." Myrddin's gazed raked Rhys intently. Rhys resisted the urge to smooth his hair and adjust his borrowed clothing.

"Aye. I found the remnants of your spell and followed it. How did you know?"

Myrddin glanced out the window. The merlin Rhys had seen earlier was still perched on the branch, preening one long wing. "You might say a bird told me."

"You communicate with the merlin. You send it forth as a spy." Much as Rhys did with Hefin.

"Among other animals."

Rhys regarded him impassively. "Can you shift as well?"

Myrddin hesitated. "I do have that power. I do not use it often." He sighed. "I tell you, I was stunned when I found you had entered this time. I would not have thought you had the courage to cast such deep magic. I should have guessed, though, you would be an idiot."

Anger heated Rhys's blood. "It is not I who am the idiot, old man. It is you! You've manipulated the most dangerous force imaginable—time itself. How dare you risk Breena in such a scheme? She does not belong in this world. Nor do I."

"We are in agreement on that point. If there had been any other way . . ." He sighed. "But there was not. Breena alone possessed the magic I needed."

"For what purpose? What sort of cursed plot are you brewing?"

"I protect Igraine, of course. I failed once, and nearly lost her. If I fail a second time, the future will turn to blood and ashes. I needed a Seer. One who could link her magic to Igraine's repressed power."

"Because your own Seer—your wife—no longer could," Rhys guessed.

Myrddin ran a hand down his face, ending with a yank on his long beard. His voice shook. "Precisely. Most likely, I should have let Vivian go, and done the job of protecting Igraine myself. I should have sacrificed my wife to my duty. *Our* duty. She would have been the first to tell me to do so."

The old man's shoulders seemed to crumple. "I found . . . I could not. I could not let her die! I thought, if I found another Seer, one who could keep Igraine safe for a few days, I could buy some time in which to save Vivian."

"How did you know to search for Breena?"

"Vivian can See into the past as well as into the future," Myrddin replied. "She is well acquainted with your time, and with the settlement on Avalon."

"She's watched us?"

"Yes, for years. I traveled to your time to fetch Breena. I did not expect to lure you here as well." He gave an unexpected snort of amusement. "I should have guessed at the possibility, though. I should have known losing Breena would turn your honor to dust. Your grandfather, I think, would not be pleased."

"You know of Cyric as well?"

Myrddin nodded. "His legacy and prophecies survive, even if Avalon has not. He was a great Druid. But his fear of deep magic twisted his judgment."

"Only an idiot would not fear deep magic."

"Only an idiot would let himself be ruled by that fear." Myrddin's lips pressed into a line. He turned abruptly. He paced to the hearth, and jabbed at the smoldering logs with his staff.

Rhys was silent. Myrddin spoke the truth. Fear and guilt had ruled Cyric's life. Rhys had not fully understood what evil those destructive emotions had wrought until shortly before his grandfather's death.

Myrddin spoke into the ashes of the hearth. "One cannot cower when evil rears its head, Rhys. Cyric Saw two versions of Britain's destiny—one light, one dark. I have worked all my life to ensure the prophecy of Light overwhelms its darker counterpart. I have cast magic of the Light, and deep magic as well, to that end. But the future remains uncertain."

"Perhaps the Light has already failed. From what I can see, this Britain already contains every darkness my grandfather feared."

Myrddin turned from the hearth. His expression was grave. "I assure you, as dark as things are now, they can get much worse. There are forces at work here, Rhys, that you do not understand. Evil is eager to doom Britain to a future of violence and misery. The land's fate hinges on deep magic. How could I refuse to take up the fight?"

A muscle in Rhys's jaw locked. "Your reckless actions could easily pull both sides of this conflict into the void. Fate belongs to the gods. Mere humans should not interfere."

"When I was young, I thought as you do," Myrddin said quietly. "Since then, life has taught me that good and evil are woven into one cloth. It is not so easy to separate the strands. Not without destroying the world. Our hope lies in the knowledge that gods war with each other, as humans do. With magic, fate itself can be changed. Each man must choose his loyalty, and act on it."

"I will not argue with you, old man, except to say

that whatever your struggle, you had no right to involved Breena in it. She is young and sheltered. Little more than a child."

To Rhys's surprise, Myrddin laughed. "Ah, Rhys. You do Breena such disservice. She is no child. She is a woman—a willful and beautiful one. Any man—save you, apparently—can see that."

Rhys swore. "You go too far—"

"Breena carries the strength of her Celtic ancestors, and the shrewdness of her Roman ones. It is a formidable combination. One you do not fully appreciate."

"She is an innocent!"

Myrddin sent Rhys a long, thoughtful look. Rhys resisted the urge to squirm under the Druid's scrutiny.

"Not so innocent any longer, I would wager," Myrddin said at last.

Heat flooded Rhys's face, his anger fleeing before a wave of guilt. "I . . . I have dishonored Breena, it is true. I did not mean to. I tried to stay away, but—"

Myrddin chuckled. "Breena has told me how much trouble you are to her. I see that she did not stretch the truth."

"Breena told you of me?" The notion did not please Rhys at all.

"She mentioned you when we first met at the Great Mother's stone. She was crying. I believe you were to blame."

"Most probably," Rhys muttered.

Myrddin's tone softened. "Do you not realize that you could never dishonor Breena with your love? Nor even with your lust—no, not even with the darkest aspect of it?"

Rhys's face burned. "You do not know what you are talking about, old man."

"Perhaps not. Just remember, Rhys, that I have lived a long life. Little shocks me. I may understand more than you guess. And I am telling you, your love and your lust are rare gifts, one I believe Breena would welcome. The only dishonor comes in not allowing her to return those same gifts to you."

"She believes herself in love with me. But I would ruin her life, should I be weak enough to claim her heart. She would come to hate me. I could not bear that." Unsettled, Rhys turned and paced the width of the small room.

Myrddin's voice followed him. "Did you ever consider, Rhys, that when you look at Breena, you see not her weaknesses, but your own? Do you think her so inconstant as to betray the man she loves at the first sign of hardship?" He made a sound of disgust. "You are the worst of fools if you allow your misplaced guilt to blind you to her strength."

Rhys halted, his spine stiffening. "I do not need your advice where Breena is concerned."

"I believe you do. You may have all the arrogance of youth, but I possess the wisdom of age. You are so certain you are right in this. I tell you, you are not."

"I will discuss this with you no further," Rhys said tersely. "It is not your affair, and there are more immediate concerns to deal with. Any discussion of Breena's future is moot unless we remove her from Tintagel."

"And Igraine with her. The duchess cannot be risked."

"And Igraine as well," Rhys agreed impatiently, "but only because Breena will not leave the castle without her. Now that your wife is safe, you must come with me to Tintagel, and lift Dafyd's pall."

"Do you not think that if I could travel to Tintagel, I would be there already?" Leaning heavily on his staff, Myrddin made his way from the hearth to the table. He sat. Rhys experienced a wave of apprehension as he realized for the first time the depth of the old Druid's weariness.

"I have spent the last sennight fighting for my life, and Vivian's, in the Lost Lands. The magic I cast there was very deep, and very dangerous. It absorbed every last dram of my strength." His hand, gripping his staff, shook. "Indeed, I believed myself lost forever. I still do not know, precisely, why I was spared. I emerged from the abyss, but my magic remains very far away. I do not know how long it might be before it returns. Or if it ever will." He sighed. "Perhaps it was wrong of me to place Vivian's welfare before Igraine's. But I did, and I do not regret it. And the Goddess must have given me her blessing, for she has sent you to save Igraine's life in my place."

Rhys frowned. "Why is the duchess's life so important? Who is she? Why is her Druid magic caged?"

Myrddin hesitated. "It is better you do not know. You do not belong in this time."

"I am in it up to my neck, nevertheless. If I am to abandon my principals in support of your scheme, I have a right to understand why."

The old Druid tugged on his beard, considering this. "Perhaps you are right." He gestured to the chair opposite. "Sit, Rhys, and I will tell you."

Rhys sat, not moving his gaze from Myrddin's face. The lamp flame flickered between them. The Druid glanced down at his clasped hands before speaking.

"Igraine is Vivian's distant kin. When Igraine's mother died in childbirth, Vivian raised the babe. She knew even before the birth that the child would be important." The old Druid raised his eyes to Rhys's. "Igraine's mother, you see, was a direct descendant, on the female line, of the woman you know as the Lady."

"Avalon's Lady? The woman who brought the Carpenter Prophet's Grail from the east?"

"Yes."

Rhys sat back in his chair. "Then Igraine's mother was a Daughter of the Lady." A Druidess with the immense power of her legendary ancestor. Like Gwen, and like Owein's wife, Clara. "And Igraine is a Daughter as well."

"She is. Igraine is descended from Breena's uncle, Owein, and his wife, Clara."

"Gods. She should be the most powerful woman in Britain!"

Myrddin nodded. "Even when she was a babe, Igraine's Seer power shone brightly. Vivian is also a Seer, though not a Daughter. My wife linked her magic to Igraine's, for Igraine's protection. Dark forces were abroad. One by one, they had eliminated the children of the Lady's line. We could not risk Igraine meeting the same fate."

"That is not the end of the tale," Rhys declared. Myrddin had yet to explain the spell caging Igraine's magic.

"No. It is not. Three years later, a second child was born, to the only other surviving Daughter. This child was male."

"Uther."

"Yes." Myrddin smiled slightly. "You have seen the high king. Surely you can guess his ancestry."

"He is the son, many generations removed, of Marcus Aquila," Rhys said.

"Yes. Of Marcus and your own sister, Gwen. Uther is your own distant nephew, Rhys. A son of the Lady. As you are."

"If all you say is true," Rhys said, "then Uther and Igraine should be the most powerful Druids in the land. But they are barely aware of their magic. Igraine is timid and weak-willed. Uther is brash and arrogant. Their magic is bound by a powerful spell."

"Those spells were cast shortly after Uther's birth. It stifles their power, as you have noted. Unfortunately, it also magnifies their faults."

"Who could have committed such a crime? It could not have been Dafyd. He is too young to have done it. Was there another enemy, before him?"

Infinite weariness passed through Myrddin's eyes. "The spells were not cast by an enemy."

Rhys stared. "It was you. You did it."

Myrddin inclined his head.

"I suspected as much," Rhys said grimly. "But . . . why, if you serve the Light? How could you possibly justify such a heinous act?"

"The spells were necessary, to protect the line of the Lady. Some of the effects of the magic were . . . unanticipated."

Rhys crossed his arms. "That is always the case with deep magic. You should not have taken such risk."

Myrddin's fist hit the table, causing the lamp to jump. "I had to act! If I had not, darkness would have crushed Cyric's prophecy of Light! Do you realize, Rhys, that there is almost no Druid magic left in Britain? Already, in your own time, you've seen it begin to fade. That is why your grandfather sacrificed your life to Avalon's cause. You brought Druid initiates to the sacred isle. You kept Avalon strong for many years, but in the end, outside forces were stronger. The Druids scattered. Their magic seeped away.

"Now, three centuries later, the Light is all but gone. When Uther was born, I hoped he was destined to be the king Cyric envisioned. I realized almost immediately that he was not. His father had not been Druid; his magic was not strong enough. If Cyric's Druid king was to be born, he must claim a magical heritage though both mother and father. He must be the son of Uther and Igraine. But even that might not be enough. I took steps to ensure that Britain's future king will wield light magic beyond measure. I will not apologize for that."

Rhys had begun to believe Myrddin was mad. "How can any son be so powerful, when his parents' magic is crippled?"

Myrddin leaned forward, his eyes intent. "Don't you see, Rhys? Can you not guess? Magic denied is magic enhanced. It is precisely because Uther and Igraine's power is trapped that their son's power will be great. He will wield not only his own Druid power, but that of his parents as well."

"You mean to say you have *sacrificed* them?" Rhys was aghast. "You altered their destinies, in order to hand their magic to a son who is not yet born? You seek to create a Druid king who will possess power far beyond what any man should wield? By all the gods in Annwyn, old man, I cannot fathom your arrogance! You must be insane!"

"Not insane, Rhys. Desperate. In your short time here, you cannot begin to imagine what Britain has become. You see the decay around you. Well, I tell you, Cornwall is paradise compared to the east of Britain! On the eastern shores, Saxons raid with impunity. They slaughter our men, rape our women, enslave our people. The brutes are a never-ending tide of cruelty, breaking upon our shores in waves of blood and misery. Britain is a broken land, abandoned by Rome and ruled by petty lords who care for nothing but their own power. Only a strong king—a man who is all but a god—can save Britain. Uther is not that king. But his son, born of Igraine, raised in the power of the Old Ones, will be that leader. I swear it on my life."

"It is madness," Rhys whispered. "Pure madness."

"Then madness is Britain's last hope." Myrddin gripped his staff and rose. "I caged Uther's and Igraine's Druid magic, but I did not abandon them. Time and again, evil has sought to destroy the line of the Lady. Vivian and I have given our lives to protect the last of her children. I am Uther's protector; Vivian is Igraine's. As they grew, we did everything in our power to see ensure they would eventually wed. But it was a difficult prospect, because of the difference in their ages. When Igraine was ready to marry, Uther was barely a man. And yet, the pair fell in love nonetheless."

"But they did not wed."

"No. Uther had not yet seen his seventeenth summer when he left Gaul to lead his brother's army to war. I rode with him. Igraine, already past twenty, vowed to wait for Uther's return. Then war spread to Dumnonia, and Igraine's cousin, Prince Geraint, fell at the battle of Llongborth. And King Erbin gave Igraine to Gerlois."

Myrddin dragged a hand down his face and tugged at his beard. "Vivian could not prevent the union. Her magical connection with Igraine had inexplicably begun to weaken. It was some time before we traced the source of the disturbance to Gerlois's brother, newly installed as a bishop of the Roman church."

"Dafyd," Rhys said. "He knew Igraine was Druid."

The leap of lamp flame deepened the lines on the old Druid's face. "Yes. And it seemed he wanted to destroy any offspring she produced. When Igraine bore Gerlois a daughter, the duke was enraged. Dafyd stole the child before Vivian and I could stop him. Then came Vivian's vision of Igraine's death."

"The same vision Breena Saw?" Rhys asked.

Myrddin hesitated. "One very like it. We could not allow the tragedy to come to pass. We hatched a plan. Uther called all his dukes and lords to court in Caer-Lundein. The king planned to reveal his secret betrothal to Igraine, and claim it took precedence over her marriage to Gerlois. Uther was fresh off a stunning series of battlefield victories; Britain's lords would have agreed to anything their king proposed. But they never got the chance. Bishop Dafyd was part of Gerlois's retinue. The strength of his magic caught Vivian and me unaware. He cast a noxious spell over the court; every man and woman, save Gerlois and Igraine, fell ill. Vivian and I were by far the worst affected."

"You recovered."

Myrddin's lips twisted. "Oh, yes, I recovered. To find that Gerlois had fled with Igraine to Cornwall. As Uther prepared for the chase, Saxons sailed up the Thamesis and attacked Caer-Lundein—emboldened, I do not doubt, by Gerlois's message that Uther's court had been stricken with illness. Uther and I had no choice but to stand and defend the city. All the while, Vivian lay near death.

"The battles raged all summer. They have only just subsided. I could not leave Uther's side until very recently. I'd hired a local woman to care for Vivian; eventually, her body recovered. But her mind did not."

Myrddin placed his hands, palms up, on the table. "She is my wife. My helpmate. My very soul. Without her, I would gladly die. Tell me, Rhys, if Breena's soul were snatched from her body, would you not do whatever you must to bring her back?"

"Aye," Rhys said quietly. "I would."

Relief flared in the old man's eyes. "So you do understand, then." The point seemed very important to him.

"I sense you are a man who does not explain yourself to anyone," Rhys said. "Why do you seek to justify your actions to me?"

"Why, indeed?" Myrddin murmured. "I hardly know. I am what my life and my circumstances have created. I do not need your approval."

He sighed. "This place—this land, and this cottage, is the place Vivian loves best. I hoped being here would help her come back to me. It did not. I realized I had to go after her in the Lost Lands, and quickly. Her body could not exist long without her soul. Igraine, who had been left unguarded when Vivian fell ill, was in grave danger. With Dafyd headed to Cornwall for the harvest festival, I dared not delay in hastening to Tintagel. Vivian herself would have insisted upon it, even if it meant her own death. But I could not risk my wife, not even for Igraine."

"So you brought Breena from the past to take Vivian's place at Igraine's side," Rhys said.

"Breena is Igraine's kin, and a Seer. She possessed the magic I needed. I did not anticipate you would follow, Rhys, but now I see the Great Mother's hand in your presence. The Goddess knew I would fail in my duty to Igraine. And so she has brought you here to act in my stead."

Rhys stiffened. "I am not your lackey. You play the god in this drama—I want nothing to do with it."

At that, Myrddin surprised Rhys with a chuckle.

"You think I jest?" Rhys demanded.

"No. I know you do not. Forgive me. I forget how young, how earnest and righteous you are. You still believe in absolutes. Someday you will no longer enjoy that luxury." He struck the ground with his staff. "But enough debate. Dafyd's pall over Tintagel must be broken. You are the only one who can do it."

"Me? If that were true, I would not be here. I have already tried to enter the castle. I failed. I cannot do it."

"Ah, Rhys. The power is yours. Your shortcoming is that you use it far too honestly. What is wanted is deceit. Deceit, and deep magic."

Rhys stared. "I do not understand."

Myrddin smiled grimly. "You will."

* * *

Breena, standing on the roof terrace, stared toward the east, over the ridge where Gerlois and his knights had disappeared two days before. The duke's departure had lightened the burden weighing on her shoulders. She might be trapped in the castle, worried beyond reason for Rhys and Gareth, and dodging Bishop Dafyd at every turn, but at least Duke Gerlois was gone. Igraine was safe, for a time.

The harvest moon would rise tonight however. Would Breena's vision unfold? How could it, with Gerlois gone? Perhaps she had changed Igraine's destiny already. Once Uther defeated Gerlois, the high king would ride to Tintagel and claim his lost bride. Myrddin would be found, Gareth would recover from his injuries, and Rhys would appear before her and declare his undying love.

And rocks would float, and horses fly. She could not bring herself to believe everything would fall into place so neatly.

"Lady Antonia?"

She turned to find Brother Morfen standing behind her. His cowl was up, but not so far forward as to hide his face. She was pleased that he no longer felt the need to hide his scars from her. "Morfen. What are you doing here?"

"The bishop wishes me to lead Lady Igraine in prayer for her husband's safety." His sigh was heartfelt. "War. It is an ugly business."

"Yes."

They stood side by side for a time, not speaking. The wind kicked up. Breena shivered and rubbed her arms.

"It is cold here on the roof, my lady. And you wear no cloak. Allow me to escort you inside." Morfen offered her his arm.

"Thank you." Breena turned, then gasped as sudden pain stabbed between her eyes. She clutched at Morfen as the floor of the terrace lurched.

"Lady Antonia? What is it? Are you ill—"

She couldn't answer. The pain was too great. She pressed her fingers to the bridge of her nose and squeezed her eyes shut. Her next breath was a shard of glass in her lungs. Morfen's presence wavered. His voice faded into deep, fathomless silence.

The vision began as it had since she'd entered this time. A falcon, circling the tower. Wine, spilling from a goblet. Window glass, cracking. She turned and looked through the broken pane. The harvest moon, split in two behind the fissure, rose bloodred over the cliffs.

Gerlois's reflection appeared, merging eerily with the fractured moon. Breena whirled about. The duke stood in the doorway, his large frame obscured by a cloud of silver fog. Igraine, standing before the painting of the Christos, shrank back as he advanced.

Gerlois shouted something Breena could not hear. She tried to cry out as the duke's open hand connected with his wife's cheek. Igraine's head whipped hard to the right; she stumbled as Gerlois's hands went to her throat.

In her past visions, Breena had been paralyzed as well as mute. This time, however, when she willed herself to Igraine's side, her limbs jerked forward. She stretched out her arm. Her hand closed on the back of Gerlois's robe.

He turned, a snarl baring his teeth. Breena gasped.

Not the duke. Not Gerlois.

Dafyd.

The bishop's lips moved. His eyes were two hard black orbs. He was shouting, his face red with rage. Breena could hear none of it. Breena grabbed the front of his robe with both hands. She tried to haul him across the room, but his weight was like a boulder. She did not succeed in moving him a single step.

She did not see the blow coming. Dafyd's fist connected with her ear. Pain exploded; her vision shattered in a shower of red stars. She couldn't see. Couldn't breathe. She tried to shout. . . .

"Lady Antonia?" Fingers dug into her upper arms. The world gave a sickening lurch. Someone was shaking her.

"Lady Antonia! By the Christos, answer me!"

"Wha—" She opened her eyes to find Brother Morfen looking down at her.

"Lady Antonia. Do you know me?"

"Of . . . of course. You are Brother Morfen."

His cowl hung down his back, leaving his head exposed to the air. He did not seem to notice. "I thought . . . I do not know what I thought. That a demon had taken hold of you, perhaps. Your eyes had gone blank. . . ."

"No." Breena fought the pounding in her head. "No demon. I . . . I just felt a bit faint for a moment. I am fine."

Morfen released her shoulders. When she wavered on her feet, he cupped her elbow. "You should lie down for a time, I think."

She looked up at him. "Morfen, where is Bishop Dafyd now?"

"I left him in the duke's library."

"Do you . . ." She hesitated. She knew Morfen owed his loyalty to the bishop. But surely he would not stand by and let his master murder Igraine.

"Do I what, Lady Antonia?"

"Do you honor the duchess, Morfen?"

"Lady Igraine? Why of course."

"And you would not allow any harm to come to her?"

"I would not."

She exhaled. "Thank you." She hesitated. "Will you spend the evening in Bishop Dafyd's company?"

Morfen's expression showed his confusion. "I am most often at my lord bishop's side in the evenings."

"Promise me, then, that tonight, you will not let him out of your sight." She gripped his arm. "Not for an instant."

"Lady Antonia. I do not think—"

"Just promise me. Please."

He regarded her in silence for a moment. Then he nodded. "As you wish. If you promise you will retire for the afternoon. Clearly, the events of the last few days have exhausted you. You are in quite desperate need of rest."

Uther Pendragon looked so much like his ancestor, Marcus Aquila, that Rhys half expected Britain's high king to grin and declare his pretension of royalty an elaborate jest.

He did not.

The king's expression was grim. The battle had been engaged, and lacking Myrddin's support of Uther's army, the fighting was fierce, with casualties high on both sides. Uther, upon learning Rhys had returned, withdrew from the field. He glanced down at Rhys from atop his warhorse as Rhys finished donning his borrowed clothing. "You did not find Myrddin."

"I did find him, Your Majesty."

"Why is he not with you?"

"He could not make the journey. His magic is gone."

The color drained from Uther's face. "Gone?"

"I assure you, I speak the truth. Myrddin's magic has fled. He sent me in his stead."

The corners of Uther's mouth slashed downward. "You do not have half of Myrddin's power."

"That may be true," Rhys said evenly. "But at the moment, I am your only choice of Druid ally. I have received Myrddin's instructions, and I am prepared to remove Igraine from Tintagel. That is the objective of this war, is it not?"

"It is." Uther regarded Rhys gravely. A soldier's death cry bled from the battlefield. Uther's stallion shied at the sound. The king, his expression grim, controlled the great beast with one hand.

"Let us hope, Druid, that your battle magic can turn the tide of this skirmish."

"It will not. I have no intention of entering this war with battle magic."

Uther spit a curse. "Then you are less than useless. You waste my time! Take yourself out of my path." His mount reared as he spun the beast about.

Rhys lunged, catching the bridle before the beast could charge the field. "You arrogant idiot! War is not your solution. Do you imagine you will be able to fight your way into Tintagel in time to save the duchess? You will not."

Uther snarled down at him. "I can and I will. Drop the reins, Druid. I will win this war, with or without your help. Once Gerlois is dead, no man will dare bar my entrance to Tintagel."

"Perhaps not." Rhys anchored his grip on the leather. "But what will you find when you enter? At this moment, Lady Igraine is at Dafyd's mercy. He will kill her this very night if you are not there to prevent it."

Panic flashed in Uther's eyes. "That is why I must fight!"

"Nay. That is why you must not. Believe me when I tell you, Myrddin is in agreement. The scheme I am about to propose to you is his."

Uther's eyes narrowed. "Tell me."

"Dismount," Rhys countered, "and I will."

Uther did not even blink as Rhys described the dangers of Myrddin's plan.

"Cast the illusion," he said when Rhys fell silent. "I am not afraid."

A wiser man, or a less arrogant one, would have been very afraid, Rhys thought. His own fear was manifested as a tightening of his chest that would not relent. The spell Myrddin had proposed was not a simple illusion. Light magic alone would not pierce Dafyd's pall. The bishop's evil had repelled even Rhys's deep magic.

What Myrddin had proposed was something far more sinister. Deep magic, aye, but deep magic wound with dark magic. This was far different from Rhys slipping a light magic illusion into Dafyd's pall, as he'd done during Gareth's duel. This time, he would claim dark magic as his own. The thought of casting such a spell opened up a pit of dread in Rhys's stomach.

But he would do it. For Breena. Despite the howling of his conscience, he did not for a moment consider turning away. His honor lay in a heap of dust before his love for Breena. He very much feared there was no magic he would not cast, no depravity he would not entertain, to ensure her safety. And if that realization brought searing guilt, it also, paradoxically, created an oasis of calm in the center of his turbulent emotions. A feeling of profound rightness.

Loving Breena was the single aspect of Rhys's life he had never once doubted.

"You must understand what you are about to undertake," he told Uther. "This spell is not an illusion. It is a transformation."

Myrddin's scheme wove Rhys's shape-shifting deep magic with dark magic. "You will not simply look like Gerlois. You will *become* Gerlois. The spell will not be stable. The shifting will be very painful; it may even kill you outright." He would not proceed unless Uther knew what he risked. "Even if the spell is successful, you may find that you will not be able to return to your own form afterward. You may be forced to live out your life as Gerlois, and put it about that Uther was killed in battle. I do not know what that will do to your political alliances. Even worse, you cannot risk leaving Gerlois alive in such an instance. There cannot be two men with the duke's name and face."

"I will kill the bastard in any case," Uther said. "If you mean that requirement to be a deterrent, it is a poor one. As for the rest, I will take whatever risk is necessary to see Igraine safe."

In truth, Uther's unwavering resolve surprised Rhys. The man went up a notch in Rhys's estimation. Perhaps the high king was even worthy of the throne upon which he sat. Uther was the distant progeny of Gwen and Marcus, after all.

Uther raised his hand and spoke to the dozen knights waiting nearby. None were strangers to Myrddin's magic, but Rhys fervently hoped none of them would fully understand the nature of the spell he was about to cast on their king. All the warriors, and Uther himself, had exchanged their red tunics for clothing bearing Cornwall's colors, which they had stripped from Gerlois's dead.

Rhys also wore mail and a green tunic emblazoned with the black tower of Cornwall. A sword hung at his hip. He could not get used to the unbalanced sensation. He nodded at Uther. "Ready?"

"Yes. Get on with it. Time is growing short. By your own assertion, we must reach Tintagel before dark."

Rhys was well aware of the position of the sun, and the full moon that would rise with the sun's setting. He was also aware that Uther's men were watching him with wary eyes. He wanted to cast the spell out of the sight of Uther's men, but the king refused.

"They must witness the change," he'd asserted. "If they do not, there is the risk they will not believe."

Rhys had agreed with some reluctance. "Very well. Close your eyes, and brace yourself for the pain."

He cleared his mind. It was not difficult to find his shape-shifter magic. It was a part of him that was never far from his consciousness. Casting that magic upon someone else, and controlling the form it would take, was far more complicated. Before Myrddin had described in detail exactly how such a feat could be accomplished, Rhys had not even known enough to dream of the possibility.

Simply transferring his own shape-shifting power to Uther, difficult as that was, would not be enough. Rhys's deep magic alone could not pass through Dafyd's pall. Dark magic was needed.

He cast his mind out over the battlefield. It took but a moment to sift through the tangled life essences on the field and locate the soul unique to Gerlois. The duke, pressed upon by a contingent of Uther's best warriors, was caught in the frenzy of battle. With his concentration overwhelmed, his grip on his life essence had loosened.

Rhys called Myrddin's dark spell into his thoughts. His lips did not want to form the Words; his tongue felt swollen and thick. Bile rose in his throat. His stomach threatened to heave. He concentrated on Breena, on an image of her held captive by Dafyd. He would do what he had to do. If it was wrong, so be it.

His body shuddered with revulsion as his lips formed the Words. He cast the spell quickly. A fragment of Gerlois's soul separated from his body. Rhys wove the glowing strand with the fabric of his shape-shifting spell. He bound the result to Uther's life essence.

The transformation struck with a vengeance. Uther gasped with the first shock of it. He dropped to his knees. As one, his men surged forward; the king held them back with one raised hand. Uther gritted his teeth, bowed his head, and bore the rest of the transformation in silence.

Fearful murmurs ran through Uther's knights. Before their eyes, Uther's handsome face melted into Gerlois's bitter features. His body thickened with age and corpulence. When at last he stood, and faced his men, Rhys realized Uther had been very wise to force his knights to witness this magic. If he had not, the twelve men would have raised a dozen swords against the enemy standing before them.

Uther looked at Rhys with Gerlois's eyes. "Will the guard allow me to pass as Gerlois?"

Rhys fought a surge of nausea. "I have no doubt."

He only hoped Dafyd's magic would be fooled as easily.

Chapter Nineteen

Waiting was torture.

Breena sat with Igraine, alone in the solar; Nesta had fetched Lady Bertrice to mediate some squabble in the kitchens. The dying sun glinted through the western window, painting the walls crimson. Breena could not tear her eyes from the cracked pane in the eastern window. The full moon would soon rise, directly behind it.

Surely Morfen would keep his promise to stay close to Dafyd's side. The bishop would not enter the room alone, as he had in Breena's vision. If reality began differently from her nightmare, did that mean it would end differently as well? Breena clung to that hope.

She paced to the window and peered through the broken pane. Dark clouds scudded above the land, but a slice of clear sky showed just above the sea cliffs. She stood, transfixed, as crimson, lifting from the horizon, bled into blue. The leading arch of the moon rose like a bloodstained sphere. As the orb traversed the fissure in the glass, it looked as though it had been sliced in two.

Breena sucked in a breath. Perhaps she should have told Igraine the whole truth—that Breena had Seen the duchess's death, and that she very much feared there was nothing she could do to stop it. If death was to be Igraine's certain fate, the duchess had the right to prepare herself for it. But Breena could not bring herself to give up that last thin thread of hope that her vision had been wrong. Closing her eyes, she braced for what she knew would happen next, even as she fervently prayed destiny would be thwarted.

She opened her eyes. Magic thickened the air. It had begun, then. Much as she wished this was a dream, another vision from which she would awaken, she knew it was not. Silence had not descended. The wail of the wind outside the window was plainly audible, as was the hitch of Igraine's breath, and the thudding of Breena's own heart.

She stared into the glass. A soft snick sounded as the door to Igraine's solar opened. A man's reflection appeared in the glass, eerily framed within the split moon.

Breena turned. Igraine had risen to greet Bishop Dafyd. Her spine was straight, but her hands trembled. Breena's gaze darted into the gloom beyond his shoulder. Where was Brother Morfen?

Dafyd stepped fully into the room. Breena could not see the sorcerer's aura, but she could feel his magic—reaching, expanding, snaking around her limbs and torso. Her stomach roiled. She tried to walk forward, to rush to Igraine's side. She could not move.

Dafyd approached Igraine. The gnawing fear in Breena's gut became a full burn. "No," Breena whispered. "No."

"My lady," Dafyd said, halting before the duchess.

Igraine's gaze darted to Breena, then back to her visitor. "Excellency. To what do we owe the honor of your presence?"

"Need I a reason to offer succor to my brother's—" Dafyd's gaze raked Igraine's body with an insolence Breena had never before witnessed. "—whore?"

Igraine gasped. "I am no whore. I have been faithful to my husband."

Breena struggled to move. Struggled to speak. Frantically, she looked through the door. Morfen had still not arrived.

"A faithful wife does not plot betrayal," Dafyd said. "A faithful wife does not encourage the attentions of her husband's enemy. You, my dear, have done both. My brother is a blind fool. He loves you too well. He is too soft."

"Too soft with his fists?" Igraine said. "I think not."

"Insolent whore. Devil's harlot. You question your husband's right to chastise you? If only Gerlois had listened to me, and thrown you from the cliffs upon your return from Caer-Lundein. Or better yet, killed you as soon as you became his wife! You are far too dangerous to live, my dear, even with your magic bound."

"My . . . my magic?"

"Do not pretend you do not know what you are!" With sudden violence, Dafyd's open palm connected with Igraine's cheek. Her head whipped to the side. As she cried out, he grasped the neckline of her gown, and ripped it open. "Do not lie to me. There! You wear the mark of Satan."

Breena's Druid pendant glinted silver against Igraine's alabaster skin. The duchess cried out, and wrested the edges of her torn tunic from the duke's hand.

"Harlot." He thrust her away from him.

She fell hard upon her knees. "Please. Do not hurt—"

Her plea fell on deaf ears. With a snarl, Dafyd fell upon her, his hands closing about her throat. It was happening, just as Breena had foreseen. She stood frozen with horror. She could not allow this tragedy. She had come to this time to prevent it. There must be a way. Surely the Great Mother would not have given her an impossible task.

Her body would not move. In desperation, Breena threw her mind toward Igraine. Her magic collided with Dafyd's, to little effect. His evil was an impenetrable wall, thick and oozing with malice. It surrounded Igraine, wrapping her with filth. But through it all, one point of Light remained.

A glow encircled Breena's Druid pendant. Avalon's mark. The symbol of the Great Mother, merged with the sign of the Carpenter Prophet. Protection and Light. Breena reached for the magic of the charm. Somehow, through the pall of Dafyd's spell, she touched it.

A burst of white light arced like lightning. Breena's magic, and Igraine's, joined as one. A shower of white sparks burst forth. Dafyd jerked back. And Breena found herself suddenly free of her paralysis.

She stumbled forward. Igraine was bent double, coughing. She raised her head as Breena grabbed her arm and hauled her to her feet. Red smudges marred the skin of Igraine's neck. Breena's rage surged. She shoved the duchess behind her and spun to face her adversary.

"You will not touch her."

"You think to stop me?" Dafyd's lips parted in a sneer. "With your paltry magic?" He laughed. "This bitch's usefulness ended when she birthed her daughter. I would have killed her then, if Gerlois had not stopped me. He claimed to love her too well, even though her disdain shriveled his cock. My brother is a fool. But he is not here now, to interfere with what must be done."

"I will fight you," Breena whispered. "With every breath in my body."

Dafyd laughed again. "Then do so, by all means." He spread his arms. "I am waiting."

Breena had never in her life cast deep magic. Would

her spell go terribly awry, as Rhys's had on the tournament field? She did not have time to consider the risk. The risk of not acting was far greater.

She let her rage rise. It surged with her magic and her will. A great gust swept through her body. She trembled with its power. She knew her mortal form could not contain it for long.

She flung the power outward. It struck Dafyd's chest. Sparks flew.

The bishop stood unharmed. "Is that the worst your magic can do? I am disappoint—"

The words choked in his throat. Breena watched in bewilderment as Dafyd jerked forward, eyes wide, mouth open. He hung suspended in that grotesque pose for a single heartbeat. Then he crumpled slowly to the ground.

Breena leaped backward with a cry as his heavy body thudded at her feet. She collided with Igraine. The two women sought to steady each other; when Breena regained her balance she looked up. Igraine gave a soft cry. Brother Morfen stood over Dafyd's body.

"You came," Breena breathed.

The monk's good eye blinked. "Yes."

"Thank you."

He gave a tight smile, the ruined side of his mouth turning it into a grimace. He bent and grasped the cowl of Dafyd's robe. Standing, he tossed the bishop aside as if he weighed nothing. Dafyd's neck issued a horrifying crack as his body hit the ground.

Breena gasped, and backed away.

"It does not seem," Morfen said softly, "that you truly wish to thank me."

"What . . . what do you mean?"

Morfen advanced a step. Instinctively, Breena tightened her grip on Igraine's arm.

"Do you not know me, Breena? Did you not guess at my identity when I bade the fair minstrel sing my mother's song?"

"The minstrel . . ." Her eyes widened. "You . . . you claim the goddess Ceridwen as your mother? But . . . but that is not possible."

"All things are possible," he said. "I am Afagduu." His single eye flashed with dark emotion. "You believed me pitiful. You believed I was the captive of this soft, sorry priest. I assure you, it was he who was *my* slave. He who did *my* bidding. And he did not even know."

He nudged Dafyd's body with his foot. "I grew tired of his stupidity. I find I wish to complete his task with my own hands." His gaze touched on Igraine. "It will be blissful pleasure to kill the last Daughter of the Lady, and watch the Light fade from Britain permanently."

"You are truly evil," Breena whispered. "As ugly as your face."

Afagduu laughed. "Men call evil ugly. But that is not right. Evil is lovely. Seductive. Darkness holds unbounded beauty."

His eyes flicked over Breena, leaving a dirty trail of shame. He lifted a hand. A black haze seeped from the ground.

"Once Igraine is dead, I will show you."

If not for the bloodred moon rising, Rhys would have laughed at how easily Uther's party passed through Tintagel's gates. The high king had only to shout a command, and the guards jumped to grant their duke entrance. Uther rode into the forecourt, swung from the saddle, and tossed the reins to a waiting stable lad.

The head of the castle guards hovered nearby, as did Tintagel's steward. Uther ignored them. Jaw set, he strode through the great hall and into the inner courtyard, his knights at his heels. The soldiers guarding the tower door hastened to lift the crossbar. Boots thudded across the garden and onto the stone stair.

A poisonous wave of magic met them on the ascent. Red sparks mingled with darkness. The knights stumbled. Only Uther and Rhys kept moving through the pall. The king unsheathed his sword and took the last steps at a run.

Uther burst into the duchess's solar, Rhys on his heels. Thick black smoke obscured the room. "Breena!" Rhys shouted.

A form emerged from the gloom. Through the haze, Rhys recognized the ruined face of Dafyd's acolyte. Magic swirled around the monk—magic that Rhys had believed was Dafyd's. With a shock, he realized the power belonged to the slave, not the master.

His throat closed. Where was Breena? Frantically, he cast his senses into the gloom. He shuddered with relief when he touched her power. She'd wrapped it around Igraine. The two women crouched in the far corner of the room

There was still time to save the future.

"Welcome, my king." The monk greeted Uther with mocking laughter. "You are surprised your paltry disguise does not fool me? Ah, well. Perhaps Myrddin is not as clever as he thinks."

Rhys was not certain the monk had even noticed his own presence. He gave no sign of knowing what Rhys was. He fought to keep his magic muted as he edged along the perimeter of the room toward Breena.

Uther, with a cry of rage, lunged at his enemy. The monk halted the attack with nothing more than a raised hand. Uther's sword froze in midair, as if it had struck stone. Before the king could react, a shaft of crimson light shot from the monk's palm, to explode in Uther's face.

The king howled. His sword clattered to the tile as

he staggered backward. Rhys ran the last steps toward Breena. Her white magic provided a fragile shield against the sorcerer's fury. Without hesitation, Rhys dove through it. He knew Breena's magic would never reject him.

She gasped. "Rhys! Gods! What is happening? You and Gerlois—"

"Not Gerlois," he grunted. "Uther. He is disguised by magic."

"Dear Christos!" Igraine cried out as Uther's body hit the ground. She struggled against Breena's grip. "Release me! I must go to him!"

"No," Breena said. "You—"

Her words died in a shower of red sparks. With the explosion came a roll of black smoke. A feeling of unfathomable hopelessness descended, crushing the air from Rhys's lungs. He struggled to breathe, struggled to find a spell to fight the sorcerer's attack. His light magic was too far away. He could not reach it, could not cast it.

He reached for his deep magic instead.

Icy blue sparks shot from his fingertips. Whether the blast hit its mark or not, he could not tell. A surge of crimson malevolence responded. A noxious stench, dung and sulfur, filled his nostrils. As Rhys prepared a counterstrike, he became aware of Breena standing at his side. She held out her hand. Deep magic gathered, rippling in her palm like a living river.

"What are you doing?" Rhys rasped. "Get back. Protect Igraine. I will deal with the monk."

"No! Rhys, you don't understand. He is not a monk. He is not a man! He is Afagddu. You cannot hope to defeat him alone."

Shock slammed into Rhys's brain. "Afagddu? The . . . the son of Ceridwen?"

"The same."

Rhys swore. He felt Breena's magic expand. It spread in a white mist toward Afagduu's darkness. He sent his own magic, bright blue and pulsing, to intertwine with hers. She spoke the truth. United, they were far stronger than they were apart. But would their combined magic be enough to smite a god?

Afagduu met their attack with a stream of fire. The flames blasted Breena's protection, licking at the edges of her spell. The resulting heat was sweltering. Rhys felt like an insect caught under glass.

If his fate was to fight to the death, so be it. Why should he have any choice in death, when he'd had so little in all his life? But Breena did not deserve such a fate.

Rhys launched a stream of cooling blue at Afagduu's fire. Breena added a torrent of icy white. The power flowing through them was heady, and dangerous. He and Breena had bound themselves together in a union that, in a way, was far more intimate than their physical joining had been. He wanted to grasp the power, and Breena with it, and never let either go.

But there was vast danger in the deep magic as well. With each pulse of the attack he wielded, Rhys felt a piece of his soul sink into a bottomless abyss. This was the void Rhys's grandfather had feared more than anything in his long life.

Rhys did not care. He would be willing to brave the bowels of the earth to defend Breena. He would sell his soul if necessary. What he would not do was allow her to be destroyed with him.

Afagduu's hideous power surged. Searing heat consumed Rhys's senses. Breena's magic held steady, as did Rhys's own. They repelled the assault, but they did not weaken the attack. Rhys was all too aware that they could not hold Afagduu at bay forever.

Rhys could not afford to hesitate. He sank his mind

into his deepest power. Into the darkest aspects of his essence. All his loneliness, all his despair, all his shameful passion. All the ugliness of his soul. He wove all the darkness into a spell that was deeper than any he'd ever known. And then he bound his own life essence to the magic, and fashioned a curse that even a god could not escape.

He was well aware it would be the last spell he ever cast.

So be it.

He tore himself from Breena's magic an instant before he launched his blight upon Afagduu. Dimly, he heard Breena scream as the magic exploded. He saw a flash of light; felt his soul fly apart.

And then, nothing.

Chapter Twenty

Breena realized what Rhys intended a scant instant before he acted. She threw all her magic into an attempt to stop him.

She was too late. Bright light flashed in the tower room, illuminating smoke and magic. The outline of Rhys's body appeared, briefly, caught in a halo of pure blue light.

Afagduu howled as the spell hit. He staggered backward under the force of Rhys's power. The very stones of the tower trembled. Breena could do nothing but cling to Igraine, and pray, as Rhys's body crumpled slowly to the ground. He lay facedown next to the sprawled form that Rhys had said was Uther, and did not move. She cast her senses, seeking Rhys's magic. It was gone.

A sob clogged her throat. He was gone.

Afagduu raised his hideous face. A sneer was upon his lips as he looked down at Rhys's corpse. "Fool. Did you think you could defeat a god? Your sacrifice was for naught."

"I would not agree." The words were spoken in a rich, masculine voice. "For this human bard's magic brought me."

Breena blinked as a man came forward from the shadows by the doorway. The dark mist of Afagduu's magic scattered before him. Breena gaped at the newcomer. He wore the simple garb of a minstrel, and carried a harp not unlike Rhys's own. He was tall and fair, with noble features and the bearing of a king. His face, and especially his brow, seemed to shine from within.

Afagduu spun around. The expression that flitted across his face as he looked upon the newcomer was one of intense hatred, searing anger, and abject shock.

"Taliesin. Take yourself away from here. You are not wanted."

Taliesin? The bard of the gods? Breena began to tremble.

The man with the shining brow stepped forward. "I have been searching for you, brother."

Afagduu's ugly face twisted. "Do not call me that. We are not brothers."

"I assure you, I have even less love of the notion than you," Taliesin replied. "However, that does not change the truth. Come now. It is time to leave this human realm."

Afagduu gathered his magic like a building storm. "I have no intention of leaving." He looked toward Igraine and Breena. "Not when I am a breath away from snuffing the last of the Lady's Light from the world."

"You want earth to be as dark and ugly as your face and your soul. You will not succeed. Light must balance dark. That is the law upon which life itself depends."

"Go back to Annwyn," Afagduu spat. "Go back and hide behind our mother's skirts. What do you care about these pitiful humans? They are bred for misery. I only grant them their fate."

Taliesin's expression was grave. "You know I cannot allow that."

He lifted his harp and plucked a single sweet note. The last of Afagduu's magic vanished in a burst of light. Afagduu stood with fists clenched, his face contorted in a rictus of hate.

Taliesin turned to Breena and Igraine, and bowed. "My ladies."

"M-my lord," Breena stuttered.

The bard smiled. "No lord. I am simply a minstrel." His gaze fell on Rhys's body. "Like this man, who gave his life to save you. In so doing, he turned dark magic to Light."

Tears filled Breena's eyes. "I never wanted him to sacrifice himself."

"He did not wish it, either. And yet, when it became clear that it was necessary, he did not hesitate." He smiled. "He is a great man. Many stories will be told of him, for many years. What tragedy, were his legend to die when he has only begun to live."

Taliesin bent his head over his harp. His long fingers caressed the strings, creating a melody so beautiful Breena thought her heart would break.

A slit of light appeared in the air. As the bard played, it widened into a shining doorway. Taliesin looked at Afagduu.

"It is time, brother, to return."

"I'll go nowhere with you."

"You will."

The bard plucked a string. A high, pure note sounded. White light flashed through the room. Breena stumbled backward, blinded. A sound like a rushing wind blotted out the otherworldly music of Taliesin's harp. All sound, all movement, ceased.

After a long moment, Breena dared to uncover her eyes. The full moon, now shining white in the night sky, was the only illumination in the tower room. Taliesin was gone.

Afagduu was gone as well.

On the floor, Uther stirred. Igraine flew to his side, and the high king enfolded his long lost love in his arms.

When their lips met in a kiss, Breena turned slowly

away. Rhys's body had not moved. It never would. She had felt his life essence leave his body as he'd cast his spell upon Afagddu. He had traded his life for hers. A great grief welled up on the far side of a thick, numb wall. Breena did not want that wall to crack; she did not want to feel the despair that waited on the other side. But she knew she would have no choice.

Woodenly, she moved to Rhys's side and knelt. She laid a hand on his head and stroked his fair hair. "I . . . I love you, Rhys." Her voice broke on the words. "I will always love you."

A soft groan answered her declaration. Breena's hand froze in midstroke. "Rhys?"

It was not possible. He was dead! Then he groaned a second time, and his head stirred imperceptibly before once again going still.

"Rhys?" Tears streaming down her face, Breena grasped his shoulders and shook him. When he did not move again, she heaved him over onto his back.

His eyes fluttered open, and a long breath escaped between his teeth. He brought one hand up to touch his temple, and winced. "Breena."

She flung herself upon him. "Rhys! You're alive." She kissed his cheeks, his forehead, his chin. "But how—?"

He shoved himself into a sitting position, his arm going around her waist. He held her to him, tightly, as she sobbed into his chest. "The bard with the shining brow," he said. "Taliesin. He sang my soul back to me."

"You . . . you saw him?"

"Yes. In the Lost Lands. He told me . . ." He hesitated. "He told me my time in the land of men was not finished."

Breena sobbed all the harder. "Oh, gods, Rhys. You were dead! I could not bear it."

He smoothed his hand down her back. "Do not think on it. I am not dead now. Thank the gods that Uther and Igraine are alive as well."

Breena blinked at the man with Igraine. When he had first burst into the room, he had worn the visage of Gerlois. Now she noticed, as she had not before, that his features, and his body, had changed. Rhys claimed the warrior was Uther. But he looked like . . .

"Marcus?"

"Nay," Rhys said as the warrior who looked so much like Breena's brother drew Igraine to her feet. Rhys rose as well, and offered Breena his hand. "Not Marcus. Uther Pendragon. High King of Britain."

At that moment, the door to the solar burst open. A dozen knights crowded into the room, swords drawn.

"Sire!" The lead man shouted. "We could not gain entrance through that foul magic! What has happened—"

"All is well, Vaughn," Uther said. The king's arm was anchored firmly around Igraine's shoulders. The duchess's face was alight with joy.

The soldier stopped in his tracks. "My lady," he said, bowing to Igraine. He turned to Uther. "Your Highness. The enchantment on your features. It is gone."

"I have no more need of it," Uther declared. He indicated Dafyd's body with a sweep of his hand. "Remove this corpse, and burn it. Take the men and secure the castle in my name."

"At once, sire." Two of the soldiers lifted Dafyd's body. Vaughn led the entire contingent back down the tower stair.

"His resemblance to Marcus is remarkable, is it not?" Rhys said when the knights were gone. Uther and Igraine entwined their bodies in an embrace, oblivious to Rhys and Breena's presence. "And not by chance. Uther Pendragon is Marcus's and Gwen's many-times great grandson."

"How do you know that?" Breena asked, stunned.

"Myrddin. He claims Igraine is your kin as well, and I have every reason to believe that is true. She is descended from Owein and Clara. Her marriage to Uther will unite the last remaining ancestral lines of the Lady's magic."

"So that was Myrddin's goal, all along."

"Aye."

"Why did he not tell me?" Breena asked.

"He thought it better that you know as little as possible of this time," Rhys said. "He was afraid what the knowledge would mean for Cyric's prophecy of Light."

Breena raised her brows. "Are you saying that you now believe Myrddin is a Druid of Avalon? That he serves the Light?"

Rhys grimaced. "Aye. I have come to believe that is true."

A look of wonder stole over Breena's face. "And not only that, I think. Rhys, if Uther is Marcus's descendant, and Igraine is Owein's, then Myrddin himself . . . Why, he can only be yours."

Rhys jerked back as if struck. "You think Myrddin is my descendant? Breena, that's . . . absurd."

"On the contrary. It's entirely likely! It explains so much. His magic, his drive. Why, he even looks like you."

Rhys's expression was comical. "You think I look like an old man?"

Breena laughed. "At nearly thirty, you are, of course, just this side of decrepit, but no, you do not look it. Yet I can well imagine you looking much like Myrddin someday. He has your height, and your eyes. His hair may be white now, but it might easily have been fair when he was younger."

"I do not see it. The man cannot possibly be my descendant! No progeny of mine could be so reckless with deep magic."

"Rhys, that makes no sense. You did not raise the man, after all. He was born long after your death, and has dealt with magic far greater than what we know."

Rhys made a chopping motion with his hand. "It's still impossible. Breena, I have no children."

"How can you be sure?" She tried to keep her voice neutral, and failed. "You've bedded many women. Odds are that at least one of them has conceived."

"Nay. It has not happened. Believe me, I made very sure of it."

Comprehension dawned. "You used magic? To prevent conception? Did you . . . did you do that with me?"

He did not look at her. "Of course. It would have been a disaster if our joining resulted in a child. Then you could never be free of me."

She gasped. "You mean *you* could never be free of *me!* You do not want the responsibility of a child!"

"Breena." He ran a hand down his face. "I have been nothing in my life if not responsible." He pronounced the virtue as if it were the worst vice. "That is why I have never allowed any woman to conceive my child."

"But you will," Breena insisted. "Someday. Because Myrddin is your descendant. I am sure of it."

"The randy idiot," Rhys exclaimed a short time later. He sent a dark glance in the direction of the stair. The instant Uther's men had withdrewn, the king had scooped Igraine into his arms and carried her up the stairs to her bedchamber.

"Could he not have at least waited until the castle was secure to bed her?" he complained.

Breena laughed. "Apparently not."

A reluctant smile touched Rhys's lips. "I very much fear three centuries have wiped all good sense from the Aquila line."

"Do not judge Uther too harshly," Breena said. "He is, after all, a man in love."

Rhys met Breena's gaze. A mischievous sparkle lit her blue eyes. Her hair had long since escaped its braid. Freckles danced across her nose. She was so beautiful, it made his chest hurt.

"Uther is a fortunate man, then."

She reached up and cradled the side of his face in her palm. "I am fortunate as well. For I love you."

He caught her hand. His kiss brushed the back of her knuckles. "I am sure I do not know what I ever did to deserve that."

"Oh, Rhys." Her eyes softened. "Don't you know? You didn't have to *do* anything. You just had to *be*."

A hot rush of emotion closed his throat. "You are too good. Too trusting. Too loyal. I know I should not claim you, but—"

"But you have no choice." Breena rose on her toes and wrapped her arms around his neck. "Because I have chosen you. And I am telling you, Rhys, your days of dodging me, of denying our love, are over."

"Bree—"

She stopped his protest with a kiss. "Do not tell me how difficult our life will be. I know there will be hard circumstances to face. But we will face them. Together."

He searched her gaze and found no doubt, no hesitation. Only love, steady and true, purely offered. He let out a long sigh. Tension drained from his shoulders. For once, he was glad to have no choices. It made the surrender to his own hopes and dreams so much easier.

"I love you." His throat burned with emotion. "I

have always loved you." He pressed his forehead to hers. "But I am a difficult man, Bree."

He felt her amusement. "No one knows that better than I, Rhys, I assure you! You are proud, and stubborn. You will not talk about your feelings, and you have great trouble admitting you are wrong." She gave an exaggerated sigh. "I will just have to deal with your shortcomings, I suppose."

His laugh was genuine. "I will try not to be so objectionable in the future."

"Oh, do not trouble yourself. I find I do not mind those traits, really." Her hands left his shoulders to smooth a path down his chest and stomach. Her fingers tangled in the ties of his breeches. Before he quite knew what had happened, he felt her small, hot hand encircling his shaft. "As long as you do not disappoint me in other ways."

He went instantly hard in her palm. She stroked firmly from the base of his rod to the tip. At the same time, she planted kisses along his jaw. When her tongue slid into his ear, he thought his knees would fail him.

"Bree," he rasped. "Gods."

"Take off your clothes, Rhys. And lie down on the chaise."

He gaped. "What did you say?"

Her eyes flashed with laughter. "You heard me."

He stared blankly for a long moment. No woman had ever ordered him to do such a thing. "Breena. Uther and Igraine are just above stairs. Uther's knights are stomping about the castle. We cannot just—"

"If Uther and Igraine can, I see no reason why we cannot." She moved to the door and dropped the latch. "There. Now no one will disturb us."

She sent him her most enticing smile as she moved around the room, lighting lamps. When she'd finished, she turned to face him.

"Now please, Rhys. Undress. I want to see you completely bare."

Laughter shook his chest as he obeyed. Naked, he sprawled on the chaise, watching her from under hooded eyes. For the first time in his life, he was content to enjoy his passivity.

She stayed out of reach as she slowly removed her own blouse and skirt. His amusement faded as her tunic dropped, revealing creamy breasts, a gently rounded stomach, and a triangle of red curls. The garment puddled at her feet.

She stepped out of it and came to him. Kneeling on the floor by his side, she slid her hands over his chest and kissed him deeply. She tasted of honey, and smelled like roses. But when he moved to take her in his arms, she pulled away.

"No, Rhys. You made love to me before. Now, I want to make love to you. I think . . . I think perhaps that no one has ever done that for you before."

He closed his eyes against the sudden emotion twisting his heart. "I think perhaps you are right," he whispered.

"Lie still. Let me love you."

Her lips pressed against his chest. His stomach clenched when they wandered lower. And lower still. She took his shaft in her hand. He tangled his fingers in her hair.

"Breena—"

She sent a quick glance his way. Her eyes were dancing. "Quiet."

But when her lips opened and slid over the head of his cock, he could not suppress a groan. His hand tightened in her hair. He wanted to drag her off him; he could not do it. The pleasure clogged his brain. His muscles would not obey. He could only lie captive to the bliss.

When her lips and tongue and teeth left him, too soon, his hips arched, wanting them back. He forced himself to loosen his grip on her hair. She shifted, coming fully atop him.

It took but a small surge of his hips to bury himself inside her. She gasped as she seated herself fully. Her spine arched; her hair cascaded down her back. He looked up at her, his heart filled with awe. Gods, she was beautiful. And she was *his*. He would not fight that truth any longer. He could not.

He gripped her hip with one hand. He brought the other up to cup her breast. He flicked his thumb over her nipple, fascinated by the expression that blossomed on her face.

"You are a dream," he whispered. "One from which I do not wish to wake."

"You never will," she said.

Chapter Twenty-one

"Tis hard luck Duke Gerlois died before he had a chance to pay us in coin," Trent said. Standing atop a crate, he leaned on the side of the boat, watching the sea cliffs drift past. Breena nearly laughed outright. The little man had such an outsized ego!

"Aye," the giant—Howell—said dryly. He tossed a stone into the waves. "I'm sure the oversight disturbed him greatly as the sword ran through his gut."

"Better to die in battle, then to be strung up as a traitor," the rotund singer put in.

"And quite convenient for the king and his intended queen, is it not," the young flautist added, "that one of Uther's knights should have dispatched the duke on the battlefield, even before Uther entered Tintagel castle? Though exactly how the king fashioned a disguise so convincing as to fool the guards at the gate, I cannot fathom. Some say it could only have been by sorcery."

"Idle gossip." Trent eyed Rhys, who leaned casually against the ship's rail at Breena's side. "Some might even say Sir Gareth's swift recovery was sped by magic," he added. "But as for me, I put the knight's continued good health down to Howell's tender care."

Rhys offered a small shrug. Breena chuckled. She had been relieved beyond all measure to learn Gareth was alive. And Rhys's magic aside, Howell's care did have much to do with the knight's recuperation.

Trent grinned. "Ah, well. What's a little sorcery performed for a good cause? At least my man Rhys here made sure we did not go completely unpaid for that outstanding performance before the duke's table. Sea passage to Glastonbury, and an invitation to the king's court in Caer-Lundein! The future of the Brothers Stupendous is a spring garden waiting to bloom."

"I regret I will not see it," Rhys said.

"Ah, but you could, if you would only reconsider your foolish plan to travel to Gwynedd," Howell retorted. "Winter is in the air, man! You and Antonia will be lucky if you do not end up frozen in a ditch. My lady, please," he added to Breena. "Reconsider. Rhys may have carried you to safety during the battle for Tintagel, but surely that is no reason to throw your life's lot in with this scruffy wanderer."

"But he is such a handsome scruffy wanderer," Breena protested with a smile. "I count myself very lucky to be his betrothed."

The words brought a thrill. She could not get used to the notion. She and Rhys had pledged to each other in private, amid an intimacy so deep it was if they shared one soul. He was to be hers. Forever. At last.

The boat put in at Brean Island, near Glastonbury. Hearty farewells were given. The troupe collected its belongings and set out in the direction of the abbey, to beg lodging for the night. Rhys hitched his pack onto his shoulder—the troupe had kept his harp safe—and turned to address Breena.

"Ready?"

She nodded. "Are you sure you can get us back?"

"I am not sure of anything," he admitted. "Not where deep magic is concerned. But Myrddin's spell is burned into my brain. I will cast it, and pray the Lost Lands lead us home."

The day was overcast. It had rained in the night; the

path to the high meadow was slick with mud. Rhys offered Breena his hand as they negotiated a tight curve. She clasped it, and felt a deep rightness in the connection.

She supposed she should not have been surprised to find Myrddin waiting for them in the shadow of the Great Mother's stone. He looked much as he had when she'd first seen him there. Was it truly only a fortnight ago since she'd come to this time? She felt like a different person—as though she'd lived every day of the three centuries that divided her time from his.

A woman stood at his side, hands folded before her waist. Vivian was round and tiny, with white hair and an aura of calm that balanced Myrddin's intense energy.

"Ah," Myrddin said as they approached. He turned to his wife. "At midday. Just as you Saw, my dear."

Vivian smiled, and hooked a hand over her husband's arm. "You doubt my Sight, even after all this time?"

"I would be a fool to do so," he answered. He nodded to Rhys and Breena in turn. "Well met. I present my wife, Vivian."

Breena nodded at the woman. Their eyes met, and something like a spark seemed to fly between them.

"We have come to offer our assistance in returning you to your home," Myrddin said smoothly, capturing her attention. "It has been a fruitful journey, has it not?"

"Of a certainty," Breena replied.

"Let us hope it has not been in vain," Rhys said with a note of belligerence in his voice.

Vivian smiled, her blue eyes crinkling at the corners. Again, Breena felt that odd feeling of affinity. Their Seer's magic, touching? She frowned. No. It was more than that.

"Your efforts have not been in vain," Vivian told

Rhys. "Far from it. The queen has already conceived. Uther and Igraine's son will be born on midsummer's day."

"The child will be the king Britain so desperately needs," Myrddin said. "The king of Cyric's prophecy of Light."

Rhys held up his hand. "I do not wish to know more. I do not agree with your methods, Myrddin, but I recognize the hard choices that drove you to them. I am content to leave the child and his future in your hands. Breena and I wish only to return to our own time."

"As well you should," the old Druid murmured. "As well you should." He swept an arm toward the stone. "Shall we?"

"Wait," Breena said. "First, I'd like to ask a question."

Myrddin exchanged a glance with Vivian. "What is it, child?"

"You have said that Uther is Marcus's descendant. And that Igraine is Owein's. I've wondered . . . I've wondered if you are Rhys's. And mine. Are you?"

An odd look flitted across Myrddin's face.

"No, my dear." It was Vivian's quiet voice that answered. "You and Rhys are not my husband's ancestors."

The eyes of the two women met. And once again, that odd sense of . . . of *knowing* stole over Breena.

The truth struck with the force of a gale wind. She reached out a hand to Myrddin's wife. A sense of unfathomable wonder washed through her.

"Why, you are . . . you are *me*," Breena breathed.

Beside her, Rhys stiffened. "Nay," he choked out. "That is not—"

"And you . . ." Breena grabbed Myrddin's arm. She stared into his gray eyes, and saw reluctant acknowledgment.

"*You!*" she breathed. "You are *Rhys*."

Myrddin sent a disgruntled look toward his wife. "You were always too clever, my dear, for your own good."

The Druid lifted his staff. Whatever Breena might have replied to his revelation was lost in a surge of deep magic.

Chapter Twenty-two

Rhys woke flat on his back in the tall grass, his limbs aching, his ears buzzing.

Nay. Not his ears. *Bees.* Bees were buzzing about his head. He swatted them away, and opened his eyes. The blue-gray of the Great Mother's stone loomed tall in his vision. He fought through the haze in his mind.

Breena . . .

She stirred beside him. He reached for her, and she for him, at the same moment. He laughed as he pulled her into his arms and kissed her soundly.

"Are we home?" she asked, looking around.

A screech had him looking skyward. A merlin falcon circled, then swooped low, to land atop the standing stone. The bird spread its wings and scolded the humans sprawled on the grass below.

"Hefin," Rhys said, his smiled broadening. He craned his neck to look out over the swamps. Gwen's white mist was thick on the water, obscuring the slopes of the sacred isle. "Aye, I'd say we landed in the right place."

He jumped to his feet and offered his hand to Breena. His smile faded as she rose. The memory of his last moments in the future were emerging from the fog in his brain.

"Is it true?" he asked. "Was . . . is . . . Myrddin truly . . . me?"

"I believe he is." Breena sounded far calmer than Rhys felt. "And Vivian is me."

Rhys dragged a hand down his face. "It's too fantastic. There are more than three centuries, Bree, between our time and theirs. How could we possibly still be alive?"

"Magic," she said. "Very deep magic."

"Aye, very deep indeed. But why? And how?"

"As to why," Breena said, "I can only think it is because of Myrddin's—and your—duty to the Light, and the line of the Lady. As to how . . ." She spread her hands. "I cannot say. But I suppose we will find out, eventually."

"I cannot fathom it," Rhys said. "Every time I try, my mind balks. How is it, if we are . . . if we will be . . . Myrddin and Vivian, they did not seem to remember traveling to the future, as we have just done?"

"Perhaps the memory faded," Breena said. "Or perhaps their history was different from ours, because our presence in the future changed the past."

"That is hardly logical," Rhys protested.

Breena smiled. "And when has logic ever been a part of magic?"

"But, Bree, am I doomed to make the same choices in my future as Myrddin did in his past? Or will I find a different way to keep the Light alive in Britain?"

"I think . . . I think that only the Great Mother knows the answer to that question. All we can do, Rhys, is live our lives and face each day as it comes."

He sighed. "I suppose you are right."

"Of course I am." Breena's eyes went soft. She reached up and brushed a strand of hair off his forehead. "Wasn't I right about us, all along?"

He grinned and tweaked her nose. "Aye, you were, Bug."

She caught his hand. "You offered your life to save me from Afagduu."

"And Myrddin offered his life for Vivian's in the Lost Lands." Rhys regarded her steadily. "Three hundred years, it seems, will not dim my love for you."

Tears glistened in her eyes. "I am honored beyond words, Rhys."

His heart was so full it seemed to have expanded into his throat. Unable to speak, Rhys simply nodded. He loved everything about Breena—her sky blue eyes, the Roman nose he knew she detested, the spatter of freckles on her cheeks, the gap between her front teeth, her firm, determined chin. Her intelligence, her impulsive and loyal nature. Her good heart.

His gaze drifted downward. Her beautifully lush breasts, and her round hips and bottom. The welcoming heat between her thighs . . .

How could he have persisted in thinking of her as a girl these past few years? Breena was no longer a child; she was a woman. He would ever carry the image of an impish, wild-haired lass in his mind, but he would never again confuse that memory with the woman who stood before him now.

He was no longer the desperately lonely lad who had soaked up her childish adoration. He was a man who had found true treasure in Breena's mature love. Aye, their future would be a difficult one, but they would take each hardship as it came. Even if he had never seen Myrddin and Vivian, Rhys would have had no doubt his love for Breena would stand the test of time—three hundred years into the future, and more.

He cupped the side of her face. "If you are willing to stand by my side for so long," he said quietly, "I am willing to offer you all that is mine to give—my love, my magic, my music, and my life."

In answer, she went up on her toes and offered him a kiss. He drew her close, and returned her promise of a life filled with love.

"Breena! Breena are you here?"

Rhys broke the kiss. Gwen's call had come from the path leading down the mountain; a moment later, his sister came into view at the edge of the meadow.

"Breena! Where—oh!" Gwen, spying them with arms entwined, halted abruptly.

"Rhys? What . . . what are you doing here? Trevor said you had gone to Isca Dumnoniorum." Her gaze touched on Breena, then moved back to Rhys. "And Breena disappeared at the same time. Marcus and Owein are frantic." She crossed her arms. "What in the name of Annwyn is happening?"

Rhys stared at his sister, unable to think of what to say. He and Breena had been gone for a fortnight. Gwen was annoyed, aye, but nowhere near as distraught as she should have been.

Breena's fingers dug into his arm. "I think . . ." she whispered. "I think we must have returned on the same day that we left."

"Myrddin's doing, no doubt," Rhys whispered back.

"Rhys," Gwen demanded. "Stop muttering and look at me. What is going on?"

He met his sister's gaze. "Breena and I . . . we are to be handfasted."

His sister's eyes went round. "Truly?"

"Yes." Breena broke from Rhys's embrace and went to her sister-in-law. "Please wish us well."

Gwen embraced her. "Of course I will! I just . . ." She shook her head. "This is very sudden, is it not?"

Rhys laughed. "I would not say that. On the contrary, it has been a long time in coming."

"I've wanted to be Rhys's wife since I was three." Breena bit her lower lip. "But I do wonder what Marcus will have to say about it."

"He will be shocked," Gwen declared. "And I am not at all sure he will be pleased. He will have many questions and, I imagine, many requirements for your future." She grinned. "But you must ignore him, Breena. You are a grown woman, after all. It is time your brother faced that fact."

Gwen turned to Rhys, her eyes suddenly wet. She grasped his hand. "I have been so worried about you these last few years. You were so distant, almost like a stranger."

"I felt like one," he confessed. "But no longer. Though I cannot dwell all my life in Avalon, it is the place I love best, filled with the people nearest to my heart."

"You are always welcome here. We return your love a thousandfold."

"I know that." Bending, he picked up his pack and slung it onto his back. Wrapping one arm around Breena, and the other around Gwen, he looked out over the misty swamp.

"Let us go home," he said. "To Avalon."

Epilogue

*H*e is beautiful, Myrddin."

Myrddin gazed down at the infant in his wife's arms. Blue eyes, filled with wonder and innocence, stared back at him, unblinking. He extended a finger, and a tiny fist closed around it.

"Arthur is strong," Myrddin said. "In body as well as in magic." The babe's rainbow aura shone like the sun, the moon, and the stars, all wrapped up together. The possibilities of the small prince's life were endless.

Briefly, Myrddin wondered what color—what magic—would eventually overwhelm Arthur's aura. What sort of man would the infant prince grow to be? Would he truly become the great king Britain so desperately needed? Myrddin was prepared to do everything in his power to ensure that he did. He was not at all sure he would succeed. But he had hope.

The babe gazed up at him with eyes so innocent and pure that Myrddin's chest hurt. How long would Arthur's innocence last? He wished it might stretch into forever.

Gently, he pried the infant's grip from his forefinger. "I wonder which is wiser," he mused. "Youth or age?"

Vivian's lips brushed the top of Arthur's downy head. Would this child grow to be the man—the king—who would lead Britain through chaos to peace? It was a daunting prospect. He was just a babe.

But in every babe, as in every seed, one power ruled all others.

"Both youth and age are wise in their way," she told her husband, "and foolish in their turn. But hope . . ." She smiled. "Hope is the greatest power of all."

Afterword

What's truly wonderful about Arthurian legend is that it exists in so many forms—and with so many contradictions—that each new author who revisits the tale enjoys a great amount of freedom in writing his or her particular twist on the story.

King Arthur's supposed birth date is a moving target, but for the purposes of *Silver Silence,* I've chosen the traditional date of AD 465, less than fifty years after the final withdraw of the Roman Army from Britain, and just a few years before the fall of the city of Rome itself. The isle of Avalon, and the real monastery that replaced my fictional Druid settlement, is located on Glastonbury Tor in southwest England. Tintagel Island, on the northern Cornish coast, boasts castle ruins that postdate my story, but there is evidence of an older settlement beneath the visible one. A Roman road marker has been discovered in the vicinity, so it is not out of the question to imagine the island may have seen an earlier Roman presence.

Silver Silence remains close to the accepted mythology surrounding Arthur's conception. As the legend goes, when Uther insisted he wanted to steal the beautiful Igraine from her husband, the Duke of Cornwall, the wizard Merlin assisted his king by creating a powerful illusion that allowed Uther to walk unchallenged into Gerlois's impregnable fortress—as Gerlois himself. In the traditional tale, Igraine believes the man in her bed is her husband. In *Silver Silence,* I've created a previous history and love between Uther and Igraine, and an abusive marriage for Igraine and Gerlois.

Arthurian scholars generally agree that the Sword in the Stone and Excalibur are two separate weapons. Popular film, especially for children, has found it convenient to merge the two into one magical sword, with the result that many people consider the two to be one and the same. In my Druids of Avalon series, they are separate weapons. The magical sword Exchalybur is forged by Marcus Aquila in the book *Deep Magic.* The Sword in the Stone of *Silver Silence* is an ordinary sword that is accidentally cast into a stone by Rhys's magic.

If you find yourself wanting to linger in Rhys's and Breena's romance, I invite you to visit my Web site, www.joynash.com, where you'll find free "Before the Book" stories that tell of their early relationship. You'll also find many other Druids of Avalon special features.

Thanks so much for picking up *Silver Silence.* This book, and all my others, could not exist without readers like you.

All the best,

Joy Nash

DENEANE CLARK

It was divinely providential, acknowledged most mamas of the *ton*, how time could change a man. A mere younger son the year before, a notorious prankster and womanizer, Gareth Lloyd was now the dignified Marquess of Roth. And the sudden possession of such a large fortune made him the catch of the Season.

He was also everything Miss Faith Ackerly despised. To her, a rake and a libertine could no more become a pillar of society than a leopard could change its spots. For a maid as prim as she was pretty, Gareth's wealth was no more an inducement to wed than his title. Yet those warm brown eyes did not show the soul of a scoundrel. They promised to protect and cherish, to fend off any foe . . . though they indeed tempted her with the pleasures of the bedroom. No, no act of God could make her desire Gareth. But a leap of faith could lead to true love.

Faith

ISBN 13: 978-0-8439-6352-6

Bandit Queen

Overnight, she became a media sensation. Pearl Hart, "the Bandit Queen." The first woman sentenced to the infamous Yuma Penitentiary. To the newspapers, she was nothing more than a sassy firebrand who held up a stagecoach in daring fashion. They didn't understand the desperation that led her to hit the outlaw trail. They didn't see the bruises behind her tough façade. They didn't know she'd do anything to escape. . . .

Jane Candia Coleman

Award-winning Author
of *The Silver Queen*

ISBN 13: 978-0-8439-6345-8

INTERACT WITH DORCHESTER ONLINE!

Want to learn more about your favorite books and authors?
Want to talk with other readers that like to read the same books as you?
Want to see up-to-the-minute Dorchester news?

VISIT DORCHESTER AT:
DorchesterPub.com
Twitter.com/DorchesterPub
Facebook.com (Search Pages)

DISCUSS DORCHESTER'S NOVELS AT:
Dorchester Forums at DorchesterPub.com
GoodReads.com
LibraryThing.com
Myspace.com/books
Shelfari.com
WeRead.com

☐ **YES!**

Sign me up for the Historical Romance Book Club and send my FREE BOOKS! If I choose to stay in the club, I will pay only $8.50* each month, a savings of $6.48!

NAME: _____

ADDRESS: _____

TELEPHONE: _____

EMAIL: _____

☐ I want to pay by credit card.

☐ VISA   ☐ MasterCard   ☐ DISCOVER

ACCOUNT #: _____

EXPIRATION DATE: _____

SIGNATURE: _____

Mail this page along with $2.00 shipping and handling to:
Historical Romance Book Club
PO Box 6640
Wayne, PA 19087
Or fax (must include credit card information) to:
610-995-9274
You can also sign up online at **www.dorchesterpub.com**.
*Plus $2.00 for shipping. Offer open to residents of the U.S. and Canada only.
Canadian residents please call 1-800-481-9191 for pricing information.
If under 18, a parent or guardian must sign. Terms, prices and conditions subject to change. Subscription subject to acceptance. Dorchester Publishing reserves the right to reject any order or cancel any subscription.